THE COMPLETE ADVENTURES OF
SINGAPORE SAMMY, VOLUME 3

George F. Worts

THE MONSTER
OF THE LAGOON

THE COMPLETE ADVENTURES OF
SINGAPORE SAMMY, VOLUME 3

GEORGE F. WORTS

COVER BY

PAUL STAHR

ILLUSTRATED BY

SAMUEL CAHAN

STEEGER BOOKS • 2021

PUBLISHING HISTORY

"The Monster of the Lagoon" originally appeared in the February 23–March 30, 1935 issues of *Argosy* magazine (Vol. 253, No. 5–Vol. 254, No. 4). Copyright © 1935 by The Frank A. Munsey Company. Copyright renewed © 1962 and assigned to Steeger Properties, LLC. All rights reserved.

"Shark Bait" originally appeared in the June 22–July 6, 1935 issues of *Argosy* magazine (Vol. 256, Nos. 4–6). Copyright © 1935 by The Frank A. Munsey Company. Copyright renewed © 1962 and assigned to Steeger Properties, LLC. All rights reserved.

"About the Author" originally appeared in the January 25, 1930 issue of *Argosy* magazine (Vol. 209, No. 5). Copyright © 1930 by The Frank A. Munsey Company. Copyright renewed © 1957 and assigned to Steeger Properties, LLC. All rights reserved.

Visit argosymagazine.com for more books like this.

TABLE OF CONTENTS

THE MONSTER OF THE LAGOON

Singapore Sammy Shay was only one of several adventurers heading toward the weirdest mystery of the South Seas

CHAPTER I

JUNGLE GAUNTLET

THE LAGOON AT Little Nicobar was like a staring Cyclopean eye, an eye that was all pupil and a mile in diameter, as blue as the sapphire, as round as the moon, with a narrow rim of white, which was the coral beach, and for lashes a curving row of coconut palms leaning to the southeast trade.

It was an evil eye, this blue lagoon, for it contained—as a human eye can contain a hideous thought—a creature so monstrous that it was feared and shunned by all men.

Perhaps the blood-chilling legend of the monster was encouraged by the appearance at night of thin clouds of steam from bubbling volcanic mud-pots in the jungle. With the coming of night, these bubbling vats sent their greasy vapors out over the lagoon, as if to veil its obscenity. And this drifting mist gave the lagoon, by moonlight, the appearance of an eye filmy with cataract. In such uneasy vapors legends become truths, myths become history, and the horror of any unsolved mystery is magnified and distorted.

Among the native islanders in this little known corner of the Indian Ocean, the legend was old—older than the memory of the oldest tribes. They believed that the monster was inhabited by a human soul—the soul of the first man to walk the earth. And they believed that the soul of this earliest man was a hateful, foul and monstrous thing.

Intrepid adventurers as long ago as the Fourteenth Century mentioned the monster in their writings. Sir John Mandeville,

There was a scurrying among the brown men

whose travels took place between 1325 and 1355, refers as follows to the legend: "In all my voiages and traveils the most strange intelligence to come to me is of an isle that men clepe Small Nicobarre. Hereon grows all manner of spicery, as of giner, cloves, gilofre, canell, seedwall, nutmegs and maces, and flowers that are big as men. And also on this isle there do be hot mud wells that no man may suffer his hand within, and there be also a great monster in a lagoon. This Beeste is a strange and dreadful creature that does eat men."

In the Sixteenth Century a Portuguese named Sequira brought back strange tales of his voyages. He told of people with tails like sheep, of hens that laid eggs nine feet underground, of a strange and awful monster in a lake fed by the sea. In the logs of Captain James Cook's first and third voyages to Polynesia, in the late Eighteenth Century, we find several allusions to "the most horrible and hungriest monster ever known to mankind."

Thus the monster of the lagoon at Little Nicobar became, with the passage of time, a legend of noble proportions. It had existed since time began. It was the largest creature ever to

The blond young man, still laughing, swung the revolver

inhabit the earth or the waters of the earth. It was by far the most terrifying monster of ancient or modern mythology—a horrible gargantuan beast without name or description, since only one man had been known through all the ages to see The Thing and survive.

This one man was a modern, a Dutchman named Gurt Vandernoot. And Gurt Vandernoot has been the source of wildest conjecture. How he came to build himself a small fortress of a house on the very edge of the lagoon no man can say. Shrouded likewise in mystery is the life this man lived there for upwards of fifteen years. Some say he was a pearler; others ascribe to him the practice of the blackest arts. He was not on friendly terms with the natives of Little Nicobar. Why they tolerated him on their island is a mystery in itself.

Just as Bluebeard's forbidden room piqued the curiosity of

his successive brides, so did the lagoon at Little Nicobar, with its legendary tabu, grip the imagination of pearlers. No man dared enter it, yet in its depths were believed to be fabulous deposits of shell—an accumulation of ages. Pearlers, tempted beyond the limits of human prudence, had ventured into the lagoon in their luggers—and neither men nor luggers had ever been seen again! Though the monster never appeared in the daytime, the lagoon was evidently perilous by night or by day.

THE FACT remains that Gurt Vandernoot lived unmolested in his stout little fortress on the lagoon for many years, and it must be presumed that he saw the monster frequently, was familiar with its nature and its habits, and could have described it to the world had he wished. Only one other fact is known: some time during the year 1907 Gurt Vandernoot mysteriously vanished, and was never seen again. There were rumors of vast stores of pearls which he spent those fifteen years fishing for in the lagoon.

There were rumors of a strange, mystical bond between man and monster. There were rumors that the monster had at last devoured him. Even with most of the known facts now in hand, few of these rumors can be affirmed or denied. Gurt Vandernoot lived and died a man of mystery. And his little stone fortress of a house still stands, in a cluster of coconut palms, on the shore of the blue lagoon.

With the exception of Gurt Vandernoot, no one in all the centuries apparently had the curiosity or the audacity to visit the island and verify or disprove the legend of the nameless monster of the lagoon or the old stories of the cruel "Gauntlet of Death" which appears to have been the islanders' favorite diversion, when a shipwreck victim fell into their ghoulish hands.

Luther Thorwald, a British able seaman, is believed to have been the last of the long succession of unfortunates who were castaways on Little Nicobar, and who were, according to age-old tribal custom, sent to assuage the monster's awful appetite. We shall see that this appetite was so gross, so insatiable, so terrible that it surpassed human imagination.

The last days, hours, and minutes of the British seaman cannot be described here with the authority of any official records. What befell him must be pieced together from hearsay and scraps of evidence mustered from a variety of sources, some dependable, others too tinged with the scarlet of horror to be taken without a grain of salt.

We know definitely that Luther Thorwald was washed ashore on a hatch cover on the island from the wreck of the British tramp freighter Nellie Blarston, of Liverpool, some time between the afternoon of November 12th and the evening of November 13th, 1933. The rest we can assume with reasonable certainty, so that the subsequent steps of the ill-starred wretch toward a hideous doom can be set down with fair accuracy.

We can picture the late Luther Thorwald drifting closer and closer to the inviting silver strand of Little Nicobar, no doubt blinded by the glare of the equatorial sun on the glassy ocean, his skin lobster-red and blistered, his tongue parched or black with thirst. A "wooden man in an iron ship," he had possibly never heard of Little Nicobar or its fantastic legends.

Eventually, the hatch cover, carried by coastal and tidal currents and the wash of the sea, was deposited on the beach of Little Nicobar. The luckless white man was instantly swarmed upon by native blacks with spears and shields, and prodded into the presence of a most amazing individual—a white man with a black beard, who ruled the Little Nicobar tribe.

The presence of a white chieftain might well have increased the host of Little Nicobar legends had not an American expedition in the early spring of 1934 visited the island for the purpose of capturing the monster of the lagoon, of "bringing it back alive"—an expedition which is the chief concern of this chronicle.

OF LUTHER Thorwald they learned very little except that he enjoyed the doubtful distinction of being the last man to run that "Gauntlet of Death"—into the digestive system of the nameless monster.

Like all his predecessors, he was held captive until his strength returned. He was treated as if he were an honored guest. He was given his choice of the island maidens, and he was fed and fattened for a period of two weeks.

At the end of this time he became the central figure in as bizarre a ceremony as the Far East can afford. A great central camp fire was built. Tom-toms and native musical instruments were played at faster and faster tempo as the tribesmen danced. At midnight, or when the dancing reached its most frenzied pitch, Luther Thorwald was told *he must attempt to escape from the island.*

The black-bearded white chieftain gave him instructions. The tribesmen, armed with spears, would scatter through the jungle. At a signal, Luther Thorwald was to run for it. He was to run for the lagoon. If he reached a small boat, a canoe, he would gain his freedom.

He must run this gauntlet of death, through the jungle to the canoe, which contained, so he was told, an adequate supply of water and food to suffice him until he reached Sumatra.

The odds, the startled and horrified seaman was told, were possibly a hundred to one against him. The odds against him were actually in the neighborhood of a million to one. Through the centuries the monster of the lagoon, with its diabolical intelligence, had learned the meaning of the great camp fire and the frenzied dancing. It meant but one thing to the monster—a morsel for its gargantuan appetite. Always, when the fleeing man reached the lagoon, the monster was waiting.

So, on this night of nights in the life of Luther Thorwald, when he was told to make his dash for freedom—he dashed. He had come to know the island fairly well. Doubtless, as he ran the length of the island, toward the lagoon, he congratulated himself on his cleverness in eluding the savages. He had been warned that if he failed to reach the end of the gantlet, if he were captured, he would be broiled alive and eaten; for the tribesmen of Little Nicobar have always been cannibals.

He could not guess that this threat was part of the unholy farce, that every man who had made that mad dash for liberty always complimented himself on his cleverness in eluding the spearmen when he saw ahead of him, through the steaming jungle, the loom of the lagoon.

Luther Thorwald saw it as in a misty mirror. Off to his right, the panting, plunging man heard the sinister bubbling of the volcanic mud pots. And he saw the thin clouds of steam trailing in spectral plumes over the lagoon.

A moon in its last quarter sent a pale and ghostly green light into this mist. Ahead, the racing man saw the vagueness of the Dutchman's little fortress, abandoned these many years. At the edge of the beach he saw the promised canoe.

In a last burst of energy he sprinted toward the beach, plunging through the heavy, sickly sweet odor of the man-size pale-blue orchids, the monster flowers of the Little Nicobar jungles.

He doubtless reached the beach. The grinning black watchers in the jungle did not know. They did not look. Fear handed down through generations made them face in the opposite direction, for no islander dared look upon the monster.

The doomed man must have stopped at the water's edge, paralyzed with terror. His awful scream was an announcement that he had seen the monster. Then came a horrified babbling, as of a man suddenly bereft of his sanity. This was followed by a bleating and a bubbling and the sound of crumbling bones. Then—silence, disturbed only by the eternal chuckling of the volcanic mud pots.

CHAPTER II

MEET MR. BARLING

ACCORDING TO THE marine reporter of the Penang *Daily Times,* the Wanderer, of New York, was the finest, most luxurious yacht ever to drop anchor in the harbor of Penang. She was a small edition of an ocean liner, some three hundred feet in length, with a rated value in Lloyd's Register of one million pounds, sterling. Diesel engines and twin screws gave her a cruising speed of twenty-eight knots. She had accommodations for twenty guests and she carried a crew of thirty-five, including a French chef and a doctor. She was as white and as beautiful as a king's birthday cake. Her owner was Hector Tobias Barling, the American patent medicine millionaire.

To quote from the Penang *Daily Times:* "The Wanderer is making a cruise of the world, having left New York City four months ago. Mr. Barling and his two guests, Mrs. Mabel Farrington and her daughter, Miss Julie Farrington, are following no set itinerary, but, true to the name of their luxurious craft, are wandering where the whim dictates, in the most happy-go-lucky of spirits. The Wanderer will remain two or three days in Penang, then proceed to Johor, where Mr. Barling and his guests will be entertained by the maharaja."

The account was written in a jolly vein, and the impression it gave was that Mr. Barling and his guests were three care-free adventurers on a wonderful lark, flitting willy-nilly from port to port, poking into amusing out-of-the-way places, gayly taking life as they found it.

THE TRUTH was gloomily otherwise. At the moment, Hector Tobias Barling, the multimillionaire patent medicine monarch, was striding up and down a lustrous Afghan rug in the Wanderer's palatial drawing-room, setting his heels down hard and telling Mrs. Mabel Farrington how utterly fed up he was with it all. Plump, blond, pink little Mrs. Farrington was softly weeping into a lacy handkerchief.

Mr. Barling was puffing and snorting as he paced. He was a self-made multimillionaire, and he had achieved his success by never letting others interfere with his wishes. If he wished a thing done, it was done. He was a chunky little man in his late forties, with a cherubic countenance, pale-blue eyes with lashes as white as a pig's, and a wisp of blond mustache. He had utterly no sense of humor, and when denied his wishes he pouted.

"I give it up," he declared in his high-pitched, irritable voice. "I've done my best. I've given her what amounts to a magic carpet for seeing the world. I treat her slightest whim as a command. I've thrown my heart at her feet. And she jeers at me! She has nothing but scorn and contempt for me!"

He strode up and down the rug, pouting, beating one fist into his other palm in measured slaps, his air conveying that here was a man driven to the last ditch of desperation. Mrs. Farrington continued to whimper into her lace handkerchief.

"If she wasn't the most beautiful thing in the world," Mr. Barling resumed his complaint, "it wouldn't be so hard. Oh, you don't realize how it makes me feel! I would give her anything— anything! And she treats me like the dirt under her feet. I've a notion to turn back to New York tomorrow morning!"

Mabel Farrington lowered the lace handkerchief and stared at him with wet, red eyes.

"You mustn't do that, Hector!" she sniffled. "You must realize that Julie is young. Give her a little more time to appreciate you. After all, Rome was not built in a day."

Mrs. Farrington often employed old saws to express her exact meaning.

This habit infuriated Mr. Barling. "Four months," he barked, "is long enough!"

"Julie is bored and restless, Hector, She needs diversion."

"Diversion!" he cried. "Good Lord! What could be more diverting than a cruise like this? Where could any reasonable person find more diversion than we have aboard this yacht? The most expensive radio and the most expensive phonograph money can buy. The choicest foods and wines that money can buy. The most completely equipped gymnasium afloat!"

Mrs. Farrington started sniffling again. "You've been wonderful, Hector. But Julie is young. And the young are restless. What was it Tennyson said?"

"I don't care a damn what Tennyson said," Mr. Barling answered angrily, knowing it was a proverb.

Sometimes he hated this pink, grasping, sniffling woman enough to throw her overboard. He knew she detested him. He knew she wanted him for a son-in-law only because he was a multimillionaire.

"Why not take her ashore?" Mrs. Farrington suggested.

"Now? Tonight?"

"Why not go slumming—just the two of you?"

Mr. Barling stared at her a moment, as if she had lost her senses. Then he nodded judicially and strode out of the drawing-room.

JULIE FARRINGTON was not in her accustomed deck chair, reading. He had had a reading lamp installed there especially for her—just one of those little thoughtful things he was doing all the time to please her—just another of those thankless little labors of love.

He roamed about the deck, and he found her presently in the bows, as far forward as she could get, a slim, blond girl in the moonlight, as romantic as the mysterious shore lights at which she was apparently gazing; a slim blond girl who, in any kind of light, always made Mr. Barling go hot and cold all over. She was the most beautiful girl he had ever seen. She was the most beautiful girl in the world. And it made him sick and furious again to realize that all of this loveliness wasn't his to fondle and caress.

Singapore Sammy

He approached on tiptoe. He wanted to sweep her into his arms, but he had learned that such methods were perilous. Once, on a warm night in the Mediterranean, he had tiptoed up behind her and swept her into his arms. And she had coolly sent a short jab—it didn't travel eight inches—into his midriff with such snap and vigor that he was ill for hours afterward. She didn't look strong; she looked as delicate as a flower.

"Julie!" he whispered.

She turned about quickly with her wonderful smile. It dimmed when she saw who it was. The suspicion flitted darkly over Mr. Barling's mind that she had been expecting or hoping it would be some one else, that cocky first officer of his, Mr. McTavish, or Mr. Axelrod, the chief engineer, both young men.

He had sternly instructed them to keep away from Miss Farrington. His officers, he had said, were, under no conditions, to fraternize with his guests.

Julie's smile had changed. No longer radiant, it was the patient, good-little-girl smile she seemed to reserve especially for him.

But the romantic mistiness of her eyes did not go away.

"Look, Hector," she said, and pointed.

He looked first at her slim, soft, bare arm, then at what she was indicating. It was a two-masted schooner with well-raked masts which had swung broadside to them and was now lying in a puddle of silver, a shimmering little lake laid there by the moon.

"What about it?" he said practically.

Julie Farrington sighed. "Have you ever heard of the primrose by the river's brim?" she countered.

It sounded so much like one of her mother's questions that Hector Barling's voice, when he replied, contained a note of irritation.

"Never," he said.

"Then you wouldn't understand."

He pouted. "What about the primrose? What about the schooner?"

"Oh, I don't know," Julie Farrington said in her most musical voice, the dreamy one. "What port do you suppose she's from? Where do you suppose she's going?"

Mr. Barling shrugged indifferently. "Oh, these waters are lousy with little tubs like her," he said with the contempt of a man who owned a yacht like the Wanderer. Then, as if with inspiration, "Julie! How'd you like to go ashore? How'd you like to go slumming in Penang—just the two of us?"

"Tonight?" Julie cried.

"Now!"

"Oh, I think it'd be tur-rific!"

CHAPTER III

"I CAN'T BE KILLED!"

AT AN EARLY hour of the evening, Penang's foremost sink of iniquity, the Gin & Bitters, was uproarious with revelry. The air clattered with talk and laughter. It was blue with tobacco smoke and thick with the vapors of alcohol. In one corner, a blackjack game was in progress. In another, fantan—Chinese fantan—was being played. Brown and yellow girls, lavishly lipsticked, powdered, mascarraed and rouged, drifted in and out, grotesquely rolling their eyes and smiling with seductive intent, and leaving in their wakes the spice of heady perfumes.

Men white, yellow and brown clustered about the bar. Others slept in drunken stupor or stood about with the alert air of men waiting for somebody to start something.

The two white men from the two-masted blue schooner which had anchored off Swettenham pier early in the afternoon were comfortably getting tight on gin *bijt,* or trade gin.

The red-headed man deposited his empty glass on the bar, wiped his lips on his wrist, and said, "That lad looks pale."

The tall, sardonic man with hawklike eyes and blue-black hair—he was in his late twenties and resembled a buccaneer—nodded judicially and said, "Yeah, and he's due to look plenty paler."

The man under discussion was a young man, no older than twenty-seven, who had been playing blackjack with gross, greasy Hat Gow. He was a big, loose-shouldered young man, wide there but narrow in the beam, handsome, with rough dark blond hair and eyes like brightest sapphires. He had long arms. His nose was Irish. And this strain of blood in him was now in the ascendant.

The blond unknown was finding fault with Hat Gow's manner of dealing. He was thumping the table with a fist and shouting insults into the Chinaman's fat, yellow, placid face. English or American, the young fellow evidently did not realize that he was courting trouble. And he was apparently not armed. He wore nothing but a slightly soiled white shirt unbuttoned halfway down his chest, a pair of slightly soiled white drill trousers, and a pair of slightly soiled white sneakers. His clothing clove to his leanness, and there was no bulge at pockets or hip of firearm or knife.

The red-headed man and the tall man who resembled a buccaneer put their backs to the bar and watched developments. They heard, above the uproar, the voice of the young man calling Hat Gow a dirty yellow crook, a dirty yellow cheat, and a dirty yellow so-and-so. They saw an assortment of brown men in sarongs moving gracefully toward the table with shiny eyes and pleased grins, and they knew that a Malay will hit, kick, bite or knife a white man without much provocation.

Innocent of danger, the blond man culminated his insults by punching Hat Gow, who had got up, in the nose. Then the young man began to laugh. The expression on Hat Gow's fat yellow face was comical enough, but it is never prudent to punch a Chinaman in the nose—and then laugh. Not a Chinaman of Hat Gow's dignity.

"We better get that sap outa here," the buccaneer said.

"Too late," Sam responded.

HE HAD seen the smoky shiver of light on white metal. The fat and murderous revolver in the Chinaman's fat and murderous hand disgorged a bud of red fire. But the blond young man did not fall. The revolver had been fired pointblank at his chest, or so it seemed from where the red-headed man stood, and the shot had been a miss!

There ensued an even more interesting development. The blond man, still laughing, snatched the revolver from Hat Gow's hand and raked it across his face. The hammer must have hooked out a gobbet of flesh, for the Chinaman's left cheek began oozing blood.

There was a scurrying among the brown men. They were massing about the man with the Irish nose and the hearty laugh.

"Give 'em the bench," the red-headed man barked.

His companion seized one end of a long bench on which lay a Japanese sailor, sleeping off a saki headache. The red-headed man seized the other end. They decanted the sailor to the floor and lifted the bench. They rushed across the room, battering their way through a wall of squirming humanity. Their rush carried them to the blackjack table and into the swarm of Malays.

The object of their anxiety was still erect and still laughing, although by all the rules of water-front warfare he should have been unconscious or dead.

Taking advantage of a momentary lull, the rescuing party seized the blond youth, each grasping one of his arms. Without loss of momentum, they carried him along, out through the doors and into the comparative calm and security of the moonlit Malayan evening. Their acquisition was softly chuckling.

"Walk!" the red-head panted.

"Fast!" the buccaneer gasped.

The three started off down the street at a lope. A block away, assured that they were not followed, the rescuers stopped and examined their charge for wounds. He was unscathed.

"You sure are plastered with luck," the red-head said.

"It's always that way," the young man answered cheerfully. "Perhaps I'd better introduce myself. I'm Laughing Larry McGurk, the guy who can't be killed!"

The man with red hair peered into his face, and with the aid of a nearby street lamp studied the sapphire eyes for symptoms of insanity, the mouth for symptoms of jesting. The eyes had a queer gleam to them, but it wasn't insanity. And the mouth wasn't jesting. It was thin with scorn.

"Say that again," the red-haired man growled.

"That's right," the young man attested. "I'm the guy who can't be killed."

"Yeah?" the red-headed man said.

"Yeah?" the buccaneer repeated.

"Yeah," the merry stranger answered. "Sharks tried it. A tiger tried it. Men tried it. I tried it." He glanced sharply from one bronzed, skeptical face to the other. "It's impossible."

"American, ain't you?" the buccaneer asked.

"Kansas City, Missouri."

"We're from Missouri, too, in a way of speaking," the red-haired man said.

"Who are you?"

"My name's Sam Shay," the red-headed man answered. "And this is Captain Lucifer Jones."

"I've heard about both of you," Mr. McGurk said. "They call you Singapore Sammy on account of your hair is a four-alarm fire. They call this guy Spike Jones on account of he's duck soup for pretty girls who spike his drinks with knock-out drops and take his roll. They also call him Lucky on account of he's a child of misfortune. I've heard about you wherever I've been. I heard you were a pair of notorious characters that would rather cut a throat than eat. I heard you've been run out of every port from Yokohama to Sydney."

SINGAPORE SAMMY nodded his head slowly.

"What else have you heard about us, Mr. McGurk?"

"I heard you two own that blue schooner, the Blue Goose, and that you've been chasing all over these waters in it for the past seven years. Looking for your old man who's got a will or something he won't let you have. I heard you've been stopped by every gunboat in Asia. I heard you'll run anything for anybody if the price is right. I heard you do a little trading, a little pearling, a little poaching, a little gun-running. I heard you were fast workers in many lines—just two hard guys trying to get along. I heard you cry into your beer when you get plastered, and I heard you think you're the two toughest mugs this side of Suez."

Lucky Jones was breathing heavily, but Singapore Sammy remained calm. "You keep your ears busy, don't you, Mr. McGurk?" He

Hat Gow

produced and ignited a large white Burmese cheroot.

"They smell something like burning rat hair, don't they, Red?" the blond man inquired amiably. "Why don't you swing on me? Afraid of my rep?"

Captain Jones made a sudden forward movement, but Singapore waved him back.

"Sock me!" the blond man laughed. "Try it!"

"Let me at this guy!" Lucky Jones pleaded.

Singapore said "Nix," and puffed benevolently at his cheroot. The young man with the blond hair, the Irish nose and the ready laugh seemed to interest him more and more.

"Let's hear some more about this charmed life you say you lead."

The young man grinned. "Think I'm lying? What happened back there in that clip joint was typical. You couldn't kill me if you tried! I couldn't kill myself if I tried! I've tried! I've been trying for four months."

"Did you try to get yourself killed just now?"

Mr. McGurk grinned. "Did you see what happened? No matter who or what it is I try to get killed by, something always happens. But that isn't the funny part of it. The funny part of it is that I'm going to kick off inside of a couple of months—and I can't get killed, no matter how hard I try."

"What's so funny?" Captain Jones asked heavily.

"As a fellow I saved from a gang of bandits in Hongkong said to me, it's the irony of fate. Inside of two months I'm going to kick off; the best doctor in Chicago said so."

"Yeah?" Lucky Jones said skeptically.

"I wouldn't kid you. The doctor called it a glooma."

"A what?"

"It's something that grows inside your head. It's rare. There's a little gland back in here." He patted the back of his head. "This little gland is inside a little kind of skull of its own, about the size of an English walnut. The little gland is okay. But this thing has grown around it, this glooma. It grows just so big and then—out I go!"

HIS LISTENERS stared at him. Lucky Jones burst out, "What the hell's so funny about it?"

"What should I do?" Larry McGurk retorted. "Go around with my face between my knees? Once you get used to it, you don't mind it. I'm used to it. I've got no kick. I've packed more into the past four months than most men do in a lifetime. And how do *you* know your number won't be up in a week or a month from now? Knowing makes it simple."

"I don't see it," Captain Jones growled. "I don't want to know. Tell us some more about this glooma."

"Well, I went to the best doctor in Chicago, because I had a terrible headache all the time, and other symptoms. He tested me out and said nothing could be done. He said this glooma would grow and keep on growing and all of a sudden I would go out like a light. He said there wasn't any cure, and that an operation would be one hundred per cent fatal."

"Did you try other doctors?" Singapore Sammy asked.

"What was the use? He charged me ten bucks, so he must have been good. I had the same hunch, anyway. I was getting so I could *smell* death."

"How do you feel now?" Lucky Jones broke in.

"Oh, I'm used to it now. But it was tough at first. I was first mate on a Great Lakes ore carrier, running between South Chicago and Duluth. A nice berth, a nice run, nice prospects."

"What kind of a ticket did you have?" Singapore interrupted.

"Skipper's—limited. I was studying to take the limit off it, and I was studying to go into the office. It's a fine outfit with room at the top. I chucked it, took all I'd saved, and went to Frisco. I'd always wanted to see Java, and I figured I might as well cash in there as anywhere. On the way to Honolulu I saw a fellow with a girl on deck one night—she was a million dollars' worth of hey-hey. And the more I thought about that, the worse it got me down. In less than six months I was going where there aren't any girls, and where it wouldn't do me any good if there were. It made me so low I walked to the rail and jumped overboard.

"It was a black night, and there was a big sea running. A deck-hand named Cinders saw me jump. He let out a yell and went in after me. Well, he got me by the hair and the ship heaved to and they picked us up."

"So you began thinking you led a charmed life," Singapore said.

"Hell, no. I thought that was an accident. It wasn't until I grabbed that tiger by the whiskers outside of Bombay and cut his throat that I *knew*."

"Hold on," Sammy said. "Take it easy, brother. How long ago did you say the doc gave you six months to live?"

"Four months ago. Two to go—or maybe less!"

LUCKY JONES muttered, "Let's hear about that tiger."

"Don't rush me. I'll get to the tiger. In Shanghai, I was ganged by a bunch of murderous coolies with knives a foot long. They had me right where they wanted me, but I walked right through them and didn't get a scratch. Then in Hongkong I ran into a bunch of bandits with knives and guns trying to kidnap a rich American tourist. I sailed right into the middle of them. They shot at me and they stabbed at me. But I didn't get a scratch. You guys ever been in Bangkok?"

His listeners nodded.

"You know how thick the man-eating sharks are at the mouth of the Menam River?"

"At low tide," Sam Shay affirmed, "you could walk from shore to shore on their backs."

"I took a dare and jumped right off into the midst of them!" Laughing Larry declared. "They came at me, the way they do, rolling over on their sides and showing their teeth. But when they got near me, they stopped and backed off. They'll chew through an anchor rope, but they didn't take a nick out of me!"

"Let's hear about this tiger," Lucky Jones said.

Laughing Larry seemed to think the question was uproariously funny. He began to laugh.

"This tiger," he said, choking with mirth, "was terrifying the villages about a hundred miles north of Bombay. The country-side was paralyzed with fear. He was eating natives right and left. I went up there and laid for this man-eater. One morning he came walking out of the jungle right at me. I met him half-way. When he got close he sat down and started to shiver. Did you ever see a tiger shiver? Ha ha ha ha ha ha ha!"

Singapore Sammy and Lucky Jones looked at him with suspicion and skepticism.

Choking with laughter, McGurk went on:

"I—I walked right up to him. Ha ha ha ha ha ha ha!"

"The hell you did!"

"The hell I didn't! I grabbed him by the chin whiskers—and cut his throat. Ha ha ha ha ha ha ha!"

Laughing Larry was now grasping his sides. He was gasping and choking with laughter. Singapore began to laugh, too. He laughed and laughed. Lucky Jones stared at him, then at Laughing Larry. Then he, too, began to laugh.

Just why they were laughing Singapore Sammy did not know.

When Laughing Larry McGurk could talk again, he said, "I had his head mounted and sent it to my old skipper as a souvenir."

"Did you ever pull a cobra's tail?" Captain Jones asked.

"No, but I'm still young."

"Are you game to pull a cobra's tail?" Lucky persisted.

"Don't be a sap," Sammy growled.

"Where's the cobra?" Laughing Larry inquired, with a gleam of interest in his sapphire eyes.

"A friend of mine has him," Lucky Jones answered. "A Malay by the name o' Arak Javon. He lives out by the Dhoby Ghat."

"Lead me to him!"

"You're nuts," Singapore Sammy said.

"I'll pull his tail and make him like it," Larry said.

CURIOUS BUT reluctant, Sam Shay assented to this fantastic test of the blond man's boasted luck. The three young men took a gharry, which is a small, enclosed, horse-drawn vehicle, to the bamboo and rattan residence of Arak Javon. Mr. Javon was a snake collector. He collected and sold venomous reptiles to menageries and zoos.

The bull cobra in question had been brought fresh from the jungle near Kuala Lumpur only yesterday, and was a savage and vicious specimen—a genuine hemadryad. It had not been de-fanged.

Arak Javon, a wisp of an old man, listened politely to the proposal made by the three white men, and indicated the stout bamboo cage which housed the bull cobra, deadliest snake on earth. Snake-man Javon was philosophical. In his philosophy all white men were more than a little mad. Tonight's doings merely supported his belief.

Torches were lit and set in a circle about the bamboo cage.

The bull cobra was one of the most dangerous looking speci-
mens Sammy Shay had ever seen. It was thicker than a strong
man's arm. Its hood was enormous. It hissed at the three men
and its cold little gray eyes stared at them with reptilian hatred.

When Larry McGurk went smilingly to the bamboo cage,
Sam burst out, "Don't be screwy! We'll take your word for it!"

The blond man looked at him with a grin. He lifted the lid of
the cage. The bull cobra began to leap about, to strike at shadows and bars.

With slowness and deliberation, McGurk reached into the
cage, pursued the dancing tail with nimble fingers, clutched it,
held it.

"Take your hand out of there!" Singapore roared.

The blond man smiled at them amiably. He gave the tail a
yank. The great hood reared above his hand. The pinkish-yellow
tongue darted about. Torchlight gleamed on white fang tips.
Sweat appeared in beads on Singapore's sunburned forehead.
Chills like snakes of ice were streaming along his spine. Captain
Jones was panting like an overworked tugboat.

But the bull cobra did not strike. It was evident that it wanted
to strike, but that some strange spell, or power, was preventing
that deadly lunge. It was uncanny. It was incredible.

Slowly, deliberately, Larry McGurk released the tail and with-
drew his hand. He closed the lid of the cage and turned back to
the two men. He was laughing.

"If you think it's a gag," he said, "try it yourself, Red. Do I lead
a charmed life or do I lead a charmed life?"

Singapore took him by the arm and said in a shaken voice,
"Brother, the drinks are on me. We'll go to the Mudhole. Have
you served any time in sail?"

"A year once, in a Lake Michigan lumber schooner."

"How'd you like to ship with us as mate? We're sailin' in the
mornin' to look up some pearls on an out-of-the-way island
called Little Nicobar. We need a guy who can't be killed!"

CHAPTER IV

PEGLEG'S STORY

PROFESSOR BRYCE ROBBINS was not a particularly sensitive young man nor did he possess an over-developed sense of smell, but he did not enjoy the sour-beer-and-cheap-tobacco flavor of grogshops such as the Gin & Bitters. And he hated the cheap perfumes used by the bold-eyed girls, yellow and brown, who drifted in and out, leering at him and calling him "baby" and making outrageous proposals. And he was more than a little put out because the two men for whom he had been combing Penang all afternoon and evening were so elusive. He seemed always to be just one jump behind them.

Professor Robbins was looking for the owners of the two-masted blue schooner lying off Swettenham pier. He had rented a motor boat and gone out to the Blue Goose shortly after she had dropped anchor this afternoon, and had been told by her Malay *serang* that Mr. Samuel Shay and Captain Lucifer Jones had just gone ashore on a matter of pressing business.

Somewhat familiar with the shore-going habits of seagoing men, Professor Robbins had been looking for Mr. Shay and Captain Jones in the waterfront grogshops, of which there were many. He left the Sailors Beware at about the time Singapore Sammy and Lucky Jones were rescuing Laughing Larry McGurk from what had seemed at the time to be certain death in the Gin & Bitters.

And he left the Gin & Bitters at about the time Mr. McGurk was brazenly pulling a cobra's tail. His next stop was to be the

Mudhole. The tired and impatient young man would have been amazed had he known by what means he was to be introduced to Mr. Shay and Captain Jones.

It is dangerous for a man of Professor Robbins' fabulous wealth to go about at night in a town like Penang without an armed escort. The fatigue of his long chase must have made him careless.

He had hired a gharry for the entire evening. At each stopping place the gharry waited for him, to take him on to the next. He was innocently unaware that his syce, the gharry driver, was the blackest-hearted of rogues, and that the gharry had been patiently stalked by three dark-skinned men since the moment he had left his hotel after a bite of dinner.

Professor Robbins told his syce to drive to the Mudhole. Then he opened the gharry door. The hitherto empty darkness of the gharry now contained three dark-skinned men. The instant he opened the door three pairs of claw-like hands reached out and snatched him inside.

Taken by surprise, Professor Robbins was for a moment unable to account for himself. But he was young and athletic. He had played football at Harvard not so many years previously, and he was in the pink of condition.

Strange, muffled sounds issued from the gharry as it went lurching down Kelawai Road—groans and grunts and stifled cries. Its small black, boxlike compartment shook and shivered and swayed as the tide of battle swept from seat to seat and from side to side.

About a block from the Mudhole, the gharry, with its strange cargo, passed three men, three white men, namely, Singapore Sammy, Lucky Jones, and the man who couldn't be killed.

The three young men swung to one side of the road to let the gharry pass. As it passed, they heard a smothered cry for help.

That vocal S O S was as distinct as a rifle shot.

"Help! Help!"

THE SYCE lashed the rump of his bony little horse with

a whip. The three men deployed. Larry McGurk dragged the syce out of his seat and slugged him in the jaw. Singapore and Lucky Jones each leaped to a door and jerked it open. They saw a white man with a gag only half in his mouth engaged with three thugs.

Pegleg Pyke

They addressed themselves to the thugs, freely using fists and boots. The three dark-skinned men shrieked curses in Malay and ran.

Professor Robbins brushed himself off and said irritably, "Barbarous place! It is criminal that this sort of thing can happen to a traveler!"

Lucky Jones eyed him sardonically and drawled, "Maybe the Resident would loan you a troop o' cavalry, mister!"

The professor said ungraciously, "Naturally, I'm very grateful to you gentlemen." He looked at Singapore. His eyes lighted. He said crisply, "I wonder if you aren't the man I'm looking for. Sam Shay?"

Singapore Sammy nodded. "I'm Sam Shay."

"Good!" the scientist said briskly. "This is very fortunate. Where can we talk, Mr. Shay—alone?"

Singapore studied him. "You can say anything in front of these guys. This is my partner and this is my mate."

Professor Robbins glanced at them coldly. "Very well. Where can we go?"

Singapore indicated the lights of the Mudhole.

At the bar the professor said, "My name is Bryce Robbins—Professor Bryce Robbins—of New York." He hesitated. As his name kindled no sparks in the eyes of his listeners, he went on:

"Yesterday, in Rangoon, I heard about the expedition you're planning. I chartered a plane and flew here, arriving a few minutes after you had anchored. I went out to your schooner and have been looking for you ever since."

"What expedition?" Sammy asked in his lazy drawl.

"The expedition to Little Nicobar. Is it a secret?"

"It was supposed to be," the redheaded man answered. "Lucky, have you been blowin' off at the mouth again?"

"Not me!" the buccaneer said indignantly.

Singapore returned his blue-green eyes to the stranger's face and wriggled his carrot-colored eyebrows, a trick he had when displeased. He gave the professor an inch-by-inch going over. What he saw was a tall, slender, wiry-looking man of about thirty, with alert gray eyes, a well-cared-for brown mustache, a thin-lipped mouth, and a lean, hard jaw.

"Well," Singapore drawled, "what did you hear, mister?"

"I heard you were starting on an expedition to Little Nicobar to investigate a legendary monster that is supposed to live in the lagoon there."

"What else did you hear?"

"That was all—you had fitted out to go to this island."

Sammy said fiercely, "You dead sure?"

"Why, certainly. I wanted to see you—wanted to make a practical suggestion. I don't take the slightest stock in this monster myth, but I'd like to join you. If we can come to some agreement, I'd like to underwrite the expedition."

"You mean, pay for it?" Lucky asked.

"That was my tentative idea," the professor said.

"We don't need help," Lucky said. "We ain't interested."

Sammy drawled, "Let's hear the rest of this. I am always open to a reasonable proposition."

"My idea," Professor Robbins explained, "is—if there's any truth in these tales—to bring it back alive."

Singapore Sammy compressed his lips and shook his red head. "It's a cockeyed idea, mister."

THE YOUNG scientist looked displeased. His eyes narrowed, too, and his thin mouth became stubborn. "Let me explain myself, Mr. Shay. About six months ago I inherited, unexpectedly, a fortune from an uncle I hardly knew. It was a large fortune. To be perfectly frank, it was seven million dollars."

"Yeah?" Lucky breathed.

"Yes, Captain. And it almost ruined my life. Until then I'd been doing research work in the Rockefeller Institute, in New York; perfectly content to plug along in my laboratory on my modest salary.

"I was trying to isolate the infantile paralysis bug. Suddenly, like a bolt from the blue, came this lawyer's letter. I was the sole heir to seven million dollars. Perhaps you read about it?"

"No," Sammy said, shaking his red head.

Professor Robbins sighed.

"It was the beginning of the first real trouble I'd ever known. My inheritance brought me nothing but troubles. I was pestered to death by reporters, news-reel men, threatening letters, slick promoters, beggars, and a host of men, women and children who claimed to be related to me.

"I tried keeping on with my research work. I tried to live simply, quietly, as I'd always done. It was impossible. I was hounded. And finally I was kidnaped. A gang of hoodlums grabbed me one night as I was leaving the Institute. I was ransomed for a hundred thousand. Oh, it wasn't the money I minded. It was the threat to my peace of mind.

"When I returned to work, the director advised me to chuck it. He and others told me that with my fortune I was a fool to go on dabbling in biochemistry. I must do something big, something really sensational for science! It staggered me. There was I, happy in my obscurity, told to do something big and sensational for science! But I chucked my job and started off to look the world over for—" He hesitated.

"For something to discover," Sammy suggested.

"Exactly! I have roamed Europe and Africa. I have roamed Asia from Urga to Ceylon. And it was not until I stumbled upon your trail in Rangoon that I had had the slightest hope. Of course, I am skeptical, but I am sufficiently interested in this old legend to go to Little Nicobar and defray all costs of the expedition."

"If you're skeptical," Lucky Jones broke in, "why bother?"

It was evident that Captain Jones did not approve of or like Professor Robbins, with his crisp, irritating voice, his assurance. But Singapore felt otherwise, for Singapore was always willing to turn an honest or a not-too-honest penny. And he liked the idea of Professor Robbins' footing the bill.

THEY ARGUED about it for some time. It was Lucky's contention that they didn't want interference with their plans. It was Sam's contention that a man who wanted to spend his money as badly as the professor seemed to ought to be encouraged.

Through it all Professor Robbins remained skeptical of the monster's actual existence.

He said, "Mr. Shay, just what makes you so sure this fabulous creature exists? Of course, I've heard some tales about it, but I put it down as a myth."

"It isn't a myth," Singapore declared. "I can take you to a guy who had a hand to hand encounter with it."

"In Penang?" the scientist cried.

"Right down the street. Old Pegleg Pyke. He's bartending at the Blue Grin."

"I'd like to talk to him," Bryce Robbins said crisply.

The Blue Grin was perhaps the most sordid grogshop in Penang, putting to shame the Gin & Bitters and the Mudhole. You could have cut the tobacco smoke with a knife, and the smells of sour beer must have been unaired for months.

To judge from his appearance, Pegleg Pyke was a man well into his sixties. His hair was white, what there was of it, and he wore a straggly white mustache. The few teeth remaining in his jaws were all gold-capped. And his metallic, snaggle-toothed grin was almost terrifying. From sunken, oystery eyes he stared at the four men who lined up at his bar.

Introducing the scientist to him, Singapore said, "Professor, this man lost a leg to that monster twenty years ago. Pegleg, you tell this guy what you told me about The Thing in that lagoon. Skip the part where you were shipwrecked and grabbed by the cannibals. Start in where you were running through the jungle to where the canoe was tied up on the beach of the lagoon."

Singapore had not finished making this request, when into the swirling blue smoke and ancient vapors of the Blue Grin came a man and a girl. The man was a sleek, plump man of forty-eight, looking out of place in his snow-white pea-jacket and white flannel trousers.

As for the girl— Just as Singapore finished, Captain Jones hoarsely whispered: "Pipe the blonde!"

LARRY McGURK turned his head and looked. One eyebrow went up. He had never seen a girl quite like her. She was so beautiful that she dazzled him. She wore some kind of blue dress. But he didn't notice the dress. Her hair was blonder than blond. It was silver-golden fleece. In contrast with her face, which was a golden brown, and her eyes, which were of the rich reddish brown of autumn leaves, it was sensational. Brown eyes, not blue. With that lustrous, rippling, pale-gold hair, they were epoch-making, so large, so warm, so deep. They should have been as blue as the fairest sky. With them, she outdistanced Larry McGurk's farthest conception of feminine loveliness.

Her mouth was scarlet, but slim and firm. She looked like a girl who knew her way about. A girl as good looking as that would have to know her way about.

He wondered who the pompous little pipsqueak with her might be. But Larry didn't care. The wonder of it was that she was staring straight at him and smiling a little—a friendly little smile.

It was certainly at him she was staring; not at Singapore, whose blue-green eyes looked dazzled; not at Lucky, who was contemplating her with goggle-eyed amazement; or at Professor Robbins, who was staring at her and licking his thin lips.

Then she spoke to Pegleg Pyke.

"A gin buck, please!"

A sweet voice, a voice with bells in it.

"A stengah," her companion said in a thin, important voice.

The girl now turned her back on her appreciative audience. And such a back! Slim and golden brown. Never, Larry declared to himself, had he gazed upon more delicious flesh.

Pegleg Pyke gave the newcomers their drinks and returned to the four sighing men. Rather, the three sighing men and the man who couldn't be killed.

For Larry McGurk wasn't sighing; he was grinning.

"Know her?" Sammy whispered.

"No."

"Ever see her before?"

"Only in my dreams."

This spirited byplay was interrupted by the return of Pegleg, whose eyesight was evidently impaired, for he had hardly glanced at the vision, and he now went brusquely into his story.

"IT WAS like this, mister," he said, addressing Professor Robbins in his harsh old voice. "I was escapin' from them cannibals—leastwise, I figgered I was escapin' from them cannibals—and racin' for all I was worth through the jungle toward the lagoon.

"I'd heard o' the monster o' the Little Nicobar lagoon, but I didn't take no stock in it. An old sea serpent story, I figured it was.

"I can remember it as plain as if 'twas only yesterday—the gurglin' o' the volcanic mud pots, the smell o' the big blue orchids—as big as a man, they are—and the steam driftin' out o' the jungle from the mud pots and over the lagoon.

"There was a half moon and the light was fair. But where the canoe was pulled up, they wasn't no light. It was darker there than the inside o' Adam's off ox. Account o' the coconut palms.

"I went sprintin' past the old stone house on the shore o' the lagoon. And jest when I was grabbin' the bow o' the canoe, to push her into the water and jump aboard, this—this slimy Thing reached up out o' the lagoon and grabbed me."

Pegleg Pyke was puffing with memories of that awful experience. Red spots burned on his cheek bones. His sunken old eyes had a feverish glitter. His gold-topped fangs flashed and gleamed.

"You saw it!" the scientist stepped.

"I saw nothin'! It was in the shadow o' the coconut palms. I jumped back and grabbed for the trunk o' one o' the palms. Oh, it was grabbin' my leg and squeezin' down on it, and I was tryin' to fight it off with my hands—"

"What did it feel like?" Larry McGurk said.

"Slimy rubber! And it smelled like some kind of acid—nitric, maybe. I dunno. I grabbed a piece of driftwood and bashed away at it, but it ripped off my leg right above the knee. Bone and all! Mister, do you blame me for lookin' like an old man at the age o' fifty?"

"What did you do?"

"I hopped on one leg for the canoe, with that Thing pluckin' away at my shoulder and arm. I got away somehow. Don't ask me how. I was off my nut, I was. I was screaming."

"I thought I was a brave man, but I learned that night what fear is. Yes, sir. I got into the canoe and somehow I got that canoe out o' that lagoon and into the open sea. I must have had presence of mind enough to put a tourniquet above the mangled knee. Leastwise, it was on there when they picked me up, jest at dawn."

"Who picked you up?" the professor said.

"A Javanese packet, Soerabaya bound. Why the monster didn't get the rest o' me is a mystery. It was a miracle! That

Thing had the strength of a hundred elephants. But it come up out o' the lagoon."

"It must have been a shark?"

"Do sharks come up out o' the sea?"

"Then it was a panther or some other cat animal prowling along the beach. It pounced on you."

"Do panthers smell like a fish? Do panthers smell like nitric acid? Do they feel like slimy rubber? Do they leave acid burns on you?"

"Oh, that's preposterous!"

"Is it?" Pegleg Pyke cried. "Then get a load o' this!"

He pulled up his sleeve. And there, coiling down from shoulder to elbow, was a curious depression—an old, old scar.

"If that ain't an acid burn, you name it!"

PROFESSOR ROBBINS had a stupefied look. He was shaking his head. But his eyes began to glitter with excitement. "Did it make any kind of sound?"

"No, mister. No sound whatever."

"But you must have seen something of it—just a glimpse!"

"I saw nothin' whatsoever, mister."

"It was a giant sea snake!"

"Your guess is as good as the next, mister. All I know is that it smelled like fish and it smelled like acid, and it got my leg—and nothin' but the biggest luck in the world stopped it from gettin' all o' me. I was in the Soerabaya marine hospital six months, out o' my head. And I ain't never been the same since."

The scientist and Larry McGurk were gazing at him as if hypnotized. And the radiant blond girl and her escort, sipping their drinks, were staring at Pegleg Pyke with the same breathless interest.

Professor Robbins said indignantly, "Then it must have been an octopus!"

"Nope. Nope, I didn't hear no suckers. They hiss, they do."

"I should think you'd want to get back there and try to kill it," Larry McGurk suggested.

Pegleg Pyke looked at the flushed young face and slowly nodded.

"Sure, son, I've thought of that."

"You'd better come along," Singapore said. "We're pushin' off for Little Nicobar in the morning."

"I'd like to go," the one-legged man said wistfully. "I sure would like to go back there and have a hand in killin' that monster."

"We aren't going to kill it," Professor Robbins said. "We're going to bring it back alive."

Lucky began wrathfully, "Who the hell—"

"Pipe down," Sammy stopped him. "Fix us another drink, Pegleg. Professor," he said, "I'll charter you the Blue Goose for this expedition for five thousand, gold—on certain conditions."

Professor Robbins looked at him thoughtfully and said, "That seems fair enough. What are the conditions?"

"That Captain Jones, Mate McGurk and I run the show—and that anything we take aboard, aside from the monster, is ours."

"What do you expect to find, Mr. Shay?"

"Pearls. You didn't hear *that* in Rangoon, did you?"

"No."

"This is the lay, Professor: I've got pretty fair information that the old Dutchman, a guy named Vandernoot, who lived in that little stone house on the lagoon for fifteen years, was pearling. He never left the island with his pearls. My understanding is, he cached his pearls in a little coral cave below his house. Maybe it's only a rumor, but I want those pearls."

"I understand."

"Okay. But here's the hitch. Old Vandernoot vanished in 1907. In 1908 there was a volcanic disturbance on Little Nicobar. The east end of the island, where the lagoon is, sank about fifteen feet. This cave is now under about ten feet of water. I can't get those pearls without getting rid of the monster in the lagoon."

PROFESSOR ROBBINS was nodding. "I think I understand. You want the pearls. You don't want to share them if you find them. Is that it?"

"That's it," Lucky said grimly.

"There won't be a quarrel about that," the scientist said. "I have no interest in profits. All I care about is—to bring that Thing back alive—if it exists in actuality. On this basis, I will charter your schooner for five thousand, gold. Does that sum it up?"

Singapore nodded. "That sums it up, brother. Pegleg, you grew up in sail. Come along and I'll sign you on at quartermaster's pay, American scale."

The old man was looking through him, beyond him, at something remotely distant, invisible and fearful. He was still living that horrible experience on the shore of the Little Nicobar lagoon. His cheeks still burned redly and in his eyes smoldered the fires of that old hatred.

"You're on!" he cried harshly. "I'll sign!"

Professor Robbins said with dreamy eyes, through clenched teeth, "If it exists! If it only exists!"

A whisper floated to the four men from the doorway. One word reached Larry McGurk's ears—"Tur-rific!"

He glanced in that direction. The blond girl was going. Evidently she was going with reluctance. Her escort was holding her arm. She was looking back. Under the golden brown of her cheeks was the high pink of excitement. Her brown eyes were dazzled with it. Her smile was like a thrilling challenge to the four men at the bar.

CHAPTER V

ANCHORS AWEIGH!

PROFESSOR BRYCE ROBBINS came aboard the Blue Goose early the following morning to discuss with Singapore Sammy the special equipment which would be needed for the expedition to Little Nicobar.

He inspected the schooner from cutwater to counter and expressed his approval of her slim lines, her staunchness and the shipshape condition in which her owners maintained her.

Captain Jones followed the tall, lean-jawed man about, listened to his remarks and scowled continuously.

The young scientist was crisp and decisive. He knew just what he wanted, and he did not hesitate to speak his mind. When he learned there were two tons of dynamite in the forward hold, with which Singapore and Lucky Jones had planned to blast the lagoon and shock the monster to death, the professor decisively ordered that the explosive be set ashore—or thrown overboard.

He let it be known that he was financing this expedition, chartering the Blue Goose, for the sole purpose of bringing the monster back alive.

"It must be brought back alive, and we must prepare to bring it back alive."

"Sure," Sammy agreed. "But I've got to look after the lives of my crew."

Professor Robbins asked him what steps he was taking to safeguard his crew.

By way of answer, Sammy told the Malay *serang* and a deck-

"Who let you aboard?" Singapore demanded

hand to open the 'midships cargo hatch. Stacked in neat piles at the bottom of the hold were steel bars about a yard in length which resembled bayonets. At one end they were sharply pointed. The other end was flat and contained holes.

Singapore explained that these bayonets were to be fastened all about the deck rail, with the pointed ends sticking out about two feet over the water. The flat ends were to be lugged to the rail. The bayonets were to be spaced about six inches apart.

"I heard from an old pearler," the red-haired man explained, "that pearling luggers have gone into the lagoon—and never came out again. That's why, when we go into that lagoon, this old hooker is going to bristle with steel like a porcupine. If any deep-sea fish tries to wrap itself around the Blue Goose, it won't get far."

The professor was reluctant to approve of this arrangement. He seemed to have more solicitude for the monster than he did for the schooner's crew. He had found, in a Penang shipyard, a diving suit which he thought might be useful. It had been left there by an outfit that had gone broke trying to salvage a sunken treasure ship in the Strait of Malacca.

"It was made for deep-sea work," the professor said. "It's steel—and uncrushable. It has articulating joints, a face plate of glass almost two inches thick, a steel armored air hose—and it looks like a man from Mars. Shall I buy it?"

"We might use it," Sammy said. "I'll show you the arms locker."

He took Professor Robbins down into the main salon. Laughing Larry McGurk, the man who couldn't be killed, was at work with oiled rags and cleaning rods. The Pelican's mate was oiling and cleaning a sub-machine gun.

"We've got six of 'em," Sammy said, "also some sawed-off shotguns, plenty of small arms and a dozen cutlasses."

They discussed ways and means of capturing the monster of which nothing was known regards size, shape or weight. They agreed, however, that the strongest tackle available should be purchased.

The professor, Singapore and Lucky Jones went ashore to attend to tackle and to inspect the deep-sea diving suit. Larry McGurk remained aboard to check off supplies from the supply boat which had just come alongside.

THE REST of the morning he spent reclining in a Bombay chair, studying the beautiful white yacht that was anchored a half mile astern—the Wanderer. He saw men holystoning her decks and polishing her brightwork. He saw a man and two women descend her accommodation ladder and enter the immaculate white tender alongside. All three were in white. The man was a chunky little figure who wore a snow white sun helmet. Of the two women, one was slim and young and one was stout and middle-aged. Both were blond.

The slim, young one stirred vague memories, but McGurk could not distinguish her features because of the distance. But he wondered, sighing, if she was the girl, the dazzling little beauty, who had come into the Blue Grin last night.

He watched the tender proceed to the landing stage at the foot of Beach Street, and he watched the trio disembark. With binoculars he confirmed his suspicions that the girl had beautiful legs. The trio vanished.

Early in the afternoon a motor boat brought out the tackle, the armored diving suit, and the professor's dunnage, including a dozen large and small chests containing scientific apparatus and supplies.

Pegleg Pyke, flashing his gold-tipped fangs with excitement, arrived in a sampan shortly before dark with his sea chest and a case of Demerara rum.

The Blue Goose, completely outfitted and manned, was ready to start, but Captain Jones waited for the night wind and ebb tide. At eight bells, midnight, he ordered sails up and anchor aweigh. The sails filled to the steady breeze from the north, masts strained against the slim and beautiful hull, the schooner slipped through hissing water, aflame with the green phosphorus, and passing the yacht Wanderer, with its rows of glittering white lights, started down the Strait of Malacca—toward what dark and ominous destiny!

CHAPTER VI

GONE OVERBOARD

HECTOR BARLING WAS in a beastly temper. He was peevish and disgruntled. He was indignant. He had been grossly mistreated and he resented it. He was, indeed, so upset that he had been unable to sleep all night.

His guests were responsible. He had spent most of the day with Julie Farrington and her impossible mother in the bazaars of Penang. He had bought Julie every *sarong*, every trinket she had expressed a liking for. And he had done almost as well for her mother.

The day had been very fatiguing to Mr. Barling. The strong tropical sunlight had given him one of his headaches, and he had acquired another bad sunburn—one that would certainly blister. And his personal physician, Dr. Nelson Plank, who always accompanied Mr. Barling on his cruises, had rather coldly informed him that if he continued taking veronal for headaches he would have something worse than headaches to contend with.

As a consequence of all this, Mr. Barling's dinner had not agreed with him. He shouldn't have had that third serving of golden pheasant casserole, or drunk that fifth glass of champagne.

All in all, it had not been Mr. Barling's day. Nor his evening. It was really the evening that rankled and kept Mr. Barling awake throughout the night.

In the evening he had gone looking for Julie—this had been

shortly after dinner—and found her again standing in the bows, staring across the magical moonlit night at that little tub of a schooner.

Perhaps because of the accumulating vexations of the day, he gave way to the impulse which he had stifled so nobly the previous evening. He swept Julie into his arms—and tried to kiss those sweet, soft, seductive lips.

A punch in the nose had been his reward. It spoiled his maneuver and sent him backward with such force that he tripped over a neat pancake of rope and sat down so heartily that his headache almost leaped out of his head. But it returned like a thousand white-hot spears. And the other extremity of his spine hurt even worse.

But that wasn't the worst of it. The worst of it was that Julie had gazed down at him with the utmost abhorrence and said, slowly and distinctly, "You pig! I detest you!"—and had walked away, leaving him sitting there, stunned, as it were, before and behind, and pouting as his indignation kindled.

"A pig!" he panted. "So that's how the land lies! So that's how the wind blows!"

He remained in the bows, glaring malevolently at the blue schooner for almost two hours, trying to adjust himself to the finality of this disappointment. But Hector Barling was not a man easily discouraged, or he would not have been the multi-millionaire he was today.

He made up his mind to tell Julie just what he thought of her. He went to the door of her suite, intending to tell that high-handed and ungrateful young lady a number of things calculated to benefit her. He found a note on the door, saying that she was not to be disturbed. Angered by this, he pounded on the door with his fists. But Julie did not answer.

MUTTERING TO himself, the owner of the Wanderer retired to his own suite, undressed for bed, and attempted to sleep. Sleep was, of course, impossible. His kindnesses to Julie kept flowing through his mind, while in a parallel channel flowed her acts of ungraciousness.

Mr. Barling leaped from bed presently, switched on the lights, and began to pace up and down his luxurious parlor. He didn't see the moon go down. He didn't see the Blue Goose slip past in the night. But he did see the sunrise.

The glow of salmon-pink at portholes and windows seemed to give him an inspiration. He lit a cigar—a dollar cigar, made to his specifications in lots of five thousand, kept at the proper degree of moisture by an electrical humidifier—and tasting this morning like burning sheep's wool—he lit this cigar and went storming into his captain's quarters.

"We're getting under way at once," he informed Captain Milikin, who was too sleepy to grasp the importance of his owner's pout. "We are starting for New York immediately!"

"Not Johor?" the captain said, knuckling his eyes.

"Not Johor," his owner shouted. "New York! At once! Now! This instant!"

"Very well, sir," the captain said, and did as he was bid.

Mr. Barling went to the bridge to take personal charge of the departure. His red-rimmed eyes saw the awakening tropical world with hatred and disgust. Stamping up and down the bridge, as the Wanderer spurned it all with her beautiful white-enameled stern, he felt a species of mean pleasure stealing over him.

Julie would be sorry. Ah, yes, indeed! How she had been looking forward to that visit with the Maharaja of Johor! How she had been anticipating the fun they would have in Singapore! How keenly she had been wanting to see the old temples in Java!

A pig, was he? Well, he'd show her! He'd make her suffer for calling him that. He'd make her suffer for that punch in the nose! He touched the nose. It was tender and swollen. The Wanderer wouldn't, he decided, stop anywhere on the way home. They'd only pause. They'd hesitate only long enough, when it was absolutely necessary, to take on oil for the Diesels.

Thinking of Julie's disappointment made him feel better. He almost smiled, thinking of Julie's disappointment. It was what she needed and richly deserved. He decided on his new attitude toward her. He would be haughty and aloof. He would treat her coldly. He would smile at her suffering.

His pleasing reveries were suddenly intruded upon by a woman's scream. The scream came closer. A moment later, Mrs. Farrington, with her hair in kid curlers, her complexion blotchy and unhealthily inflamed, came screaming onto the bridge. In her pink dressing gown she was awful to look upon.

"Julie!" she screamed. "She isn't on board!"

"What's this?" Mr. Barling squealed, after a moment of dreadful silence.

"She isn't aboard! She's not in her suite! She's gone! She packed a suitcase! She left a note saying not to worry but to go on and forget her! Forget her! I'm going to have one of my heart attacks! Why don't you do something? Why don't you say something?"

"Hell," Mr. Barling said.

CHAPTER VII

STOWAWAYS

UNDER A MORNING sky of dazzling blue, the Blue Goose was bowling down the Strait of Malacca with sails tight as drumheads, with a wake as straight as an arrow feathering out astern. Off to port, the Malayan Peninsula was a sharp green line on which whipped cream clouds were piled. Off to starboard, the island of Sumatra was a thread of misty heliotrope.

Mate Larry McGurk was at the wheel, bare-headed and bare-footed, his rough blond hair spilling about in the spanking breeze, his feet planted wide apart against the roll of the deck. He was getting the feel of the schooner, and deciding that she was a perfect lady. Now and then he glanced off to the weather horizon, which looked a little squally.

Singapore and Lucky Jones were below, checking off stores in the lazaret. Professor Robbins was in his cabin, unpacking his boxes of scientific paraphernalia. And Pegleg Pyke was stumping about forward, coiling down ropes, singing an old chantey, happy to be at sea again.

It was Senga, the *serang*, who found the stowaway. Larry heard his hoarse yell. Then Senga and Pegleg Pyke came aft with the stowaway between them. He was hardly more than a boy—a thin, homely, black-freckled boy of nineteen, with a button nose, bright little black eyes which danced with derision, and an insolent young mouth.

His black hair was shaggy and flecked with bits of oakum and straw. The suit he wore was shabby, shiny and out at knee and elbow. His denim shirt was in rags. He was grinning impudently.

Pegleg said, "Caught him hidin' in the for'ard hold, mate."

"Take the wheel," the mate said. He looked the stowaway over and the boy's grin slowly faded. Larry McGurk's sapphire Irish eyes were cold and unwelcoming. But the little black eyes stared without wavering.

"WHO THE hell are you?"

"Who, me?" the boy retorted. "I guess I'm just a bird o' passage, mate. I ain't afraid o' nothin'. I'll work my way."

Professor Robbins, Sam Shay and Captain Jones came up from below. Lucky's blue-black brows met in a fierce scowl.

"What's this?" he asked.

"A stowaway," Larry McGurk said. And: "What's your name?"

"Pete Cringle."

"Where you from?"

"Who, me? Most everywheres, mate. I'm a deep-sea diver by profession. I was in Penang yesterday when this guy here"—his dirty thumb indicated the scowling scientist—"bought that deep-sea divin' outfit off of Hin Jok. I was figgerin' you might want the guy who went inside it."

"Keep on talkin'," Lucky advised him. "You ain't said nothin' yet."

"I'm an American citizen, mister, if that's what you mean," the boy said. "I was in Australia, but I didn't like them Limies. An American don't stand a chance there. I bummed my way on a copra boat from Sydney to Macassar, and I stowed away on a Chinese trader from Macassar to Penang. That was six months ago. Since then," with dignity, "I've been associated with this salvagin' bunch that was tryin' to salvage the gold ingots off the old City o' Benares. She went down off Cape Tamuntalang somewheres, but we didn't even find her. That's how come I was on the beach in Penang and saw this guy here buy my old suit."

"How deep water did you work in in that suit?" Lucky asked.

"Ninety fathoms."

"You're a liar."

"I ain't. That suit's good for more pressure than that."

Sam Shay said sharply, "Do you know where we're headed?"

"Who, me? Yes, sir. We're headed for Little Nicobar."

"Who told you that?"

"A guy in The Mudhole—a souse. Little Nicobar is okay with me, Mr. Shay. I don't care where we go. I'm the best deep-sea diver on the Indian Ocean and I ain't afraid o' no monster in no lagoon. I'm lucky. And you guys can use plenty o' luck."

"How'd you get aboard?" Pegleg growled.

"I swum out last night while you was eatin' and snuck aboard."

"Put him to work, Larry," Singapore said, "chippin' anchor chain. Professor, it looks like this expedition is about as secret as an active volcano. When did you eat last, mutt?"

"I can't remember back that far," Pete Cringle said.

"Tell Ah Fong to fix him some breakfast," Sammy instructed Pegleg.

"You can use me in that divin' suit, cantcha, Mr. Shay?" the ratty-looking youth eagerly asked.

"I'll wrassle with the idea," Sam said. Lucky Jones, a diver of long experience, questioned the stowaway and reported his talk to Sammy with the recommendation that the "fresh little mug" be enrolled in the crew.

"He knows divin' and he seems game," Lucky said, "even if he has got a lip a mile long." Thus did Pete Cringle, who had run away from his home in Hoboken at the age of eleven and been wandering since, become a member of the schooner's crew.

FOUR BELLS in the morning watch had just sounded when the presence of another stowaway was announced. Singapore Sammy was taking a turn at the wheel when the shriek of terror rang out, muffled, from the forward end of the ship.

The shriek was long and lusty. It was followed by muffled yelps and howls.

Gripping the wheel, Sam stared forward at the point from which these disturbances seemed to originate.

Hidden by the jibs, a woman was hysterically saying, "It was a spider the size of an eagle!"

Accompanied by Pegleg Pyke and the best deep-sea diver on the Indian Ocean, the second stowaway appeared. Pegleg Pyke was in a state of blustering anger. Pete Cringle was grinning evilly. This stowaway was as trim a figure of a girl as ever graced a quarterdeck. She wore a sailor's suit of white duck which was rumpled and smeared with green and buff paint.

"She was hidin' in the paint locker, Mr. Shay," Pegleg Pyke remarked in the voice he might have used to say, "She was openin' the sea-cocks, Mr. Shay."

"Take the wheel," the red-headed man growled. With fists on hips he slowly advanced on the slim girl in ducks. She had recovered from her alarm and was smiling radiantly. Her hair was blonder than blond. It was silver-golden fleece. Her eyes were of the rich reddish brown of autumn leaves. And her color was golden-brown. She was quite as dazzling as he remembered her.

As if mocking him, she placed her small browned hands on her hips and grinned up at his stern face.

"Good morning, Mr. Shay!"

Professor Robbins, Larry McGurk and Captain Jones came up the stairs, followed by Ah Fong, the cook, ordinarily the most imperturbable of men. The stowaway disbursed her smile among them.

"Another stowaway!" Sammy grimly announced.

"Good morning!" the girl laughed. "Good morning, everybody! Fancy meeting you gentlemen in the Strait of Malacca! I think it's simply tur-rific!"

"Who let you aboard?" Sam asked.

"Nobody. I just came aboard."

Singapore was glowering from wriggling red brows. A girl named Sally Lavender had been the latest to destroy his faith in women. Professor Robbins was staring at the blond girl with dazzled gray eyes.

"You're the girl in The Mudhole!" he said triumphantly.

THE STOWAWAY mimicked his astonishment and said, "Yes, indeed! Mudhole Queenie! Will somebody be big and give Queenie some breakfast? Queenie is starving."

"Come 'long," said Ah Fong. "Can fixum."

"Wait a minute," Sam said. "What are you doing here?"

"Escaping," she answered. And her brightly tanned young face became grave. "Escaping from a life of boredom on a yacht."

"What yacht?"

"Wanderer."

"That big white Diesel yacht that was anchored astern of us in Penang?" Singapore asked.

"Yes, Mr. Shay."

"You ran away from *her?*"

"I certainly did, Mr. Shay!"

"You mean you ran away from your husband?"

"Dear, merciful heaven, no," the stowaway said. "I merely ran away from the man who wanted to be my husband. I heard you men discussing this cruise and the monster at Little Nicobar. I was carried away! I was spellbound! It was tur-rific!"

"Pegleg," Sam said, "take a look around this ship and see how many more deadheads we've got aboard."

"Women," Pegleg muttered, "bring bad luck to a ship. And women stowaways is the unluckiest of all."

"But I'm terribly lucky!" the girl cried.

"Stowaways always sing that song," Singapore said. "What are we going to do with her, Lucky?"

"Put her ashore in Singapore," Captain Jones promptly answered.

"Oh, no!" the girl wailed. "You wouldn't be so brutal! You wouldn't let me fall into that little beast's clutches again!"

"Oil," Lucky jeered.

"Oil?" the stowaway cried. "Oh, really?" She was angry now. There was a pink flush under the golden tan. The wonderful brown eyes were snapping. The gay smile was gone. "Maybe you'd like to be dragged off on a cruise around the world by a revolting little pipsqueak like Hector Barling!"

"Who is the other dame?" Lucky interrupted.

"My mother! She engineered it all! Dying to have me marry that pompous little squirt! Having heart attacks if things didn't go just her way!"

"Who is this Barling?" Larry McGurk said.

"You've never heard of Hector Barling—the patent medicine king? The Emperor of Dyspepsia? Barling's Elixir? Barling's Tummy Tabs? Barling's Liver Livener? Why! People cry for it!"

"Never heard of him," Sammy said.

"We will," Lucky growled, "if we run off with his girl. A guy like that would hire a navy. And maybe she's lyin'. Maybe she *is* his wife. Lady, if you think you're goin' to Little Nicobar with us, you're nuts."

For a moment the wonderful eyes became misty. Then this cleared and she smiled. Sammy sensed that she was putting up a game fight—and trying not to let them see that it was a fight.

"I can pay my passage—or I'll work," she said. "I'll be delighted to do the most menial work! I can cook!"

SAM GLANCED at those small, beautifully-kept hands, with their long, shiny, pink nails and said, "I'll bet you never cooked a meal in your life."

"I can scrub floors."

"Or scrubbed a floor."

"I'll bet," Lucky said scornfully, "you never did a lick of any kind of work in your life."

She whirled on him. That whirl verified Sam's guess. It went with music.

"Watch me," she said. "If you think this isn't work, try it."

She snapped her fingers and, raising her elbows, swung into

a lively tap dance. Her small slippers twinkled and clattered in the steps of a fast and smooth routine. She flung her arms. She whirled. She stomped. She was as abandoned, as graceful as a young palm tree in a gale.

Mate McGurk cried, "Hot dog!" The girl flashed a grin at him. She ended her dance, and with feet apart and hands on hips said: "Well?"

Professor Robbins yelped: "I know you! You're Julie Farrington, of the Follies!"

"Hey-hey!" the dancer laughed.

"If there's one thing we need in a bad way on this hooker," the sardonic skipper said, "it's a tap dancer."

The girl laughed: "I'm good for raising the morale!"

"How about the blood pressure?" the professor drawled. "Do you do a strip tease?"

Her smile faded. She looked at him wearily and said, "I don't think I care much for that remark."

"How," Singapore asked, "did you wiggle aboard?"

"About an hour before we sailed, Mr. Shay, I rowed alongside in a dinghy from the Wanderer. You were all aft or below, so I went forward, climbed aboard with my suitcase, kicked the dinghy off, and hid in the paint locker. I'd have been there all day if it hadn't been for that spider. Oh, how I loathe spiders."

Laughing Larry McGurk said gravely, "Did you bring your lunch?"

"Only some water."

"Ah Fong," Singapore said, "will get you something to eat."

"A caviar omelette, Ah Fong," Laughing Larry said, "some anchovy hearts, and a bottle of the Nineteen-Twelve Chateau Yquem."

Julie Farrington stopped smiling again. She looked at him with steady brown eyes. "Mister," she said, "I'll bet my stomach has traveled as far on beans as yours has. You're talking to a working girl."

Ah Fong brought her suitcase from the paint locker and installed it in an empty stateroom. Miss Farrington breakfasted and reappeared on deck, more alluring than ever in silk lounging pajamas of navy blue. The deep blue brought out the golden color of her clear young skin and contrasted sensationally with the pale-gold excitement of her hair.

Lucky Jones was at the wheel. She told him she simply adored sailing vessels, and she tried to make him talk. But she made little progress with the black-browed, scowling skipper. Lucifer Jones answered her with grunts, shrugs, and other revelations of an unyielding nature.

He said bluntly, "You're wastin' your time on me, baby. If you think that's oil, take a look at the course."

She looked tired. But she went forward with fresh determination to where Singapore Sammy was sitting on a hatch cover, smoking his calabash, watching the gyrations of a flock of sea gulls off to starboard, and letting the breeze blow through his red hair.

"**MR. SHAY**," she said, seating herself beside him, "you must have led a terribly interesting life."

"Kid," said the owner of the Blue Goose, "I quit falling for that line before you quit wearing square-rigged underwear."

"You aren't a day older than twenty-seven!"

"I learned young."

She tried persuasion. Singapore Sammy puffed at his calabash, watched the sea gulls and grunted his answers or made none at all. Her voice became husky with effort.

She said, "When I was a little girl, in Amityville, Long Island, I used to throw pebbles at a granite rock; in the back yard, wondering how long it would take to wear it down. Now I know."

"Singapore tomorrow," Sammy said unfeelingly.

She retired to her stateroom to weep. But when she reappeared for tiffin she was her gay, charming, debonair self. She was radiant and she was witty. She poked fun at them all. She poked fun at Ah Fong. She gave a marvelous imitation of Hector Tobias Barling, his pompousness, his pouting.

Her audience was with her every inch of the way, but when tiffin was over, Lucky Jones said, "We hit Singapore early tomorrow morning. Be sure you're packed, lady."

Singapore went to his cabin. Larry McGurk followed him in, and closed the door. He seated himself on Sam's bunk and said, "What are you going to do about the sweetheart of the South Seas?"

"What is there to do?"

"I'm asking you."

"Yeah. I figured you might. As far as I go, she walks the plank in Singapore."

"Sure about that?"

Singapore Sammy was looking out a porthole. He turned and looked at Larry. The blue-green eyes were troubled.

"Are you falling for this skirt, Larry?"

"She kills at fifty rods."

"That makes a way to get killed you haven't tried."

"You're going to have a shipload of corpses!"

"You won't find mine among 'em, Larry. She isn't my type."

Laughing Larry grinned. "I've heard all about your type. Her name is Sally Lavender. They call her Shanghai Sal, and she's given you the run-around so many times you feel like a pin wheel. She's the one who gave Lucky such a raw deal."

"If she wasn't a crook," Singapore Sammy said, "I'd marry her tomorrow. The last time I almost proposed to her, she put knockout drops in my beer and stole the Malobar pearl."

"But you got it back."

"She's the only woman I ever knew I wanted to kill and kiss at the same time. But never mind Shanghai Sal. This little blonde is falling for you. If you want her to stay, I'll let her. What do you say?"

"Put her ashore, Sam. I want to keep on laughing."

CHAPTER VIII

BOTH BARRELS

THE WIND WAS falling. By early afternoon the Blue Goose was ghosting along in light airs. By mid afternoon a dead calm had set in.

Because Sammy wished to conserve their gasoline supply, he did not order the engine started.

A merciless equatorial sun beat down on a painted ship on a painted ocean. Pitch softened in seams. The Blue Goose rolled lazily in the ground swell and drifted with antic currents.

After studying the blazing blue furnace of the sky, Pegleg Pyke said to Larry McGurk: "What did I tell you, mate? A woman brings doldrums and trouble every time." And he stuck a dirk into the mainmast and whistled an eerie bar, but no wind came.

Julie came up from her cabin, dressed for hot weather. She wore a soft white shirt and white shorts and was demurely unaware of herself.

Lounging under the after deck awning, Sammy drawled, "Well, the last doubts are cleared up."

"Yes," she said sweetly. "It shows what fate will do to help a deserving girl along."

"Fate or nature?" he asked lazily.

"The minute you say I'm welcome, a spanking breeze will blow. Try it!"

He grinned. "You're a better salesman when you don't say

anything. Lucky said he's going to take you ashore under his own power if we don't find a breeze."

"Some sculptor ought to do a statue of all of you in chromium—to show how soft chromium is by comparison."

"Give Lucky an eyeful and stop talking."

Her eyes darkened. She said, "Oh," coldly and went below. She returned in a few minutes in her blue deck pajamas. Her eyes were still stormy.

"Am I less offensive now?"

"Every little wave is saying, 'She's wonderful!'"

"By the way, Mr. Shay, I'm a terribly nice girl."

"Are you telling me, Miss Farrington?"

"Why can't I stay, Sam?"

"We'd be spending all our time protecting you."

"Would you?" She doubled up her fist, crooked her arm and said, "Feel this!"

The red-headed man grinned and felt it. His grin vanished. The girl's returned.

"Does this girl walk home from a boat ride?"

"The girl snapped at the wrong hook. I was talking about our friend in the lagoon."

"I'd rather be eaten by it than marry the Gaekwar of Gastritis. Sam, it's the first time I've been out from under my mother's thumb. You don't know what courage it took."

"You're wasting time. It isn't my say-so. It's up to Bryce Robbins and the skipper—and Larry."

"If I can persuade them, can I count on you?"

"I make no promises to women after 1 P.M."

"All right, by golly; I'll sell all of them!"

PROFESSOR ROBBINS came on deck. He and Julie talked in low murmurs, but Sammy caught a word now and then, and grinned. Julie was giving him high pressure, with a few hey-heys thrown in. Turning on the personality. He liked the girl and admired her courage, but the Blue Goose, enlarged ten times, would still have been too small.

The dancing lady and the millionaire scientist presently went forward.

Pegleg Pyke came stumping aft from the fo'c's'le.

"Mr. Shay," he said ominously, "that woman's gonna turn this ship keel fer trucks to make you let her stay. Better the rats to leave than a woman to come."

"She goes overboard tomorrow, old timer."

They were startled by the sound of a sharp, small report forward, bouncing off the limp sails. A blue wraith came swiftly aft. She passed the binnacle. Her hair was different. Her eyes were wrathful. She was white. Her lovely mouth was a storm flag.

She passed without speaking, went to the stairs, disappeared.

Professor Robbins came aft more leisurely. Just then Sammy heard a stateroom door slam. Soft, smothered sobbing came up the ventilator. This dwindled. A girl had buried her face, unless he was mistaken, in a pillow.

Sam glanced at the professor. He saw a trickle of blood from the scientist's nose.

"And to look at her," Sam drawled, "you'd think she wasn't any stronger than a kitten."

"Damn her," Robbins said. He didn't sound angry. He sounded sick.

The beautiful stowaway remained in her cabin until Ah Fong rang the dinner gong. She appeared in a slim, frilly white frock, so dazzlingly lovely that the men welcomed her with a stunned silence. She was perfection glorified. She was so radiant that she hurt the eyes.

Dinner began in an uneasy silence, but this ended when Julie went into her performance. There was a light in her soft brown eyes, and Larry McGurk suspected that this was the stowaway's last stand. She was giving them both barrels, the works. She was wittier, gayer, more entertaining than she had been at noon. And

Singapore Sammy observed that, throughout dinner, Larry McGurk's face was a dark and shining crimson and that Lucky Jones looked more sardonic than usual.

Larry McGurk was sitting in his Bombay chair on the after-deck smoking a cigarette when Julie came up. She saw him sitting there and walked to the taffrail. She sighed, stretched her arms to the stars and said, "Ah, how much sweller it is from this schooner than from that floating penthouse!"

Her voice was that of an exhausted girl. Slim and romantic in the starglow, she looked up at the Southern Cross, an eerie blaze in the sky. "Larry, will you swing your vote if I can line up just one other?"

He was re-lighting his cigarette. In the light of the match he looked at her anxious mouth, her pleading eyes.

"Sure!"

"All right!" she snapped. "Watch me get your vote!"

WHEN BRYCE ROBBINS came on deck, she strolled forward with him. The night was so still Larry could hear the murmur of their voices in the bows. They were there perhaps eight minutes. Then Julie slipped aft. Once again she was pale, her hair was disarrayed, her eyes were wrathful, and her lovely mouth was thin. She stopped near his chair.

"The professor," she said, in a choking voice, "says I can stay."

Larry laughed. "You kissed him into submission."

She seated herself on the broad arm of his chair, with her back to him. The night was as hot as the day, but Julie was shivering.

"How many more people do I have to kiss?"

"You might give Pegleg a whirl."

"All the monsters in all the lagoons in the world aren't worth it. Put me ashore in Singapore!" Her voice was hysterical. "I'm sick of it! I'm worn out!"

"Hold it, baby. My sales resistance might be at a low ebb."

"Not really!" she said, looking around at him.

He got up, clapped his hands to her shoulders, lifted her

off the chair arm, and brought her hard against his chest. He lowered his face and kissed her.

Even in the starglow, he could see the wrath in her eyes. But her self-restraint was wonderful.

"That ought to rate a trip around the world," she said huskily.

"You won't need any more votes."

"You don't mean I can stay!"

"Hold everything." He went below. Singapore Sammy was at the desk in his cabin.

Larry said, "Well, Red, it's around to you again."

"I said she could stay if it was jake with you and Robbins."

"When was this?"

"Right after supper."

"So she kissed you out of your horse sense, too!"

Singapore wriggled his carrot-colored brows. "What is this game—postoffice?"

"What does Lucky say?"

"He has been in a daze since he saw her in those little-bitty white pants. He never knew a girl had legs. Tell her to come down here."

Larry went out, leaving the door open. Julie came below promptly and walked in. Her face was flushed, her eyes were brilliant. She looked almost feverish.

Singapore Sammy closed the door and said, "Sit down, sister. There's something I think you ought to know."

And when she had seated herself on the edge of his bunk, Sammy said: "I want you to answer a blunt question with the truth. Are you in love with Larry McGurk?"

Her eyes widened, then narrowed. "I'm not in love with anybody."

"There's something you ought to know. I don't want Larry hurt, and I don't want a nice kid like you hurt. Did you know that he has about six weeks or a couple of months—at the most—to live?"

Julie stared at him. The faint smile vanished. She suddenly went white. And she said huskily, "I hope this isn't a joke."

"No. It isn't a joke. There's something in his head, some kind of a growth, that is absolutely incurable. A little over four months ago the doctors gave him six months to live. He came out here because he wanted to die in the Far East. And did you hear about the charmed life he leads?"

"No"—faintly.

So Sammy told her about that, too—the sharks and the tiger, the bandits and the cobra. Her eyes were wet.

She cried: "Oh, it seems such a pity! He's so young—and such a fine fellow!"

"But you're not falling for him?"

Julie shook her head. "I like him. I like all of you. You're a grand bunch, but I'm not falling for anybody. And I don't intend to. Can I stay?"

"Yep. You can stay."

SHORTLY AFTER midnight a breeze sprang up. By morning it was blowing a half-gale. The Blue Goose charged down the Strait of Malacca under double reefs.

And with Julie accepted as a full-fledged member of that strangely assorted little company, shipboard life settled into a pattern, as shipboard life on a long voyage always does. The bright central figure was Julie, and her shipmates revealed themselves according to their natures.

Bryce Robbins was so desperately in love that he could hardly eat or sleep. He became more and more irritable and assertive. At every opportunity he made love to Julie, and was indignant when she repulsed him.

Between him and Lucky Jones a lively hatred had sprung up. Lucky, too, had fallen in love with Julie. He turned so sardonic that his former self was, by comparison, a sunny fellow.

Pete Cringle fell victim to a species of puppy love. He thought

Julie the most wonderful creature in the world—and told her so. She was so kind to him that he became bold and tried to kiss her.

Only with Singapore Sammy and Laughing Larry did she feel comfortable—and safe. These two treated her as if she were a man. Sam taught her to box the compass and to steer a straight course. But of them all, she seemed to prefer Larry's companionship. Perhaps it was because he had so short a time to live, perhaps because he seemed so immune to her charms.

Little else was discussed these days but the monster of the lagoon: how large the creature was, and how dangerous; how much of the legends they had heard was lies and how much was truth; what its nature might prove to be; how they would go about capturing it.

They agreed—hoped—that it wasn't large enough, powerful enough to sink a hundred and twenty foot schooner.

Lucky came out of the chartroom one morning to announce that, if the wind held, they would anchor inside the barrier reef, off the lagoon at Little Nicobar, the following dawn.

The rest of the day was spent in bolting into place the steel bayonets. They were spaced along the rail from stem to stern on both sides of the ship.

The wind held. Julie Farrington awoke next morning to the rumbling of anchor chain, the flapping of sails, the rattling of blocks, the distant booming of surf on the barrier reef.

CHAPTER IX

THE ISLAND

SHE LOOKED OUT the porthole. Save for bleakly glittering stars and a strange green glow in the distance, the world was still in blackness. The green glow puzzled her, and it made her uneasy. Indefinitely, it was oval in shape—a long, thin oval that seemed to lie mistily on the water about a half-mile away. It glowed and waned and glowed again like an opal or, rather, an emerald with an uncertain pale and mystic fire in its heart.

She heard, in that direction, above the muted thunder of surf on the barrier reef, a low and sustained bubbling.

A breath of sickly-sweet fragrance floated in at the porthole, and she wondered if it was the perfume given off so freely by the pale-blue monster orchids which Pegleg had mentioned.

The very air seemed charged with uneasiness. Julie shivered and clasped her breast in her arms.

She presently discerned a black mass to the right of the misty pool of glowing green, and she presumed that this was Little Nicobar. She supposed the smoky green oval was the lagoon, and she supposed that it was alive with those mysterious microscopic creatures which are the cause of phosphorescence. She had heard that in some parts of the South Seas the phosphorescent glow is so bright that you can distinguish a face a dozen feet away.

The world was growing light. Soon she could see the dark loom of the island against the burnished black metal of rain clouds. The oval wraith faded and she saw the uneasy glimmer of stormlight on the lagoon and the pale glow of the encircling sand arms and the silhouettes of palm trees.

The sickly-sweet fragrance and the faraway bubbling sounds continued. Wisps and plumes of steam were stealing out of the jungle and floating across the lagoon.

The Blue Goose had evidently made her anchorage under light airs, for there was no wind now. Glassy water, slowly undulating, stretched from the schooner to the island. The dark mirror of the lagoon was shattered by a million dancing feet.

A column of purple darkness stretched from the lagoon to the low-hanging black clouds. The column moved swiftly on the schooner, lashing the calm surface to milky froth. And rain drummed on the deck over the girl's head.

She dressed in her ducks, slipped into the sticky yellow slicker Singapore had given her, and went on deck. The men were standing in a group in the stern, looking at the island. As she joined them it vanished behind a brown curtain that seemed to rise out of the water. The squall whipped the sea into racing white.

Julie went to where Singapore Sammy was standing with binoculars to his eyes, peering at the brownness where the lagoon had been. She glanced at the wet faces of the other men. She was trying not to feel uneasy. Her intelligence said that those old, old legends must be, at least, terribly exaggerated; that Pegleg Pyke's story must have been, in a large part, a product of a sailorman's imagination.

This island was, after all, very much like the hundreds of tropical islands they had passed in the Java and Flores Seas.

Yet she sensed in the very air an uneasiness, a sinister something that could not be defined, and this was not imagination. Studying the intent, dripping faces of the men, she saw reflected the same uncertainty, the same struggle with doubt and skepticism. And when the brown curtain vanished and the island was again revealed under the low-hanging dark clouds, her feeling and the look in the men's faces did not vanish.

A drumlike roll of distant thunder made her jump. She was

looking at the lagoon, trying to visualize what manner of creature might live in that inkily blue water, and in her imagination she was picturing a hideous, dragon-like monster of green and yellow, with an enormous head about which lappets and tentacles of awful flesh hung. In actuality, mankind's old conception of a sea serpent. Each ripple, each swift-moving color on the surface of the lagoon made her catch her breath. And she could see in the faces of the men, as they stared at the lagoon, this same wonder and expectancy.

JULIE ASKED Sam, in an uneven voice, if he had seen anything. And he nervously answered, "Not yet."

"We aren't going in there?"

"No."

The clouds presently lifted a little, the light grew brighter, and the Dutchman's house at the edge of the lagoon became visible in its setting of coconut palms.

Sammy studied it through his binoculars and saw a square gray lump of stone. It resembled a tomb, a very lonely tomb. Until breakfast was ready, he scrutinized the lagoon, raked now and then by showers. He climbed the mainmast ratlines and perched in the cross-tree. Using the glasses, he saw no sign of life in or upon the lagoon. Sea gulls and flamingoes wheeled above it, but he saw none of them light in the water.

He studied the white coral rim of the lagoon, beginning at the Dutchman's house and moving his glasses slowly until he had completed the circle. He saw no sign of life except for one large, sluggish crab, and he saw only one entrance to the lagoon—the narrow inlet off which the Blue Goose was anchored. The tide was running out in a swollen blue current. He saw a school of porpoises swimming leisurely against the current midway through the inlet. He watched them until they entered the lagoon and disappeared.

At breakfast, Bryce Robbins alone was skeptical. He wanted to take the Blue Goose into the lagoon under power and explore.

Pegleg Pyke said harshly, "Only a fool sets sail for a place where an angel wouldn't dast show a keel."

"Oh, there's no danger," the scientist irritably answered. "It's all in your imaginations."

"That tribe o' head-hunters ain't in our imaginations," the one-legged old sailor retorted.

"Bosh!"

Lucky said angrily, "Yeah! Yeah! You know everything."

"I don't take stock in childish legends."

Sammy cried, "Oh, pipe down. We're on each other's nerves. We aren't going into the lagoon. We will send a party ashore in the small boat and the shore party will take pistols and cutlasses. Pegleg has been here before and will take charge. Who do you want?"

Pegleg looked about the table. He passes Julie's pale, hopeful young face. His glance lingered on the freckled, pug-nosed face of Pete Cringle. "The best deep-sea diver on the Indian Ocean." He glanced at Bryce Robbins, at Larry, at Lucky and back to Sammy.

"I'll take you, Lucky and Larry."

"And me," Julie muttered.

"I'm going, of course," Professor Robbins said firmly. He looked as if he was prepared to add that it was his right, inasmuch as he was underwriting the expedition.

He had said this in settling several other disputes.

Sammy said hastily, "Of course, Bryce."

"How about me?" Julie huskily asked. "I can shoot as straight as any man on board!"

"Don't be silly," Larry said.

She sent him a furious glance and tightened her lips.

Pegleg fixed his sunken, oystery old eyes on the pale, lovely face, the resentful brown eyes.

"They ain't no women in the shore party," he snarled.

"I go if I have to swim!"

SINGAPORE WENT on deck and instructed Senga, the *serang*, to put the small boat over. He went to his cabin for his automatic pistol. When he returned, a lively argument was taking place between Pegleg, on deck, and Julie, who sat in the stern of the small boat alongside and refused to move.

Julie was saying, "I defy anyone to put me off this boat."

Pegleg implored: "Sam, for God's sake reason with her!"

"But she isn't reasonable," Sam said. "Julie, will you be a good little egg and get out of that boat?"

"No."

"Do I have to grab you by the scruff of the neck?"

"I'll bite!"

"Larry, talk to her."

"Listen, brat," Larry said. "The gentlemen want to *use* the little boat. Will you kindly haul yourself out of it?"

"No."

When the small boat started for the beach, it contained Larry, Pegleg Pyke, Professor Robbins, Lucky, Sam and Julie. Larry took the oars and drove the boat toward a landing place on the beach near a grove of coconut palms.

Julie, in the bows, stared at the island through the drizzling rain. Her heart was thumping. At each surge of the bows her excitement grew. She wasn't using her imagination. There was something, in the air that frightened her. It wasn't the low clouds. It wasn't the smell of the jungle. Yet it was as definite as an odor, a sound, a moving object.

The keel grated on the sand. She leaped out, stared through the palms at the white sand dune beyond which was the lagoon and Gurt Vandernoot's old stone cabin. She expected to see something appear at the top of the dune. She tried not to feel so frightened, but her heart was beating against the wall of her chest, and she was as white as a ghost.

She waited for the others to land. She was glad she was so well armed. There had been a moment when it had seemed a trifle ridiculous to be holding a cutlass in one hand, a pistol in the other. But it didn't seem ridiculous now. It seemed eminently sensible.

Even Bryce Robbins, the scoffer, pale and watchful-eyed, carried his cutlass and pistol ashore, although he had said, leaving the ship, that such precautions were fantastic and childish.

And she observed that Larry McGurk, who took nothing seriously, was pale and that a tightness had settled about his mouth.

Sam and the scowling Lucky were grim and watchful. They had spent many years in these islands and they had the look of men prepared for any kind of treachery or trouble.

Pegleg Pyke led the way to the top of the sand dune. The old sailor was still peevish because Julie had come along. In his harsh voice, using his cutlass as a pointer, he told them where he had come through the jungle and out onto the beach.

The clouds had lifted a little, and the base of the black mountain in the middle of the island could be seen mistily. Julie glanced at the mountain, but her eyes were snatched back to the shimmering surface of the lagoon below her. Her eyes roved about, darted here and there over the water. She would have been horrified—but not surprised—to see the water part and a beast of unearthly appearance and dimensions rise up and stare at them boldly from lidless eyes. Her heart beat faster as she pictured it staring at them, then come plunging to shore with great and horrible writhings and lashings. It would churn the water to suds. It would come plunging to shore and up the hill and overtake them, gripped in the paralysis of terror, before they could escape.

Shivering, she stared at the little gray block of stone near the edge of the lagoon, where Gurt Vandernoot had mysteriously lived and mysteriously died. She wondered what his end had been.

PEGLEG PYKE was brandishing his cutlass. "From the base o' that mountain and right down through there is where I run that night—twenty years ago! Right down there past that little stone house I run. The island's sunk fifteen foot since then. There was palms growin' close to the water then. They're gone now. It was one o' them palms I grabbed when the thing grabbed me."

Julie shuddered but said nothing. If she said she was afraid, if she said anything, they would make her wait in the boat.

Sam said, "I suppose it's safe enough to go down there."

"Safe enough in the daytime," Pegleg said.

"How about these natives?" Lucky asked.

"Just keep clear o' the trees."

Bryce Robbins made a sound of impatience in his nose and started briskly down the slope toward the lagoon. He called back, "There's nothing to be afraid of. You can see there's nothing to be afraid of."

Julie glanced quickly at Sammy. He was looking at the lagoon, frowning a little, a doubtful man struggling to be skeptical. He felt her eyes on him, and flashed her a grin.

They followed Pegleg and Bryce down the slope to the Dutchman's house, but Julie kept wary eyes on the lagoon. She wasn't afraid of the natives, but the lagoon, in its blue innocence, frightened her as nothing had in all her life.

The Dutchman's house was no farther than twenty feet from the water's edge. It had been built of slabs of coral rock neatly fitted together and it had the look of a structure that would last forever. Shaped like a paving block, it was about twenty feet long by fifteen wide.

On the lagoon side, about five feet from the ground, was a row of eight equally-spaced five-inch loopholes. Julie caught the glint of light on them and saw that they were not loopholes but peepholes covered with thick glass.

A whirring sound behind her made her spin about with a cry which she quickly stifled. But it was only the sound of flamingoes circling out over the lagoon from the jungle.

Bryce Robbins said impatiently, "You people act as if you expect to see a ghost. Let's have a look inside." But his voice was none too sure.

They went around to the rear of the stone cabin, where the door was. It was open. It was a narrow door of iron or steel an inch thick, hung on hinges like those of a bank vault.

It was caked with rust. There was a heavy bolt on the inner side, and there was a steel socket set into the masonry to accommodate this bolt.

Singapore said, "Someone had better stand guard."

Lucky said, "Watch out for snakes. It's blacker in there than the heart of hell."

Julie was staring into the darkness, wondering about the mysterious man who had lived here so many years.

Larry said, "That roof was built to last, too." It was reënforced concrete, constructed by laying small iron pipes crosswise in layers, then flowing on cement. Successive layers of pipes and cement made a roof eighteen inches thick.

The cabin doorway exhaled a breath of dampness and mold— the characteristic smell of poorly ventilated stone houses in the tropics.

SINGAPORE FLASHED on an electric torch. Julie saw a floor littered with rubbish. She saw dust, mold, fungus, spiders, crabs and scorpions. Large nameless shiny insects scurried to cover. Presumably this cabin was, except for the ravages of time, just as it had been twenty-six years ago when Gurt Vandernoot died in it or abandoned it.

Sammy said, "There's two rooms. There's a stone wall down the middle, dividing the cabin. And there's another iron door."

Sammy, Bryce Robbins, Pegleg and Lucky went inside. When they announced that there were no snakes, Julie followed them. Larry remained outside to keep an eye on the lagoon and the jungle.

The door in the stone wall was closed. About five feet from the bottom was a round hole, probably a peephole, three inches in diameter. Below it, near an edge, was a large keyhole.

Sam put one eye to the peephole, but saw nothing. He put

his fingers into the hole and tried to pull the door open. He said, "It's locked. When Vandernoot left, he locked that room."

Lucky growled, "We gotta see what's in that room. How do you know the Dutchman's skeleton ain't in that room? I'm goin' back to the ship for the acetylene torch."

"And leave us here, marooned?" Julie cried.

"Maybe you better come along."

"Oh, I'm not afraid!"

"Naw, you don't look afraid," he jeered, but he didn't persist.

When he was gone, Julie said, "How did Vandernoot build this house? He dared work only by daylight. Where did he go at night?"

"He may have had a ship," Bryce guessed.

"Or slept in a tree," Singapore said.

"Why he wanted to live here at all," the scientist murmured, "is a mystery."

"Pearls ain't a mystery," Pegleg said.

They explored the room. They found fragments of books printed in Dutch. They found the spot against the wall where a bookcase had stood. Termites had destroyed all wooden furniture and woodwork.

"This room," Bryce Robbins said, "was undoubtedly his living room and kitchen. That pile of rust was doubtless his cook-stove. I presume he lived in this room and slept in the front room."

"At night," Julie said, "he would go in there and lock himself in. Walls a yard thick, that roof and this steel door kept the thing out—if it tried to get him. The thing may have caught him unexpectedly. It may have fooled him and come out in the daytime!"

She started to shiver and called, "Larry, are you all right?"

His voice answered, "Everything's okay. It's going to stop raining."

They investigated the room until Lucky returned with the oxy-acetylene blowtorch and set to work cutting through the steel door. It took him more than an hour to cut around the massive lock which was riveted inside the steel slab.

He said presently, "Here she goes." With a mechanic's hammer he dealt a sharp blow to the semicircle of steel he had cut with the torch. The steel half-disc fell inward.

He pulled the door open.

The five of them crowded about the narrow doorway and stared into the darkness of the front room. The floor was littered with rubbish. Against one wall were the remains of an iron single bed. The mattress was nothing more than shredded fragments. The legs were columns of red rust.

There was no skeleton.

Pegleg panted: "It got him! I knew it got him! He was careless. He went outside when he should 'a' been locked up in here—and it got him!"

Bryce said irritably, "He may have died a thousand miles from here."

"No, he didn't. He got careless. He was here fifteen years. I've heard tell he was a friend o' the monster's. Mebbe he was and mebbe he wasn't. But it got him in the end."

The one-legged old sailor was puffing with excitement. His voice was shrill. "Sam," he shrilled, "I'm goin' to spend the night in this room!"

CHAPTER X

PEGLEG'S PLAN

JULIE UTTERED A shriek. Sammy growled, "Don't be foolish, Pegleg."

"Foolish?" the old sailor panted. "It's what I've wanted to do for the past twenty years—see the thing with my own eyes! I'll do what Vandernoot did. I'll lock meself in this room. I'll clean off them peepholes. There's a moon tonight. Here I stay!"

Lucky entered the argument. He declared it was damned foolishness.

"You boys don't understand," Pegleg pleaded. "How would you feel if year after year you wondered what kind of a critter it was mashed your leg off? What if it's foolish? Call me anything—but here I stay tonight!"

"The lock's gone," Sam said.

"Lucky can fix another."

"No."

"Fiery hell," Pegleg cried, "ain't I the only man in the world who met the thing face to face—and lived to tell it? Ain't it my right to have first look at it? And it won't be risky. Because *you're* gonna lock me in!"

"Oh, Pegleg," Julie groaned.

"Weld it up," he shouted, "and put a padlock on the outside. There's a good big padlock in the paint locker. I want to be locked in, and I don't want to be let out till tomorrow mornin'."

"Why?" Singapore growled.

"'Cause I'm scairt o' meself. I don't trust meself. I might give in to temptation and rush out and give battle to it. Once I see it, I might go daffy. So lock me in. I'll bring ashore a cot, drinking water, rations and rum."

"What makes you think you'll see it?" Julie asked.

"Don't it come out o' the lagoon every night?"

"Does it?"

He ignored the question. He looked hopefully at the semi-circle of faces in the dimness.

"Am I bein' selfish?" he cried.

Julie gave a hysterical little laugh, and Lucky jeered:

"Maybe the professor would like to stay with you."

"I don't want comp'ny."

"We won't quarrel," Bryce said. "My only request is that you don't kill it."

"I promise you I won't kill it!"

"Then your proposal is satisfactory to me."

But Sammy was reluctant to give his consent. He wanted to size things up first. He went outside. Larry was walking along the beach, shading his eyes against the glare of tie clouds, and: looking into the water. Sammy asked him is he'd found the cave.

"I think so. But these cloud shadows fool you."

What he believed was the cave was a patch of darkness a dozen feet under water. The beach here was not sand but a solid formation of white coral.

Sam found rocks and threw them in the water. The shadow did not move or change.

Lucky joined them. He studied the shadow and said it looked like a cave to him.

JULIE, COMING out of the cabin with Pegleg, saw the three men standing at the edge of the lagoon. She cried hysterically, "Come away from there!"

Her eyes suddenly filled with tears. Angrily, she got rid of them. Her nerves, she discovered, were in tatters. Her heart was still racing, her mouth and throat were dry. Not once since she had put foot on Little Nicobar had she been rid of a feeling that a sinister something threatened her and all of them. It evaded her normal senses, yet it remained in the air, and the air tingled with the threat of it.

Not until the small boat was well away from the island did the feeling withdraw from her senses. She was so relieved she could have cried. Her face began to burn as if with a high fever.

Once again aboard, the discussion continued. And Pegleg Pyke remained belligerently determined to spend the night in the Dutchman's cabin.

At tiffin, Bryce Robbins settled the argument by saying, "Pegleg's findings may be exceedingly useful. We must know what this creature is like. If you talk him out of it, I will spend the night there myself."

Pegleg Pyke grinned his evil, gold-fanged grin. He assembled supplies and equipment. He loaded and tested one of the submachine rifles. He stowed a cot, bedding, candles, a jug of water, a bottle of rum, tobacco, a cutlass and the submachine gun in the small boat. Sam and Larry went ashore with him.

Julie did not ask to go ashore. Her morning on Little Nicobar had exhausted her. She felt panicky when the three men started off in the small boat She climbed to the cross-tree with binoculars and perched there until they returned, but she saw nothing in the lagoon to frighten her, and she saw no unfriendly black faces peering out from the trees at the edge of the jungle.

When the three men reached the stone house, Lucky repaired the door and welded a strong steel ring to the plate that replaced the old lock. He set another ring into the masonry, so that the door could be held shut with the padlock.

Pegleg cleared a space for his cot and placed a grocery box beside it. On the box he arranged the bottle of rum, the submachine gun and an old gin bottle with a candle in the neck.

It was late afternoon when the door was finished. Pegleg was ready to be locked in for the night.

"If you hear me yell," he said, "don't worry. When I clap eyes on the thing, if it's as horrible, as I think, I may git scairt and yell blue murder. But don't pay no attention. Don't come ashore."

"You'll probably be a ravin' lunatic in the mornin'," Lucky said.

The one-legged man laughed shrilly. His oystery old eyes were watery.

"Don't you worry, son," he cackled, and flashed his gold-capped fangs. "I'll be here and, with luck, I'll be tellin' you how it looks. I was never so doggoned excited in all my life. It's like havin' the curtain pulled back and lookin' into the hereafter. Sure you lads ain't jealous?"

Larry grinned and said, "Remember to keep your head on, old timer. No matter what it is, remember you're safe. We'll see you in the morning."

Lucky closed and padlocked the steel door on the old sailor, and the two men returned to the schooner. Julie climbed down from the cross-tree and Sammy took her place. He was uneasy about the natives, he told her. According to all accounts, the Little Nicobar tribe had never been civilized. And there was the rumor of a white chieftain. White chieftains were, as a rule, not to be trusted. But he saw no sign of natives.

He watched Little Nicobar sink into the smoky blue-lavender of dusk. Then the last remaining light ebbed away, and the lagoon became a ghostly emerald glow. Dimly, through the coconut palms, he saw the row of lighted discs in the front wall of the Dutchman's shanty. Pegleg had lit the candle, was waiting.

For what? Sam wished that he had not let that bull-headed old man stay in the stone cabin.

There was very little wind. He could hear the bubbling of the volcanic mud pots clearly above the noise of the surf on the barrier reef. A pale moon in its second quarter rose and floated like a wraith above the mist which now covered the lagoon.

The bubbling of the mud pots, the fragrance of the mammoth orchids, the gleam of the swollen moon in the mist, and the black loom of the jungle shoreline made him definitely uneasy.

He had had that feeling, like an unresolved premonition, since the Blue Goose had anchored.

He climbed down the ratlines and joined the group under the afterdeck awning. They were watching the island with the air of people enchanted. It was actually as if that dark and brooding mass was possessed of an ominous, sinister presence which filled the night with the effluvia of menace.

At midnight, Julie tiptoed down the stairs to her room. Lucky, Larry, Bryce and Pete Cringle turned in a little later.

Singapore remained on deck. Near him, in the stern, Senga stood guard with a submachine rifle. Oangi was on lookout forward.

Stretched out in the lazy man's chair, Sammy must have dozed. Senga's brown hand on his shoulder brought him to alertness.

Far away in the night, Sammy heard a dull, slow booming. It was not the surf. It seemed to come from the mountain. He saw, or fancied he saw, a faint, deep-red glow in that direction. It might have been a fire. It might have been the reflection of the moon on a porphyry cliff. The reverberations, low and distant, might have been those of a drum. They presently stopped. He dozed again.

A shrill sound wrenched Sammy from sleep. He sprang from the chair and grasped the taffrail, staring dazedly at the dark mass of Little Nicobar.

Far away, a man was screaming. Muffled as it was, and dimmed by distance, the sound came clear and throbbing. The blood-chilling screams emanated, there was little doubt, from the stone cabin.

CHAPTER XI

VANISHED

FEET HAMMERED ON the stairs. Larry and Lucky came plunging up. Lucky gasped: "What the hell is it?" Julie appeared, struggling into a dressing gown, crying, "What's happening?" Pete Cringle came running from the fo'c's'le.

Sam ran forward to the mainmast rigging and began to climb. At the cross-tree he braced his legs and stared out over the dark water. The moon was gone. The reflections of stars slid over undulations like darting silver knives. The sinister sweetness of the giant orchids perfumed the warm night. The mist-shrouded lagoon glowed and shimmered. He could see the row of lighted peepholes in the stone cabin. Suddenly came the rapid, stuttering fire of the submachine gun. Perhaps a dozen shots were fired. There was a bar of silence, ripped by another awful scream. There were no more shots.

Sam's legs were trembling so that the shrouds and ratlines shook. The row of peepholes suddenly went dark and he groaned. The screams were shorter and fainter, as if they were wrenched from a man in mortal terror. Suddenly they ceased. As if they had been withholding their sound, the bubbling of the mud pots was resumed.

Sammy descended the ratlines and walked to the group huddled on the afterdeck. A bitter argument was in progress. Pete Cringle was determined to go ashore at once. If they didn't let him have a boat, he'd swim.

Lucky said, "Nobody leaves this ship till sun-up."

In frantic wrath, the boy rushed at him. Lucky struck him in the jaw with his fist and Pete Cringle fell to hands and knees, whimpering curses.

Sam panted: "Lucky, could anything happen? Doesn't that door open out? All the pressure there is couldn't smash that door in on him, could it? He's safe. He must be safe. He saw it and got scared. That's all."

In a shivering little voice the girl said, "What could it be to make any man scream so—just the sight of it?"

Bryce Robbins made that familiar sound of exasperation with his nose. "Bosh. You're forgetting the old fellow has been in a pathologic state of mind. He would have screamed at anything."

Sammy shook his head. "Why did he shoot that gun?"

"Nerves!"

Lucky growled, "Oh, you know so damned much!"

"Who heard that strange booming sound earlier?" Julie asked.

They compared notes. Pete Cringle picked himself up from the deck and muttered that he had heard it, too. He had also heard a queer swishing sound after Pegleg had stopped screaming. It had sounded like monstrous wings.

Bryce said peevishly, "Oh, that's absurd. I was listening and I heard nothing but the mud vats and the reef."

"I heard that swishing, too," Lucky said. "It seemed like it came from the beach by the cabin."

"It could be a dragon," Pete Cringle muttered.

Julie said, "Will somebody get me a drink? I feel just sick."

Larry went to get her a drink. Sam said, "The poor old fellow must have got an awful scare. It may have driven him out of his wits."

And Julie repeated, shivering: "What could it be to scare any man so?"

"Pegleg has seen every kind of fish that grows in the sea," Singapore said. "If we find, in the morning, that he went stark staring mad at the very sight of it—"

"Nonsense!" Bryce snapped. "I'll grant that he's had a bad scare, but you're making mountains of molehills. Pegleg was not rational. His phobia is only natural. For twenty years he's been obsessed—"

Captain Jones said jeeringly, "Oh, nuts. Our hunch is as good as yours. You want to measure off everything with your damned tape measure. Maybe you'll find this don't answer to laws."

But Bryce Robbins took no stock in mythological monsters, mysterious creatures with wings, sea serpents, dragons, with any beast, in fact, that did not knuckle down to natural laws. He declared they would find Pegleg sound of limb and mind— and it would be thrilling to listen to his account of a stirring experience.

BRYCE SWAYED no one. The discussion raged until a steely glow appeared on the eastern horizon. The glow brightened until the sky was filled with a cool, clean, colorless radiance, then blazed with the purple and gold of tropical sunrise. But the island lost none of its strangely sinister character with the coming of sunlight. The mist vanished from the lagoon. The oppressive sweetness of the giant orchids evaporated from the air. The song of birds floated out. But Little Nicobar remained an island of doubt, with an aura of mystery and fear.

At a conference from which Julie was absent, it was decided that Sam, Lucky and Bryce Robbins would slip ashore, leaving Larry aboard to guard Julie. The scientist was not afraid of what she might find at the stone cabin, but the others were. After those screams, the least they expected was a madman.

While Julie and Larry were forward, the three men left in the small boat. Julie yelled in protest, but the small boat, with Lucky at the oars, drove on toward the beach. When they neared their yesterday's landing place, Singapore Sammy did not wait for the keel to scrape sand, but leaped out and splashed through shallow water to the beach and ran up and over the dune.

Sprinting down the other side, he shouted, "Pegleg!" And

*Suddenly the shark
smashed down
upon the water*

when no answering shout came, he shouted wrathfully, "Pegleg! Answer me!"

But Pegleg did not answer. And as Sammy ran on to the cabin, he saw great grooves in the sand, running from the edge of the lagoon to the shrubbery which formed a thick undergrowth about the cabin, as if heavy objects had been dragged there.

Panting, he stopped and stared at them. They were wide swaths in the sand, perhaps a dozen in number, and of varying depths and widths, some a foot wide, others as wide as a yard, and some were shallow while others were perhaps a foot deep. He saw that all of them were coated with a drying, colorless slime. And he saw that some of the bushes nearest the cabin had been crushed, as if some massive creature had crawled over them. Leaves and twigs of these crushed bushes were dripping with slime.

In sudden panic, the red-headed man wheeled about and stared at the lagoon, but its smooth blue innocence was unruffled by so much as a light breeze. He saw no strange shadows or shapes.

But he backed away from it with loathing and trepidation until his groping hand found the corner of the cabin. Breathing loudly, he ran around to the back and to the doorway. When he saw that the inner steel door was still shut, and that the padlock was still in place, he gave a great groan of relief and panted, "Pegleg! Wake up, old fellow! We're here!"

But Pegleg did not answer. With the breath wheezing in and out of his windpipe, Singapore went to the steel door and peered in through the peephole. But he saw nothing. And he became aware of a queer, sharp odor. It was reminiscent of acid fumes, but it was unlike any acid he had ever smelled.

He ran to the outer door and saw Lucky and the scientist floundering toward him through the soft sand. He yelled, "Hurry up with that key!"

And Lucky shouted, "How is he?"

"He won't answer!"

SAMMY BECAME aware simultaneously of two sensations, the one localized and sharp, the other quite as definite but nameless. One was fear of unseen, lurking peril, the other was a stinging in the palm of his hand. It was the palm he had pressed against the steel door. He looked swiftly from his palm to the door, hissing curses. His palm was flushed an angry red. The steel door was wet. This wetness formed a triangle from the bottom to the keyhole, as if the nameless thing which had left those swaths in the sand had pressed a flank or some other portion of its slimy anatomy against that area. And Sammy saw that this wet area was gently fizzing, as metal fizzes when diluted acid is poured on it.

He wiped his hand frantically, with repugnance, on his pants leg. Bryce Robbins, plunging ahead of Lucky, had reached the grooves in the sand. He dropped to his knees beside them.

Sammy roared: "Watch out for that slime! It'll rot your hide!"

Lucky ran past the scientist, his face yellow and contorted.

Violently shaking his head, Sam groaned, "I don't know! Get it open! Watch out for that slime! It burns!"

Lucky had the key in his right hand. He was grasping the padlock with the left, but his hands shook so violently that he could not at first insert key into lock. When he had unlocked it, he seized the iron ring on the door and gave a wrench and heave.

The heavy door swung open. Sammy had a bundle of matches in his hand. He scrubbed the heads down the masonry and held the small torch aloft.

Shoulder to shoulder, the two men entered the room.

Pegleg Pyke was not there.

CHAPTER XII

WHERE IS PEGLEG?

WITH THE FLAME over his head, Sammy sent glances about the empty room. He took in the ceiling and the walls. They were intact.

His brain thought it out before the realization bit home. He said, methodically: "He could not have get out. That door was padlocked on the outside. He could not have got out through walls or floor or ceiling. He could not possibly get out of this room." Then he hoarsely cried: "Good God!"

The man beside him made a metallic sound in his throat. He beat at the air with his hands, with fingers distended like claws. He turned about and, with that strange rattling sound, ran out of the cabin.

The red-haired man dropped the matches, spun about and sped after him. Through the watery blur of panic, he saw Lucky running, floundering, through the sand toward the top of the dune.

Bryce Robbins shouted: "What is it?"

And Sam yelled: "Get out of here!"

He followed Lucky Jones through the sand, over the dune and to the small boat, with the scientist legging it after him and hoarsely shouting questions. Bryce dashed through the water and climbed into the boat as the bows started to swing. The two men, each with an oar, were poling it away from the land with the desperate strength of insane men. Their eyes were glassy with panic, and their color was that of fresh clay.

Bryce said harshly, "Is Pegleg dead?"

Lucky, in a voice thinned by fury and terror, answered, "Oh, God, is he dead?"

"What was it?"

Sam answered: "He's gone!"

"Out of that locked room?"

"Sure!" Sammy panted.

"Oh, that's impossible!"

"Oh, hell!" Lucky yelled. "Don't start an argument or I'll murder you!"

Furiously, Bryce shouted: "I'm going to find out what happened!"

Sam dropped down to a thwart and fitted an oar to an oarlock.

"He wasn't there," he gasped. "He was gone."

"And that door was locked?"

"That door was locked," Lucky panted. "Don't tell me it wasn't locked. I locked it myself last night and I had the only key!"

"Nothing was broken in?"

"No!"

The scientist stared from one sweating, yellow face to the other.

"You—you looked thoroughly?"

"He wasn't in that room," Lucky said.

"He was gone," Sam added. "And there was no way for him to get out! My God, I think I must be nuts! But he wasn't there!"

"Is that why you ran?"

"Oh, Lord," Lucky groaned. "Is that why we ran!"

Bryce looked at him with hatred and tightened his lips.

"I'm naturally curious to know just what happened. A man was locked in that cabin last night, behind a steel door, in a room with three-foot stone walls and an eighteen-inch reënforced concrete roof. In shore, it was physically impossible for him to get out of that room. Yet you say he did. What you're saying is beyond the bounds of wildest fantasy."

Sammy heavily nodded his head. "Yes. Far beyond."

"Didn't you see anything—didn't you run because of anything you saw?"

"We didn't see anything!"

SHOUTS WERE reaching them now from the schooner. Larry, Julie and Pete Cringle were on the afterdeck yelling questions.

Sam shouted in answer: "Wait till we get aboard. Pegleg's gone! He's vanished!"

They heard Julie cry out faintly, and saw her grasp the rail. But she was at the accommodation ladder when they pulled alongside, staring down at them with frightened dark eyes.

Bryce said concisely: "Sam and Lucky found the door still locked but Pegleg gone."

Julie looked ill. "Dead?"

"Gone."

She swallowed. Her mouth had a curious, limp shape.

"How could he?"

"He couldn't! But he's gone!"

Julie made a little whimpering sound. "Sam, what happened?"

He shrugged his shoulders and wiped his forehead.

"You couldn't have looked thoroughly!"

"We both looked. I lit a bundle of matches and we took a good look. If I'd been alone, I'd think I was nuts. But we both saw that room. There was no one in it!"

"Oh, how could he be gone!"

"Your guess," Lucky said shakily, "is as good as mine!"

Julie dropped into a chair with a sick little moan. The three men came aboard. They looked confused and ill. Even the scientist was pale.

Larry drawled, "Was there anything else unusual?"

"Tracks," Lucky growled. "That thing came up out o' the lagoon durin' the night."

"What was it?" Julie gasped.

"We don't know anything," Bryce answered.

Lucky gave a jeering laugh. "Say it again, mister!"

Bryce flashed a look of hatred at him. "They weren't tracks," he said, "in the usual sense. They were deep grooves, about ten of them, running from the water to the cabin. They were coated with slime."

"That slime is full of acid," Singapore said. And he showed Julie his hand. It was inflamed and beginning to blister on the heel. "The door was wet with that stuff."

Julie shivered. "Soak it in antiseptic, Sam. Bryce, do you know what it is?"

He shook his head. "I've got a pocketful of the sand. I want to analyze it."

Larry had gone below. He returned with a bottle of trade gin. He and Sammy each took generous swigs from the bottle, then Sammy went to the ladder and said: "Come on, fella. Back we go! We're going to get to the bottom of this!"

"Yeah?" Lucky said. "I've had enough for one mornin'. Take Larry along. This is a fine chance for a guy who can't get killed. But he won't grab this tiger by the chin whiskers!"

"You men aren't going ashore!" Julie protested.

Lucky jeered, "Let 'em go! After all, it's nothin' but a pair o' human lives. If they lose 'em, they won't miss 'em."

THE TWO men went down the ladder. Larry cast off and picked up the oars. Ah they started off, Lucky called: "I'll post a lookout. If he fires two shots—run!"

"Okay."

Reaching shore, the two young men proceeded cautiously over the dune and to the cabin. Larry had brought along a pocket electric torch.

Sam said, as they entered the cabin: "We're going over this joint with a fine-tooth comb. When you come right down to it, there's nothing to be scared about."

"Nothing," Larry said.

"It makes my skin creep, but we're going to make two and two come out even. Now, look. Pegleg couldn't have got out through the walls or the roof or the floor. All we have to do is use our noodles. How did he get out?"

Larry gasped: "Good Lord! Did you see that cot?"

The cot was crushed—flattened to the floor. The grocery box was crushed into splinters. The gin and rum bottles were in fragments.

"He put up an awful fight."

Sam gasped: "Throw your light into that corner!"

Larry swung the beam into the corner and gave a sharp grunt.

In the corner was Pegleg Pyke's wooden leg.

Sam said, "Don't touch anything. Everything is covered with that slime. And here's a tough one. The straps are not unbuckled!"

"It was ripped off!"

"These straps are badly eaten, and the buckles are corroded as if they'd been in salt water for years. It's that stuff. Watch out for it."

"How could Pegleg have been taken out of this room?" And when Sam made no answer, Larry said, "There is no logical explanation. I'm convinced of that. I'm convinced we're dealing with something that doesn't conform to natural laws."

"Do you believe in ghosts?"

"Hell, no."

"If you're going to take stock in a spooky explanation, you might as well call it a ghost."

"But how do you explain it?"

"I don't. Let's look around some more."

The wooden leg was the first of several shocking but unedifying discoveries. The next was Pegleg's old silver watch. It had stopped at 2.24, the time at which they had heard the old man scream. The crystal was smashed and the case was green with corrosion.

Sam bent down to examine tie submachine gun, which lay on the floor near the crushed cot.

He gave a sharper grunt. "The barrel's bent! Something grabbed it and bent it! Do you know how much strength it takes to bend that kind of steel?"

"What could have bent it?"

"Fifteen shots were fired."

"At what?"

"Let's see where they went."

THEY EXAMINED the door for bullet marks. On the inner side, near the peephole, they found five. They kicked about in the litter and found a number of bullets. Several were flattened and gouged, as if they had struck the door or the wall, and ricocheted. But others were only slightly mushroomed, as if they had expended their force in softer substance—flesh of some kind.

"But what kind of flesh?" Larry asked.

"Ghosts don't stop bullets."

"Can't you make a guess?"

"Teeth!" Sam exclaimed.

They lay in a small group, six of them, each within a few inches of the other. Each was gold-capped.

Squatting down, Sam looked up at the man who couldn't be killed. "Any question about them?"

"No! They're Pegleg's!"

They looked further. They found fragments of shoes, badly eaten and covered with slime. They found rotting fragments of cloth. They found another collection of teeth and another watch.

Sam cried: "These aren't Pegleg's!"

The watch was thick, of gold, with the name Van Huyt, Amsterdam, on the dial, and the initials G.V. engraved on the back.

"Gurt Vandernoot! He died in this room, too!"

Sam said, unsteadily, "Now, let's try to be reasonable. Let's use our heads. So far we haven't found anything that doesn't make some kind of sense."

"Oh, yeah?"

"We haven't!" Sam declared. "Let's keep on using our heads."

"Okay. Two men were locked in this room, one of them twenty-six years ago, the other last night. Both disappear. Nothing is left but teeth and watches—and a wooden leg. Whoever or whatever got them could not get into—or out of—this room. So what?"

"The peephole," Sam said in a stronger voice. "That's it! Of course that's it! Look here!" He played the flashlight beam on the inner side of the door. "It's wet and slimy in a triangular pattern, the same as on the other side!"

Larry shouted: "My God! It crawled through that hole!"

CHAPTER XIII

WILD THEORIES

IN THE LIGHT from the outer door, each stared into the other's pale face.

"A sea-snake!" Larry cried. "It crawled through that hole twenty-six years ago and ate Gurt Vandernoot! It crawled through that hole last night and ate Pegleg!"

Sam looked at him with half-open eyes, then he looked at the peephole.

"How could a sea-snake crawl through that hole, eat a man—and crawl out again? No snake digests food so quickly. I've seen a python eat a pig. It took days for the lump to go down. And how about those tracks in the sand?"

"It could have been—" Larry stopped. "Listen!" he whispered.

Sam had heard the shot faintly, rounded, like the thump of a hand on a leather cushion. They heard a second shot.

Larry ran out. Sam unfolded a handkerchief and scooped into it the teeth, the watches and several of the bullets. When he went out, Larry was facing the lagoon with hands outstretched rigidly.

"What is it?"

He growled, "I don't know! Why did they fire those shots?"

Sam scanned the lagoon, which was innocently blue mid calm, then the edge of the jungle. There was no breath of wind. The equatorial sun beat down in a vibrant, merciless glare.

The red-headed man saw no motion, no life, but he said, "Let's go." And they walked rapidly back to the small boat. Sam pushed it out, jumped in and rowed vigorously until they were well offshore. He rested on the oars, then, and looked around at the Blue Goose. A figure was in black silhouette at the cross-tree. Sam looked shoreward again, but saw no sign of life, no movement.

Julie called through a megaphone; "You were gone so long we got worried."

BRYCE ROBBINS came above as Sam and the mate climbed the accommodation ladder. He said eagerly, "Find anything?"

"Plenty. It got in that peephole, it got Pegleg, and it got out the same way."

"That's incredible!"

Pale-lipped, Larry said, "It was a sea-snake, Bryce. It had to be."

Lucky Jones was stretched out under the awning, with his eyes closed and an empty trade gin bottle in the curl of his fingers.

When Sam started describing what they had found, Lucky rolled over and peered at the grisly souvenirs spread out on the handkerchief. He nodded sagely and said: "Sure. It had to be an eel."

The scientist shook his head. "I don't see an eel going through a three-inch hole, eating a man and getting out, in spite of the fastest digestion probably ever known to science."

"I see an eel," Lucky said obstinately.

Sam asked Bryce if he had analyzed the slime.

"That's what I was talking about. I don't know what it is. It might be an external secretion, but that seems unlikely. It is probably a digestive fluid. But none of my reagents are any good for it. It's a rare acid, with some of the characteristics of hydro-chloric, which is the basis of most digestive processes. Yet it isn't hydrochloric. Whatever it is, it's a powerful solvent. It would dissolve—or digest—almost any ordinary substance. We've seen how it attacks leather and metal—and human flesh."

"I see an electric eel," Captain Jones stated.

Bryce Robbins was irritated. "If you drank less of that rotgut, you might see less reptilian activity."

Lucky started to his feet, with jutting lip and fierce black brows. Sammy barked, "Steady, you sap!"

"I'm fed up with this smart aleck!"

"Then lay off him. We're all on edge. Julie, you better have a drink. You, too, Larry. You're a pair of ghosts."

Julie said, "Pete passed out while you were ashore."

"I'm okay now," the boy muttered. "Who wouldn't pass out? I thought that thing had got them."

Larry gave him a grin. "There wasn't anything to worry about, Pete—at least, nothing visible."

"Well, how do you know it isn't invisible?"

Bryce said: "What's your opinion, mate?"

Larry shrugged. "I'm stumped."

The scientist tightened his lips. He, too, was colorless and tense. "I'm inclined to suspect an octopus. It must answer to natural laws." He glanced coldly at Lucky, but Lucky was staring stonily at the handkerchief. "Doesn't the octopus secrete a fluid with which it stains the water when it attacks?"

"How," Julie asked tremulously, "could an octopus get their skulls through such a small hole?"

"Easily! A tentacle of a large octopus is strong enough to crush a man's skull into fragments, and no eel could have made those tracks."

PETE CRINGLE mumbled an objection. "I've done a lot o' divin' in these waters and I never seen an octopus that could stick an arm far into a three-inch hole."

"It may be a rare variety."

"I've seen all the varieties there are. And I never seen a land-going variety."

"Neither have I," Lucky grunted.

"Why do you keep thinkin' of octopuses and eels?" the diver

persisted. "What if it ain't either? What if it's somethin' you never saw and never thought of? What if it's some kind o' dragon that makes itself invisible or somethin'? How do you know?"

"It wasn't an octopus," Sammy said. "It was something worse than any octopus. The black stuff an octopus shoots out isn't acid. It's coloring matter."

"Don't octopi sometimes board ships?"

"I've heard old sailors say so, but I never saw it happen."

The scientist looked displeased. "What do you think it is?"

"I'd hate to say. It's got me up a tree, Bryce. I've sailed among these islands going on seven years. I've run into queer riddles, but never one like this. Tell me: If that acid's strong enough to eat my hide, why doesn't it eat the thing itself?"

Bryce Robbins smiled thinly. "Why doesn't a cobra's venom kill the cobra? Why don't your own digestive juices digest you? This octopus merely ejects acidulous fluid as a process of digestion."

"Was it," Lucky sneered, "tryin' to digest that door?"

The scientist scorned his question. In his crisp, cool, irritating voice, he said, "I'd like to have a definite understanding. I know how all of you feel about Pegleg. You'd like to avenge his death by killing this octopus. Undoubtedly, one or all of us will in due course have opportunities to destroy it. I insist that you restrain yourselves. It must be taken alive."

Lucky jeered: "Aw, go sing a hymn!"

Julie gave a little groan. "Oh, Lucky, stop it. Sam, what are your plans, anyway?"

"To wait a while and give our nervous systems a chance to catch up. We're nervous wrecks."

A shout from Senga, perched on the crosstree, was so startling that they all jumped. He had seen a ship.

Julie ran to the rail, that bulwark of steel bayonets.

At first she saw nothing in that direction but the barrier reef, then she made out a fleck of white far in the distance where the blue became purple.

Sammy, beside her, was adjusting his binoculars. He looked through them steadily for a long time, then grunted.

"It's a yacht—a white one."

"Not the Wanderer," Julie moaned. "Oh, not the Wanderer, Sam!"

"It looks like her."

"Let me see."

He gave her the glasses, but she was too jumpy to hold them steady. She saw nothing but a white blur that danced about on the deep blue field.

Singapore said, "She had two exhaust stacks, didn't she?"

Julie began to cry. She knew she was on the very brink of hysterics, for she wanted to cry and she wanted to laugh, too. Some nerve in the small of her back was giving way. And there was a ticklish, biting feeling in the back of her mouth. She wanted to scream. She couldn't stand seeing Hector Barling and her mother now. Not now. She wished Sammy would thump her on the back.

"You'd better get packed, pardner," he said.

Julie shrieked: "I won't go back to that yacht!"

CHAPTER XIV

JULIE DECIDES

THE WANDERER, AT far range, was a ship carved of alabaster upon a sea of kingfisher jade. She cleaved through the water toward the barrier reef at a speed of not less than thirty knots, the snow-white hull and the buff exhaust stacks smartly delineated against the vivid, intense blue of the sea with its purple distances. The beautifully flared bows sent up wings of white in which rainbows hung. For a moment she held against the barrier reef with its jade shallows, its two lonely, tattered palms, the spume which shot into the air like jets of milk.

Those aboard the Blue Goose could see the crew lined along the deck rail, and they could see a small group on the bridge, men in snowy white and a plump woman in pink, with glasses to her eyes.

When the yacht was so close that you could read the gold lettering on her prow without the aid of binoculars, a bell tinkled; the bow waves subsided. The Wanderer seemed to settle a little. Hot sunlight glistened on bright-work as she hove to, with engines in reverse churning the sea to turquoise foam—not more than a hundred yards from the schooner.

A red megaphone appeared in the hands of one of the men in white; a short, chunky one. A high-pitched voice hurtled across the gap.

"Julie, are you all right?"

She tried to answer, but her voice refused. She nodded.

Larry shouted: "She's fine!"

"Those guys," Lucky muttered, "have all got guns. What is this—a hold-up?"

The megaphone changed hands. A woman's hysterical voice called: "Julie, are you quite all right?"

Unable to speak, Julie bobbed her head.

"She says," Larry shouted, "she never felt better in her life."

A consultation was taking place on the Wanderer's bridge. The megaphone appeared again, and a deep, strong voice called: "Mr. Barling and Mrs. Farrington are going over for Miss Farrington. I want to warn you men I have guns trained on you."

"That's Captain Miliken," Julie whispered. "He's really awfully nice."

Larry said, "He sounds like a hospitable soul."

"Hector told him to say that. Listen, Larry—Sam—Lucky—Bryce. You're going to back me up, aren't you?"

"It looks like a tough spot, baby," Singapore said.

"Why?" She seized Sam's arm. "You'll stand by me, Sam!"

He shrugged. "I hate to see a member of my crew desert in a foreign port, but I think you'd better get packed."

She made a little squeaking sound. Sam saw tears coursing down her cheeks.

Julie didn't leave the rail. She stopped weeping and watched them put over the little tender. The Wanderer's accommodation ladder was lowered. Mr. Barling and Mrs. Farrington went down it and got into the tender. Two members of the crew followed. The engine purred. With a smart little flourish the tender started toward the Blue Goose.

Sam studied Mr. Barling in the stern: a plump, important figure in a snowy sun helmet; a man with a pink, round face adorned with a wisp of blond mustache. Sam had seen Mr. Barling in the Mudhole, but he had actually not seen him at all, because of the radiance of the slim blond girl who had accompanied him. There was no such distraction now. Certainly, the flushed, perspiring, wet-eyed woman beside Mr. Barling was not a distraction.

THE TENDER swung neatly alongside the schooner's accommodation ladder platform. Mr. Barling looked up at the row of faces above the steel bayonets. He looked wrathful. Fixing his pale blue eyes at Julie, he said sternly, "Julie, are you coming?"

She shook her head.

"I thought so!" Mr. Barling snapped.

Sam said lazily, "What did you think, mister?"

Mr. Barling glared at him a moment, then said to the plump woman in pink, "We are going aboard. You men will follow."

"Yes, sir," the two men said.

Mr. Barling helped Mrs. Farrington up to the platform, and aided her up the steps to the afterdeck. The two men, looking uneasy, with black holsters at their hips, followed.

With a whimpering sound, Mrs. Farrington went to Julie and, sobbing loudly, embraced her.

"Poor mother!" Julie murmured. "I'm horribly sorry you worried so."

Mr. Barling, standing straight and stiff, was glaring at the schooner's assembled company. In his fresh, starched ducks, he looked pompous. His bodyguard stood behind him, pale, sheepish, uncertain.

"Who is the master of this ship?" Mr. Barling barked.

"I'm the skipper," Lucky drawled.

"I demand the instant release of this young woman!"

Captain Jones's thick black brows bent down and his breath whistled out of his nostrils. But before he could speak, the owner of the Wanderer said in the same stern measures, "If you do not release her instantly, I will have you in the nearest admiralty court!"

"Yeah?" Lucky's mouth seemed to be pushed to one side. "Are you an admiral?"

Julie giggled nervously. She was still on the brink of hysterics, but she tried to make her voice calm. "Hector, I'm not a prisoner. These men are my friends."

"You mean you're afraid to tell the truth! I am not! This gang of cutthroats will learn that kidnaping is a serious offense!"

"But I wasn't kidnaped. Mother—"

"Oh, Julie, my poor darling, how could you!"

"Pack your things!" Mr. Barling snapped.

"I am not leaving this schooner!"

"I'll have every man on this dirty little tub clapped in irons!"

"What have we done?" Sam asked lazily.

"You're guilty of abduction!"

Lucky bared his large white teeth and with a rolling gait approached the patent medicine king. "You use another word like that in the presence of this lady, and I'll knock your teeth out through the soles of your feet!"

"You men," Mr. Barling panted, "keep this fellow covered!"

Lucky looked at the bodyguard. "You guys pull a gun on this ship and you'll be crab-food!"

Mrs. Farrington screamed weakly.

"Lucky!" Julie cried. "Let me handle this. Mother, I am perfectly well and perfectly happy. Must I say that my morals are unimpaired?"

"It's—it's indecent," her mother wailed. "A young girl like you all alone with these men!"

"If every man I knew, including Hector, were as decent, it would be a swell world for any girl!"

"Hector," Mrs. Farrington implored, "talk to her. Make her leave this awful boat!"

"She ain't leavin'," Lucky said. "She's our mascot. Now—get off this ship!"

MR. BARLING backed away from that belligerent glare. He was pale. His pugnacity was suddenly and definitely of the past.

But he said firmly, "Captain, you must admit that a young girl has no business on a ship of this kind."

"You heard me, sucker."

Julie sighed with despair. "Hector, stop trying to bluff these men."

"I am not bluffing."

Lucky folded his arms. "Then clear out and leave us alone."

"I am simply saying that it is, to say the least, highly unconventional for a young girl—"

"These men have treated me with as much respect as you ever gave your own mother."

"How about the respect you owe your own mother?"

"She brought this on herself!"

"Julie!" Mrs. Farrington wailed. "Julie! How can you!"

"I've a right to carve out my own life," Julie said stoutly. "I'm doing what I want to do. I'm not afraid of what people will say."

"That isn't the point," Mr. Barling blustered, perhaps because it was, in his eyes, an important point. "I know you're shielding someone. Which of these men brought you aboard?"

"I stowed away. They found me and were determined to put me off in Singapore. I—I bullied them into letting me stay. I'm going to stay."

Mr. Barling had the look of a man who suddenly finds himself in an unstrategic position. He could not go forward, and his pride would not permit his retreat. He stood, friendless and alone, on his two stout legs.

Compelled to temporize, he said pompously, "Just how long, may I ask, do you intend to take this attitude?"

"Until we've captured the thing in the lagoon."

"Are you referring to the preposterous lies that one-legged bartender was telling these men in the Mudhole?"

"If you'll look at that handkerchief," Julie replied, "you will see all that remains of that one-legged man. Those are his teeth— the gold ones. He was killed and eaten last night by this horrible, unknown creature that lives in the lagoon."

Mrs. Farrington screamed again.

Mr. Barling looked at the assortment of teeth. He looked

quickly back at Julie's pale, lovely face with its shining brown eyes. He swallowed. He looked suspiciously at the other faces. Lucky Jones, black-browed and jutting-lipped, was regarding him sardonically. Singapore Sammy, stolid and solemn, contemplated him with steady, blue-green eyes. Larry McGurk, his dark blond hair tousled, his face flushed, eyed him expectantly. Professor Robbins, lean-jawed, cold-eyed, met his probing glance with scorn. Pete Cringle, so pale that his freckles resembled spatters of dried mud, stared at him insolently.

Back went his little pale-blue eyes to Julie. His straw-colored lashes flickered. "What happened?"

"He insisted on sleeping ashore, in a little stone cabin that was built on the edge of the lagoon by a Dutchman who mysteriously vanished twenty-six years ago. You can see the cabin through those palms—that little gray block. It has stone walls three feet thick and a reënforced concrete roof eighteen inches thick. He was locked behind a steel door an inch thick—the only door. There are no windows. A little after two this morning we heard him screaming and firing a submachine rifle. This morning when we went to look for him he was gone. The thing, whatever it is, crawled through a three-inch peephole in the steel door, killed and ate him, and got out again."

MR. BARLING had stopped pouting. His face had gone slack, open-mouthed, with incredulity. He looked stupid.

"Impossible!" he gasped, but his eyes were no longer fuzzy with anger. "Utterly impossible!"

"Twenty-six years ago," Julie went on, "the man who built the cabin—Gurt Vandernoot—was killed in just the same way. There are his teeth and his watch—all that the creature left."

Mr. Barling's round, cherubic countenance had become flushed, and there was a strange glitter in his little pale-blue eyes. He was softly panting.

"How could any creature swallow a man and get out through a three-inch hole? It's impossible!"

"You explain it," Singapore said.

"Somebody is playing a trick on you. A—a practical joke. Isn't it obvious? Your one-legged man himself! Wasn't it on the strength of his wild story that you came here?"

Julie said patiently, in a tired voice, "Hector, these are his teeth. Lucky—Captain Jones—locked him into that room last night. The padlock was on the outside. There was absolutely no way for Pegleg to get out. Houdini couldn't have gotten out. We found the monster's tracks in the sand, running from the lagoon to the cabin."

"Tracks?"

"Gouges, or grooves; some deep, some shallow."

"Hector," Mrs. Farrington bleated, "take me back to the yacht."

He ignored her. He looked wildly about the semi-circle of pale, grave faces.

"It's utterly too fantastic to believe," he panted. "A three-inch hole! It defies every natural law!"

Senga, at the crosstree, interrupted with a yell. He babbled in Malay.

Mr. Barling gasped, "What's that? What's he say?"

"He says watch the lagoon," Singapore answered. "He says the seagulls are vanishing in the lagoon!"

Julie ran to the rail. The others joined her. They lined up along the rail and stared at the lagoon and the flock of seagulls wheeling and diving and raucously crying above it.

They saw a seagull drop down to the water. They saw it paddling about, looking for whatever food it had seen from the air. Suddenly, with a flapping of wings, a screech, the seagull vanished under water. It was as if an invisible hand had reached up and seized it!

CHAPTER XV

INTO THE LAGOON

THEY WATCHED THE spot where the gull had gone under, but the bird did not reappear.

Sam watched the spot with his binoculars. The seagulls were flying wildly about, wildly screaming. They dived and swooped, but they did not alight. Sammy saw one of them coasting along a few inches above the water. In mid-flight, it stopped. With frantically beating wings, it went under.

Julie screamed: "What is it, Sam?"

"I can't see anything!"

"Something must have reached up and grabbed it!"

"Hector," Mrs. Farrington wailed, "take me away from this loathsome place!"

Julie was beating on the rail with her fists. "Bryce, do you still call it an octopus? Do you realize those two gulls went under at least a hundred feet apart?"

"The octopus we're dealing with might have a stretch of a hundred feet."

"Did you see it send up a tentacle?"

"It might have been too quick for the naked eye."

"Nonsense!" Mr. Barling blustered. "I was looking at that bird—at that precise spot. Whatever it was that grabbed that bird was invisible!"

"You can't see it," Pete Cringle said defiantly. "And you'll never see it."

Flushed and starry-eyed, Julie cried, "Well, Hector? Is somebody playing a practical joke?"

Mr. Barling answered feebly, "It—it stuns me."

The *serang* gave another yell.

The black dorsal fin of a large shark was slicing the surface in the inlet. It was traveling rapidly toward the center of the lagoon. They could see its body. It must have been fully twenty feet in length—a sleek brown shadow.

The black fin sliced through the water toward the spot above which the squawking gulls were still wheeling. The fin suddenly went under. And there was immediately a violent agitation in the water where the fin had last been seen. The deep blue of the lagoon at that spot became a mad churning of foam.

Sammy kept his glasses trained on that spot. The tail of the shark suddenly appeared above water. It seemed to slide into the air, as a sunken plank will rise from depth, as if propelled by a hidden force.

Up and up rose the slim, brown shape, with its tremendous flukes. Most of the shark was out of water now—fully fifteen feet of it. The flukes lashed about, the slender brown column shaking and heaving in a frenzy of fury. It was being held there as if by some irresistible, immovable force. For fully forty seconds it remained there, lashing about helplessly. Then, suddenly, the long brown body was brought smashing down upon the water. Spray shot fifty feet into the air.

Sam said quietly, "That broke its back."

THE GREAT fish had vanished into the welter of foam. The agitation subsided. Pinkness stained the snowy foam. That area quieted until only a pink patch on the blue water remained to mark the site of that battle of giants.

Bryce Robbins said huskily, with the accents of relief, "It ate the shark."

"Hector," Mrs. Farrington sobbed, "we are leaving instantly. This moment! Julie, pack your things."

With firmness, Julie said, "No, mother."

"The tender will take you," Mr. Barling panted. "I am staying. You men may go with Mrs. Farrington. Julie, that shark was all of twenty-five feet long!"

"Julie, are you coming?"

"No, mother. I'll see you later."

"But you—you don't intend to stay!"

"I do, indeed, mother."

The lady in pink pressed her hand to her side. Her tear-streaked face was making grimaces. "My heart!" she groaned. "My heart!"

"Poor dear! I'll help you into the tender."

"But aren't you coming?"

"No, dear."

Julie helped her aboard the tender. When it had gone, Mr. Barling lit a cigar and walked excitedly up and down the deck, watching the lagoon. His face was flushed and perspiring. He said presently, "This is stupendous! It's absolutely stupendous!"

He wanted to know more about Peg-leg's death. He asked numerous questions. Julie had never seen him so excited.

"I'd like to see that cabin."

"Too dangerous," Singapore said. "You've seen that thing in action."

"But it doesn't come ashore in the daytime."

"It might," Julie said. "And the natives are cannibals."

"I don't believe it."

"You're a hard man to convince," Sam said.

"But, my dear fellow, cannibalism is a thing of the past! Years ago, there were cannibals in the South Seas. But these islands have all been civilized."

"Little Nicobar," Singapore said, "isn't civilized. It's too far off the beaten path."

"They don't eat you," Julie said. "They feed you to the thing in the lagoon—make you run a gantlet."

"Have you seen them?"

"No."

The patent medicine millionaire looked expectantly along the shoreline, the wall of the jungle with its many shades of green. He had an uneasy look. His pinkness had gone. He was pale and nervous. He was falling victim to the threat of danger that hung over Little Nicobar like a haze. He said suddenly:

"Let's kill that thing! Let's blow it to smithereens!"

"The purpose of this expedition," Bryce Robbins said coolly, "is to bring it back alive. It is, under no circumstances, to be killed."

"How'll you do it?"

"I really don't know, I'm sure."

"But s'pose you capture it?" Mr. Barling said eagerly. "How will you carry it? It must weigh enough to sink this schooner."

"We'll find a way."

MR. BARLING became thoughtful. Those who knew him well, his mannerisms, his tricks of eyes and mouth and hands, would have said that he was applying his genius to a problem. He was like a man in a trance except that his color, perhaps fired by the whisky, gradually returned and denied the glassiness of his pale-blue eyes. He pursed his lips and delicately nibbled at them.

He said suddenly, "Gentlemen, as I understand it, you have come here because of a report that Gurt Vandernoot left hidden a considerable fortune in pearls. Is that correct?"

"Only partly," Bryce Robbins said. "I am primarily interested—"

"Yes. I know. Bringing it back alive. You take the monster— Mr. Shay takes the pearls. Frankly, I'd like to get in on this. I'd like to help."

Bryce was coldly eyeing him. "How, Mr. Barling?"

"What we have here," Mr. Barling said briskly, "is a somewhat complex problem. The problem is, to outwit and capture an amphibious creature of which we so far know very little. In spite of the most plausible theories, no one has yet advanced a plausible description. We know that it is powerful enough to kill a thirty-five foot shark, swift enough to pluck birds from the air, and ingenious enough to kill a man locked in a room the only access to which is a three-inch hole. We know, in short, that we are dealing with a devilish creature."

"So what?" Lucky drawled.

"So this: We cannot capture the creature with ordinary nets or tackles. We must have elaborate equipment. We may have to charter a fleet of ships. We may have to charter a fleet of amphibian planes. And that is where I come in. I have thought it over, and I will gladly back this expedition to the limit."

"You apparently haven't heard," Bryce Robbins said frigidly, "that I am underwriting this expedition."

"Personally—or as the representative of some foundation?"

"Personally."

"But, my dear fellow, you can't possibly afford it. If necessary, I can comfortably afford to spend a hundred thousand dollars, perhaps even more."

"Why?" Bryce asked.

"Why? Why not? It would be a pleasure to contribute such a sum to such a worthy cause!"

"Applesauce! You want your name in the papers. That's all. You want to be known as the patron of the Bryce Robbins Expedition to Little Nicobar!"

The patent medicine king said angrily, "Young man, it is sometimes inadvisable to look a gift horse—"

"You can take your gift horse—" the scientist began, when Mr. Barling stopped him with a shouted, "Why are you so damned anxious to hog all the credit?"

"My interest is purely scientific!"

"Nuts," Lucky jeered.

Mr. Barling sent him a thin smile. "You express my sentiments perfectly, captain. Gentlemen, I am not a piker. This opportunity must not be fumbled. If necessary, I am willing to put one million dollars on the line to assure the success of this expedition!"

"If necessary," Bryce said coldly, "I am willing to put *seven* million dollars on the line!"

Mr. Barling looked at him and began to laugh. "Really?" he chuckled.

"Really."

"It's news to me that science pays so well."

"It doesn't."

"Hector," Julie said wearily, "Professor Robbins is the Rockefeller Institute man who inherited a fortune six months ago from an uncle. Don't you remember discussing it at the time?"

THE PATENT medicine monarch suddenly looked tired and old. But he rose nobly to the occasion. "I hope," he said, "you won't mind my staying and just looking on, professor?"

"As long as you don't interfere."

"I might even be helpful! Gentlemen! I have an idea! Under the Wanderer's afterdeck is a big swimming tank. This tank is thirty feet long, twenty feet wide, and ten feet deep. The deck lifts out in sections and is stored, aft. It would contain your monster! And I would be delighted to put the Wanderer at your disposal."

Julie said, without attempting to conceal her disappointment: "Then you aren't pulling out?"

"Not much! None of you object, I hope."

"If you play ball," Sammy said, "nobody will object. This island is a Dutch possession. The Dutch are touchy about their islands. Once let them get wind that an American outfit is monkeying around Little Nicobar, and this place will crawl with gunboats. We'll get bogged down in a million yards of red tape. While you're here, don't use your wireless transmitter."

Mr. Barling cried affably, "That's a promise, Mr. Shay! Anything else?"

"Good Lord!
What is it?"

"You'd better take Julie aboard the Wanderer."

"Never!" Julie squealed. "I'm a member of this crew!"

"Your mother needs you, Julie," Mr. Barling purred.

"It's a trick!" she cried.

"No, Julie. I promise we won't sail off. We're going to stay here to the finish. Do you mind telling me, Mr. Shay, what your plans are?"

Singapore Sammy had been gazing dreamily at the stone cabin. "We're taking the Blue Goose into the lagoon tonight. We're going to find out what that thing looks like."

Julie wailed: "Without me?"

"Yes—without you; it's too dangerous. We don't know what we'll be up against."

Mr. Barling protested: "But can you see it at night?"

"Yes. Better than in the daytime. This lagoon is so bright with phosphorus at night you can almost read a paper by it. Did you ever look at your hand with an X-ray machine? You get the same kind of effect. Anything moving in the lagoon you can see as a clean-cut shadow against the green glow. We'll find out what this thing is, then we can make plans for trapping it."

AS IF she were being prepared for sea battle, the Blue Goose was made ready for that dubious expedition into the lagoon. The deck was cleared of all unnecessary objects. All the firearms on board were brought on deck, oiled and loaded. The cutlasses were sharpened.

Each man was assigned his station, and Sammy gave them station drill.

He said, "We don't know what this thing is going to be. We will probably get the scare of our lives. This isn't going to be a Sunday-school picnic."

Bryce said, "Remember this: the creature is not to be killed." He objected to the use of pistols, revolvers and Thompson guns.

"It looks to me more like an errand of slaughter than an expedition of investigation."

"Don't worry," Lucky said, jeeringly, "we'll promise to handle it with kid gloves."

The remainder of the day was spent in bolting into place all the rail bayonets that had not been used—on the theory that if the creature could send a tentacle through a three-inch peephole, or thrust its entire body through, a six-inch space between the bars was too generous.

When this task had been finished, the sun was setting. Ah Fong served supper on deck. The crew of the Blue Goose, pale and apprehensive, ate little. They watched night creep over the lagoon. Mist appeared in wisps and banners. As the darkness increased, the smoky green of the phosphorescence glowed more and more brightly.

The tide would turn at a few minutes after eight. It was Sammy's intention to take the Blue Goose into the lagoon at precisely eight thirty.

Sammy had a final talk with the assembled men. He said: "There's no telling how dangerous this will be, because we don't know what we're up against. If any of you think we're running too big chances, you can duck now—and nobody will hold it against you. You can stay on the Wanderer. Speak up!"

No one spoke. He said: "Don't kid yourselves. This is danger-ous. None of us may come back alive. The thing may even sink this schooner. And it wouldn't be a pleasant death. I'm not trying to scare you, but I'm telling you—it's dangerous."

Still no one spoke. Every man was gazing through the black night at the swimming green haze of the lagoon. The bubbling of the mud pots came clearly. It was like a giant's sardonic chuck-ling. And on the night breeze, the sinister odor of the great orchids came floating out.

Lucky said, "It's eight twenty."

Singapore asked him if he had checked the engine thor-oughly.

"Yeah. Every square inch of her. Senga—Oangi—Pete! Stand by to raise the anchor."

Lucky went below and started the engine. The muttering and blubbering of the exhaust drowned the sound of oars alongside. Sammy did not know that Julie was anywhere in the vicinity until he saw her blond head shining like a halo in the light of a deck lamp.

A moment later Mr. Barling came aboard from another boat.

JULIE WAS looking about her with shining, excited eyes. She saw men, like the ghosts of pirates, flitting about the deck. They were stripped to the waist. Each had a cutlass in his hand, a revolver or pistol strapped to his waist.

Sammy reached her just as Mr. Barling, puffing and gasping, said, "Julie! This isn't fair! You promised—"

"I promised to sleep aboard the yacht. I'm needed here. If any of these men get hurt, there's no one to nurse them."

Singapore told her curtly to get off the ship. Julie ran forward and hid in the shadows. A rumbling forward indicated that the anchor was up. A moment later Pete Cringle yelled: "She's up and down."

Senga, having returned aft, advanced the throttle and let in the clutch. The schooner forged ahead, the bows dipped slightly, then the anchor came clear of the bottom, and the chain was windlassed in.

Julie could not be found. Sam barked at Mr. Barling: "You'd better clear out, mister. We're going into the lagoon."

He saw that the patent medicine king was sweating and white. Mr. Barling was scared. Mr. Barling was terrified.

"I'll s-stay!" he chattered.

He was going to be brave, Sam supposed, to impress Julie. But there was no time now for arguments. Oangi and Pete Cringle came aft, took in the accommodation ladder, stowed it below and closed the gap in the rail.

Julie did not reappear until the schooner was well into the inlet. Sam said: "The place for you, baby, is in the crosstree. Scramble up there and keep a lookout."

She picked up a cutlass and climbed to the crosstree. Sammy took a quick turn about the deck, to make sure everything was in readiness. Lucky Jones and Ah Fong were stationed in the bows. Sam gave Mr. Barling a station amidships, and furnished him with cutlass and revolver. Oangi and Pete Cringle were stationed amidships, one on the port, one on the starboard side. Senga was at the wheel. Bryce and Larry were at the taffrail.

Sammy had no station. He would go where he was needed.

He went forward. The schooner was now entering the thin mist. It was cold.

With engine at slow speed, the Blue Goose entered the lagoon.

CHAPTER XVI

THE MONSTER STRIKES

SINGAPORE SAMMY MOVED restlessly about the deck. The thin, sinister mist dimmed the stars and reduced the glittering lights of the Wanderer, at anchor a mile away, to a blur.

There was something dreamlike, unreal about it all. It was as if the water were giving off the steam, and, with its strange, faintly acrid smell, it was easy to imagine that the beginnings of the world had been like this, with this queer smell and with mist obscuring everything, the water glowing ghostly green with phosphorescence.

All the tales he had heard of the monster were going through his brain now. He tried to picture it as a definite, familiar beast of the sea. But he could not hold any picture. Swarming into his mind came monsters of mythology—sea serpents and creatures slimy and green with fins like the dragons of Chinese legend.

At the crosstree, Julie suddenly cried: "Something in the water dead ahead! Moving this way! Coming to meet us!"

Sam shouted: "Can you make it out?"

Her answer was a hysterical scream: "No! No! It hasn't a shape!"

He had run forward. Standing beside Lucky, he stared into the swirl of the mist, illuminated by the phosphorescence as if by green hell-fire.

Perfectly silhouetted against the bright green of the depths was the clear-cut black body of a small shark. It streaked off to starboard, leaving a trail of black bubbles in the green, and a swirling of the luminous water marking its passage.

Lucky said tensely: "I can't see it!"

And Sam called: "Julie! Do you make it out?"

She cried: "It—it seems to be everywhere—a weird kind of dark—writhing around. But I can't make it out. *We're on it!*"

She stopped. In the emerald green effulgence he could see her slim body clearly. She was holding to the shrouds, leaning out, staring.

The green luminance bathed the masts to their tips and it gave to every face a corpselike glow.

The schooner seemed to stagger slightly.

Lucky roared: "We're aground! Senga! Hard a-starboard!"

And Sammy shouted, "No! Steady on!"

Ah Fong, that placid Chinaman, suddenly uttered a scream. And Sammy simultaneously made a hideous discovery. A slimy ooze was creeping up about the ship, sliding up the sides, sliding between and past and over the steel bayonets!

Worse than any nightmare was this amazing, horrifying invasion.

Slipping, sliding, oozing through the bristling row of bayonets, the slime came aboard. It gleamed and glowed with a pale green fire of its own. It formed tentacles. These instantly became snakes, or eels, without heads, without eyes, without apparent guiding intelligence. The air was felled with that strange acid stench.

Sammy started aft at a run, shouting: "Full speed ahead! Shake this thing off!"

Behind him, Lucky yelled, "Good Lord, what is it?"

All about the ship men were shouting and hacking at the writhing, snake-like tentacles. As Sammy raced aft, he saw a great colorless column rise out of the sea at least twenty feet astern. It resembled a waterspout. It was a pillar of the smoldering green slime! It rose up, headless and horrible, just as the bodies of legendary sea serpents were said to rise.

IT SHOT up swiftly with splayed ends to attain a height of perhaps twenty feet, then it plunged unerringly at the schooner's stem. It touched the rail with a thud which Sammy could hear above the shouts of the men and Julie's horrified screams. Then it came arching and writhing aboard.

The splayed ends were like the forked tongue of a snake—a snake as large as a mountain.

They struck down at Senga. He darted away from the wheel, but he could not escape. The headless thing reached his head with incredible alacrity. It wound and enfolded his head. The Malay screamed once. Sammy saw his head vanish—mysteriously and horribly crushed and torn into fragments. He saw the Malay's arms torn out and he saw them disintegrate.

He leaped at that twisting column. He slashed at it with his cutlass. He could not sever that terrible snake-like arm. He had supposed that the stuff was a soft slime. It was not a soft slime. It was as tough as the hide of a shark.

Senga had entirely vanished—swiftly destroyed and mysteriously and dreadfully consumed by this hideous unknown thing.

The arm had coiled about Sammy. He felt the sharp sting, the pressure of it on his back. He slashed and hacked. He did not know that he was cursing and shrieking like a madman. He did not know that all over the ship men were cursing and shrieking like madmen.

It was as if they had sailed from the world of men into a world of nightmare.

Hacking and slashing, Sammy presently severed the head of the tentacle. He hacked at the clinging mass about his chest. The stuff fell away from him to the deck. Instantly it changed shape. It became a pool of slime with live tentacles reaching out frantically in all directions.

And this was the most shocking discovery so far. This awful

slime, of tough consistency, had no central brain. Each part of it was its own center of energy and motion.

Desperately, he hacked at the writhing pool of the stuff at his feet. It was reaching out for the main body, or mass. Suddenly, a tentacle joined it. Miraculously, the puddle of slime flowed into the tentacle; instantly became part of it. And this re-formed tentacle struck at him again!

Sammy leaped back and ran to the other side of the ship. Bryce Robbins was hacking away at a mass of tentacles of all sizes, some as thick as a man's wrist, some as thick as a man's thigh, which came flowing aboard and which seemed determined to enfold and destroy him.

Sammy had a momentary fear that none of them would leave the lagoon alive. Every man aboard was fighting for his life. Even Hector Barling, with his white dinner jacket in shreds, was cursing and slashing at the oncoming tentacles.

Stopping at the mainmast shrouds, Sammy received the most sickening shock so far. A tentacle at least five inches in diameter had swarmed up the shrouds to where Julie clung. She was striking at it with her cutlass. Below her, Larry McGurk was similarly engaged, trying to free her.

SAMMY LENT his help. He began chopping at the tentacle as a man would chop at a tree. With a better purchase for his feet than either Julie or the mate had, he severed it swiftly.

The slender column of phosphorescent slime came slithering down. He did not wait for it all to reach the deck, but hacked at it as it came. He severed it again. He kicked the chunks away from each other. He continued to bring the cutlass down as if it were an ax. When he had cut the column into a half dozen lengths, he hacked at them.

Someone shouted hoarsely: "It's going! We're leaving it astern!"

Sammy ran aft. Bryce Robbins had taken the wheel. One of his hands was limp. He was panting and weakly cursing.

Streaming aft, the mass of the thing was dragging through

the water. Perhaps a hundred tentacles ran like hawsers from the rail and the hull to the shapeless great mass.

Sammy chopped away at these. Lucky Jones came limping aft to join him. Larry McGurk came aft and aided them. Tentacles when they snapped formed pools on deck and were joined by other pools. Some of these reached the rail and slithered overboard.

The Blue Goose suddenly seemed to leap ahead. This was due to the fact that the last of the clinging tentacles had been chopped through, or had snapped.

They were, for the present at least, free of that hideous, shapeless thing.

The schooner forged through the water. And behind it came the thing, a wallowing, churning, monstrous mass—of what? There existed no question, at least, of its disposition.

It was fury incarnate. It was as if the emotion of wrath had been reduced to this animate and horrible stuff.

The thing followed them, churning the lagoon to foam, shooting out long tentacles like arms of lightning at the escaping hull. But the Blue Goose, at eleven knots, could not be overtaken.

When Singapore realized this, he laughed and sobbed with relief. He knew that they were dead men who had been miraculously spared.

Senga's last living act had spared them. By giving the engine full throttle, he had defeated the thing.

But now came another danger. The schooner was lost in the mist from the volcanic mudpots. It was impossible, from deck, to see a hundred yards into the mist. The engine speed could not be checked, or they would be overtaken and annihilated by the thing.

Sammy knew that he could fight no more. He was exhausted by his efforts and the nervous strain. Yet the Blue Goose could not be checked, could not be anchored until dawn came and they found the inlet. And they could not safely maneuver about in the lagoon. The thing might corner them in a cove, or they might run aground. In either case, they would be annihilated.

Looking aloft, he saw that Julie was still clinging to the shrouds at the crosstree.

He shouted: "Julie! What can you see from up there? Can you see the inlet?"

She called down, faintly: "No. But it's off over there to starboard. I saw it a moment ago. I can just see the Wanderer's lights."

A thud on deck behind him made him turn about. Bryce had fainted at the wheel.

Sammy took his place while Larry McGurk joined Julie at the crosstree. She was afraid, she said, that she would faint.

But she didn't faint. Only two of that company were unconscious from the horror they had been through. One was Bryce. The other was Hector Barling.

NOT DARING to let a sharp, sudden turn reduce the schooner's speed, Sammy put the wheel over easily, a few spokes, and made a long, wide circle. Then, as the mate called down directions, he headed the Blue Goose for the inlet.

The wake was almost a perfect semicircle. Threshing and churning about in it, lashing the water into liquid green fire with its tentacles and the writhing and lungings of its great central mass, the nameless horror followed.

Bryce Robbins regained consciousness as Sammy piloted the schooner through the inlet. He sat up and saw Lucky, standing near by in the stern, shouting oaths and taunts and emptying the last of three machine guns into the frenzied, threshing mass astern.

The scientist came weakly to his feet and shouted: "Stop that!"

Lucky jeered: "What the hell? If you expect to take that thing back alive, you're nuts!"

Bryce staggered to the taffrail. Panting, he rested his hands on it.

Lucky snarled: "Yah! There's your octopus, smart guy!"

The scientist, gasping and uttering shorty sharp groans, grasped the rail and stared at the frantically pursuing mass of radiant green.

Then he glared at Captain Jones.

"You fool!" he panted: "Octopus! Eel! It's greater than anything we imagined! It's stupendous! It's the greatest living wonder of the world!"

"Aw, you're screwy!"

SOMEONE FORWARD announced that the Wanderer had come close inshore, was lying broadside off the mouth of the inlet. Through the thinning mist, Sammy heard the hysterical screams of Mrs. Partington. Later, Sammy learned that Captain Milikin had heard their shouts and cries and had come close in to render what assistance he could, but had not dared take the yacht into the lagoon.

Sammy estimated his distances. It looked to him as if there was insufficient room for the schooner to squeeze out past the yacht, and he must keep the engine turning over at top speed. He was certain that incredible, tentacled mass, in its malignant fury, would pursue them out into the sea.

But it did not. The tide had turned. There was a sharp green line marking the tiderip. The lagoon water was vividly green, while the ingoing water from the sea was only faintly luminous. At that sharp line, the nameless monster stopped. Not only did it stop, but it began to move away—toward the center of the lagoon.

Bryce shouted, "I knew it! It checks with my theory! That lagoon water has some element in which that thing exists. It cannot exist in ordinary sea water. We must go back! We must prove it!"

"Like hell," Lucky panted.

"Go back!" the scientist insisted. "I'm paying for this show!"

"You're crazy," Singapore said. "We're lucky to be out of there with our skins."

Bryce came toward him, with the glassy, dark eyes, the snow-white skin of a man insane.

"Get away from that wheel!" he shouted. "I'll take her in!"

Lucky sprang at him; struck him twice in the head with fists like hobnail boots. The scientist went down to hands and knees, shaking his head as a punch drunk fighter does in the ring, muttering and almost sobbing, with blood drooling from his lips.

One hand pounced on an automatic pistol lying in the slime on the deck. But before he could aim it, Lucky kicked it out of his hand and Bryce groaned: "Before we're through, I'm going to kill you!"

Sam told Lucky to take the wheel. When Lucky relieved him, Sam helped the scientist to his feet. He said sternly, "Keep your head on, fella. You saw what happened to Senga. Anyhow, why prove your theory all over again?"

He took Bryce down to his cabin and gave him a stiff drink of whisky. Then, he went on deck and took inventory. Senga was the only outright casualty. Senga had died instantly and horri-bly—doubtless as Pegleg Pyke had died and, twenty-six years before him, Gurt Vandernoot.

Julie and Larry McGurk had come down from the crosstree. The lower part of her white sailor's jacket had been torn-off. The tentacle had encircled her waist, had burned her skin on the left hip in a patch as large as her hand.

Bryce had suffered a broken wrist bone. Ah Fang had lost two of the fingers of his left hand, and an ear. Mr. Barling's right arm was broken at the elbow. Oangi's right foot was smashed. Lucky's left ankle was sprained. And Singapore Sammy had a wrenched back. It was beginning to hurt. And it was going to hurt worse.

Strangely—or not so strangely, perhaps—the man who was doomed to die, the man who couldn't be killed, had not been hurt in the least!

BRYCE EXPLAINS

JULIE CALLED TO the Wanderer for immediate medical assistance. Mr. Barling's personal physician was too ill to leave his cabin. Dr. Plank was suffering from sun fever, was running a high temperature, and was almost delirious. But he came.

He bound up sprains, sewed up wounds, set broken bones and smeared acid burns with unguents. When he had finished his work, Dr. Plank collapsed. So did Mr. Barling. The doctor and Mr. Barling, the latter suffering from complete exhaustion, were taken aboard the Wanderer.

And the survivors of that fantastic battle with the most dangerous, most horrible creature that ever lived in the sea, huddled in the stern of the schooner, drank whisky in an attempt to restore their shattered nerves, and hysterically discussed what they had individually seen and experienced.

It was like the babbling of men after a night of nightmare. What they had been through was too incredible to be grasped. It would take them days to sort out their experiences and to become normal.

Bryce Robbins was not among them. Immediately after the Blue Goose anchored, be took two stiff drinks of whisky and went to his stateroom with samples of that strange, tough, slimy substance.

He returned to the afterdeck with the announcement that they had all taken part in one of the most amazing discoveries in the history of science.

Flushed with this new excitement, stuttering in his eagerness, he burst out: "An anomaly! An absolute anomaly!"

And Lucky Jones growled: "What the hell is an anomaly?"

"An exception—a reversal of rules. This is a reversal of all the rules I know. Do you know what that thing is?" he cried. "It's an amœba! A giant, monstrous amœba! It revolutionizes all scientific concepts. It is utterly and stupendously amazing! It is a giant mass of protoplasm—a unicellular organism of tremendous size!"

"Keep it simple," Julie advised. "We aren't scientists."

He tried to explain it to them in simple layman's language.

"Men, animals, are composed of billions of cells. An amœba is a microscopic creature, composed of one cell. An amœba reproduces by splitting in halves. This thing in the lagoon is an amœba, but it is a freak. Instead of reproducing, it grew from a speck of life invisible except under a microscope, to this incredible size! Why, I don't know. Perhaps some curious freak of its structure caused it—aided by the strange acid in the lagoon water. In other words, a tiny, single cell has become this hideous and horrible thing—a single cell weighing many tons, possessed of a shrewd and horrible intelligence. It is probably millions of years old. It is the most amazing thing the world has ever known!"

JULIE SAID, "Why, it's tur-rific! Does this thing look like an amœba, Bryce? Does it act the same?"

He cried: "It *is* an amœba, only with these astounding differences. The amœba changes form continually. Short processes flow out from the cell body in different directions, and the rest of the protoplasm appears to flow or be pulled along after them. In this way the amœba is able to progress slowly, by means of these *pseudopodia*, or false feet. They are protruded at any part of the cell body or on several parts at the same time. I am talking about the microscopic amœba.

"When this amœba encounters a vagrant bacterium or other food, it throws out these false feet, on both sides of the object;

they flow around it, feet beyond, and thus swallow into the body the wandering bacterium. The food has been *ingested.* Inside the amœba are products secreted which *digest* it. The parts of the food which are indigestible the amœba rejects by a reverse process called egesting. These three processes are not localized, but take place in any part of the body.

"Now this monster is the same amœba, only of terrific size, invested with a shrewd and malignant intelligence, and of remarkable speed. It shoots out *pseudopodia,* or tentacles, with almost lightning swiftness. We saw it shoot a tentacle up the shrouds and attempt to seize and ingest Julie. We saw it shoot a tentacle out of the water to a height of twenty-five feet and attack the *serang.* It enclosed his head and shoulders. It ingested his body, tearing it into little fragments, so swiftly that the eye could hardly follow. It was the same with Pegleg.

"Such parts of him as were unfit for food were rejected—his clothing, his teeth, his wooden leg, the buttons of his clothes, his shoes, and so forth.

"We know now how it devoured Pegleg. It sent a tentacle into the room through that three-inch hole. It fairly poured itself through that hole. Once inside that room, it took new forms—shooting out large and small tentacles to overcome and devour Pegleg. Once he was consumed, it simply flowed itself out of that peephole again. No wonder we were amazed and terrified!"

Larry McGurk interrupted: "Is this anything like that fragment of chicken heart which Dr. Carrol is keeping alive in broth in New York, and which would grow to the size of the earth if it weren't kept under control and constantly cut away?"

Bryce said, "There is no similarity. That fragment of chicken's heart consists of millions of cells. This—this thing consists of but one cell. Yet I must contradict myself. It brings us to the most amazing, most fantastic phase of this creature's structure and being. You will hardly believe me, yet I am sure I am speaking the truth."

He paused. He shook a finger at the semi-circle of upraised faces as if he were addressing students in a classroom.

"I said that this creature, this thing, this monstrous amœba, consists of one cell. But let me tell you a horrible thing. Floating, or somehow moving about within this strange, tough, slimy mass, are brain cells! They are not the type of cells, or centers, found in the ordinary amœba. In the ordinary amœba, the center is called the nucleus. This monster has, strictly speaking, no nucleus.

"But scattered about in the mass of it are free, or independent, brain cells—*and these brain cells are the brain cells of men it has ingested!*"

JULIE PROTESTED: "Oh, Bryce! After all, you've told us that it secretes a powerful kind of acid, and that this acid is the stuff with which it digests things so quickly. If it digests skulls and fingernails, how can a brain cell escape?"

Bryce smiled excitedly. "You're getting into deep water. I can explain it, but not simply. In this tough, slimy stuff of which it consists there are small patches or clusters of a neutral kind of stuff—I mean they contain no acid. They have the power to digest nothing. If this creature wished, it could surround any object—your finger, let us say—with this neutral stuff—and your finger would not be digested. That is what happens with occasional brain cells of men it ingests."

Sammy interrupted: "Are you trying to tell us that that—that thing does its thinking with the brain cells of men it has killed and ingested?"

"Exactly!"

"How horrible!" Julie wailed.

"But," Bryce said, "and get this straight: it has no central brain. There are strings, or clusters, of these human brain cells scattered throughout it like—like raisins in a cake! I don't say that this monster thinks, in the sense with which we use the word.

"But with these brain cells it is enabled shrewdly, even cleverly, to carry out its purpose on earth."

Lucky jeered: "This is gettin' good. Tell us what its purpose is on earth."

"To eat! That's all! It has no other purpose or function. Its sole job on earth is to keep itself supplied with food. Since time began—since its time began—it has had no other job. It is nothing but appetite incarnate. You saw it attack us. You saw it furiously, with a horrible eagerness, thresh and plunge after us in the water. It did not attack us because we are its enemy. It recognizes us only as food—food for an appetite so ravenous, so horrible that you could not possibly imagine hunger like it."

Sam stopped him with: "What do you mean—it recognizes us? Can it see us?"

"Positively not. It has no eyes, no ears, no taste, no smell. It has nothing but supersensitive feeling. To this sensitive surface, all things are alike—sound, waves, light waves and other vibrations. I question whether it could distinguish between heat and cold. Its surface is supersensitive, however, to the nearness of anything fit for food. Once it senses the imminence of food, it attacks. It can attack with horrible wrath, as we saw it attack, or it can attack with diabolical ingenuity, as we know it attacked Pegleg.

"We saw the sureness and fury with which it seized and ingested the shark. We saw the speed and cleverness with which it plucked birds from the air. And that's all it is—stark, insensate, insatiable hunger!"

Julie said: "It's horrible!"

"I doubt if this appetite has ever been appeased. I now believe the stories we have beard of its devouring a whale, of its swarming over and sinking pearling luggers—devouring every man, every edible thing aboard.

"This strange acidity in the lagoon may have developed other freaks of nature, but this monster amœba would have eaten them before they could grow. It has always been master of the lagoon."

HE LOOKED at Singapore Sammy and shook his head. "I'm afraid you're going to be disappointed about your pearls, Sam. In its search for food, this monster has, I think you'll find, literally scrubbed the floor of the lagoon clean. Any clam or other bivalve wouldn't have a chance. It would absorb them, digest the meat and reject the shell."

"The other rumors are true," Sam said doggedly. "We've proved they're true. And I heard the pearl rumor on good authority."

"There are no bivalves in this lagoon," Bryce said in his didactic way.

Pete Cringle muttered: "Just the same, we're gonna look."

"If there ain't pearls," Lucky said, "then the whole expedition is a flop. How do you figure we're goin' to capture that thing?"

"We don't have to capture all of it," Bryce answered. "A good-sized chunk will do. You saw it in action. What happened when you chopped off a piece of tentacle? Didn't you see it form a pool on deck? Didn't you see these pools shoot out tentacles until they found and rejoined the main body? But wait! In some cases you didn't see this occur. Why not? I'll tell you! The pools that remained lifeless, that did not shoot out tentacles, that made no attempt at rejoining the main mass were without brain cells!"

"All you want then," Larry said, "is a good-sized chunk full of brain cells."

"Exactly! I'll take it back to New York! I'll give the scientific world a greater surprise than Dr. Carrol's chicken's heart did!"

"But," Julie argued, "you say it will stay alive only in water containing this funny acid."

"That's easy. I'll take the chunk in lagoon water. I'll take a supply of the water along. I'll have it analyzed by the best chemists on earth. We'll find what the acid is. We'll duplicate it!"

"How," Julie asked, "will you get the chunk you want? We don't dare let it attack us again."

Bryce said optimistically, "We'll find a way."

"We'll rest up a few days," Lucky said. "We won't monkey with that thing again until we're up to it."

The voice of Captain Milikin floated across the water from the Deisel yacht.

"Miss Farrington! Your mother wants to know if you'll come over. She's having hysterics."

Julie answered, "Okay. Send over the tender."

Singapore Sammy started up out of his deck chair. He fell back with a groan, collapsing.

He said, "My back got a bad wrench. Somebody had better help me to my cabin. I can't walk."

Bryce and Larry helped him down the stairs to his cabin. They undressed him and rubbed his back with liniment, but the pain did not ease.

When Larry had gone, Bryce, staring down at the pale, red-headed man in the bunk, said, "Look here, Sam. You're game to go through with this, aren't you?"

"Sure."

"If it's a question of more money—"

"It isn't. I'll go through with it. But we've got to be more careful. I want no more men killed. Senga sailed with me for six years. He was like a brother."

"There'll be no more casualties," Bryce said. "We'll take every precaution."

The two young men gravely shook hands on it. But they were reckoning without the impulses of men driven by shattered nerves and hatred—and the horrible hunger of the most amazing monster the world has ever known.

CHAPTER XVIII

KING OF THE ISLAND

ON THE FOLLOWING morning, Mr. Barling, Julie and her
mother were at breakfast under the canopy on the afterdeck
when First Mate Bevan McTavish came aft to inform them that
a native canoe was approaching from the island.

They could see it from where they sat. It contained but one
man, who sat in the stern, vigorously wielding a crude paddle.
They watched his progress with excitement.

"He must have put out from that point of land," McTavish
said.

Mr. Barling studied the mysterious stranger through the
mate's binoculars and exclaimed: "He's a white man!"

The canoe passed some distance astern of the Blue Goose.

"He's coming here!" Julie said excitedly.

The canoe stopped two hundred yards away. Its occupant
removed binoculars from a case slung over his shoulder, placed
them to his eyes and studied the Wanderer for some time. Then
he returned the glasses to their case and resumed paddling.

When he was a hundred feet away, he shouted, "Wanderer
ahoy! Can I come aboard and pay my respects?"

Mr. McTavish, at the head of the accommodation ladder,
answered, "Who are you?"

The reply came clear and lusty: "I am Jason Rebb—the king
of Little Nicobar!"

"Tell him, by all means, to come aboard," Mr. Barling said.

The king of Little Nicobar paddled alongside the accommodation ladder, made his canoe fast, and came springing up the steps. He was a soiled and sun-blackened specimen of forty-five, with a scraggly black beard, bold brown eyes and a wet red mouth. He wore a stained and battered old sun helmet shaped like a mushroom, so wide that it overlapped his narrow, square shoulders. His blue denim shirt and his white drill pants were in rags. He *wore* nothing on his feet. His shiny, new-looking binoculars case lent a striking note to that strange, Robinson Crusoe costume.

For a moment, as he came on deck, he stared at the breakfast table, with its snowy linen and sparkling silver. He was grinning. Certainly, there was nothing bashful or repressed about the king of Little Nicobar.

Bold of eye, insolent of smile, he approached. Mr. Barling and Mrs. Farrington he dismissed with a glance. Grinning, he stared at Julie, fresh and cool and lovely in white deck pajamas. His eyes reminded her of bees, so busy they were prowling over her. He stared at her until she dropped her eyes with a feeling of shame.

"I just wanted to welcome you folks to my island," Mr. Rebb said. "I just wanted to tell you if there was anything I could do, don't hesitate to call on me. But from the looks of things, you don't stand in need of much." He let out a roar of laughter.

His accent was Australian. Julie had never seen a man with so much self-assurance. He stood with his naked brown feet planted fully two feet apart, and with his fists planted on his thick waist, staring at her and grinning.

MRS. FARRINGTON was eyeing him with apprehension. But Mr. Barling was apparently delighted with the informality of this dirty, insolent stranger. He said: "We heard something about a white chieftain here, didn't we, Julie?"

Julie nodded.

"The main reason I came out," said the king of Little Nicobar, "was, I thought you might be interested in seein' my tribe. They're puttin' on a show tonight—the big yearly orchid ceremony. They dance and they eat one o' the orchids. You seen 'em yet?" he asked eagerly.

"Not yet," Mr. Barling, replied.

"Well, you've missed something, brother! They grow as big as a full grown man, and they smell like nothin' this side o' heaven. The ceremony goes on at ten o'clock tonight, and I'd like to have you come and see it. You'll never see anything like it as long as you live."

Mrs. Farrington shrank from the very glance of this strange, ragged creature, but Julie was fascinated and so was Mr. Barling.

They asked him questions. He answered willingly and with a complete absence of shyness and modesty.

Julie asked him how he had come to be king of Little Nicobar.

"Why," he said, "I used to be a magician. I had a variety act—what you call vaudeville in the States. I was goin' from Java to Malaya in a little hooker. A typhoon turned her inside out, and I got washed ashore here. I'd heard of Little Nicobar—and I was ready. I had some odds and ends in my pockets. When I got ashore and these black fellahs grabbed me, I kept yellin' 'Sambio! Sambio!' Then I gave 'em the treat of their lives. I took glass marbles out of their beards and coins out of their ears till they were rollin' on the beach in hysterics. It's a pipe when you know how."

He was still addressing himself to Julie, still prowling over her with those bee-like eyes.

"What does 'sambio' mean?" Julie asked.

"Peace! Peace! There was a native chieftain. I took beads out of his whiskers and a jackknife out of his hair—and he adopted me! He thought I was the greatest man that ever lived! And when he died, I became the king."

"When was this?" Mr. Barling politely inquired.

"I was shipwrecked here twelve years ago. The old man died two years later."

"Isn't it lonesome?" Mis. Farrington timidly asked.

"Sometimes. But I like it."

"But—but aren't these people cannibals?"

Mr. Rebb threw back his head and laughed. He said, "Aw, that's old sailors' talk. There's no cannibalism in the South Seas any more. It's been stamped out."

Looking at him steadily, Julie said, "We've heard that these natives send shipwrecked men into the lagoon, to be eaten by that horrible thing."

"Before my time, maybe," said Mr. Rebb. "But not since I've civilized them. Why! They're just like children!"

He was gazing at the bandage and splints about Mr. Barling's arm. And Mr. Rebb said: "Ho! You were in that fight last night! I heard you two miles away—hollering and shooting."

"Have you ever seen that thing?" Julie asked.

"No, thank you, ma'am. It's somethin' not to see. There's an old legend in my tribe that the man who looks on that thing walks in trouble the rest of his days. It's death and insanity and trouble—pukka trouble—to look on that thing. What happened?"

MR. BARLING told him dramatically of their adventure. And the king of Little Nicobar, with a sad head shake, commented: "You were lucky to come out alive."

He smoked several of Mr. Barling's dollar cigars.

And abruptly took his departure, after repeating his invitation.

"It's somethin' you'll never see the likes of as long as you live. No white man in the world but me has ever seen that orchid ceremony. You see that little point of land down there?"

Mr. Barling nodded.

"Meet me there at nine-thirty tonight. You ladies—" he bowed—"will be as safe as if you was at a lawn party in Devon. Have any of you been to Lake Howard, in the swamps of Puma?"

"No," Mr. Barling said.

"Well, they're somethin' like the natives there. You'll notice their strong Jewish cast. I tell you, folks, I honestly believe this is one o' the lost tribes o' Israel."

Julie said, "Gosh! That's interesting."

Even Mrs. Farrington was interested, although she detested men in dirty shirts.

And when the king of Little Nicobar had paddled away in his dugout canoe, she said, "Hector, you—you're not thinking seriously of going ashore tonight?"

"I'm tempted," Mr. Barling admitted.

"But he's such a ruffian!"

Julie left them arguing it, and went over to the Blue Goose. Larry and Oangi were at work dismantling the steel bayonets, which had so thoroughly proved their uselessness last night. Lucky Jones and Pete Cringle were busy in the stern with the deep-sea diving outfit.

SHE ASKED them what they were going to do with it, and Lucky said, "Just lookin' it over, baby."

"Where's Sam?"

"Still laid up with that bum back."

She went below and entered Sam's stateroom. He was lying in his bunk, his face wan with pain. But he grinned and said, "Slumming again, eh? I hear you had a visitor."

Julie told him about the amazing Mr. Rebb.

She had not said much when the red-headed man's eyes narrowed and his mouth hardened.

"I've met plenty of his kind," he said. "They'd steal the pennies off their dead grandmother's eyelids."

"I'd like to see that ceremony," Julie said wistfully.

"Don't be a little sap!"

She cried: "Who's being a little sap? It's a chance in a lifetime!"

"Guys like him eat little girls like you."

"I'm not afraid of him!"

"No? I'd rather have a date with a bubonic rat!"

For the first time in their friendship they were having harsh words.

Julie said angrily, "I'm sorry about your back. But I think it's given you a grouch. And I'll see that ceremony tonight!"

Their nerves were still finely drawn from last night's terrifying adventure. Julie left in a huff. When the tender had gone, Sam shouted for Larry. And when the mate came in, Sam said, "She's off her nut. It's that white chieftain. That slimy rat came out and asked them to go ashore tonight. You go over there and argue with Barling. Tell him I said it was too dangerous."

Shortly after Larry had gone, Lucky came below. He, too, had a grim, tense look. Larry had told him about Julie's threat to go ashore tonight.

"I'm gettin' fed up, Sam. Let's make a try for them pearls and get to hell out of here."

Sam said, "Keep your shirt on, fellow. We've got an agreement with Bryce."

"To hell with him! Let him keep his five grand! Pete Cringle is game to make a try for them pearls now."

"How?"

"We're goin' ashore. We're gonna send him down off the beach in that suit."

Sam rose up on one elbow and grimaced with pain. "Nothing stirring. Send that kid down here."

Lucky yelled, "Pete!" and the boy came below, grinning.

"You listen to me, sap," Sammy said. "You're not going down in that suit."

"But it's safe, Mr. Shay."

"Safe! Good Lord! It was safe for Pegleg, and it was safe for Senga, too!"

"But that thing don't go near the beach in the daytime, Mr. Shay. We proved it."

"You saw what it did last night. You saw how fast it is. Stay away from that lagoon!"

"But I just tried the suit and the pump, Mr. Shay. They work fine. And that thing isn't strong enough to smash that suit. It's built for pressure. I been down fifty fathoms in that suit. You know how much pressure there is at fifty fathoms?"

Sammy, still on an elbow, stared at him and he stared at Lucifer Jones.

"What happened last night must have worked a lot of screws loose. You guys are all on edge. You're rarin' for action. Take it easy. Let's study this thing some more."

"If he don't go," Lucky said grimly, "I will."

Sammy tried to sit up, but his back was full of knives. He shouted for Bryce, and when the scientist came down told him to "talk this pair of saps out of pure suicide."

Lucky said, "This guy's got nothin' to say to me. Come on, kid."

SAM FELL back with a groan and the three of them went out. He heard Bryce arguing with them, and he heard Lucky's snarling responses. He heard them loading the small boat, and he heard them start for the beach. He dragged himself up, almost fainting with pain, and looked out the porthole. Oangi was with them.

If it had not been for their blood-chilling adventure last night, he might not have been so concerned. It was hard to imagine that danger of any kind threatened on a day as beautiful as this. The cloudless sky was innocent, a lovely blue. The sea, gently undulating, was as bright, as blue as a Chantaboun sapphire, sparkling pleasantly under the hot sun. There was no breath of wind.

He saw the three men land on the beach, unload the diving suit and the pump, and carry it over the dune to the lagoon. With an agony of effort, he secured his binoculars and placed them to his eyes.

Pete Cringle was getting into the clumsy steel suit. Now Lucky was bolting down the face-plate. Oangi was working the pump.

Clumsily, the boy in the steel suit walked across the coral ledge beyond the stone cabin and entered the water, with Lucky standing at the edge, paying out hose and line, holding them up so that they would not drag on the knife-edged coral.

The steel suit flashed and glinted hotly in the sunlight. It was a fantastic sight—the shining steel suit, like the armor of a knight, against the white of the beach and the sapphire blue of the water.

He was going down now. Gripping the porthole, with the sweat of pain streaming down his face, Sammy watched. His eyes darted along the wall of jungle. He didn't trust Jason Rebb and his savages. But he trusted the lagoon less.

The steel suit went slowly into the blue water. Pete Cringle was apparently proceeding with caution. He was facing the lagoon as he went into the water, taking slow steps. Now he was waist deep. He went on. Lucky, at the water's edge, paid out the rope and hose slowly, merely keeping the slack out of them.

Now the water was lapping about the face-plate. The great, grotesque helmet went under. Bubbles came surging up.

Watching the lagoon, Sam let out his breath. Oangi was methodically working the pump. Lucky was holding the hose in one hand, the rope in the other. The diver was going down.

Sam's heart was thumping. Unknown to himself, he was growling curses. Nothing was happening. Nothing was going to happen, but he wished that kid would hurry.

And suddenly he saw the ripple on the calm face of the lagoon. It was moving swiftly from the center toward the shore, toward the stone cabin. An icy pain gripped Sam's heart. He shouted at the top of his lungs: "Get him out! Get him out!"

Bryce Robbins, on the deck above, took up the shout. His voice was a thin scream: "Get him out!"

The ripple was not a tiderip. It was rounder, smoother, and it hadn't a broken side, as tiderips always do.

There was sudden activity on the beach. Lucky was hauling in on the line. He was being dragged in to the edge. He ran across the beach to a coconut palm and took a turn with the line about it. The line tightened. The fronds began to shiver as if a ghostly wind were stirring them. Then the tree bent. Suddenly the line snapped. It slid like a snake into the water. The hose followed it, dragging the pump along. Hose, rope and pump vanished into the lagoon.

Above the frantic hammering of his heart, Sammy heard Lucky's and Oangi's yells. Then he saw a gray glimmer, like a wave of slime, on the beach. Sun glistened on shooting tentacles.

Lucky and Oangi ran back from the beach. With a sick groan, Sammy relinquished the rim of the porthole, dropped his binoculars, and fell back upon his bunk.

CHAPTER XIX

DEVIL DANCE

BRYCE CAME CLATTERING down the stairs. He burst, white-faced and grimacing, into the room. He panted: "It got Pete! It went after Lucky and Oangi! Oh, those damn fools! Those idiots!"

Sam said weakly, "Yeah. Look out and see if they're getting away."

Bryce looked out the porthole. "They're just coming over the dune, running like mad."

"Is that thing after them?"

"No. They're getting into the boat… they're shoving out."

Sam groaned, "Oh, that poor damned kid. That poor little sap!"

He could hear the oars splashing. Bryce said: "Lucky's at the oars, rowing like a madman."

The small boat came alongside. Lucky's panting and cursing could be clearly heard. Then his unsteady feet were on the stairs. He came down, white-faced, with horrified eyes, and snatched up the bottle of trade gin on the table beside the bunk. He drank a half pint of it and, panting, faced Sammy.

"It—it got him, Sam!"

"Yeah, I was watching."

"It—it crushed that suit like it was made of wet paper! You—you could see the blood squirtin' out. It squashed that suit flat and it just tore it to pieces! Oh, that poor kid! Then it come up on the beach after us. You never saw anything happen so fast.

There was a hundred of them tentacles in the air at once! It almost got Oangi."

"It's a damned shame," Bryce said wrathfully, "it didn't get you, you fool, you damned utter senseless idiot!"

Lucky swayed a little, with fists gripped at his sides. His lower lip jutted, his black brows came down and in and met.

"Yeah," he said. "It don't cost a dime to say that!" He started toward Bryce and Sam barked: "Steady as you go, you ape! You've done enough for one afternoon!"

Lucky turned, like a man in a drunken daze. His eyes were worse than mad. They were stark and horrible and empty.

He suddenly shouted, "I'm gonna kill that thing! I'm gonna take this ship to Singapore and load it to the rail with powder, and I'm gonna blast that son-of-a—"

"Steady!" Sammy stopped him. "We aren't going to kill it. We aren't going to drop our plan for any crazy man. Get in there and take a cold shower. Then get yourself drunk and stop raving."

Lucky lurched out of the room with the bottle in his hand. He ignored only one of Sammy's suggestions: he didn't take a shower.

Larry returned from the Wanderer, wanting to know what had happened at the island.

Sammy said, "Pete went down in that suit to try for the pearls in the cave—and it got him."

"Oh, God. That poor kid."

Sammy repeated portions of Lucky's description of the gruesome and hideous end of "the best deep-sea diver on the Indian Ocean."

And Larry said, "Hell, Sam. You can't blame Lucky. After what happened last night, it's a wonder we all aren't crazy. Over there, everybody on board is on the verge of cracking. It's fierce. The crew is ready to mutiny. That woman is having hysterics. And Julie and Barling insist they're going ashore tonight."

Drearily, Sam said, "Oh, nuts."

"I've been talking to them ever since I went over. There's something gotten into them. That Barling is a little screwy, anyway. But I didn't think Julie'd go haywire on us."

"All women," Sam said, "are screwy. Show them some excitement and they go nuts. Well, what are you going to do about it?"

BRYCE CAME in. He had overheard enough of the conversation to grasp its essentials.

Sam said, "You'd better both go over there and try to talk sense into them. Tell 'em I said it's risky. Tell 'em these white chieftains are rats—always rats. This Rebb is poison."

Lucky came in, staggering, with the look of a man awash. He said heavily, "You guys can listen to me now. I'm fed up. Do you get it? I'm fed up. I'm through. I've seen three good men killed by that thing. It's got a jinx on us."

Bryce said coldly: "What happened to Pete Cringle was needless. It was murder. It was—"

"Stow it!" Sam barked. "We're all in this. We're all to blame. We could have stopped Pegleg from going ashore. It was my fault for losing Senga. We were too damned reckless. From now on, we use our heads."

"We're through!" Lucky snarled. "We're pullin' out!"

"No," Bryce snapped.

"By God, I'll take you to pieces the way that thing took Pete—"

"Pipe down!" Sammy shouted.

Lucky glared blearily at him. "Who's runnin' this show?"

Bryce said icily, "We have an agreement!"

"To hell with the agreement! You agreed in the Mudhole for Sam and me and Larry to have the say. We're sayin' it now. We're through!"

"You're out-voted," Sam quietly answered. "Now, clear out and finish getting yourself plastered. And if you sober up inside of two days, I'll put it into you with a force pump."

Growling, Lucky staggered out. And Sam said, "Bryce, will you go back to the yacht with Larry and argue with Barling?"

"No," the scientist snapped. "They ought to know now how safe this place is. Tell them about Pete, Larry. Let them use their judgment."

Larry went to his room. He shaved, bathed, got into clean whites and returned to the Wanderer. When darkness fell and he had not come back to the schooner, Sammy supposed he was staying over there for dinner. And he presumed that Larry had talked them out of going ashore.

But at a little after nine-thirty he heard the soft exhaust of the tender. And when the soft purring receded until it was finally lost in the far rumble of the barrier reef, he called Bryce below. The scientist said, "They went ashore at the mangrove point."

And Sam growled, "I have a feeling we'll all be dead before this is through."

MR. BARLING, Julie and Larry McGurk had gone ashore. There was no moon, but the stars were so bright that a man's face could be distinguished six or eight feet distant.

Julie wore a sailor's suit and a Sam Browne belt with an automatic pistol in the holster. Mr. Barling carried an automatic rifle, and Larry had a revolver in his hip pocket.

It was Julie who had insisted on going. All day she had been in a reckless mood. She couldn't sit still for five minutes. She could hardly eat. And when Larry told her of Pete Cringle's fate she had not been subdued. She had burst into tears, and when this fit of hysterical sobbing had gone its way, she was more restless than ever. She must, she declared, have action.

A half-dozen times Larry had argued Mr. Barling around to the point where he would have called off tonight's trip ashore, if Julie had only backed down. But Julie would not back down. She wanted action.

When the keel of the tender scraped the sand, Jason Rebb, more mysterious and certainly more sinister by starlight than by sunlight, stepped out onto a patch of sand between the black mangroves.

He greeted them heartily. He said he had been looking forward all day to their visit, but he addressed himself exclusively to Julie. Then he saw that she was armed.

"My dear young lady," Mr. Rebb said, in the accents of alarm, "you don't want to be hurt, do you? And the same goes for you gents, too. My people are just like children, but they know what firearms mean. Firearms mean trouble. I've told them you're coming in a friendly spirit, but if you have firearms, they'll think I lied to them. They'll think you mean to kill them."

Peering into the black wall of jungle, Julie said huskily, "Where are they?"

The king of Little Nicobar chuckled. "Oh, they're scared. Some of 'em ain't more than twenty feet away, peekin' at you. But most of them are down at the old crater. The ceremony is on. Now, folks, if you'll just leave your guns in the boat and follow me—"

"But why," Mr. Barling plaintively interrupted, "are you carrying that cutlass?"

"I'll show you. It's part of the orchid ceremony."

Larry was averse to leaving their guns behind, but Julie, once again, overrode him. They left their weapons in the tender and followed Mr. Rebb along a jungle trail toward a blood-red glow in the night.

Perhaps an eighth of a mile from the beach they passed the village, now dark. There were thatched huts on bamboo poles, after the Malay fashion, and there was one huge structure of riata, interlaced palm fronds and palm boles. It measured perhaps one hundred feet across the front, and must have been two hundred feet long, by thirty in height, with an arched roof and a floor made of logs from the goru palm.

This, Mr. Rebb explained, was the *dobu*, or communal house, where everyone except the sick lived. It was partitioned into stalls or small rooms.

The embers of cook fires smoldered in front of the *dobu*. They passed this and re-entered the jungle. Sharp yells accompanied by a barbaric thumping made it difficult to talk. The glare became brighter until they could see the fire through thinning trees.

The king of Little Nicobar shouted to his guests, "You better start yellin' *sambio* now! Yell it good and loud and keep on yellin' it."

So Julie, Mr. Barling and Larry started yelling, *"Sambio! Sambio!"* The yelling and the rhythm ahead of them did not diminish, but yells of *"Sambio! Sambio!"* were flung back at them.

MR. REBB and his guests entered the clearing. In the center of a wide, shallow depression which strangely reminded Julie of the craters of the moon, was a fire of blazing faggots. On the far side, half-naked men were beating on gourds and empty kerosene tins, setting up a barbaric clamor. Black men and women were dancing about the fire, hopping first on one foot, then on the other, and chanting as they hopped.

A small roar greeted Mr. Rebb and his guests. He shouted to Julie, "They're all ready now. They're all set, my dear. You better stop right here. Don't move. If anybody comes close, just yell *sambio.*"

Julie was shivering. She felt a little faint. She was more than a little scared. It was her first glimpse of any kind of barbaric ritual. The sharp sounds, the thud of men's feet as they hopped, pounded at her nerves and set them jangling.

Mr. Rebb left her side and walked part of the way around the enclosure to a great black tree from which hung a white and softly gleaming object as large as a man. It might have been, in fact, a man hanging.

It was Julie's first glimpse of the fabulous and monstrous blue orchids of Little Nicobar. She had grown so accustomed to the sickening sweetness of them that she had not particularly observed it tonight until now. And now she realized that the perfume was overpoweringly strong, a scent so powerful that she wanted to fight it off.

Mr. Rebb was climbing upon a structure of some sort beside the gleaming white mass. He began chopping at the top of it with his cutlass. The natives stopped dancing and gathered around him until Mr. Rebb was lost from view.

The great orchid suddenly dropped. There was a milling in the crowd. Six men were carrying the orchid toward Julie, Larry and Mr. Barling.

When they were twenty-five feet away, they dropped it. The savage rhythm started again, and the black men and women again began to dance.

Staring at the monstrous orchid, Julie shuddered. In the wavering firelight, it reminded her of the torso of a woman. It was much longer, but it had that shape. Its pale-blue flesh gleamed pinkly-white in the firelight.

A woman leaped at the great orchid, threw herself across it, and, with her teeth, tore out great shreds of the sweetly reeking flesh. She tore out handfuls and leaped up, hopping back, in rhythm to the gourds and the kerosene tins. She held her long skinny black arms over her head and squeezed the handfuls of fragrant flesh-like stuff until juice ran down her arms and spattered into her upturned face.

A black man had hurled himself down on the orchid. He, too, bit into the flesh of it, and tore out handfuls of the fibrous pale-blue stuff and leaped up, with hands held stiffly overhead.

Julie grasped Larry's elbow to steady herself. She felt sick. It was hideous. It was obscene.

The natives were yelling more loudly now, and dancing with greater abandon, working themselves to a higher and higher emotional pitch. The din was deafening.

JASON REBB rejoined them. He threw down his cutlass. He grinned and clapped his hands with the beat of the gourds and tins. The firelight in his eyes made them resemble glowing coals. And the fireplay on his impudent profile gave it a saturnine look.

He shot out of the water fantastically

To Julie, he was suddenly an ogre—a human turned monster, offensive, loathsome.

She tried, through her fright, to be polite. She shouted at him, "We must go! We've seen enough! It's been wonderful!"

He caught one of her hands and squeezed and held it. He stared at her face, baring his teeth, and playfully shook his head, not releasing her hand. "You can't go tonight!"

Larry seized his shoulder and spun him roughly about. "Why can't she go tonight?"

The king of Little Nicobar lost his grin. His fiery eyes seemed to glitter. He shook Larry's hand away and snarled, "She is their guest of honor. They would be offended if she left now."

Larry gave him another push and shouted: "Let go her hand! We're going!"

"You're going to hell!" shouted Mr. Rebb. "But she's staying here! She's staying with me! From now on! Get it?" And to Julie, with that satanic grin, "We need a queen. I need a queen."

But he had released Julie's hand. She cried: "Larry! Hector! What are we going to do?"

Mr. Barling was too shocked, too horrified, to answer. Mr. Rebb made another lunge at Julie. Larry met him with a shoulder and butted him back. All day he had anticipated something of this sort, and yet he had made no plans for meeting it. What could three unarmed people do in the midst of savages famed for their cruelty, ruled by a white rascal?

Some of the black men, perhaps a dozen, had stopped jumping about the fire and were now gathering in a semi-circle between Jason Rebb and the dancing fire, as if they were acting on a signal from him. Many of them carried spears—black-handled weapons with points elaborately and cruelly barked with native thorns and the spines of fish. They would rend and rip and tear flesh in a hideous manner.

The king of Little Nicobar yelled, "Try it! Try and get away!"

Julie had gone behind Larry. She was standing as close to him as she could, clasping him about the chest. He could feel the tremors running through her, he could hear the chattering of her teeth.

Behind her, Mr. Barling panted: "Do something, McGurk! For God's sake get us out of this!"

Jason Rebb heard part of it. "Yah!" he jeered. "Do something, McGurk! One move—and you get a spear in your belly! Go on, McGurk! Do something!"

LARRY McGURK was not at all afraid for himself. He was a man who had been forced to accept the fact that he was to die very soon. He wished there was some way in which he could deliver Julie from this predicament. If he could do that, he would die gladly.

Suddenly, in the midst of these somber reflections, he grinned. It was a hard and ferocious grin.

He said to Rebb, "You call yourself a magician! I'm going to make you look like a tinhorn! Tell 'em that! Tell 'em I'm the man who can't be killed. Tell 'em I defy 'em to kill me! They can't do it! Tell 'em!" And over his shoulder, "Beat it!"

Julie whimpered, "I won't desert you!"

"Barling, get her out of here! Get her aboard that boat!"

Jason Rebb did not hear this. The king of Little Nicobar was shouting at the semicircle of spearmen. He was evidently translating Larry's boast. For the black men were beginning to laugh. And those who had spears grasped them firmly and advanced on Larry McGurk.

Larry had wanted to focus all attention upon himself. He had succeeded. For he was aware that Julie no longer clutched him. He assumed that Mr. Barling had acted without hesitation, and that he and Julie were making their way toward safety.

Though he was sweating a little, he wasn't afraid. But his stomach shrank as several of the spearmen raised their spears to the throwing position—slightly above and off the shoulder.

Jason Rebb shouted a curt order. A spear plunged through the air. It started, accurately enough, for Larry's chest. Then it was as if some magic diverted it in its flight. Mysteriously, the throw was wild—by inches.

A yell went up. That had been, of course, an accident. The next spear grazed his chest on the left side, but it drew no blood. The dancers were stopping now, gathering about, grinning, watching the warriors at their target practice.

Mr. Rebb shouted wrathfully. A third spear, at the moment of leaving a tall, black man's hand, seemed to slip. At all events, it plunged into the ground between Larry McGurk's feet.

A fourth spear whizzed past his neck, but did not even tick him. And now there was bedlam.

The king of Little Nicobar was roaring. He snatched the cutlass from the ground and sprang at Larry, swinging the wicked, curved sword over his head. A spear handle thumped on Jason Rebb's head as he swung the blade. He fell to the ground at Larry's feet and lay there, unconscious.

The black giant who had hurled the last spear plucked from his loin cloth a knife with a bone handle. The blade, narrow and wickedly curved, like the blade of the Malay *parang*, was a full ten inches in length.

With a savage yell he hurled himself at Larry McGurk, his eyes smoky-red, saliva frothing from his thick, dull-red lips.

It was more than Larry McGurk could stand—but he stood it. He could feel the bite of that wicked blade in his heart. But, once again, providence magically intervened. The black giant, racing toward him, unexpectedly caught one foot in the protruding loop of a root.

He went crashing to the ground. The knife, clutched in his big fist, struck the ground four inches from Larry's foot.

But it did not strike into the ground. The keen blade struck a stone—and snapped off at the hilt!

And when the mass of yelling black men and women saw this, the yelling stopped. A sound like a deep, unearthly moan rose from the islanders. A woman ran forward, snatched up the bladeless handle and held it above her head with a shriek. Then she grovelled at Larry McGurk's feet.

THE MOAN persisted. It was like the humming of a million bees. The tribe of Little Nicobar dropped to knees and elbows and noses and grovelled before Larry, as if he were a god—or a demon. And above the moaning, he heard Hector Barling's faraway yells. Larry was starting to back away, down the path. He supposed Hector Barling and Julie had been captured. Abandoning his leisurely retreat, he turned to run. He collided with Julie.

"I couldn't go!" she cried. "I couldn't leave you!"

"Barling?"

"He went when you told him to—ran!"

"Come on!"

And as they ran, Jason Rebb came drunkenly to his feet and staggered down the path after them.

But Hector Barling had not been captured. He had reached the tender and was screaming at them in a panic to hurry.

The engine was purring when Larry and Julie reached the boat. Larry gave it a heavy shove, when Julie had climbed in, and jumped aboard.

"My God!" Hector Barling shrilled. "I thought you'd never come!"

The king of Little Nicobar came running into view. As the boat backed swiftly into deep water, he ran down to the edge of the beach, waving his arms and hoarsely shouting.

The crack of a rifle behind him deafened Larry's left ear.

Mr. Barling was clumsily holding the rifle with the aid of his bandaged-and-splintered arm. As Larry glanced at him, the automatic rifle cracked thrice, swiftly.

The king of Little Nicobar plunged forward and buried his face to the ears in the water and lay there.

Mr. Barling shouted exultantly, "I got him, I got him!"

Larry barked: "You damned fool! Why did you do that?"

"Why did I do it?" the patent medicine king crowed. "He had it coming, didn't he? He was going to kill us and take Julie, wasn't he? Wasn't it justice?"

"There's no telling what that mob will do," Larry said. "We're going to have enough trouble without them."

Julie said, "You didn't have to shoot him, Hector. After all, we were safe."

Mr. Barling blew up. He raved. His nervous system had collapsed after last night's adventure. Tonight's excitement had shattered him again. He called Larry a conceited ass and a smart Aleck. Julie, in hysterics, laughed and sobbed.

"A show-off!" Mr. Barling yelled at Larry. "That's all you are! The man who can't be killed!"

"Oh, let's drop it," Larry said.

"Oh, no! We won't drop it!" the millionaire panted. "I see right through you. I see through both of you."

Julie stopped sobbing to say, "Oh, stop talking like a lunatic."

"I'm not crazy enough not to know the truth when I see it. And I defy you to deny it!"

"What?" Julie wailed.

"That you're madly in love with him—and he's just as goofy about you!"

"Who?"

"This fellow here!"

"Larry?"

"Yes—Larry!"

"Oh, you poor sap," Larry groaned. "In love with me? Don't you know I'm going to be dead in a month?"

"What difference does that make?"

"Hector," Julie said, "stop being an ass."

"It's true!"

"It isn't true. You're crazy."

"You don't love him?"

"No, no, no. Calm down."

But Mr. Barling did not, or could not, calm down. He shook and shivered and jabbered and babbled. Most of it didn't make sense.

"When you get him aboard," Larry said, "you'd better have the doctor give him a shot."

He saw them safely aboard the Wanderer, rowed back to the schooner, and made his report to Sam Shay.

"We ought to pull out," the red-headed man said. "The expedition is jinxed. We've lost three good men. Lucky and Bryce are at each other's throat. Barling has cracked wide open. Julie has gone primitive on us. But," he said grimly, "we aren't pulling out. Before we leave this damned place, we're going to get what we came for—the Dutchman's pearls and a live sample of that murdering jellyfish!"

LARRY SWIMS IN

EARLY THE NEXT morning Julie came over to the Blue Goose. Obviously, she hadn't slept. There were dark patches under her eyes, her lips were pale, her face was wan.

Larry went below and brought her a cup of strong black coffee and told her to drink it down. She asked him what they were going to do.

"Sam says we stay."

"So does Hector. He's a madman. He didn't sleep a wink. He paced up and down the deck. He got me out and made a fool of himself. He had the wireless operator up all night. He's snapping everybody's head off. Poor Dr. Plank came on deck for the first time today. He wanted to give Hector morphine or something to quiet him. Hector insulted him. It was awful. And of course mother's having one attack of hysterics after another."

The tender, having left Julie on the schooner, had returned to the yacht. It was coming back to the Blue Goose. And in the stern squatted Mr. Barling. He clutched a handful of yellow sheets of paper, which he brandished. He came up the schooner's ladder, waving them.

He yelled at Julie: "Look at this! Here's your sweetheart!"

Julie wearily asked him what he was talking about.

"I got a report on him from my Chicago office," Mr. Barling cried. "I've got all the dope on him!"

"On whom?"

"This Laughing Larry of yours!"

"You promised not to use the wireless."

"Never mind that. Nothing but a mate on a filthy old ore carrier!"

"Is that a disgrace?" Julie cried.

"Ah! Then you admit you're in love with him!"

"I admit nothing of the kind. I am not in love with him. Or anybody else."

"That—that business last night!" Mr. Barling panted. "Just showing off! That's all! Just a show-off! Oh, it makes me sick. It makes me nauseated."

"Well," Julie said, in a calm voice, "he got away with it, Hector. You must admit he saved our lives."

"The man who can't be killed!" Hector sneered.

"Shut up," Julie said. "Everybody's nerves are snapping. It isn't fair to take your grouch out on everybody else. Go on back to your yacht."

"And sail away," Larry said.

"You'd like me to, wouldn't you? You'd like to see me sail away and leave her here!" He uttered bitter, mirthless laughter. "So you're the fellow who can't be killed!"

"That's right," Larry said stolidly. "Bandits tried it. Sharks tried it. A tiger tried it. A cobra tried it. Natives with spears tried it. Why don't you try it, you pompous little pipsqueak?"

"All right!" Mr. Barling cried. "Let's give it a real test! Let's see you swim across the lagoon! Let's let that monster try it!"

"Don't be an ass!" Julie said.

"You don't dare!" Mr. Barling shouted. "I'll bet you don't!"

LARRY BEGAN unbuttoning his shirt. "How much'll you bet?"

"One—million—dollars! But maybe dirty deckhands on filthy ore carriers don't save that much!"

"No," Larry said. "This dirty deckhand doesn't happen to have that much."

"All right. I'll leave you a million in my will if you swim to the middle of that lagoon and come back alive!" He laughed again.

Bryce came on deck. He, too, was pale and irritable.

"Sam says to cut it out," he said. "Sam says to tell you you're all screwy and to get drunk or do something."

"Listen, fellow," Larry said. "This pompous little squirt bets me a million I can't swim the lagoon."

"I heard him. Anybody within ten miles heard him."

"But I haven't a million, so he'll leave me a million in his will. A month is a long time. I have a hunch I'm going to outlive him. You know all about wills. Draw up a document. Make it legal and binding. I have a hunch I can spend a lot of that million—"

Julie angrily broke in: "Don't be idiots!"

"I can't get killed," Larry said. "I've tried every way there is. I'm not afraid of that thing. Draw it up."

Bryce went below. They heard Sam roaring at him. Bryce came above with paper and ink and a pen. He drew up the strange document.

Julie cried, "Larry, you're not going into that lagoon!"

His eyes were hard and his lips were thin.

Bryce said: "Sign it, Barling."

Mr. Barling signed it. Bryce witnessed it. Larry was taking off his clothes. He removed everything but his underclothes.

Julie wailed: "Larry, you can't do it!" And when she saw that he meant to go through with this suicidal plan, she ran down to Sam's cabin.

He was sitting up in his bunk, with his feet on the floor.

She cried: "Sam! You've got to stop him!"

"I'll try," Sam said. With an effort, he stood up. Groaning, he started for the stairs, with Julie helping him.

They were halfway up when they heard the splash as Larry McGurk dived. When they reached the bows, where Mr. Barling and the scientist were standing, Larry was swimming toward the inlet. Julie screamed at him to stop, but he did not even look around. He was using a trudgeon, pulling his powerful brown body through the water with long, sure strokes.

The tide was beginning to ebb, but the current was not strong enough to retard him. Julie dropped her elbows to the rail and buried her face in her hands. She would not look. She could not look.

"That's number four," Singapore said.

"Five," Bryce said. "Or don't we count the king of Little Nicobar?"

Julie took her hands from her eyes. The world was swimming. Her heart was beating slowly, like a gong, in her chest. She felt her strength, like a current, oozing out of her arms and legs. She could feel perspiration gathering, wet and clammy, on her upper lip and her forehead and the palms of her hands. She fought off faintness. Through a reeling blue-and-white blur she saw the bronzed arms of the swimmer against the heavenly blue of the lagoon.

Singapore Sammy dropped his arm clumsily about her shoulders and gave her a hug.

"Don't take it so tough, baby," he said. "How do you know he didn't want it to happen like this—quick?"

Julie leaned heavily against Sam and watched the swimmer.

"Maybe he'll make it," she whispered.

THE MAN who couldn't be killed did not reach the center of the lagoon, which was more than a half mile from the inlet. When he was less than a third of the way, there was a sudden disturbance in the water all about him—such as is made by a school of small fish trying to escape from a larger fish—a rippling commotion.

And he instantly vanished, as the sea gulls had vanished, as if a great hand had reached up and plucked him below the surface.

Julie's weight against Sam's side had become complete. She had fainted and was limp in his arm.

Sam tightened his hold and watched the lagoon.

"That's all," he said.

But the agitation in the water had not subsided. And suddenly Larry reappeared. It was a grotesque and horrible spectacle. He was under water for fully forty seconds. And when he reappeared, it was to shoot into the air. The swiftness of his flight, some trick of vision, made him seem twice the length of an ordinary man—twice his own length. He shot out of the water fantastically, gleaming wet in the sun. It was like the leap of a salmon after a fly.

He disappeared. Again he was under water for many seconds. And again he shot into the air, with arms flattened at his sides, his legs straight, his head thrown back. He looked as stiff, as unyielding, as a steel beam.

He disappeared again. Lucifer Jones came lurching forward. His eyes were bloodshot. He was unshaven and dirty. He stared at the group, then at the lagoon, and just then Larry McGurk was cast into the air again.

Lucky said, "That's Larry! What's the idea?"

Bryce Robbins briefly told him. Lucky looked at Barling with the brooding intensity of the very drunk. He said, "You didn't do that, did you, Barling? You didn't dare the kid to do that?"

And Mr. Barling snarled: "Go to hell! If he can't be killed, he won't be killed!"

Lucky reached out with one hand, snatched at and secured a fold of Mr. Barling's white silk shirt, lifted him off his feet—all with the one hamlike hand—and with the other he punched the patent medicine king in the nose.

Mr. Barling fell flat on his back, with arms and legs asprawl, and with blood spurting from his smashed nose.

Sam, at that instant, shouted: "Get that engine started! Bryce, help me get this anchor up! Barling, damn you, give us a hand!" He shook Julie. She opened sick eyes. Her head wobbled on her neck.

He shook her again. "He's swimming back! It didn't get him!"

Lucky, momentarily snapped into soberness, ran aft and

started the engine. Oangi appeared miraculously and helped windlass the anchor in.

Larry was swimming toward the inlet. Swimming feebly. Hardly able to lift one hand ahead of the other, or to kick his legs. But he was still alive. Still swimming!

Even at that distance he looked white. His head was low in the water. His arms followed one another in the trudgen slowly, weakly, as if their strength was going fast.

But the miracle had happened. He had escaped.

They met him midway through the inlet, a swimmer spent. But he gave them a white grin as hands reached down, grabbed his hair, grabbed his shoulders.

Utterly spent, he was hauled aboard. Ah Fong met him at the rail with his bathrobe and wrapped it about him.

AND THEN Julie proved herself a liar. She refuted what she had been solemnly swearing. She pushed the rest of them aside and gathered the limp swimmer into her arms and said, "Oh, my darling, my darling! I was so afraid!"

She cuddled his head to her breast and kissed him. And Mr. Barling, holding a silk handkerchief to his smashed nose, bleated: "Hah! I told you so! She's madly in love with him!"

"I admit it," Julie said.

"But he's still a liar," Larry muttered.

"Don't say you don't love me!" Julie wailed.

"Yes, I will. I like you. I like you a lot. But I don't love you."

"You're a liar," Julie said. "You love me."

"Try," Sammy said wearily, "and make her believe you don't. If you do, you don't know Julie."

Bryce Robbins was staring at him, and staring at Julie with eyes of amazement and shock. He said queerly: "Here's your million-dollar will, mate."

Larry took the fantastic document and looked at it, and looked at Mr. Barling. "All I've got to do now," he said, "is kill you, Barling."

And the patent medicine monarch panted, "It wouldn't do you much good, would it?"

"Rub it in!" Julie said angrily.

Larry went limping aft and below to get dressed. His left knee was wrenched and beginning to swell. But aside from this, he had escaped from that astonishing encounter unharmed. The strange destiny which watched over the life of Laughing Larry McGurk was still, ironically, guiding and guarding him.

CHAPTER XXI

WAR CANOES

TROUBLE WAS BREWING in many quarters. It was in the air, like the sensation of thickness, of tensely-drawn electricity, before a thunder storm. To Singapore Sammy, trying to think clearly, the situation was comparable to that in a volcanic area which has given warnings of eruption.

With Julie's emotional declaration of her love for Larry McGurk, the situation was made even more delicate and dangerous. Bryce Robbins was infatuated with the brown-eyed blond girl. So was Lucky Jones. Heretofore, these two men had been on the friendliest terms with Larry. Now, they suddenly hated him. Under the present nervous stress, anything might happen.

And Mr. Barling had definitely shown his intention to make trouble. He was going to stay. He said he was going to stay to the bitter end, and he meant it. And a man in his nervous condition might do anything.

One by one, Sammy had seen his little company go haywire. Bryce Robbins, the cold scientist, was now a creature of uncontrolled impulses. Lucifer Jones, always so dependable, had cracked, too. Julie, once a gay and lighthearted companion, was now the victim of a dangerous restlessness and recklessness—in love with a man who could live no longer than a month. It was enough to crack the morale of any girl. Just the same, Sammy wished she hadn't cracked. Even Larry, on whose levelheadedness Sam would have banked his last dollar, had gone haywire.

Deliberately swimming into that lagoon! Taking that idiotic dare!

Sam had the feeling that hell was going to pop at any moment; that he would see murder before this ill-fated expedition up-anchored and sailed away.

Trouble came from an unexpected source. Oangi came gibbering aft at tiffin time. The Kanaka sailor was flinging his arms toward the island, but what he said was too incoherent to make sense. They were having tiffin under the afterdeck awning. The tide had swung the schooner around, so that the stern pointed toward the Wanderer and the barrier reef.

Sammy hobbled forward to investigate. He saw five large war canoes, bristling with spears, making out from the mangrove point. The canoes were loaded with men whose faces were painted with white and blue and red.

As Sam returned aft, he called to Larry to break out the machine guns. Obviously, the warriors of Little Nicobar were on their way to avenge the death of their white chieftain.

The five canoes crossed the schooner's bows a full quarter mile away. They were headed for the Wanderer. They had presumably been watching, and knew that the murderer of their white chief was aboard the Diesel yacht.

And apparently the crew of the yacht were fully aware of the impending danger. Sammy saw men running about the decks. Some had guns in their hands. And Mr. Barling was running about among them shouting orders. His voice was once again shrill with hysteria.

The five great canoes—each of them was possibly seventy feet long—were approaching abreast and about forty feet apart. It was their apparent intention to mass their attack, to swarm upon the Wanderer and no doubt to annihilate everyone aboard.

THE FIVE canoes were about a quarter of a mile away from the Wanderer when a machine gun on her bridge began rattling. Sammy, watching through his glasses, saw that the gun was in the hands of Captain Milikin, and he was relieved; for Captain Milikin was a cool-thinking, solid individual.

The water across the bows of the five war canoes was suddenly a-churn with plunging lead. There was immediate confusion aboard the war canoes. Spears waved and wabbled as men scrambled about. But Sammy was certain that none of the bullets had entered the boats; that Captain Milikin had merely wished to show the black warriors that it would be imprudent to venture closer.

That sensible idea was not, however, being shared by Mr. Barling. Five boatloads of savages had the effrontery to threaten his life! And he was evidently determined to show them what happened to men insolent enough to threaten the life of Hector T. Barling.

Sammy watched that pantomime on the Wanderer's beautiful flying bridge. Mr. Barling started emptying a gun at the boats. Captain Milikin knocked the muzzle of the gun upward with his fist.

But some damage had been done. Several of the black men had fallen to the bottom of the boat at which Mr. Barling had shot.

The five boats had stopped their advance. The paddlers were evidently demoralized. By this time, Captain Milikin had disarmed his owner, and Mr. Barling had disappeared from the bridge.

No more shots were fired. It took the natives upwards of half an hour to restore order. And when their yelling and milling about had stopped, and the paddlers resumed their work, the canoes were put about and headed back to the point.

Julie had gone to the Wanderer for tiffin. She returned during the siesta hour with a report on Mr. Barling's latest outbreak.

"He wanted to wipe them out. He wanted Captain Milikin to break out the one-pounder he carries and shoot grapnel at them—destroy every one. But Captain Milikin is sensible. He had a talk with Dr. Plank, and they practically used force in giving Hector some kind of hypodermic injection—morphine or something to calm him down. He's a lot calmer, but he's still dangerous. I think this is the first time in his life anybody ever really opposed him. Certainly, he's never had any real excitement before. And it's too much for him."

Sammy asked her how her mother was.

"In bed—prostrated. All she can do is wring her hands and whimper. Hector almost struck her when she begged him to leave this place and go home."

"Why," Sammy drawled, "didn't you back her up?"

"Do you think I'd go—now?" Julie cried.

"I'd like to see you get that little squirt away from here," Sammy said.

"But he wouldn't dream of it, Sammy. Don't you realize that he can't go—that he's got to stay? It's in his blood now. It's like dope."

"It's worse than dope," Sam said. "What's he planning to do?"

"He has ordered the captain to have the crew serve day and night as sentries. Larry," she said suddenly, "I want to talk to you."

SAMMY WATCHED them go forward. He hadn't liked the feverish look in Julie's eyes, the wild flush in her cheeks. Larry, however, appeared to be calm, restrained, uneasy.

Lucky snarled, "Watch that guy be noble!"

And Bryce said coldly, "What would you do in his boots?"

"I'd grab her if I was gonna kick off tomorrow! If she was as nuts about me as that, I'd make hay till the sun went out!"

"Perhaps his principles happen to differ from yours."

"Is that a dirty crack?"

"You can take it as you wish."

Both men had clenched fists. Sammy said, "Step it down, you lunks. I'll have no more fighting on this ship."

The two men glared at him, but the tension was momentarily broken. Bryce went to his cabin and Lucky went aft to sulk.

Julie came aft, alone, a few minutes later. Her head was high, her face was pale, her eyes were blazing. She evidently intended to pass by Sam without speaking.

He said, "Baby, you ought to know better."

She whirled on him. Her eyes filled with tears. She sniffled. "S-Sam, you—you talk to him."

"What's the good? He's a decent lad. I don't pretend to be as decent as he is, but I'd do the same."

"Captain Milikin could marry us!"

"Sure—and then what? You'd have him for a month—or less. You'd see him sicken and die, as he's going to. You couldn't help. He'd die—and there'd never be room in your life for another man."

"I don't care!"

"You would later. Larry sees that. There aren't many men in this world decent enough to do what he's doing."

"He says he doesn't love me."

"Maybe he doesn't."

"He's lying! O-h-h-h-h, Sam!" She almost fell into his arms. She sobbed. He patted her shoulder. She lifted a tear-streaked face and howled, "Oh, I love him so!"

Sam said uncomfortably, "I don't know what to do about it. If you were a man, I'd tell you to get plastered. I don't know what to tell you. But go ahead and have a good cry. Listen! Listen to that! War drums!"

She stopped crying. She went to the taffrail, where Lucky stood glowering at the island. The sound of the drums was actually something less than sound. Rather, it was a soft, measured thudding on some sense below hearing. It was like the steady beating of a heart, yet its rhythm was as genuinely barbaric as the festival of the juggernaut.

Tumpa-tump-tump—*tumpa*-tump-tump.

"You'll hear it," Sam said, "for a long time. It'll get into your brain and into your blood. Fifty years from now, if you listen

right, you'll hear that drum. It's worse than that bird in Siam—
The Bird That Beats on Gold." He sighed. "It's going to help
a lot."

"What will they do?"

"After a few hours of it, you won't mind what they do—if
they'll only stop that drum. But they won't. We'll hear that drum
till we leave—if we're lucky enough to leave."

JULIE RETURNED to the Wanderer soon afterward. She
told Sam she intended to lock herself in her room, with the
phonograph, turn it on, and have hysterics until she felt better.

He went to the head of the ladder with her and said quietly,
"Listen, kid. I suppose I'm a sap to say such a thing, but can't
you—couldn't you use will power or something? You're going
to make it pretty tough for Larry."

"No," she said firmly. "I love him."

"Yeah. You must."

"You—you can't realize how it is, Sam. You—you can't understand. From the minute I saw him in the Mudhole! Why do you
suppose I stowed away? I'd follow him to the end of the earth!
Don't you suppose I'd help it if I could? Feeling as I do, what
do you suppose I've been through since I came aboard? I wasn't
going to say anything. I swore I wouldn't. But when he swam
into the lagoon, I knew I couldn't keep it a secret any longer.
How do you suppose I felt?"

"It's tough, Julie."

"I love him so damned much! Just the way he holds a cigarette. The lazy way he looks out over the sea. The way he holds
his hands when he's at the wheel. And his voice. And his shoulders. And his eyes. And his sense of humor. Lord!—and you tell
me to use will power!"

She ran down the stairs to the platform and went aboard
the tender. Watching it go, Sammy felt low and pretty useless.
Yet he said nothing to Larry McGurk. Larry was handling the
problem as a man should handle it.

The drums made Sam uneasy and restless. He had heard such drums before, once in Borneo, once in Papua. They got under your skin and into your sleep. Even the most civilized ears, attuned to that dull, constant pulsing of sound, would know its meaning. Their tempo was the slow, insinuating tempo of menace. You did not grow used to it. It was as insistent, as ruthless as the gnawing of an insect buried in your flesh.

CHAPTER XXII

A MAD SCHEME

ALL THAT NIGHT, men armed with machine guns patrolled the deck of the Wanderer, and from dusk to dawn the searchlight on her bridge sent its blue-white beam swivelling about the water. And all that night the drums beat out their slow, deliberate rhythm.

Mr. Barling visited the Blue Goose shortly after breakfast. His eyes had a glazed look, his movements were slow and curiously measured, and Sammy correctly assumed that the patent medicine king was under the influence of sedatives.

These sedatives, whatever they may have been, had taken the rough edge off Mr. Barling's hysteria, but he was still in an ugly mood.

The man was touchy and irritable. He flared into bursts of petty rage at the slightest provocation.

It was all keyed to a single obsession. All the hatred stored up in him, all his resentments—the resentments, it seemed, of a lifetime—were directed against the murderous thing in the lagoon. It was an epic hatred—a seething, blistering hatred. Everyone in contact with him was scorched, as bystanders might be scorched by flames from the mouth of a cannon fired at a distant target.

Foremost among them was Bryce Robbins. For it was Mr. Barling's fierce and fixed purpose to destroy the thing in the lagoon.

Their discussion became a wrangle which went on for hours.

Lucky Jones sided with Mr. Barling. He, too, had a truly blasphemous hatred of the hungry, nameless monster. He disapproved of Bryce's plan to secure a live portion of it to take back to civilization. He wanted to blow it to smithereens.

Singapore Sammy and Larry McGurk sided with Bryce Robbins. And from time to time that argument had the aspects of a pitched battle, with men shouting and yelling insults and taunts and curses.

It went on through tiffin and lasted well into the afternoon. The scientist, the redheaded man and the man who couldn't be killed stood their ground, and, in the end, won.

The ravenous beast of the lagoon was not to be killed!

"But we are to waste no more time," Mr. Barling said. "I will place the Wanderer across the inlet, as close inshore as it is safe. We will study it. We will somehow lure it aboard the Wanderer, into the swimming tank. The tank is large enough to hold all of it, or most of it. Once it's aboard, we will sail immediately for New York. Is that satisfactory?"

"Having that thing aboard, in that tank," Sammy said, "will be worse than having a tiger by the tail. But it's your risk. I wouldn't have more than a hundred pounds of it aboard this schooner. It's powerful."

"So's the tank."

"How'll you get it in?"

"Easy! Get it used to meat. Put meat over. Lure it aboard! I'll have the engineers reënforce the hatch covering. We'll leave a hole in the hatch—and fill the tank with meat and all the fish we can catch. We'll lay a trail of meat to the hole, and it will pour itself inside. Once we have it inside, we'll slam a lid over that hole. Trapped!"

Sam said dubiously: "According to Bryce, it won't live in ordinary sea water."

"That's easy," said Mr. Barling. "Once it's in the tank, we'll take the Wanderer into the lagoon and pump that tank full of lagoon water. And we have enough storage tanks on board for a fresh supply."

"How will you transfer it when you reach New York?"

"That's a problem for clever engineers to worry about."

"How does your crew feel about staying here?"

"My crew feels as intensely as I do about it. They want the thing killed. But I can talk them around to this. What they really want is action."

"They're going to get plenty," Larry predicted.

THE WANDERER'S anchorage was changed that afternoon. She was placed across the inlet, a few hundred feet offshore, with bow and stern anchors down so that she would not swing ashore with the changing tides. And her crew fell in readily with Mr. Barling's rather mad plan. All but the captain. Captain Milikin declared that he had had a premonition, a dream in which he had seen that horrible thing swarm aboard and devour them all.

But Mr. Barling's scheme to strengthen the hatch cover of the tank was enthusiastically carried out by his engineers. They strengthened it to such a degree that even Sammy was forced to admit that it might hold the monster, although he was still dubious of the plan. It took the engineroom crew five days to complete their work.

And in this time, a number of interesting facts were discovered concerning that diabolical mass of hungry protoplasm in the lagoon. One was that it could be enticed out of the lagoon if the tide was ebbing, so that the sea water was sufficiently diluted with lagoon water. Another was that it had apparently centered on Julie as the tidbit it wanted most!

This discovery was made soon after the monster began making daylight appearances. Ordinarily, it spent most of its time in the precise center of that round body of water. But when the crew of the yacht began throwing in chunks of meat and fish which they had caught, the filmy gray mass would come into the inlet, provided the tide was ebbing. It could be seen clearly in the water, a shapeless mass, always changing, always shooting out and drawing in its cloudlike tentacles, searching, always searching for food.

Mr. Barling had organized regular fishing expeditions. He had excellent deep-sea gear. And every day, several of the crew would go to the barrier reef in the tender. In an hour of fishing, they would always fill two or more barrels with their catch.

First Mate McTavish rigged up an ingenious catapult, by which a thirty-pound fish could be hurled several hundred feet. With this device, fish were hurled to the monster. And it was always fascinating to watch. A fish would be hurled. It would strike the water, say, a hundred feet from the monster. Instantly, often before the fish landed, a tentacle would shoot out and seize and ingest the fish. Then the tentacle would leisurely return and be absorbed by the central mass.

When no fish were being thrown, the filmy, horrible body would lie there, close to the surface, moving about with an awful restiveness. And one day Mr. Barling discovered that the thing became curiously agitated whenever Julie walked along the deck. It would shoot out long tentacles following her passage, no matter whether she was alone or in the company of someone, and no matter how many accompanied her or were scattered along the rail.

Mr. Barling thought at first that it was due to the color of the pajamas Julie was wearing when he made the discovery. They were of satin, with a sapphire-blue top and white trousers. Dismayed by the monster's particular interest in her, Julie was reluctant to try experiments, but she finally consented. And she proved that it made no difference what color clothes she wore.

Mr. Barling even tried others in Julie's clothes. A small deckhand walked up and down the deck in the blue-and-white pajamas—and the waiting monster paid no heed. But when Julie appeared on deck in pink pajamas, it instantly became excited.

Its agitation every time she appeared was very pronounced. And no question could exist that that revolting, jellylike mass in the lagoon wanted Julie more than it wanted anything.

Mr. Barling said, "We could use you, Julie, to lure it aboard."

And she said hysterically, "I honestly believe you would! I honestly believe you'd sacrifice anybody for this mania!"

YET JULIE was not the only person singled out by the monster. It grew to know Mr. Barling, too, and in the most amazing way. Mr. Barling, as Sammy learned much later, could not quite restrain his hatred of the thing, nor could he put down impulses, typical of him, to express that hatred.

Secretly, he would slip out of his suite, in the dead of night, and, with the catapult, would hurl at the monster various edibles—chunks of meat from the diminishing store in the great refrigerators, and fish.

On several occasions he catapulted to that malignant mass chunks of beef in which he had wrapped up several pounds of dry mustard. And on several occasions, he disemboweled a large bonita and filled it with red pepper.

On receipt of these delicacies, the monster would go into a sensational fury. It would lash about until the water resembled green flames.

And amazingly enough, it identified Mr. Barling as the perpetrator of these insults. Thus it was that when Mr. Barling appeared on deck, it would seem to grow frantic. It would shoot out tentacles and lash the water into foam. But this was different from its agitation when it "saw" or "felt" Julie's presence on the yacht's deck. It reacted to her in a sinisterly deliberate way, as if it merely hungered for her. Mr. Barling, however, it seemed to wish to destroy.

The work of the engineroom crew was finally finished. The hatch covering the steel swimming tank was so strong, at least in Mr. Barling's estimation, that no creature on earth could dislodge it. At one end of it, in the center, a hole had been cut in a steel plate an inch thick. Through this hole, if Mr. Barling's plan worked, the giant amœba would flow, in seeking the food with which the tank was to be filled. An electro-magnet, actually a solenoid, had been rigged there, so that the closing of a switch would shoot a thick bolt over the hole, covering it and blocking any attempt on the part of the monster at escaping. This bolt was operated electrically by remote control. One switch was on the bridge, the other on the boat deck, aft.

Unknown to them at the time, the changing of the Wanderer's anchorage had accidentally furthered Mr. Barling's mad scheme. It blocked the entrance of the lagoon to a certain extent, so that the tidal currents themselves were diverted, making it more difficult, or inconvenient, for fish to swim in. So, little by little, the monster's food supply was curtailed, and by the time Mr. Barling was ready to trap it, its hunger had increased to the point where it would go well out of its way for any food.

Unaware of this, however, Mr. Barling planned to capture the horrible, slimy mass at night. He reasoned that it was always bolder in the night, although Bryce Robbins argued that it was not a case of boldness but of the creature's sensitivity to the direct rays of the sun. He maintained that it shrank from direct sunlight.

IN ANY event, having decided upon the night for the capture, Mr. Barling proceeded with his elaborate plans. Ever since the yacht had anchored across the entrance to the inlet, the monster had become bolder and bolder. At least it had, day by day, been coming closer and closer for the fish and chunks of meat the sailors catapulted to it. One afternoon, when Julie appeared on deck, the great filmy, slimy mass surged out of the inlet and a large cluster of tentacles shot out from the central mass to within forty feet of the Wanderer's hull.

With a shriek, Julie ran into the music room. Mr. Barling, however, was wildly enthusiastic. He marked the time: two forty-five. The tide was ebbing rapidly, so that it could be assumed that the water all about the yacht was strongly diluted with lagoon water. Tonight's ebb-tide, occurring approximately twelve hours later, would set the time for the experiment at between two-thirty and three.

Mr. Barling laid his plans accordingly. All of the crew of the

Blue Goose, with the exception of Ah Fong, who remained aboard with a machine gun in case the natives made a surprise attack, came aboard the yacht.

All afternoon the crew of the Wanderer fished at the barrier reef. At dusk they came in with their catch—eight barrels of assorted deep-sea fish. Seven barrels were emptied into the tank. The other barrel was used for bait. A one-inch Manila line a thousand feet long had been softened by soaking and stretching. It was the baitline. At yard intervals along it, hunks of meat and whole fish were lashed with twine.

During the making tide, just before sunset, Mr. Barling set the baitline. At the outer end of the baitline was fastened a small kedge anchor. The other end of the line was made fast to a cleat set for the purpose in the hatch cover close to the small hole through which, if all went well, the monster would flow. And—again if all went well—the investigating tentacle would reach the hole and sense the presence of the great store of food in the tank.

With the inboard end of the line made fast to the cleat, Mr. Barling coiled up the thousand feet of line, with bait lashed in place, into the tender. Then, with the tender slowly moving toward the lagoon, he payed out the line. When the end of it was reached, he dropped the kedge anchor. Theoretically, the hungry monster would work tentacles up the long line and eventually work itself entirely aboard and into the tank.

It was the opinion of the assembled company, with the lone exception of Singapore Sammy, that Mr. Barling's scheme was wonderful. Sammy took exception to it on the ground that the monster might not be so readily managed. True, it might come aboard the yacht. But suppose it decided not to flow into the tank? Suppose it decided on a tour of inspection first?

But he was quite alone in that opinion. Even Mrs. Farrington, after three days of hysterics, had fallen into the universal madness and was anxious to see the monster captured. The persistent beating of the drums seemed to soothe that high-strung lady.

While the sound irritated the others and made them restless and touchy, that unremitting pulsing had a curiously calming effect on her. True, she would burst into tears on little provocation; but for the most part she entered into the spirit of the game—what Mr. Barling called "the greatest fishing expedition the world has ever known"—and she even worked the catapult and screamed with delight when the most horrible beast ever to dwell in the sea snatched and ingested the barracuda she sent it.

IT WAS decided that, when the zero hour approached, the decks would be cleared, and all doors closed and bolted against possible intrusion by the slimy thing. Everyone would gather on the boat deck aft, where they could overlook the arrival of the giant amœba and watch its descent into the tank. Mr. Barling was to stand beside the switch with which the hole in the hatch would be electrically sealed when all of the monster was in the tank.

Thus was Mr. Barling's mad plan executed. Flood lights were arranged over the after deck, so that the creature would be clearly seen.

At two o'clock they gathered along the rail of the boat deck. All but Dr. Plank were there. He was still confined to his bed by fever.

Cutlasses were served out, in case the monster did not go into the tank.

It was, once again, a moonless night. Close at hand, the lagoon glowed, a smoky emerald, clouded by mist from the bubbling volcanic mud pots. And once again the air was sickly sweet with the fragrance of the great orchids.

In a growing atmosphere of tension, the watchers waited. A sailor suddenly cried: "It's takin' up the slack!"

They saw the monster, deep in the water. It had dropped down for the bait nearest the lagoon. The inlet was a swift current of green fire, lashed by tentacles which were sharply delineated.

Mrs. Farrington cried: "I can't stand it! I can't stand it!" And rushed to her suite.

Sammy watched the line. There was a cry along the rail as the first fish tied to the line above water disappeared. He watched it come—an endless gray python, six inches in diameter. It swarmed up the line, coating it, surrounding it, moving upward with a swift wriggling like that of an earthworm, with the rope as its core, absorbing fish and hunks of meat as it came.

No one was crying out now. In a hush, broken only by the heavy breathing of the watchers, that transparent, palely-gray endless python came aboard. Tentacles shot out here and there like the antennæ of a great caterpillar as it slithered across the afterdeck to the hatch. It reached the last tidbit lashed to the line. And it did not hesitate. It began to flow into the hole!

Mr. Barling gave a little gasp of gratification. His scheme was working. It was working perfectly! The monster, strung into an apparently endless rod, was coming aboard and flowing into the tank!

Sammy clocked it. It began to enter the tank at two thirty-five. For one hour and sixteen minutes that seemingly endless mass of protoplasm flowed into the tank. He began to wonder if it would never come to an end.

Try as he would, he could not consider any of it dispassionately. Occasionally, as he stared at the flowing, snake-like, wriggling thing, he saw green sparks in it, and he wondered if these were the brain cells Bryce had mentioned.

And be wondered what would happen if the great slimy mass completely filled the tank before the greater portion of it was aboard. But his fears were groundless. At precisely three fifty-one the seemingly endless python of gray, transparent slime entered the tank. The python became smaller and smaller. All of it—the very last inch of it—went into the tank.

WITH A triumphant shout, Mr. Barling closed the switch. There was a metallic thump as the stout steel bolt shot across the hole. The monster was trapped!

He cried: "We've got it! It worked! It's trapped! It's ours!"

Sammy said, "Yeah. I hope so, I certainly hope so."

Mr. Barling yelped. "Aw, don't be such a gloom. It can't get out. It's practically hermetically sealed in there. I saw to that. There isn't a crack anywhere big enough to insert a hair!"

Sammy watched the tank. He hoped Mr. Barling was right. But none of the others were so dubious. Like people suddenly and unexpectedly released from prison, they were leaping about and shouting. Julie was executing a dance, snapping her fingers, flinging her arms about. Mr. Barling was laughing like a madman, going about and thumping men on the back. Bryce Robbins was laughing hysterically.

For a few moments the unremitting sound of the drums was drowned out. The brains of the most advanced of all living creatures on earth had triumphed over the brute strength of the most horrible, most malignant creature ever to inhabit the earth or the waters of the earth.

Over the heady tumult, Mr. Barling presently made himself heard. "We're going to celebrate! We're all going to get as drunk as owls. Steward! Henry! Jim! Clyde! Bring all the liquor you can carry into the main saloon! We've won! We've won! Sam, you can get your pearls in the morning. For the first time in millions of years that lagoon is safe for any man! Tomorrow we clear for New York! When Hector T. Barling puts his mind to a job, that job gets done! Who's afraid now?"

Laughing, Julie cried, "Who's afraid of the big bad monster!"

She tossed her cutlass to the deck below, climbed over the rail and slid down a stanchion. With a shout, Mr. Barling followed. The others swarmed after him.

Mocking their enemy, taunting its malignant hunger, its horrible appetite, its hideous potentialities, Julie leaped on the hatch. She began a tap dance. Her feet twinkled and clattered. Sailors began clapping their hands in time, unaware that they were keeping time to the beat of drums.

Sam Shay was the fast to join that excited mob. He did not go down a stanchion, but went forward, and down the stairway. His back was still bothering him, and he wasn't yet up to athletics.

Walking aft, he saw, in the floodlights, the beautiful blond girl, her silver-golden hair flying about her head, her cheeks feverishly flushed, spinning and spinning and spinning on her little nimble feet.

And he saw what no one else saw at the moment. He saw that the great lid on which she danced was swelling, that it was beginning to bulge ever so slightly in the middle.

Then a deckhand saw it and shrieked: "That thing is bustin' loose! Look out!"

CHAPTER XXIII

THE MONSTER'S FURY

NO ONE HEARD him. No one heard Singapore Sammy's shouts of warning. He ran aft and seized Julie about the waist and carried her off the hatch.

Mr. Barling was staring at the hatch with bulging eyes. Sammy grabbed his arm and the millionaire cried: "It can't get out!"

"What would it do to this ship!"

"But it can't get out! I tell you, that hatch is too strong! It's almost solid steel!"

"So was Pete Cringle's diving suit!"

There was a deep and sinister ripping sound. The hatch cover bulged more. The planks were beginning to splinter.

Sammy shouted to Julie: "There isn't time to get off the ship. Go to your room. Larry! Take her to her room! And make her stay there! Don't let her out until I tell you!"

Still under that spell, Julie cried: "What if it does bulge? It can't get out! Nothing is strong enough to get out of there!"

Larry scooped her into his arms and ran with her to the main corridor door. He vanished into the corridor and the door slammed behind him.

But none of the others had moved. As if hypnotized, as if refusing to accept the evidence of their eyes, they stood, cutlasses in hand, and watched the swelling hatch.

It burst off with a sudden explosion of splintering planks and tortured steel. It seemed to vanish into the air. Sam backed away in horror. Where the hatch cover had been was now a huge, gray, greasy bubble welling up and out.

One of the deckhands had been knocked unconscious or dead by a chunk of flying metal or wood. Unerringly, a tentacle a foot in diameter shot up from that pulsing gray pulp and enveloped him. As the *serang* of the Blue Goose had done, the unfortunate man vanished into the tentacle, his body disappearing down the tentacle in a swift stream of fragments of bone and flesh and gobbets and long threads of blood.

With the swiftness of lightning striking, the insatiable pulp in the tank reached out and dealt death and mortal injury.

Sam Shay was in the heart of it, wielding his cutlass, slashing and hacking, each effort an agony to the torn muscles in his back. It was worse than the nightmare he had gone through on the night when the Blue Goose ventured into the lagoon.

In this crowded space it was more difficult for men to escape. And the monster, at closer quarters, a more compact mass, had many of the men at its mercy.

Sammy saw Captain Milikin, a dozen feet away, entangled in at least a score of agile, milky-gray arms of the hideous stuff. The captain was a powerful man. He chopped at the tentacles, but no sooner had he freed himself of one clinging mass than other flashing, slimy arms wrapped about him.

Sammy tried to fight his way to Captain Milikin's side. Before he could reach him, he saw the captain's arms and legs disjointed, his head crunched and dissolved. In an instant, that living, breathing, gallant man was utterly non-existent.

Others were going in the same incredible, horrible way. Fighting now for his own life, Sammy saw a steward lift a steamer chair to beat off a looping tentacle. The chair vanished magically in a cloud of splinters. The steward dived down and tried to crawl away. He was engulfed in a veritable wave of the protoplasmic slime—engulfed and absorbed!

A TENTACLE encircled Sammy's waist. He hacked it through, leaped away from snakelike reinforcements—and saw two deckhands seized by the same splaying tentacle, wrapped in a crushing embrace. Their heads vanished, their arms vanished, their torsos dissolved into the wrenching, crushing, sucking mass.

Men, screaming, were dying—and some were escaping. Sammy saw them swarming up the stanchions to the boat deck, saw slimy creepers go looping after them. A deckhand was dragged back. An oiler escaped.

A four-inch tentacle shot out of the tank and twined about Bryce Robbins' left arm between elbow and shoulder. He saw that arm wrenched and twisted and pinched off. He saw Lucky Jones do a perfect back somersault to escape a lunging, three-headed tentacle. He saw Lucky seize the scientist's legs as he sprawled back. Sam ran to them and grasped a handful of Bryce's hair.

The after deck was now clear of everyone but Bryce Robbins, Lucky and Sam Shay. The monster was coming out of the tank. A great lip of slime was welling up over the edge toward the three men.

Sam and Lucky dragged the wounded man into the corridor. They ran down the corridor to Dr. Plank's suite and ran in. As he closed and bolted the door behind him, Sam saw that the wave of slime was swiftly following, sending great tendrils and shoots into the corridor.

Dr. Plank was sitting on the edge of his bunk in pajamas, his eyes wide and his skin white and blotchy with terror.

Lucky panted: "It's coming down the corridor! Is there a way out of here?"

The sick doctor dazedly shook his head. "No, no!"

Sam helped the half-conscious scientist across the room and barked: "You've got to fix up this man quick."

The doctor staggered from the bed. He was like a man in a trance. But he fashioned a tourniquet above the amputation and checked the bleeding.

All the time he babbled. What a fool Barling had been not to get out of here when he had the chance! What would become of them now—with that hideous thing aboard?

"It won't leave until it's got all of us!"

Sammy ran back to the door and placed his ear to the panel. The doctor shrieked: "Don't open that door!"

The red-headed man had no intention of opening the door. With his ear flattened against the wood, he heard a splintering crash near by. This sound was followed by agonized screams.

Sammy had his hand on the knob. He jerked it away. Through the keyhole, a thin tentacle of the gray slime was oozing. And slime was oozing in a thin layer through the crack under the door. He trampled the stuff under his feet and kicked it about, but it continued to ooze in, yet not in dangerous quantities. Evidently this room was not its objective.

He shouted: "Is Julie's room next door?"

Dr. Plank said, "Yes. Is it going there?"

"It's broken in there! It's got her!"

"Don't open that door!" Lucky shouted.

Listening, Sam heard a steady swishing sound. The monster was flowing, writhing, wriggling through the corridor.

SAM LEFT the door and said, "No matter what else happens, doctor, you've got to fix this man's arm. Now!"

Dr. Plank, white and shaking, answered, "Yes. I'll operate. This minute. But someone must help."

Sammy said grimly, "I'll help."

And while he dribbled ether into a cone, Dr. Plank cut and sewed. Lucky Jones stayed at the door, trampling on the slime as it trickled through the keyhole and oozed under the door.

Suddenly he shouted: "It's stopped. It isn't coming in any more!"

Dr. Plank said to Sammy, "All right—I won't need you any more."

Sammy ran to the door, listened, unbolted it, and jerked it open. The corridor was empty save for a thick coating of slime

Lucky slashed at the imprisoning tentacles

on floor and walls to a height of four feet. The carpet runner was already in rotting threads. Paint was blistering from the walls.

Sammy ran into the hall and, with Lucky, entered the room adjoining. The door had been smashed in. The monster had forced its way into that room—into Julie's parlor. The parlor was in ruins. Every piece of furniture it had contained was in rotting splinters and shreds. The floor and walls to a height of six feet were coated with slime.

Behind him, Lucky panted: "It got her! It got her and Larry and it went out that porthole!"

The two young men ran to the porthole, which was open. The two other portholes were closed. A familiar triangular pattern of slime from the floor to the porthole indicated how the monster had escaped.

They peered out the porthole into the night. And they saw the thing, a bulbous mass in the green flames of phosphorescence, as it writhed and twisted and wriggled and wallowed and churned through the inlet and into the lagoon.

They went into an adjoining room, the door of which had likewise been demolished. It had been Julie's bedroom; every object it had contained had been shattered, or twisted, or somehow wrecked and ruined. The bed was a tangle of splinters and springs. The closet door was in fragments—all her clothing in shreds. The mattress had been tore into threads. Slime was everywhere and the reek of acid was suffocating.

They suddenly heard yells. And Sam gasped: "Julie! It didn't get her!"

A door across the room had not been smashed. It opened into Mrs. Farrington's parlor. Here, the monster had not visited. The two young men went on through her bedroom, likewise untouched—and empty. There was a slight depression in the bed where Mrs. Farrington had been lying.

They entered another corridor, shouting as they went. They followed Julie's answering cries; climbed the stairs to the bridge. In the pilot house they found Julie and her mother clinging to Larry McGurk. Huddled on a stool near the chart table, with glazed, stupefied eyes, was Mr. Barling. His body was limp. His mouth was open. He was breathing noisily through it.

Julie cried, "Oh, Sam! I thought it had got you!" She ran to him and threw her arms around his neck and began to sob. She whimpered: "Where's Bryce?"

"He lost an arm. But Dr. Plank says he'll be all right."

A little later she told him how she had made her escape. Larry had carried her into her room and bolted the door. When the monster came surging down the corridor in pursuit, and smashed down the door, Larry had carried her into her bedroom and bolted that door.

"He had hardly shot the bolt when it smashed against that door, and we only got into mother's parlor when the door gave. We got her and came up here. Hector's arm is broken again."

"It's too bad," Lucky growled, "it wasn't his neck."

Sam left them and made a tour of the ship. There had been eight casualties: the captain, an oiler, the second engineer, two stewards and three deckhands. In less than ten seconds the monster had sucked these men into instant death. Sam did not check up on the broken arms and the lost fingers and ears.

CHAPTER XXIV

STARVATION

FIRST OFFICER BEVAN McTAVISH, now the acting captain, wasted no time in returning the Wanderer to her old anchorage. And the ill-starred expedition to Little Nicobar entered upon its final phase. Sanity and reason were virtues of the past. After that night of horror, no man among them was rational.

The horrible death of eight men in almost as many seconds had undermined coolness and judgment. They had learned the impossibility of coping with that slimy mass of insensate hunger. Reason should have told them that a thing that had, perhaps, outlived by a billion years the oldest living thing on earth could not be outwitted, captured, or easily destroyed. They had sampled its monstrous fury enough times to know that any further dealings with the thing would be suicidal.

There was but one course open to them: to leave instantly, to give time a chance to restore their sanity.

But they did not take this course. To the last man, even the last woman, they elected to stay. It has been said of that insane little company that they were far worse than the victims of a malignant drug which works spiritual and physical destruction.

The toxin was in the veins even of Mrs. Farrington. A week ago she had been hysterically pleading with them to sail away. Now she added her shrill voice to the counsels of vengeance.

The thing must be killed—destroyed—annihilated! There was no other thought in anyone's mind. Down to the last survivor in the Wanderer's crew that was the theme of all talk. No one mentioned leaving. No one mentioned the possibility of further human sacrifice to that wanton and ruthless creature. They must annihilate it! The thing in the lagoon must be exterminated!

Mr. Barling had had another nervous collapse. His heart went bad. One night he almost died. But he was soon up and about again. And he, too, was possessed of but one thought: to exterminate that murderous thing in the lagoon.

Lucky's reaction to the madness of the moment was typical of him. He got drunk and stayed drunk. But he no longer jeered. Personal feuds were put aside. He had always wanted to kill the monster. His hatred, too, became a mania.

Acting Captain McTavish, a cool-eyed and canny Scotchman, would have kept the Wanderer at Little Nicobar even if his crew had turned mutinous and demanded that they up-anchor and go—which none of them did. Bevan McTavish had sailed under Captain Milikin as mate in one ship and another for fourteen years, and had looked upon him with an almost filial affection. With Captain Milikin's death, he turned dour and taciturn, and his blue Scotch eyes burned with a cruel and fanatic light. He declared he would not leave Little Nicobar until the monster was dead.

And Jim Axelrod, the chief engineer, stoutly shared this determination with him. A happy, joking man, the chief turned even more glum and frowning than did the acting captain. He wanted to construct depth bombs and to set them about the lagoon, baited, and he swore he could build a bomb that would destroy any form of life within two hundred yards. But he was willing to work day and night on any scheme which would assure the monster's destruction.

PROFESSOR ROBBINS was the most fanatic of them all. His dreams and hopes of taking the monster, or a living specimen of it, back to America, alive, had been discarded. He became a thin and haggard apostle of vengeance. The doctor ordered him to his bed for at least a week, to give nature a chance to restore lost blood and to heal a shattered nervous system.

For two days and nights, Bryce did not go to bed at all. He paced the main deck and the luxurious halls of the Wanderer, a gaunt and spectral figure, with burning eyes, with lips raw from gnawing, with face pinched by the pain of the amputation. He drank innumerable cups of coffee, he put away quarts of whisky, he smoked cigarettes incessantly. He could not eat. He would not even sit down. All he did was pace and smoke and drink and talk. As if the barrier dam of his reserves had been broken down at last, he let loose a flood of talk. It was neither mad nor sane. Actually, it was cold and scientific—a flood of pure hatred.

The loss of his arm did this. If the monster had not torn that arm away, he doubtless would have held to his original course. But his arm had gone—a morsel for the horrible thing which he had himself described as appetite incarnate. He must avenge the loss of that arm.

He spent days talking hatred and revenge, other days of thinking and plotting and scheming. He would pace the deck, staring at the lagoon, with tobacco smoke trailing off his shoulders. He would stop by a stanchion and peer under heavy lids at the lagoon. At night, through the swirling mist, he would watch the smoky emerald of the phosphorescence and listen to the unremitting pulsing of the war drums.

It had never stopped, that drumming. Day and night it persisted, wearing down nerves, eating into brains.

One day Professor Robbins announced that he had a plan. He prefaced his explanation with the familiar statement, "I'm going to kill that thing if it's my last act on earth." Then he said, "We will block the lagoon. We will starve it, then lure it ashore near the stone cabin to its destruction!"

Because of its cruelty, the scheme, so far unfolded, appealed to them all. They wanted to see the thing suffer, to writhe and thresh about in the accesses of hunger; they wanted to punish it in the cruelest way possible. You punish a man by striking at his weakness, whatever it may be. The surest way to punish, to inflict suffering on the monster was to deprive it of food. Its single instinct was appetite. Its single purpose was to seize and ingest food. Any kind of food, so long as the eager protoplasmic mass of it was fed—birds from the air, fish from the sea, clams and oysters scrubbed from the bottom, men seized from the decks of ships. Food! Anything to assuage that tremendous, horrible, insatiable hunger!

No one bothered to ask Bryce Robbins the rest of his plan of destruction. The uppermost thought was to make the thing suffer. And every man in both crews was eager to help.

In following days, the inlet was laboriously blocked. Anchor chains were sawed into lengths and draped from shore to shore. Heavy cables were interlaced with the chains. Ropes were tangled amongst the cables. Shore parties scorned the threat of native attack and chopped down trees, which were fashioned into piles and forced into the bottom of the lagoon. Swimmers dared sharks and possible attack by the monster to dive on the seaward side of the barrier and plug up chinks and crannies with rags and bunches of oakum.

The time came when the barrier was so tight that it acted almost like a coffer dam, hardly permitting the flow of the tides. The swimmers declared there wasn't a crack big enough to admit a herring.

THEY RESTED on their labors and awaited results. Professor Robbins declared that if the blockade was ineffective, if fish were entering the lagoon by some subterranean channel, he would take other steps. He had almost seven million dollars to spend, and he would spend it. Hector Barling, only slightly less fanatical in his hatred, declared he would likewise spend every dollar of his great fortune to the end that the monster be exterminated.

Heartily enough, these two men, who hated each other, agreed on this. They would hire fleets of bombing planes. They would hire navies. They would buy thousands of tons of dynamite, if necessary. But they would destroy the monster!

But the dam did its work efficiently. On the first day following its completion, the monster began its suffering. So accustomed it had grown, through the ages, to a constant, uninterrupted supply of food, in the form of fish life, from sardines to whales, that any interruption, however brief, made it frantic. A curtailment of its food supply, caused by the yacht's being anchored across the mouth of the inlet, had been largely responsible for its eagerness to board the yacht.

Its food supply now, however, was cut off entirely. And the creature went, beginning with that first day, into a continuous convulsion of wrath. All that day they saw it clearly, near the surface, roving about, snatching at what food was left. The next day they saw it reach thirty feet into the air to snatch a flamingo on the wing. A long section of the cloudy gray filament, shaped like a ship's jib and steaming with spray, leaped into the air to seize the flamingo.

On the second day its agonies were more pronounced. It circled swiftly about the lagoon. It dashed here and there. Portions of it lapped up onto the beach. Fingerlike tentacles shot here and there, frantically, groping for any substance to appease that ravenous hunger.

Bryce Robbins was quiet that day. The more frantic the convulsions of the beast became, the calmer he became. He would watch it with his eyes crinkled, a wan smile at his bitter mouth, nodding approvingly as it lunged here and there, or lashed into the air with its amazing tentacles, possibly for insects.

But the scientist was not satisfied. That night he daringly ventured close to the barricade and tossed onto the adjacent beach chunks of beef liberally dosed with cyanide of potassium. Each chunk he salted with enough poison to exterminate a hundred men. Next morning he found a portion of the monster where he had placed the poisoned meat, a slimy mass, already rotting in the sun. He estimated that he had destroyed less than one-tenth of one per cent of the mass.

And on that day the frenzied searching of the thing for the

least morsel of food was dismaying. It flashed about the lagoon, churning the water to a mad froth. It sent tentacles a hundred feet into the air. It skimmed about the beach. As if some old memory stirred it; it writhed and squirmed up onto the beach and visited the old stone cabin. It returned frantically to the lagoon. All that day it lashed and darted and lunged about. And there was something so insane about its actions that it chilled one's blood to watch.

BRYCE ROBBINS watched and smiled and at times nodded and laughed. It was as if his appetite for revenge was an equal match for the monster's appetite for food. That night he tried another experiment. He soaked a gunnysack of rags with gasoline and tossed it on the beach. Next he threw flaming matches at the sack until it blazed. He then tossed a chunk of fish onto the beach behind the blazing fire, and waited.

The monster sensed the food, but it did not approach until the last of the flames was gone. Then, carefully, it sent tentacles encircling the spot where the fire had been—and snatched the fish!

Bryce had thus learned that the thing feared and hated fire, and this he added to his plans for its eventual destruction. But he was in no great haste.

"We will kill it in due course," he said.

"It is getting too desperate to stay in there much longer," Mr. Barling said. "First thing you know it will escape into the sea. Then it'll be lost forever."

"If it escapes into the sea," the scientist answered, "it won't live. It needs that constant supply of acid from the volcanic springs to survive."

"Do you want to let it starve to death?"

"No. The same argument applies against that scheme as against trying to blast it to death. As it starves, it will throw off portions of itself, and these will fend for themselves as they may. It might split: into a thousand parts, each with its individual brain cell centers. Some of these might survive—to grow again.

It would be the same if we used dynamite. We might destroy all but a tiny fragment. Not one tiny fragment shall survive!"

The professor continued with his torture. He threw chunks of poisoned meat into the water. Portions of the thing detached themselves, floated on the surface, turned white and gave off an offensive smell.

And Bryce was privileged to do as he wished. His suggestions were acted upon. His insanity had affected everyone else. Even Singapore Sammy, that hardened adventurer, was glad to see the nameless creature suffer all the agonies which the scientist wished to inflict upon it.

And presently Bryce Robbins announced his plan—based on his long study of the monster, his intimacy with its traits.

"A few hundred feet inshore from the Dutchman's cabin we shall dig a great pit," he announced. "We shall fill this pit almost to the brim with fish and all the meat we have left. And in the bottom of the pit, all about the walls, before we fill it with fish, we shall set drums of gasoline, on their sides; with electrical controls on their valves, so that, when a switch is closed, the gasoline will gush out of all these drums at once. Simultaneously, an electric spark will set fire to this gasoline. Instantly, four walls of flame will shoot into the air, locking that thing within them. It cannot possibly escape. It cannot possibly survive. Flaming gasoline will gush over it. Every part of it will be roasted. Every tentacle it sends out will be charred and withered and destroyed!"

Professor Robbins began to laugh. It was the laughter of a man so close to the brink of insanity that he frightened his listeners. Yet they agreed enthusiastically with the plan. It was cruel and it was horrible. It was, in short, what they wanted.

Mr. Barling, admiring the plan, interposed an objection, however. He said: "Look here, Bryce: how do you figure you can dig that pit and lug all that fish and meat ashore and put it into the pit without the thing rushing ashore and attacking you?"

Bryce was ready for that. "I proved it won't come near fire. We will build a wall of fire all along the beach."

"How about the men who go to the beach to build the fire?"

"Each will carry a ten-foot steel rod on the end of which is a burning clump of waste soaked in gasoline. Make no mistake: that thing dreads fire. It will starve to death before it will go near fire."

AND WHEN the men betrayed doubt, he demonstrated his point. He was rowed ashore near the white dune. He carried a long steel rod, with a flaming mass of gasoline-soaked waste at the end of it, and approached the lagoon. The monster came threshing to shore. It shot tentacles into the air, but it sent none of these near Bryce Robbins.

Yet there was another source of danger—the islanders. Since those drums had started their incessant pulsing, black faces had been reported seen amongst the foliage. There had been no recurrence of the war canoe, attack, but the feeling definitely prevailed that the natives; were only awaiting opportunity.

The work of preparing the death pit, as it came to be known, was distributed among three groups. One, to keep fires burning along the heach, to prevent the monster's coming ashore; another, to patrol the area inshore with submachine rifles, to keep the warlike islanders at their distance; the third, to dig the pit and to arrange its pyrotechnics.

The pit was dug carefully, with sharp walls, to a depth of twenty feet. It was thirty feet square. These dimensions were considerably greater than those of the Wanderer's swimming tank, which had once held the monster completely. The high, steep walls were provided to prevent the thing's escape when the flames started.

Bryce Robbins divided his time between the work ashore and the Wanderer's engineroom, where Jim Axelrod, the chief engineer, was fashioning the remote-control apparatus which would, at the closing of a switch, release the flood of gasoline and ignite it. There must be twelve duplicate sets, as there were to be twelve fifty-five-gallon drums of gasoline placed equally distant against the walls at the bottom of the pit. And this apparatus must perform its job perfectly—all tanks disgorging their contents simultaneously, all twelve torrents of gasoline bursting into flame at once.

And when Bryce was not engaged in the engineroom, with Jim Axelrod, or at the pit, where Singapore and Lucky Jones were in charge, he was betraying the symptoms of another kind of insanity for the benefit of Julie.

His infatuation for the lovely, brown-eyed girl had changed to obsession, and from obsession to mania. Late in the afternoon of the day when Bryce planned to complete his elaborate arrangements, Julie sent a sailor ashore for Larry, who was in charge of the "fire brigade" on the beach.

And when Larry, smoke-smudged, came out to the Wanderer, she said, "I hated to interrupt you, but I'm scared, Larry. When does Bryce plan to spring that trap?"

"Tonight, if that gang he sent fishing brings in enough bait. The refrigerators are full now, but he wants the pit filled to the brim. The gas drums are in place and the electrical apparatus is hooked up. We're all set." He looked at Julie curiously. "What's the matter?"

Julie said steadily: "Bryce told me he intends to kill you and Lucky after he has killed the monster."

CHAPTER XXV

BRYCE ATTACKS

LARRY McGURK TOOK out a cigarette and lit it. He did not seem alarmed or even surprised.

"He's screwy."

"That's why."

"When did he say this?"

"Just now. Just before he went ashore."

Larry looked away from her, toward the lagoon. For a moment he watched the agitation of the water, a great patch of threshing foam, where the starving monster was plunging about, close to the barricade. He looked back at Julie.

"I think Sam suspects something is up," he said. "He's been keeping close to Lucky all day, and watching Bryce like a hawk. If Bryce laid a hand on Lucky in anything but a fair fight, I think Sam would kill him. He doesn't say much about it, but Lucky means more to him than any brother. They've been pals for five or six years. They've saved each other's lives in a dozen wild scrapes in the Far East. They're held together by bonds that the ordinary man doesn't even dream could exist."

Julie said, "Yes, I know. They curse and snarl at each other—but they'd die for each other. That kind of affection is marvelous—and rare. I think you should warn Sam. Have him watch Lucky and Bryce. Bryce isn't sane any more. And I don't believe he will ever recover his sanity."

"But even that doesn't explain his sudden hate of me. He and

Lucky have been ready to jump each other since the night we all met in Penang. But what has Bryce got against me?"

"Isn't it fairly obvious?" Julie looked up steadily into the smudged, bronzed face. Without changing expression or moving her eyes, she said gently, "He knows I'll never love anyone else as long as I live."

"Julie, listen—"

"It's true," she said stolidly. "I'm not a child. I know my own mind and I know my own heart. I'll never love anybody else but you as long as I live. And what you've been telling me is a lie— you know it's a lie. I'm not just sorry for you. It isn't pity. I loved you long before I knew the truth."

The blond man said, with despair: "Julie, I told you—"

"You were lying," she said evenly. "You love me. You've been in love with me from the first moment. And you might say so. Isn't it about the least you can do? I honestly don't believe any of us is going to get away from here alive. We've lost our heads. We're so many lunatics. If we weren't lunatics we wouldn't be here. We're all going to die. Even you're going to die—before your time's up, too."

Her chin was quivering. Tears filled her eyes.

"Aren't you going to say it?"

"No."

"If you were going to live, would you say it?"

"How do I know what I'd say if I were going to live?" he said brusquely. "Don't worry about Bryce. He's bluffing."

"That's just what he says you're doing. He says you've told this story of your illness only to arouse my sympathy. He says you're no sicker than he is. He says it's just a line. Just a line to get sympathy."

Larry looked at her thoughtfully a moment, then took a wad of paper from his pocket, placed it in the palm of her hand and folded her fingers down upon it.

"What's this?"

"Two wills—mine and Hector's. Just a little something to remember me by. If you hang onto those two scraps of paper long enough you'll be a millionaire."

HE WALKED briskly away from her. For a moment the lovely blond girl stared at the wad of paper in the palm of her hand, then she started up the deck after him. But there was no time now, or opportunity later, for a discussion of this thing that was eating into her heart. The shore gang was coming aboard, and, as if timed to converge with them, the fishing boats were coming in from the barrier reef.

In the confusion of last-minute preparations, Julie received two ultimatums. The first was from Lucifer Jones. That black-browed, sardonic man found an opportunity to talk to her alone.

He said, "Listen, baby. We ought to be cleaned up here tonight. Tomorrow we ought to pull out. Where you headin'?"

"I don't know, Lucky."

"I want to see you some more. There's something I want to talk over with you. Is there a chance of you bein' in Singapore in about a month?"

She repeated, "I don't know, Lucky."

"I look at it like this," Lucky said. "I like Larry. I like him fine. But there's no sense kiddin' ourselves. He isn't gonna last much longer. You'll need somebody around to comfort you. I'm the guy, Julie. Meet me in Singapore in a month. That's a date."

He strode away. Hector Barling had something to say to her along similar lines.

He said, "Julie, there's no sense beating around the bush any longer. We'll be leaving here tomorrow. You'll never see any of this Blue Goose gang again. You'll forget 'em all. And you'll forget this blond fellow. We'll go on with our cruise around the world. One of these days we'll have Captain McTavish marry us. A high seas wedding, Julie!"

Julie said sadly, "Are you so sure of me, Hector?"

"I'm dead sure you'll love me in time. And understand this:

no more running away and no more stowing away. You're to stay on this ship. Understand?"

"I understand."

They were interrupted by Bryce, coming aboard. He came on deck, a wild-eyed fanatic at the brink of realizing his mad dreams. He had stopped shaving since he had lost his arm. The beard was at the "dirty" stage. It added to that look of insane wildness.

He came aboard, shouting, "We're ready. We're all set! Tonight's the night! Where's Sam? Sam!"

Singapore Sammy answered: "What's up?"

"Did you check that apparatus, Sam?"

"Yes. It works like a clock. I tested the batteries. I left a guard of five men at the pit. We're ready to go."

In the quick tropical dusk, Bryce Robbins stared at the lagoon. The swiftly waning light made of the world a shifting, changing mirage. It was like a pool of blue light, softly gleaming in the twilight. And in the midst of it the incredibly hungry monster churned and prowled and roved, lashing the blue water into patches of angry white, searching in a frenzy for food—a victim after so many centuries, of the cruelty and cleverness of man.

Then the light went out of the world and stars began to shine. In this new light, thin and cold, the blue lagoon began to glow.

WITH THE falling of the wind, sounds came clearer—the bubbling of the mud pots, the breaking surf on the barrier reef, the pulsing of the never-ceasing war drums at the base of the mystic black mountain—and the surging sound of the frantic monster, searching in a frenzy for any morsel of food. Bryce Robbins watched and smiled and sometimes softly chuckled.

Larry, with his "fire brigade," went ashore at once—the vanguard of that expedition of death. When fresh fires had been started along the beach, the tender began making trips to shore with frozen and fresh fish. Each time with a full load, it made fifteen trips. Men carried fish singly and in bags to the pit until the bottom was covered and the gasoline drums, ranged about the walls, were covered.

Bryce did not believe it would be necessary to lay a trail of bait from behind the fire line on the beach to the pit, but he had this done nevertheless. He wanted no hitch in his plans.

The remote control apparatus, which would free the gasoline and ignite it, had been set up on a platform five hundred feet from the pit.

Guards with machine guns and gasoline torches were stationed fifty feet apart in a line behind the pit, on the inshore side, to discourage attack by the islanders.

The plan was that Bryce should mount the platform and give the signal—the firing of his revolver—to Larry and his men on the beach. At this signal they were to throw water on that section of the fire line which blazed between the end of the bait line and the lagoon. Then they were to run to the platform. Well acquainted with the habits of the monster, they knew that it would swarm up onto the beach and follow the trail of fish into the pit.

Every one but Julie, her mother and Dr. Plank, who was convalescing but still confined to his quarters, would be ashore. Julie had protested, but had acquiesced when Singapore Sammy had explained to her that someone was needed to guard the two ships, in case the islanders took this opportunity to make a surprise attack.

He said to her: "With luck, we'll pull out of here at crack o' dawn. It will be a relief. Old Lucky has gone haywire on me. It'll take me a month to snap him out of it. And another month to make him forget you. But he's tough, Lucky is. You won't know him in a couple of months from now."

"Where are you two going next—to Singapore?"

"No. Back to Burma. I never told you about my old man, did I? He ran out on my mother and me when I was two—took all her savings and a will of my grandfather's leaving me almost a million. For going on eight years I've been hunting for that old rat all over the Far East. That's what I'm doing out here. And some day I'll find him!"

"What will you do to him, Sammy?"

"Oh," he said quietly, "I'll get that will. Then Lucky and I are going to buy up some ships and start a steamship line of our own. It's an old pipe dream of ours."

"Are you going to stay here long enough to look for the Dutchman's pearls?"

Sammy gave her a wan grin. "If they're in that cave, I'll have 'em by morning, baby. What are your plans?"

"I haven't a plan to my name, Sam."

HE WENT ashore with the next boatload of men. And when they had all gone ashore, Julie went to the bridge with a machine gun, switched on the searchlight, focused the beam on the mangrove point, and watched the line of fire along the beach.

She had thought that, after all the excitement she had been through, she could never again respond to excitement. But she was as thrilled and frightened now as she had been on the schooner's mad trip into the lagoon. Her heart was pounding. Her throat was dry. Her face was hotly flushed, and her spine was icy.

She knew that Bryce would not give the signal until he was satisfied that the last detail of his plan had been carried out. She waited for the sound of his pistol—and she watched the line of fire along the beach, waiting for the sudden gap of darkness to appear in it, which would mean that the horrible, ravenous thing in the lagoon was being permitted to writhe and squirm and flounder up onto the beach—and to its hideous doom.

She heard her mother sobbing in her suite, for Mrs. Farrington had once again succumbed to hysteria.

Then she saw a boat leave the beach and start toward the Wanderer. It was the tender. She swung the searchlight beam upon it, and saw that it contained one man—Bryce Robbins. When he was still some distance away, he called: "Come on down, Julie. It's important."

When she reached the accommodation ladder, he had made the tender fast and was coming up. His face was unusually pale. It reminded her of wax. And his eyes were strange fiery blurs.

"What's happened?" she cried.

He answered; "Nothing—yet. But we've decided to take no chances. We're going to put water and provisions in the tender, just in case."

"In case of what?"

He was half-running down the deck. She followed him, demanding an explanation.

In the galley, he hastily filled jugs with water and gunnysacks with food.

"But what's it all about, Bryce?"

"We decided to prepare for every possible contingency," he said.

"But what possible contingency—"

He stopped her harshly: "Julie, for God's sake, don't expect men to be reasonable in moments like this."

"Oh, all right, all right."

"Help me carry this stuff."

She helped him carry it on deck and stow it in the tender. And when this task was finished, and she started toward the ladder, he said, "Wait! You're going ashore with me."

"Sam told me to stand guard aboard."

"We've changed that plan," the scientist said. "We decided the searchlight would keep them off, and we thought you ought to be in on the fun. It didn't seem fair, making you stay aboard."

Julie thought it was strange, but she had grown accustomed to irrational men.

"Will you take the wheel, Julie?"

She went into the bows and took the wheel, facing forward. She felt the bows settle as Bryce walked toward her, but she did not turn around; She thought he was merely coming to stand beside her, to give orders, perhaps to make love to her in these last few minutes before the great excitement started.

The scientist had a club in his hand. It was wrapped in a piece of gunnysack. He lifted it carefully. He struck her sharply, once, on the side of the head, and he caught her across his arm as she collapsed.

He throttled, down the engine to its slowest point. Methodically, clumsily, the one-armed man lashed her hands behind her with rope. He lashed her feet together. He stripped off one of her silk stockings and bound it into her mouth as a gag.

Then he advanced the throttle and drove the tender toward the beach.

CHAPTER XXVI

FIERY FURNACE

SAM, MR. BARLING and Lucky were waiting for him at the platform, all three impatient and irritable.

The buccaneer snarled, "Where the hell have you been?"

And Bryce coolly answered, "I was anxious about Julie. I went out to see that everything was all right."

"Was it?" Mr. Barling asked.

"Yes. She was on the bridge. She was nervous, but she's quite all right now."

Lucky said hotly, "By God, I believe you're lyin'!"

And Singapore Sammy growled, "Pipe down, you wildcat. Let's get this going. All ready, Bryce?"

"Yes."

The four men climbed to the platform. Bryce Robbins looked carefully about him with the faint smile of a general reviewing his forces before a battle, and finding the status to his liking. Off to the right, torches glared where men with machine guns had been posted to frustrate any hostile move on the part of the savages. Bevan McTavish and Jim Axelrod were in charge of that detachment.

Off to the left the line of fire burned along the edge of the beach. On this side of it men were silhouetted blackly as they ran about piling on brush. Beyond the fire line was darkness. But even above the crackle of the flames the scientist could hear the frantic agitation of the thing he had so ingeniously schemed to destroy. It was out there, held back by the fire line, in a frenzy to get ashore, to get at the food the presence of which it sensed.

Bryce ran his eyes along the trail of dead fish, placed a foot apart, leading in the straightest possible line from the beach to the pit.

He could see into the pit. It looked as if it were half full of fish. He said, "A banquet for the condemned!" He smiled. He chuckled softly. He removed his automatic pistol from the holster and fired it twice.

Instantly, men on the beach leaped into action. He saw silver blobs of water leave buckets. He saw a fifteen-foot line of the fire die and become black. He saw men running toward the platform. They gathered about and tensely watched.

Sam Shay was suddenly aware of a sense of emptiness, having nothing to do with the giant amœba. The drums had stopped!

A greasy gray tentacle appeared on the beach, at first no thicker than six inches. Swiftly it thickened. Tentacles leaped ahead like striking snakes. A fish vanished into that amazing slime. Another.

Bryce shouted: "Come on, damn you! Get your banquet!"

And as if the thing heard that taunting invitation, it came lunging out of the lagoon, a shining, enormous bubble of slime, sending tentacles ahead of it with incredible speed. It came in waves, that floundering, hideous gray slime—eager, ravenous waves. It slithered and climbed and rippled up the slight slope of the beach faster than any man could run.

An avid tentacle a foot in diameter went darting ahead, pouncing on the row of fish, gobbling them up, snatching them in to assuage that monstrous, never satisfied appetite.

THE ADVANCING tentacle reached the edge of the pit. Not hesitating for the fraction of a second, it leaped down into the pit, into the very center of the great layer of dead fish, and these fish began swiftly to vanish, as if they were being removed by a terrific suction.

The main body of the repulsive mass ravenously followed

that tentacle. It wriggled and writhed and floundered to the trap, sending out countless tentacles to drag itself along faster.

Bryce shouted: "Glut yourself! Eat your fill!"

Mr. Barling was laughing hysterically. Lucky Jones was cursing. Sam was staring at the wriggling mass of gray slime.

All but a few laggard tentacles were in the pit now. And swiftly these were drawn in. The pit was half full of the slime, a writhing, pulsing mass.

"Now!" Mr. Barling breathed. "Now!"

"Not yet," Bryce said. "Let it eat. Let it have its last meal. For countless hundreds of centuries it has gorged that rapacious hunger. Let it gorge itself for the last time!"

His hand hovered over the switch which would release six hundred and more gallons of gasoline, which would transform that pit of slime into a blazing inferno.

And suddenly Bevan McTavish shouted: "These woods are full of savages—here they—"

His warning was interrupted by the snarling uproar of a half-dozen submachine guns cutting loose at once.

Sam Shay saw them coming—a wave of black men, with white and red and blue painted faces, with shields against their chests, with spears clutched in their hands.

He shouted: "Throw that switch!"

Bryce Robbins dropped his hand to the switch. For a moment its closing seemed to bring no result. Then there was a soft puff of sound, a faint subterranean trembling. The mass of slime in the pit underwent a sudden convulsion.

The head of a spear buried itself in the soft wood of the platform near Singapore Sammy's feet. And the air was suddenly a clamor of discordant yells as the black warriors charged.

A mass of flame and dense black smoke gushed from the pit. It leaped into the air, a solid, writhing red column, shot with spurts of black.

What now happened was in defiance of all natural laws, as

we know them. Certainly no known living creature could have survived that blast of fluid flame. Yet it had been adequately proved that this monstrous thing that had been tempted from its habitat already defied, by its very existence, its agelessness, the strongest of natural laws.

It should have died instantly and horribly in that hellish fire. Yet Bryce Robbins, who was a scientist, should have been prepared for any contingency.

The monster was not to be so easily destroyed. In it some amazing impulse to life, greater, stronger, more enduring than any like impulse the world has ever known, fought for survival. For eons of time, this protoplasmic mass had contrived to survive. For millions of years it had been embattled with nature, and it had vanquished nature in all known forms since time began. It fought now to survive as these men could never imagine any specimen of life could fight.

ALL ABOUT that fiery heat, tentacles large and small darted and sprang and leaped through the air. In a frenzy of desperation beyond the grasp of the human mind, the broiling monster fought for its existence.

The air was spangled and electrified and interwoven with a great webwork of these flashing, darting, plunging tentacles. They madly laid upon great palm trees, uprooted them and, with a strange perversity, dragged them into the pit. Tentacles withered, blackened, dropped off. Others flashed up out of that bubbling, roasting mass of protoplasm.

The result was hopeless and horrible and fantastic. Singapore Sammy saw a telescoping of events as if he were watching the effect of a runaway projection machine on a cinema screen. Time ceased to be, or its measurements were amazingly abridged. In split seconds he saw loops and coils of glistening tentacles seize palm trees, black men and white men, and snatch them—almost too swiftly for the eye to register—into that roaring hellfire. He saw a dozen islanders in one tangled, screaming, wriggling mass soar through the air and into the pit.

He saw individual men, helpless with horror, plucked in amazing jerks and despatched into the flames, as if they were shot through the air by the snapping of giant rubber bands. He saw Jim Axelrod and Ah Fong hurtle by, moving as if by magic, standing on their heads, their legs wildly waving and kicking. He saw a great loop of slime go sailing through space and settle about the neck of a deckhand at least four hundred feet from the pit.

Sam looked frantically about for Lucky Jones—saw him running toward the lagoon. A spear whizzed past Sam's head as he dashed after Lucky. Then Lucky disappeared. And Singapore plunged on toward the lagoon.

Larry McGurk had been standing beside the platform when the natives attacked and the pit burst into flames. He escaped a looping tentacle—and saw a spear which had hissed past his head plunge into a man's chest. In the confusion he did not at first identify the victim. Then he saw it was Hector Barling.

The patent medicine king had been standing not a yard away from him, babbling with terror. The spear had struck him in the center of the chest. The long, cruelly-barbed head had plunged into Hector Barling a few inches above the solar plexus. The long black handle, smooth as a rod of glass, projected: grotesquely.

But Barling did not fall. Amazingly, he stood, with feet planted apart, face streaming with sweat, both hands grasping the shiny black handle, trying to pluck it out.

His mouth worked, but no sounds came from it. And as Larry helplessly watched this erect dead man, gray slime formed about him mysteriously, as if from nowhere—as if a giant spider were wrapping him about with millions of glossy threads. And suddenly Mr. Barling was plucked into the air. With incredible speed he dwindled in size, until he was a whirling black spot against the leaping crimson flames—and then became a part of them.

Larry saw, as Sam had seen, islanders in great numbers sucked into the blazing pit. He saw men, white and black, clawing and fighting to free themselves of the menacing slime. He saw Oangi, the deckhand, break loose and run toward the lagoon.

He saw Bryce Robbins lashed to a palm tree by transparent gray ropes of the stuff. He saw Lucky Jones appear from the direction of the Dutchman's cabin, waving a cutlass, saw him stare wildly about in the glare, and faintly heard his shout: "Sam! Sam!"

THEN LUCKY Jones saw his enemy roped to the palm tree. He ran to the tree and began slashing away at the imprisoning tentacles. Other tentacles came splitting through the air like great loops of saliva. They bound Lucky against the scientist. They suddenly solidified into one great rod of gray. The tree swayed. It was uprooted. The tree and the two men went whirling into the pit!

The islanders were in retreat now. But they threw spears as they backed away. And one of the last to be thrown found Larry McGurk. It struck his left arm below the elbow with the glancing slash of a razor-sharp cleaver. Blood spurted from a severed artery.

The arm to his shoulder instantly went numb. The redly glaring world began to spin and reel. Acting Captain McTavish had him by the other arm. But before this illusion visited him, he and a little handful of men saw the death of the giant amœba. The furious heat of the gasoline was too much, at last, for that life-loving, ageless, ravenous monster.

Tentacles darted up and withered and blackened and shriveled before they could leave the purlieus of the flames. They fell back into the pit.

And now ensued the sound of a hideous bubbling. The monster of the lagoon, roasted and scorched and baked along its sides, was now boiling. Its tenacious hold upon life had not been enough, A product of the cruel and clever brain of man had despatched it at last to oblivion.

There was now no motion in the pit, save for the mad leaping and seething of the flames, A sizzling and bubbling sound arose from the crimson inferno.

The monster of the lagoon was dead!

In the instant before faintness overtook him, Larry realized this. Then acting Captain McTavish had him by the uninjured arm and was shouting, "Clear out!"

He helped Larry to the beach where the boats were. He bound a tourniquet above the gash and stopped the gush of blood. Then the acting captain of the Wanderer sat down in the wet sand close to the ocean and began to sob.

The last of the survivors came staggering to the beach—a handful of spent and terrified men. Bryce Robbins, Lucky Jones, Hector Barling, Oangi, Sam Shay, Jim Axelrod and Ah Fong were not among them.

CHAPTER XXVII

LARRY LEARNS

JULIE HAD RECOVERED consciousness soon after Bryce Robbins left the tender. She lay helpless on the bottom of the boat. She heard Bryce fire the shots which signaled the beginning of the excitement. She heard the yelling of the natives as they charged. And, lying there, with her eyes staring at the stars, in such terror as she had never known, she heard the ensuing bedlam, the soft smooth roar of the fired pit, the shouts and yells and shrieks of men snatched into the very trap they had set.

She knew, without knowing just what was happening, that that elaborate plan had gone astray. At the height of it she fainted. And when she again came to her senses, she heard the sobbing of a man close at hand. Because of the gag, she could not cry out.

A moment later the survivors of the latest Little Nicobar massacre came tumbling into the tender. She saw Larry silhouetted, against the crimson stain of the night, and the next moment he was kneeling beside her.

He removed the gag and the ropes at her hands and feet. When she saw the deep, ugly gash in his arm, she screamed. Then she gave way helplessly to hysteria. She sobbed questions. Where was Sam? Where was Lucky? Where was Hector? Bryce; Where were the rest of them?

The men talked all at once. But through this confusion, through the sobs shaking her, she glimpsed a picture of the horror they had been through.

202

When the tender reached the yacht, she had herself some-what under control. She fought back sobs and the impulse to scream. She ran up the ladder, herded the shocked men into the bar and gave them whisky.

She said what Singapore Sammy would have said under the circumstances: "Drink all you can! Get drunk!"

Then, still holding her nerves together by sheer will, she took Larry down to Dr. Plank.

Hector Barling's personal physician had heard the uproar ashore and had interpreted it, as Julie had, correctly. He knew that the elaborate and dangerous plan had miscarried somehow. But when he heard, from Julie and Larry, the full extent of the horrors, he collapsed.

And Julie gave way, too. She could restrain her sobs no longer. In a matter of seconds, so many stanch friends, so many fine men had been snatched to that hideous, flaming grave!

Larry tried to comfort her, but she would not be comforted.

Dr. Plank tried to pull himself together. He managed to get to his feet. He staggered up and down the room, cursing, raving.

White from loss of blood, Larry McGurk sat in a chair, drank excellent Bourbon and tried not to faint.

Not until he pitched out of the chair was Dr. Plank brought to a realization of the young man's urgent need.

When Larry pitched out of the chair, Julie screamed. She ran to him and lifted him up. He was not quite unconscious. His glazed eyes, visible through slits, were awake, and there was a queer grin tugging at his lips.

DR. PLANK gave him a hypo, which brought him around. But he was still weak. His danger, however, succeeded in clearing the air of emotion somewhat.

Julie knelt beside him and kissed his blood-blackened hand.

Larry said bitterly, "It's—it's ironical, isn't it? Nine of us—nine healthy men—all but me. But Pegleg went—then Senga—then

Pete—and now Oangi, Lucky, Bryce, Ah Fong, Sammy—All gone!"

Dr. Plank said, almost savagely, "What's so ironical about it?"

"Because I'm the man who's doomed to die! I'm the man who's doomed to die—and the man who can't be killed!"

"I'd say," Dr. Plank said curtly, "that you've suddenly become fairly vulnerable. You almost got it this time. I don't think you bear a charmed life any more, young man."

Larry groaned: "Oh, God, why wasn't I killed with the rest of them?"

And Julie cried: "Larry, please don't say such things!"

"What good am I to anybody? A walking dead man!"

Dr. Plank, working at the slash in the blond man's forearm, said impatiently: "What's all this talk of a walking dead man? You don't look like a walking dead man to me. If I were as healthy as you are, I'd consider myself singularly fortunate."

Julie cried, "But you don't understand, doctor. He has this growth in his head—"

Dr. Plank was bandaging the sewed-up slash. He looked sharply into Larry's face.

"Sarcoma?" he snapped.

"A glooma," Larry corrected him.

"A what?"

"A glooma."

"Do you happen to mean a glioma?"

"That's it! A glioma!"

"Have you a glioma?"

"I have."

"Who said so?"

"The best doctor in Chicago! Six months ago—almost. It's growing around a little skull that protects a gland in the back of my head."

The doctor nodded impatiently. "You mean the pituitary. But have you violent headaches?"

"I did."

"Do you vomit?"

"I used to."

"What was your occupation?"

"I was the first mate on a Great Lakes ore carrier."

"Were you getting much exercise?"

"No. What difference does that make?"

"Were you, by any chance, using your eyes in bad light?"

"Yes."

"Using them a lot?"

"Yes. I was studying to go up to get the limit taken off my license, and taking a correspondence course in business, because I had a chance to go into the office."

"Did you ever have your eyes examined?"

"No."

DR. PLANK said, almost genially, "Well, I'm glad I can save one life out of this horrible shambles. You haven't a glioma. You *had* eyestrain—a bad case of it. And that wonderful Chicago doctor gave you a wonderfully bad diagnosis. If I had as good chances of living to a hundred as you have—"

Larry McGurk struggled out of the chair. "You mean," he said huskily, "I—I'm not going to kick off?"

"I can't predict," the doctor said, "what will happen from now on if you insist on pulling tigers' beards, swimming in monster-infested lagoons, and inviting native spearmen to disembowel you; but if you live normally you'll doubtless live to a ripe old age."

Larry said harshly: "Tell it to me! I haven't got a glioma!"

Dr. Plank shouted: "You haven't got glioma! You're not going to die!"

Larry continued to look at him dazedly. He shifted his dazzled blue eyes to Julie. He stared at her with the look of a man confused, bewildered, stunned.

He turned and started for the doer. He walked unsteadily. He said nothing more. He opened the door and went out.

Julie said faintly: "Doctor, are you sure?"

"Of course I'm sure. A man in his condition couldn't possibly have had a glioma six months ago—couldn't possibly have one at this minute. He's a perfectly healthy specimen. Am I sure? Of course I'm sure!"

She was too weak to get out of the chair she was sitting in. When she was able to walk she went on deck. She saw Larry with his elbows on the rail staring at the silver gleam hovering over the island. He was clenching and opening his fists. And she believed she knew what he was thinking, if his thoughts had yet come out of their chaos, as he watched the tropical sunrise. He was thinking that he could stop counting sunrises.

She did not approach him at once. She stopped at the rail some distance away and watched him—watched him until the dawn brightened and the first red rays of sun lighted his face, which remained grim, as she had often seen it. There was no relief, no ecstasy there. It was like the face of a man pondering an insoluble riddle.

She saw his lips working, as a man's will, when he is faced by a miracle, a fact too stupendous to be grasped.

The cool, shadowless, steely radiance of dawn had been followed by the golden drama of the tropical sunrise. The lagoon was no longer obscured with mist. And the sickening sweet fragrance of the monster orchids was gone. She hoped she would never meet that perfume again as long as she lived.

She saw now that Larry was not staring at the sunrise. All this time his eyes had been fixed on the blue schooner. He swivelled his eyes around and saw her.

HE WALKED down the deck to where she was standing. There was something new in his face, and there was something new in the color of his eyes. In spite of the pallor of sleeplessness and weariness and loss of blood, shadows were gone. He was like a different man.

He said, sighing, "Come here, baby." And he took her in his arms and kissed her with gentleness. He folded his injured arm about her shoulder. The other he dropped about her waist and pulled her tight against him. "I can say it now. I'm pretty sick and shot and dazed—but I can say it."

Julie's arms clung about his neck. She could feel the beating of his heart through her thin blouse. She shut her eyes.

She whispered, "I want to hear it. I've grown thin and gaunt and deaf, listening for it!"

He laughed softly. "I love you, Julie." He rubbed his cheek against hers. "I don't rate you, but God knows I've wanted you. I can't see things straight yet. We'll be a long time getting over all this—this murderousness. And Sam—especially Sam. I'll never get over that."

He patted the small of her back. "It's going to take a long time to get organized on this new basis, too. It's hard to realize that I'm not popping off next week or the week after. I don't know what we'll do, but we'll have Captain McTavish marry us today. I suppose your mother will kick and scream."

Julie laughed softly. "Why, darling? Aren't you a millionaire?"

He said, "Good Lord, I'd forgotten about that." He held her off. "I'll bet a dime you're marrying me for my money!"

His expression suddenly changed. Color flashed into his face. His eyes went round and glittering with excitement. He dropped one of his hands. With the other he pulled her about to face the lagoon.

"Boat!" he cried.

She could not see it at first because of the white splintering light of the sun on the water. Then she made it out—one of the small boats in which the men had gone ashore last night.

It contained two men, one who sat in the stern, the other at the oars.

Julie shrieked: "It's Sammy!" She danced up and down.

"Oangi's rowing," Larry said presently.

THE SMALL boat came alongside the ladder, and Sam came on deck. His hair, his shirt, his pants, were soaked. He said, grinning wearily: "For the first time in a million centuries or so, it's safe to paddle around in the lagoon. Look what I've got!"

He removed from a pants pocket a small iron box, pitted with rust.

"The Dutchman's pearls! The treasure!"

Julie murmured, "Oh, not really!"

He opened the box. Glowing in the early sunlight were perhaps a score of pink pearls—blood pearls, perfectly matched, strung on a slender silver wire.

"Pretty, aren't they? But they didn't come from this lagoon. I think Bryce was right—the monster never let a clam or an oyster live for long on the bottom. Old Vandernoot must have spent his life matching these pearls all over the Far East—and then came here to die."

"They're lovely," Julie said.

Sammy stared at Larry McGurk and said, "What was that I saw going on on deck here a while back? She broke you down, at last, did she?"

"My luck changed," Larry said. "Dr. Plank changed it."

Sammy listened to Larry's recital of that stupendous revelation, then shook his hand and said, "Julie, you'd better see this guy stops pulling tigers' whiskers."

She said, "I'll see to it. What happened to you ashore?"

"Ever since that fire burned down, Oangi and I've been hiding in the Dutchman's cabin, waiting for a little daylight. When it was light enough, I dove in for these pearls." He looked up and down the empty deck. "Where's everybody?"

"In the bar, getting plastered," Larry answered.

"Yeah? I'll bet Lucky's outdrinking every man on board. I guess I'll just join—"

He stopped, his eyes on Julie's pale face, and stiffened a little.

"Isn't Lucky aboard this ship?" he asked quietly.

"No, Sammy."

"That thing didn't—" he began, then, harshly: "I saw him get away! I saw him get clean away!"

"He went back, looking for you," Larry said. "He tried to save Bryce. It got them both."

Singapore Sammy looked at him for fully a half minute without change of expression. His carrot-colored brows were knotted a little. His green-blue eyes were as clear as aquamarines. Then he looked at Julie.

His lower lip protruded a little. He took the wired blood-pearls out of the box and threw the box overboard. He looped the pearls about Julie's neck and twisted the wire in back.

"They look pretty nice there," he said. "It's a wedding present."

Julie started to protest, but she did not dare. The look in his eyes would tolerate no protest.

He said quietly, "So long, Larry. Congratulations!" And shook Larry's hand again. Then he turned to the ladder and said, "You can say so long to the rest of them for me."

As he started to go down the ladder, Julie flew to him, threw her arms about his neck and fiercely kissed him.

"Oh, Sam—" she sobbed.

"Be yourself, brat," he said, and went.

With tear-streaming eyes, Julie watched him go. He sat stolidly in the stern of the small boat, with the sun turning his red hair to fire. They watched him and Oangi go aboard, watched them raise the sails.

Larry growled: "I ought to be there."

"No," Julie said. "He wants to be alone."

Captain McTavish came along the deck, limping. He paused to say, "We're getting under way at once, Miss Farrington."

"Where?"

"The Mediterranean—New York. Will you serve as relief mate, Mr. McGurk, until we can pick up a new crew?"

Larry McGurk accompanied him forward. Julie, left alone,

heard the rumble of the anchor chain. She saw Sammy and Oangi getting up the schooner's anchor. She watched the two figures go aft, and she saw the sails fill with wind—white sails, white as a gull's wings. She saw rain falling in the distance, an indigo banner of it.

The blue schooner was under way. The hull under her trembled with the quick thrust of the twin engines. She watched the schooner sailing into a purple and golden magic of wind and rain and sunlight.

SHARK BAIT

Who was the mysterious giant who insisted on trying to slaughter Singapore Sammy every five minutes?—A million dollar Dutch East Indies treasure held part of the answer

CHAPTER I

SOUTH SEAS JAIL

THE RED-HEADED AMERICAN was holding three mop-squeezers and a pair of bullets when the trouble started. It was his first strong hand of the morning. He had been dealt the queens, and the two aces fell his way on the draw.

It looked as if his luck might be turning. It was high time. He had been losing money steadily. Practically the last of his personal wealth was represented by the small stacks of coins remaining in front of him. It was a tough game, with the Malay to the right of him possibly bottom-dealing, the Chinaman across from him apparently reading the backs of the cards, and the first assistant engineer from the little tramp steamer doing strange tricks with the cards every time it came his turn to shuffle and deal.

Singapore Sam gazed at his full house and looked bored. Clever eyes might have slid over his face and seen just that. But inside him was triumph. He was going to take these three pirates to the cleaners!

The black-eyed fellow from the tramp freighter had opened for a dollar, Straits. He now gave promise of action by betting two. And before Singapore Sam, his heart beating with joy, could call and raise, the trouble started.

The street door across from the poker players burst open, and a man who filled every square inch of the doorway except for a few triangles in the corners, came charging in, shouting, "Oh, there you are, you dirty, lousy, thieving bum!"

He said much more than this, but the highlights can't be printed. He was a great tall fellow, sandy-haired and just drunk enough to be belligerent. He ran to beef in chest and shoulders, his arms were cargo booms, and his close-set eyes were wrathful. These eyes, bloodshot and blurry, were riveted on Singapore Sam's mop of red hair. Singapore Sam had never seen the man before.

Play at the poker table halted. Ah Fong came out from behind the mahogany counter of the bar firmly grasping an empty whisky bottle by the neck.

The tall and powerful looking stranger came charging across the dirt floor, scattering threats and insults.

"You dirty, thieving rat!" he roared—and worse.

Singapore Sam watched him with bewilderment as he came. He raked his memory but could not recall ever having met or seen this infuriated gladiator. Yet there could be no question that the roaring stranger had him in mind and intended doing plenty about it.

One of the cargo booms, with a fist at the end of it, came sweeping up from the vicinity of the floor and would have sent the redhead's head rolling down the room like a bowling ball if he hadn't ducked and sidestepped. All he had time to say, while the furious stranger wound up again was:

The big man refused to be knocked out

Sammy realized that every broken pot meant another day in jail

"Brother, you've made a mistake."

And the blasphemous retort was that brother had, on the contrary, made no mistake, and was prepared at this double-dashed, splintering minute to make human hash of him.

Having the dislike of most men, honest or otherwise, of being called a crook, a thief, and the lowest known kind of rat, Singapore Sam met the fighting stranger this time considerably more than halfway, and an epic battle of the waterfront was on.

In fact, two epic waterfront battles were on; for, in the confusion, the Malay had reached for the redhead's dwindled stacks of coins, the Chinaman with the same brand of expediency made a grab, and the black-eyed first assistant engineer, being a white man and therefore faster at any kind of skullduggery, grasped each of them by the hair, smacked their foreheads together and pocketed the money. But this was only the beginning.

A knife appeared. A second knife appeared.

Meanwhile, Singapore Sam and the brawny unknown were systematically and methodically wrecking Ah Fong's drinking and gambling resort. And Ah Fong was making wild and empty gestures with his glass weapon.

Chairs and tables were smashed. The bar went over. Gallons of fiery beverages gurgled upon the dirt floor from smashed and toppled bottles. Fists thumped on flesh and bone as the two strong men tried to take each other apart.

WHEN THE native police finally arrived, Ah Fong's was in ruins; the Chinaman, the Malay, and the black-eyed engineer were gone, and Singapore Sam and the man who was intent on destroying him for reasons unknown were still slugging, socking, wrestling, and throwing anything they could lay hands on.

The six dark-skinned members of the police force of Buru-Waru succeeded presently in separating them and subduing them, but it took three of them to hold the red-headed man. He had been furious at the sandy-haired man, but he was even more furious at the police. He did not want to go to jail. He could not afford to be thrown in jail. His freedom for the next few hours was absolutely necessary to a plan that was vital to him.

But he could not get away from them. The brown policemen shackled the hands of the two gladiators behind their respective backs and escorted them down the waterfront to the Buru-Waru jail.

It was a fine, hot, tropical afternoon, with the sun blazing down from a blue and flawless sky, the trade wind rustling the lacy arms of the palm trees and kicking up white wavelets on the vivid sapphire blue of the harbor.

Singapore Sam, ignominiously parading through the hot and dusty town, glared across the blue at his schooner just inside the barrier reef, and decided that this could not by any stretch of the imagination be called his lucky day.

As to the stranger's grievance, Sam was completely in the dark. Singapore wondered what the big fellow's object could be, and why he had chosen to annihilate a total stranger. It was a bewildering and inconvenient mystery—just how inconvenient Sam had yet to learn.

A droning overhead increased to a roar. Sam glanced up to see the daily plane from Singapore, gleaming in the hot sunlight. As he looked, the roaring stopped. The plane was gliding into a landing at the Buru-Waru airport, just beyond the big pottery where Sam was to have kept his rendezvous with a mysterious gentleman who wanted to do business with him. The shining metal ship vanished over a cluster of tall palms, her retarded engines muttering and popping. And Sam became furious again.

The man with whom he had the date was on that ship.

THE BURU-WARU jail was a half mile down the waterfront from Ah Fong's, and it was typical of many East Indian jails in which Singapore Sam had been an unwilling guest. It was, in fact, a little worse than typical: a hot, dark, vile-smelling hole consisting of four walls, a roof, and two rows of cells which faced each other across a corridor about eight feet in width.

There was one other occupant when the two destructive white men were pushed, one at a time, into their cells, and their gyves removed. He was in the cell across from Singapore—an old and skinny Malay with wispy gray hair, who was curled up on the dirt floor, breathing heavily and noisily, no doubt sleeping off a tilt with gin-bijt or arrack.

Sam began to curse. With a complete waterfront vocabulary, and a familiarity with several languages, he did full justice to the big sandy-haired man, who had been placed in a cell diagonally opposite him.

"You numbskull! You gnatbrain!" he wrathfully concluded, grasping the bars of the door and glaring between them. "I don't know who the hell you are, but you have certainly balled things up pretty for me. Do you know what you've done, you big lunkhead?"

"Boloney," the other sneered. "I know what you done, and that's plenty."

"You've just as good as murdered a man," Sam exploded. "The best guy that ever lived. He's in that French jail in Saigon. They've got him hooked for a murder he didn't do. He wouldn't hurt a fly. They framed him. They've got him under a fifteen-thou-sand-dollar bond. I've hocked everything I owned, and I raised all but four thousand of it—and I was going to raise that on this deal you just ruined, you louse! I was going to see a guy at the pottery and make a deal that would clear ten thousand dollars, gold!"

The big man across the way stared at him dubiously through the bars, then he shouted, "Nuts!"

"Yeah," Sam panted, "nuts! That's what's the matter with you! You're screwy! And you certainly messed things up pretty for me!"

All of which was bitterly true. Jake Fordyce, one of the finest old fellows who ever breathed, a man who had been kind and helpful to Sam on a dozen occasions, had been jailed in Saigon by his enemies on a trumped-up murder charge. Sam had pawned everything he owned, including the schooner, which he had mortgaged to the limit, trying to raise enough money to bail old Jake Fordyce out, and enough more to pay for the best lawyer in the Far East to defend the old man.

Sam had been in Buru-Waru a week, waiting to contact a mystery man who wanted to give him ten thousand dollars for an undertaking of which Sam as yet knew nothing. He believed the mystery man had come in on that plane. If he had, he would go to the Buru-Waru pottery.

And Sam could not keep that appointment!

A POMPOUS little brown man in freshly starched white drill came into the jail with pad and pencil and asked questions of the two new prisoners.

He came to the redhead's
cell first. He purred his questions.

"Your name, pliz?"

"Samuel Larkin Shay."

"Address, pliz?"

"You see that schooner out
there?"

"The blue one, *mynheer?*"

"Yes. That's my address."

"But your nationality is
Americaine, no?"

Anthony Wingate

"Yair."

"Do you wish to retain legal counsel, pliz?"

"Nuts."

The other white man in the cell diagonally across from him
was even more antagonistic.

"Your name, pliz?"

"Who the hell cares?"

"But I must have—"

"Go to hell."

Somewhat huffily, the little brown official departed.

The big fellow looked heavily at Sam for a moment, and then
began again:

"You dockwalloping scum! You thieving rat! You lousy crook!
You'd steal the pennies off your dead grammaw's eyelids!"

Sam controlled his own temper.

"Yeah? What did I get of yours?"

"Yah! Stand there and rib me about it, will you? Wait till we
get out of this joint! Wait'll I lay my hands on that lousy red
dome o' yours again!"

A native jailer interrupted the flow of brimstoned eloquence
with what was supposed to be the prisoner's tiffin. It consisted
of a bowl of a kind of stew with coolie rice and bits of dubious

looking fish floating or sinking in greasy hot water. He hooked onto the middle crossbar of each cell a small shelf, and on each of these shelves he placed a bowl. A pair of chopsticks for each prisoner completed the equipment. The prisoner was supposed to manipulate the chopsticks through the bars.

It took skill. In Singapore's case, it would have taken skill if he had desired to eat the stew. One smell was sufficient. But the big sandy-haired fellow across the way fell to with relish. His clumsiness with the Far Eastern version of a knife, fork, and spoon showed that he had not been in these parts long.

The red-headed man watched him for a time in silence, then said:

"Listen, gnatbrain. There's an old gag we can work to get ourselves out of this joint."

The big fellow stopped scattering bits of fish and lumps of rice about the corridor, and glared at him. "I ain't interested."

Sam Shay went on grimly:

"We've got to get out of here. When the jailer comes back to get these bowls, he'll come to your cell first. While he's unhooking your shelf, I'll throw my bowl at his head. It must weigh five pounds. I can probably hit him, because I'm pretty good at throwing things. The minute I hit him, grab his keys and let us out. There is no one around but him, because I saw the cops go back uptown. And he hasn't a gun."

The brawny unknown looked at him without appreciation.

"You talk too fast," he growled. "You're a sneak-thief and you would double cross me somehow."

"Listen, ape," the red-headed man patiently argued. "If you're so anxious to mix it up with me some more, this is your gold-plated chance. Get his keys and let us out of here, and we will see who is a double crossing sneak-thief or a thick-headed palooka. He carries the keys on a hook on his belt."

With a sullen glare, his new acquaintance twisted his heavy, bruised mouth into a snarl and answered:

"Go clip the feathers off another horse. I'll get you when they let us out, you dockwalloping scum!"

Sam looked at him thoughtfully, but saw no promise of peace in those bloodshot pig eyes, and went to his cell window and looked out. He arrived there in time to witness some strange and inexplicable activity taking place on the blue bosom of the harbor.

CHAPTER II

ONE WAY OUT

THE CELL WINDOW was like a picture frame. In the fore-
ground was an area of white sand which glared in the equatorial brilliance of mid-afternoon. Off to the left was the small
mountain of drying copra, the fragrance of which was so annoying to the red-headed prisoner. Beyond it was a row of coconut
palms, slender and graceful and inclined from years of steady
pressure of the trade wind. Beyond the trees sparkled the Bay
of Buru-Waru, an expanse of incredibly blue water brightened
by small whitecaps.

The red-headed man's eyes focused on a spot, far offshore,
where his schooner, the Blue Goose, was anchored just inside
the Buru-Waru barrier reef.

The strong and steady trade wind ruffled his red hair as he
stared. His schooner was preparing to get under way!

He grasped the bars and stared across the white sand, the
sparkling, vivid-blue water, with amazement. Since the death
of his partner, Lucifer Jones, Singapore Sam was the sole owner
and master of the Blue Goose. His crew at present consisted of
a Malay *serang*, one Koja, who had been in his services for some
time, and an elderly Cantonese cook and handy man called
Win Lok.

The two of them were able and obedient men. He had told
them not to move the schooner under any conditions unless he
personally gave the order.

Why, then, were her sails and anchor going up?

No nightmare could have given him, on waking, a greater sense of unreality than he experienced as he watched the three white sails fill with wind, and the slender, graceful hull heel to the power of the strong breeze. It had all been done in remarkably short order. Neither he nor Lucky Jones had ever gotten the Blue Goose under way in faster time.

The dumfounded man at the cell window stared and stared. His heart was hammering. His mouth was dry and brackish. He felt a coldness steal along his spine and a sensation of sickness settle in the pit of his stomach.

Gripping the bars, he watched his beloved schooner straighten up from the first effects of the wind; saw a froth of whiteness appear at her step, then saw her bear around and head for the inlet.

She was standing out to sea!

He cursed softly in a thin, baffled voice. Try as he would, he could see no more than two men on deck, one of whom must be Koja, the *serang,* the other Win Lok, the cook.

Why were they taking the Blue Goose to sea? Why, as if impelled by some nameless terror, were they fleeing Buru-Waru?

Singapore Sam trusted his two-man crew implicitly. He knew that the Malay and the Cantonese were two of his best and most loyal friends. He dismissed the suspicion instantly that they were stealing the schooner. If they had wanted to steal her, they could have done so in the past. And he had had ample proof that both men were absolutely honest, above even the petty thievery of their kind.

Why, then, had they weighed anchor, hoisted sails, and put to sea in such a hurry?

He saw a brown speck hobbling about on the water astern of the Blue Goose. It might have been a small boat, but he couldn't be sure. The schooner grew smaller and smaller.

PRESENTLY ANOTHER object entered the picture frame, a small steamer. The schooner was through the inlet and well out to sea. The steamer, no more than a hundred and seventy feet long, came from the direction of the Buru-Waru waterfront. Sam recognized her. She had been tied up for several days at the pier which jutted out into the harbor from the P & O godowns.

Her name was the Moanga. Her skipper, Sam had learned, was a rascal named Duke Wrangle, and she was loading crude rubber and copra for trans-shipment in Soerabaya. The Moanga was connecting with a British regular-run freighter there, and was pulling out at midnight tonight, with a deadline arrival-hour in Soerabaya at 3 P.M. the day after tomorrow. Sam had gone to some pains to secure these vital statistics from that black-eyed card sharp, the first assistant engineer.

Why in the name of Buddha had her sailing plans been changed? She slid into the center of the picture, as if she intended following the Blue Goose out of the harbor. Then, for no visible reason, she executed an about-turn and started back toward the pier from which she had come!

The red-headed young man watched her vanish from the picture, then he gave way to his stored-up emotions. No bridegroom of an hour could have felt more furious, more sick, at the theft of his bride than did Singapore Sam over the mysterious departure of his schooner.

He loved that small ship as he would never be able to love any woman. She was gallant; she was a thoroughbred; she was a perfect little lady. Not only did he love this ship, but she was absolutely essential to the as yet unknown plan in connection with which he was supposed to be seeing the mysterious man at the pottery some time this afternoon!

The theft of the Blue Goose meant he would be unable to collect this money which he needed so badly for helping out old Jake Fordyce!

Watching her vanish over the horizon with a finality that might have marked the very end of all life, Singapore suddenly almost lost his mind. He cursed in a thick and strangling voice. He charged about the cell, he grabbed and shook the bars with all the awful and wasteful frenzy of a freshly caged animal. He banged about that cell as if, with sheer wanton strength, he would batter his way out. He tried the window bars, and found them still an inch thick and still solidly anchored top and bottom. He climbed on the rickety hand-made table and attacked the roof. The table swayed, lurched, squawked under his reckless hundred and eighty pounds.

Duke Wrangle

The roof consisted of palm boles adzed along the abutting sides and set as tightly together as planks in a deck. But several of them had lost their green-black look and had turned brown as if with inner rot. A dead palm tree didn't last long in this climate.

Sam attacked one with his pocket knife, jabbing the blade deep and ripping a slash in it as if it were an animal he was determined to disembowel. Payment for his effort took the form of a deluge of brownish-yellow dust, as fine as the finest sawdust, proving that his guess was right. This log and the one to the right of it were hollow with dry rot, filled with nothing more than the dust of insect gnawings. The dust spilled down into his upturned face, burned into his eyes, and a small stream of it went pouring down his back and chest through the opened collar of his blue shirt.

And while he blinked the stuff out of his eyes, his chest and face and back seemed suddenly to burst into flames. That, at least, was the sensation—fire crawling over him everywhere above his waist at once.

Ants. Fine red ants. Not unlike fire ants, but smaller, though doubtless of a close relationship, they bit and dug and burned into his flesh, freeing their hot and terrible poison all over the upper part of his body.

He wanted to yell with pain. But worse than yelling, he wanted freedom from the Buru-Waru jail.

HE SLASHED at the palm bole with the knife blade. He grasped handfuls of rotting bark and tore them away. And when he tackled the abutting log, he freed more dust and another army of the savage little red ants. They seemed to be tearing the skin from his flesh.

But he didn't give up. He hacked and clawed at the hole until it was large enough to pull himself through. In the midst of fresh agonies from fresh ant swarms, he wondered where the jailer was. It was, of course, still siesta time, and the jailer was no doubt snoozing under a tree near the beach. In fact, every one in Buru-Waru should be off the streets for some time.

Singapore Sam gave only a quick glance at the cardinal points as he emerged from his cell to the rooftop. He saw no one; no sign of life. The fiery little insects reached new territory in a savage wave of attack. They went down his abdomen and down his legs in white-hot streams.

As he eased himself down the roof, sweating and moaning with pain, it struck him with irony that he now knew the literal meaning of that expression, "I've got ants in my pants." But it didn't strike him as being in the least funny now. He dropped to the white sand, looked quickly about him, saw nothing to check him, and ran for the beach.

A small and insecure looking jetty for small boats jutted out from the beach. Singapore had heard there were sharks and stingrays in the water of Buru-Waru's harbor, but he didn't let that rumor hinder him now. He capered out onto the jetty, and made a running dive off the end of it.

The blue brine enfolded his flesh with delicious coolness. At once the fire went out. His heart was banging from the exertion of his three-hundred-yard dash, but he managed to stay under water, paddling about, for at least thirty seconds.

He scanned the waterfront as he swam in. No police were in sight. No jailer was in sight. No one was in sight. Perhaps he wasn't too late. Perhaps he could make his way to the rendezvous without being apprehended.

Rufus Pound

But what was the use? His schooner was gone. Without the schooner, he could not make the ten thousand dollars which Neil Frothingham had said was in this deal; and even if the mystery man waited at the pottery for him, Sam would probably never know just what the deal was all about.

It might be anything. Neil Frothingham had merely sent him a mysterious note saying that he could make ten thousand dollars, gold, by contacting a "Mr. Z" in Buru-Waru. A password had been given in the letter, and the pottery was named as a rendezvous. Sam was dubious. Frothingham was clever—a little too clever; often involved in some deal that was not too well within the law. Sam needed the money to help out old Jake Fordyce, but he was doubtful about taking part in a project too shady, as he was on thin ice with the authorities now because of certain enterprises in which he had figured.

Yet—he was willing to do anything for ten thousand dollars. He was willing, but how could there be a deal without the Blue Goose?

SAM MADE his way cautiously through the palms, skirting about the village until he reached the pottery. It was surrounded by a whitewashed brick wall. There was only one gate, and it was always open. Sam made his way to this gate.

All about the pottery yard were neat piles of bowls, vases, and pots of assorted shapes, sizes and colors, for a variety of uses. And just within the gate a white-haired old man, a Javanese, was skillfully spinning a potter's wheel with his feet and molding a red vase with his hands.

Sam glanced anxiously about the yard, but saw no one. He questioned the potter. The potter had seen no strangers about. Sam went to the gate and waited.

He knew he would not be a free man long. They'd get him sure, and this time the charge would be serious—jail-breaking.

He was angrily resentful at his fate. His schooner, once clear of the land, had shaped a sou'westerly course. That might mean any port along the whole northern coast of Java. Or Sumbawa, Flores, or Timor.

And there was nothing he could do. If he went to the American consul, the American consul would tell him to go to the Dutch authorities. And he could not go to the Dutch authorities as a jail-breaker.

Pale with fury, Sam watched a short, heavy figure in white coming up the road from the village. Stepping into a small dark shed, Sam waited. The approaching man wore a suit of rumpled white drill and a large, mushroom-shaped sun helmet. He looked funny, with that huge hat and his waddling gait.

As he came nearer, Sam saw that his face was heavy and red and not at all amiable. He was a hot, tired old man. He looked about him with cold, pale-blue eyes. Furthermore, he looked mean, and he looked as if he might be cruel. He had a thin mouth, drawn down at the corners. His head was set so close to bent shoulders that he looked hunch-backed.

Reaching the pottery gate, the old man stopped and looked furtively about him. Sam stepped out of the shed.

The man with the hot red face and the cold blue eyes stared at Sam a moment, then said in a tense voice:

"I wonder what the temperature is today."

Sam drawled, "Six below and getting colder."

"Ah!" the old man said harshly. He seemed relieved, but he did not smile, and his eyes lost none of their coolness. They had a penetrating, or measuring quality that made Sam uneasy. This old fellow seemed to be searching in Sam's eyes for every crime he had ever committed, for every secret he knew. And in weighing Sam, not giving him the benefit of many doubts. Sam judged that this mysterious old stranger was capable of great greed and great cruelty.

The old man said, "Can we talk here safely?"

"In here," Sam said.

"It is very important," the red-faced stranger said, "that no one sees us talking. You understand."

"Yes."

"There is not time to say much. My plane is leaving for Soerabaya in half an hour. Perhaps I should mention that Mr. Frothingham told me to meet you here—a white man with red hair, named Shay. I have letters—credentials—which I will show you in due course. It is very important that my plans remain secret until the moment we go. That may seem mystifying to you, but I think it advisable. I will wait for you in Soerabaya, at the Oranje Hotel, in Simpang. You know it?"

"On Toendjoengan Road—yes."

"When will you be there?"

"You think we'd better not both go in that plane?" Sam said hopefully.

"Decidedly not. I think there is already a leak in my plans. Your reputation coupled to my name would be fatal, I assure you."

Sam said, a little coolly, "Very well. I will be in Soerabaya day after tomorrow."

"I will not leave my rooms at the Oranje until you come."

SAM FELT his heart thumping a little. Very casually, he said, "Oh, by the way—my schooner has been stolen. Just stolen, as a matter of fact."

He waited, sure that the old man would simply turn and walk away. The stranger stared at him a moment suspiciously, then said:

"Oh, that isn't important. We can charter a boat in Soerabaya or Batavia. It's you, after all, not the schooner, I most want."

Sam grinned briefly with relief. "Who will I ask for at the Oranje?" he said.

The man in the rumpled white suit hesitated, then answered: "Ask for Mr. Z. Can I absolutely count on you?"

"You can—yes, unless the original figure has changed."

"No, Mr. Shay. It is still ten thousand, gold."

"And it's positively not gun-running, or anything of the sort?"

"Positively not—but very dangerous."

Singapore stared at him, wondering why an honest man should want to pay him ten thousand dollars, gold, for a charter that wasn't worth much more than one thousand dollars at the best. "Do you care to make some kind of a small advance now, Mr. Z?"

The pale-blue eyes seemed to go a little paler. "I am sorry, Mr. Shay. I have not a florin on my person. My funds have all been transferred to the Chartered Bank of India, in Soerabaya. If you do not reach my hotel by midnight on the day after tomorrow I will understand that you are not interested."

"I'll be there," Singapore Sam said lightly.

Without anger he watched the old man walk away. Mr. Z was merely cagy, and some of the things he had doubtless heard about Samuel Larkin Shay had not been too flattering. The redhead was puzzled. So Mr. Z's plan, while not gun-running, "or anything of the sort," was very dangerous. He felt, for the first time since his fight with that sandy-haired nitwit, that his luck wasn't so bad, after all. If only his schooner hadn't been stolen, he would have felt pretty cheerful.

The pottery was not far from the godowns where the Moanga had tied up. Over intervening buildings, Sam saw her spars approaching slowly, as if moving in the air with no support, and watched them stop moving. The Moanga was back at her berth. Why, he wondered, had she started out, as if to pursue the Blue Goose, then turned about and returned to her pier?

Beyond the tips of her spars, he saw lacy white clouds, tinged with gilt, in herringbone pattern. Sam sniffed the air, and guessed that those clouds and the faintly changed smell of the air would mean business in a big way before midnight tonight. It was hurricane season, anyway, and they often popped up from the south without even this warning.

If a heavy squall came, it would not, he believed, last long. The Moanga would sail at midnight, and he would be aboard. He would hide here until after dark, then stow away on the Moanga, and if all went well reach Soerabaya in ample time to keep his appointment with the mysterious Mr. Z.

A SMALL Malay boy had come into the yard. He was about nine, and he had the pot-bellied and spindle-shanked construction of all Malay small boys. Sam glanced at him without interest or curiosity, although he might have glanced more sharply if he had appreciated how importantly the boy was to figure in his life before the day was over.

The boy went in and began talking to the potter. There ensued a spirited argument; the boy wanted to buy a water jar—at a price. After some dickering, he paid the price he had first named, selected a large red jar from a near-by pile, placed it on his head, and started to walk out of the yard.

From his secure and comfortable hiding place, where he intended to remain until dark, Sam watched the boy and lazily marveled at his grace. How these kids carried jars on their heads had always amazed Sam.

As he passed the shed, the boy glanced at him. And though Sam had seen nothing remarkable in the boy, it was evident that the boy saw something quite remarkable in Sam. Perhaps, in his startled young mind, this white man with his flaming hair was a god. But perhaps he was merely astonished at seeing a red-headed white man in that shed.

At all events, he was startled. His large, centerless brown eyes became larger and larger. Staring up at the grinning white man, he faltered, then he stumbled. His new water jar bounded from his head, described a long and graceful arc and struck the ground, smashing into fragments.

The small Malay promptly began to weep. He didn't weep noisily, as most small boys do in the face of catastrophe, but almost in silence. Great teardrops squeezed out of his big brown eyes and trickled down his satiny cheeks.

In Malayan, the white man said, quoting a native warrior who was great before the white men came to these islands, "My son, only a woman weeps when disaster drops its long shadow."

"But it is the second one today, *birahi*," the boy whimpered. "Only this morning I stumbled and fell when I was carrying the other jar full of water for my grandmother."

"Did she whip you?"

"No, *birahi*, but she promised me a hundred lashes if I broke the new jar. I don't want to be whipped, *birahi!*"

"There are other water jars," the white man said. He plunged his hand into a pants pocket and found several coins that those human vultures at the poker table had overlooked.

The small Malay gazed up at him with wonder and dawning hope. He gulped.

"Master!" he gasped. "You are not going to buy me a new water jar!"

"Son, my rule is never to let anybody, if I can help it, put dents in the seat of my pants. And as long as you are a good guy, the same rule goes for you, too. Never let anybody put dents in the seat of your pants if you can help it. You wear a *sarong*, but it's the same idea. The skin inside a *sarong* can hurt just as bad as the skin inside a pair of pants."

"*Tuan*, you are a good man," said the boy.

"Sonny, you don't know anything about human nature."

For approximately six cents in American money, Sam bought a water jar identical to the one the boy had broken, placed it on his young friend's head, and was given a fine smile and a Malayan blessing as his reward. He watched the boy go.

In the wide doorway of the pottery he was still gazing at the clouds beyond the spars of the invisible freighter, when he heard a heavy thumping of feet along the dirt road down which the boy had just gone.

Thinking the police were coming, Sam turned, intending to hide under a pile of gunnysacks in the shed; but he was too late. And it wasn't the police. It was the sandy-haired man.

CHAPTER III

RETURN ENGAGEMENT

HE CAME RUNNING down the street, roaring. With rising wrath, Sam watched the big man come. If he did not promptly stop the big dumb-bell's bellowing, the police would certainly come, and his scheme for escaping from Buru-Waru and meeting Mr. Z in Soerabaya would be ruined.

Red-faced and out of breath, the big man came pounding up, shouting:

"Now, you lousy sneak-thief! Give it back or I'll knock your teeth out through your heels!"

Sam promptly executed the plan he had ready for this maddening emergency. The plan was to knock out the big fellow with one blow, then hide somewhere else until dark, when he would slip aboard the Moanga and hide again.

With his feet well braced, Sam put every ounce of his power into one slashing swing to the jaw. It did not land as squarely as he might have wished. But it landed with such force that his entire hand, tough, as it was, promptly went numb.

He waited for the big fellow to drop. The only thing wrong with the plan was that it did not work. The big fellow did not drop. He staggered back. He roared—and came charging.

This time Sam met him considerably more than halfway.

Furious at him for threatening his carefully laid plans, Sam lashed out with murderous wrath. Cursing and bellowing, the big man rushed and slugged, and then began another fistic epic—the battle of the pottery yard.

In spite of the difference in their sizes, they were—as they had proved in the morning—evenly matched. The sandy-haired giant knocked the tough, broad-shouldered, red-headed man down no oftener than did the redheaded man knock down the giant.

Each time a man fell, the white-haired Javanese potter would yell with rage, for each time a man fell it generally meant that more vases, pots, and bowls were broken.

The fight traveled rapidly all over the pottery yard, and the fighters left in their wake a growing litter of pottery fragments.

The fighters seemed unaware of this new bill of damages they were incurring. From time to time Singapore Sam realized it, however. He knew that it would be impossible for him to leave Buru-Waru until he had, in some way, satisfied not only the officials but the pocketbooks of Ah Fong and the old potter.

His fury at this needless damage made him fight even more savagely, for every pot or jar broken meant another day in jail or on a Javanese road gang.

With a well-aimed sock to the jaw, he knocked his sandy-haired enemy into another neat tower of red earthenware pots. The tower came crashing down into fragments. The sandy-haired man sprang up—and they fought on.

Try as he might, it was impossible for Sammy to knock him out. The man was made of India rubber—or chromium. He took all the punishment there was, then came back for more.

Sam was fighting with futile fury when the police arrived. He would have made a real effort at escape, but this time the police drew their revolvers. And they looked earnest.

So furious that he could not find profanity scarlet enough for his purpose Singapore silently let them handcuff him again and lead him and his sparring partner off to jail again. The sandy-haired giant was cursing fluently. And he was not the only disturber of the tropical tranquility of the little island.

A hot wind was rising, and palm fronds were stopping their whispering and beginning to chatter and rasp. Purple clouds were piling up on the south horizon from whence the blow was coming.

This time the jail-breakers were not to be permitted a chance to worm their way out. A brown guard, armed with bolero and rifle, was stationed in the corridor in front of each cell.

THE RED-HEADED man considered the situation and softly cursed that addlepated duckbrain across the way who had brought this real calamity about. He needed that ten thousand, gold, more than he had ever needed money in his life. If he could not secure it, that gang in Saigon would guillotine Jake Fordyce. He must get out of here! He must be aboard the Moanga before she sailed! He must reach Soerabaya!

That afternoon Sam discharged, as best he could, two obligations which were weighting his mind. He asked the guard to send a messenger to Ah Fong and to the Javanese potter, to tell them that he wanted to see them. Ah Fong was the first to appear. The Chinese had cold murder in his eyes as he stared through the bars at Sam, but he relented a little when he learned what Sam said.

"I want to know how much it's going to cost to repair the damage to your joint, Ah Fong."

"Two hund'ed dolla—gold," Ah Fong promptly said.

"That sounds reasonable. And you are going to get it, Ah Fong."

"When?"

"Some day. But you can count on it."

Ah Fong left the jail with a look of extreme doubt.

The old Javanese, who came a little later, was somewhat more moderate in his demands. He had taken inventory of the damages the fight had caused. Twenty-five dollars, gold, would cover it.

Sam said to the old potter what he had said to Ah Fong. And the Javanese, no less skeptical of Sam's intentions, departed.

The red-headed man spent the rest of the afternoon considering plans of escape. He must escape. He must be in Soerabaya on the day after tomorrow. And the only possible way of reaching Soerabaya in time was to be aboard the Moanga tonight when she sailed.

With darkness came a howling wind. And with both came a whisper at the window in Sam's cell.

"Master! Psssst!"

He went eagerly to the window. A small satiny brown face appeared in the storm-glow. A small hand held up a long earthenware vessel smelling fragrantly of fresh-cooked meat and good boiled rice. Sam accepted this votive offering with thanks and enthusiasm.

An audacious scheme occurred to Sam. He said to the Malay boy, "Son, how would you like to do me a big favor?"

"*Tuan*, you have only to command!"

Sam briefly told him what he wanted, then, "Come back when the hurricane reaches its height."

The boy eagerly nodded. "*Tuan*, you can depend on me!"

With mystery and excitement in the big brown eyes, the face vanished. The hurricane soon settled down to business. The wind rose from howls to shrieks, and now came the rain—a skyful of it, lashing the water of the unseen bay, lashing the sand and the palms and the jail with the ferocity of a million whips.

The roof roared under the deluge. And leaked. Water came trickling down in countless cataracts. Lightning flashed and thunder crashed and roared and rumbled. At intervals, through lulls in wind and thunder, Sam could hear the great waves roaring on the barrier reef, like animals growling and snarling at a closed door.

He wondered if the tramp freighter would leave on schedule—at midnight. The quickness with which the hurricane had sprung up made him suspect that it wouldn't be of long duration. It might blow itself out by midnight. He hoped the Malay boy wouldn't fail him.

The hurricane had reached its height. Spray from the bay

was spattering against the wall of the jail with the force of shot. Broken fronds were striking the roof and rattling off into the howling night.

A SMALL voice shrilled, "Master! I have come!"

The brown face at the barred window, streaming with water, was hardly visible in the dim oil light flickering in the corridor. But Sam clearly saw a trickle of blood running down with rainwater from the bridge of the boy's nose. Then he saw the end of the rope that stretched out and up and into the tumultuous blackness.

The boy said, "I have followed your orders, *tuan*. This is a very tough rope—and one end is already fastened about the top of the tallest palm, as you directed. Prepare to escape, *birahi*."

Singapore Sam grinned. He glanced behind him, into the corridor. The guard who had been stationed there was not looking. He seemed to be absorbed by the sounds of the hurricane.

The red-headed man helped the Malay boy snub the end of the rope around the two middle bars. The boy dropped to the ground again, and quickly took up all the slack. The rope stretching out and up into the darkness now looked as tight as a piano wire. There was a sudden shriek of wind. And Sam pictured the tall palm as it leaned under the terrific pressure of that blast. The rope was now stretched so taut it could have sung. Rope or bars must certainly give.

The two middle bars began to bend as if they were warm tallow. All four ends suddenly popped out of their masonry sockets, and the two bent bars were whisked out of the window.

Sam glanced at the guard again. The guard was still sitting there unoccupied, but not with him. The wind had drowned the sounds of those bars going. And as the red-headed man turned back to the window, there was a sudden faint tinkling and crashing, and the oil lamp went out. Some flying object had apparently struck the lamp and extinguished the flame. In the sudden blackness some one shouted.

Grasping the wet stone sill, Singapore Sam hoisted himself

up and let himself through the window. He dropped into water ankle-deep. Rain instantly soaked him to the skin. A small wet hand groped for his, and Sam let himself be led.

He could see nothing. Above him, trees lashed in the wind. To his left, waves roared on the beach with a continuous, grinding thunder. There was no light whatever. The village was total blackness. But as he let the boy lead him down the invisible lane, faint points of light pricked through the blackness, obscured now and then by smothers of rain, only to reappear again a little closer.

The source of these light points was the tramp freighter, which was Sam's destination. The Moanga would not, he was sure, pull out before this wind had blown itself out, yet the height of the hurricane was evidently passing already. Even in the scant half hour it took the boy to lead him through the rainswept blackness toward those pinpricks of light, the force of the wind had seemed to lessen a little, and the lulls between gusts were growing longer. East Indian hurricanes came that way and they went that way, much after the style of Siamese Gulf typhoons—they came in staccato raps, closer and closer, harder and harder, then the heavens opened and the wind screamed a while, and it went away again, rap by rap.

In the swimming black shadow of a godown, Sam gave his young Malayan friend his pocket knife as a souvenir of this eventful occasion.

The boy suddenly began to sob.

"*Tuan,* take me with you! I broke the new water jar!"

"You're a little liar! So long!"

"*Salamat tinggal!* And the blessings of Allah!"

In the blackness, the adventurers parted and went their separate ways.

CHAPTER IV

STOWAWAY

SAM TROTTED ALONG the rain-soaked planks toward the inshore end of the pier, keeping close to the black shadow cast by the large rusty iron shed.

He did not know what time it was, and he presumed that, if the wind abated only a little more, the master of the Moanga would carry out his sailing orders. The rain seemed to be stopping. The crew, now snug in their cabins, would soon come on deck to attend to the details of the departure. It therefore behooved Sam Shay to get aboard and hide as expeditiously as possible.

In the uncompromising blackness of the godown's shadow he ran into a man so unexpectedly that he almost knocked the wind out of himself. Without hesitation Sam let drive a fist into the unknown's midriff, stepped back to hear a grunt and a thud, then stepped over the victim and slipped out into the rain-streaked murk and along the heavily riveted, glistening side of the Moanga.

He climbed a springline to the deck, found it apparently deserted, and scuttled aft. A sparlight disclosed a closed manhole not far from the after of three closed and battened-down cargo hatches. The manhole lid was bolted down, but the butterfly nuts had not yet been tightened by wrench. He unscrewed them, found an iron ladder with his heels, and descended, pulling the manhole lid over him.

He lowered himself into a familiar and sickening atmosphere.

Copra! He would be sick. He would be deathly sick, but there was no way out of this. He found a dry match in his pocket, struck it, hooded the flame in his hands, and found that there was no bulkhead door into the forward hold. He made his way across the mound of odorous shell to the forward bulkhead, and softly cursed his luck. After a while he heard the drumming of rain on deck subside, then the brisk clatter of heels. An hour or two or several may have passed. He heard the ship's bell ring out eight strokes. Midnight—or 4 A.M.? Then he heard a stealthy sound behind him.

He shrank down against the copra on which he was sitting. But the sound was not repeated. It had sounded like some one moving about. The next sound was that of rattling and squealing deck engines, then the ringing of the engine-room telegraph.

Singapore Sam listened to the familiar sounds of a ship getting under way. He didn't mind a rough sea, but he did mind the sickening smell of this damp and moldering copra.

But he was so exhausted by his full day's activities that he was asleep before the little coaster was through the Buru-Waru inlet. He was awakened by the morning sun streaming into his face. He looked up to discover that the hatch cover had been removed—no doubt to air out the hold and the copra—and that the sky overhead was a clear, soft blue. The ship was rolling slightly in a long and gentle swell.

He was thirsty and hungry, but there was nothing to do about either until the Moanga docked in Soerabaya tomorrow afternoon.

Behind him, on the mound of copra, a familiar snarling voice exclaimed:

"Why, you lousy, thieving rat!"

Sam spun about as if he had heard the accents of a hated ghost, and saw the big sandy-haired fellow rising like an ape from hands and knees, preparing to leap and doubling up a fist.

THE SHOCK of seeing this mysterious and hateful apparition deprived Sam momentarily of the will to act. There was something too fateful about it, quite as if the big fellow could conjure himself into Sam's life at will. How had he twice broken jail? How had he found his way so unerringly to Sam's hiding place? There was something almost supernatural about it. He could not imagine why this evil geni was pursuing him. He had become unreal—a figure in a nightmare.

If this big dumb-bell started a fight now, Sam's plan would be ruined. He planned to remain in hiding until Soerabaya was reached, then slip ashore. A fight would certainly attract the crew's attention. The two of them would be put in irons—and turned over to the police on arrival in Soerabaya.

In a harsh whisper Sam panted:

"Wait a minute! They'll turn us over to the—"

Not hearing, or not caring, the sandy-haired giant swung.

Sam could not sidestep that one; his footing was too uneasy. The big lunatic's fist landed squarely. Sam separated himself from the ensuing constellations, and fought with fury. Their grunts, their curses, their thuds as blows landed, soon called attention to this continuation of their fistic drama.

Heads appeared over the hatch coaming above them.

A bull-like voice issued from a yellow-whiskered face. "Belay it, ye swabs!"

The gladiators paused and looked up, and saw the row of faces, some sour, some grinning. Sam cursed with futile rage.

"If they don't come up," yellow whiskers roared, "give the swabs that bucket o' hot soogey-woogey."

The two fighters had no arguments with hot soogey-woogey. They climbed the steel ladder to the deck. Fifteen men or more in a crowd watched them. Some distance forward a tall, lean man stood alone. Hatless, his raven-black hair was as smooth as lacquer in the light breeze. His eyes were cold and pale-blue like chilled steel. And his jaw, lean and hard, had a blue look.

He caught the red-headed man's eyes as the latter came on deck, and held them with a steady, ironical scrutiny. In that first glance, Sam labeled him: one tough egg. He had seen him in Singapore and once again in the port of Melbourne: Duke Wrangle, gun runner, pearl poacher, opium smuggler, all-'round opportunist. One tough egg. Carrying copra—as a blind for what?

"I'll talk to you," Captain Wrangle said quietly. "Put the other mug to work until I'm ready for him, mister."

Sam followed him forward and into his cabin, which was no more than a clean, efficient office. He wondered anxiously what was going to happen. He must somehow get out of this mess.

DUKE WRANGLE seated himself in a swivel chair bolted to the deck before his scarred and battered desk, and said, "Stand there in the doorway, so I can admire you."

He stared at the sea-green eyes of the red-headed man for perhaps ten seconds, then said softly, "You're the fellow they call Singapore Sam Shay. I know a lot about you. You came out here seven or eight years ago looking for your old man who's got a will of your grandfather's leaving you a pile of money. I guess your old man's too smart for you. Where's that big blue pearl I understand you carry in a little bag on a copper wire around your neck?"

"In hock."

"What's happened to your schooner?"

"Maybe I sent it off on an errand."

The steel-blue eyes neither relaxed nor blinked.

"Yeah. Maybe you did." Captain Wrangle suddenly sat up straight. "Well, Red, where is it?"

"My schooner?"

"You know what I mean."

"Ah," Sam said, "that."

"Yes, that."

Sam's eyes gave the impression of going cloudy.

"I wouldn't know about that," he drawled, and added in a tone of deep respect, "captain."

"You figure"—the blue-jowled man took him up as slowly

and as gently—"it wouldn't do you any good to take me into your confidence."

The red-headed man was trying to make his brain do a dozen things at once—trying to find answers to everything. What was Wrangle driving at? Did he know about Mr. Z's mysterious plans? Why had he chased the schooner? Why had he put back? What was it all about?

Sam nodded slowly. "That's right—captain."

"Of course," Duke Wrangle went on, still in that soft, quiet way, "I could make you say a lot of things."

Sam weighed this with a judicial air.

"Yeah," he agreed. "You could."

The other nodded. "Yeah, I've heard a lot about how tough and how smart you are. I think I might take a little of that out—the tough part. You're pretty cocky. By the way, Red, what are you doing on my ship?"

"Oh," Sam answered laconically, "I sort of figured a sea voyage might be good for my health. You see, I'm kind of delicate."

Captain Wrangle's eyes remained as steady as the muzzles of guns anchored in concrete. "Who is this palooka you were having the workout with?"

"If I could answer that one," Sam replied, "I would solve the biggest mystery of the universe."

"In other words," Duke Wrangle said, "you don't feel like telling me where it is, or where your schooner went, or what you're doing on board, or why you and this big mugg don't like each other."

"That's right—captain."

For the seventh or eighth time Singapore had reached the conclusion that he had never met a man who impressed him as being more wilful, more dangerous, than this quiet-spoken, steel-eyed, blue-jawed sea captain. A steel hand in a velvet glove—with the velvet badly worn in places.

Duke Wrangle pressed a button at the back of his desk, and said, "I think you're going to be my guest quite a while, Red.

You may not get to like me, but you certainly are going to get to know me."

Two men appeared in the doorway.

"See that this gentleman is shown the work we always give stowaways to do," Captain Wrangle said. "And bring that other passenger up here."

Sam was more or less satisfied with the outcome of the interview. He would work his way to Soerabaya and, once there, would somehow slip ashore before Wrangle turned him over to the Dutch authorities—if that was Wrangle's intention. Sam was extremely mystified by Wrangle.

AS SAM went aft, he verified what he had suspected about the Moanga when he had seen her from a distance. She was a converted yacht, no more than one hundred and sixty feet over-all, with plenty of speed. And as he went down the steel stairs into the Moanga's hot little engine room he wondered what Duke Wrangle meant by "it." "Where was it?" What? It looked to him, with the skimpy evidence at hand, as if there might be a leak in Mr. Z's plans, whatever they were.

The boiler room of the converted yacht proved to be hotter by far than the little engine room. It was poorly ventilated, obviously not designed for these latitudes. The Moanga, he suspected, was a man-killer.

He found it out soon enough. There happened to be a following wind. The boiler room temperature was at least 130. And the Moanga was making knots in spite of boilers so old they fairly oozed steam.

His thirst quenched, Sam shoveled coal. He shoveled a great deal of coal. He suspected that his endurance was being tested, for throughout the afternoon there was a virtual parade through the boiler room—members of the crew coming down to look him over. And he tried to show them that a red-headed man is a faster and better coal shoveler than men who are merely blond or brunette.

The sandy-haired mystery man came into the boiler room

late in the afternoon. He had evidently been cross-examined by Duke Wrangle all this time.

When he saw Sam he stopped and stared. Now, Sam reflected, was the time for a discussion of whatever it was that was bothering this big dumb brute. But he did not get the chance. He had just clanged shut a fire door with the aid of his shovel, when the big fellow came in and saw him. After staring at him for only a moment, the big fellow reached down for a chunk of coal half as large as his head—and threw it!

The man's ridiculous persistence made Sam so disgusted, so angry, that he threw the shovel, blade first, not caring whether or not it cut the big dumb-bell's head off.

The handle struck the big sandy-haired man across the forehead. He staggered back and slipped. The back of his head struck a closed fire door. A puff of smoke left his hair. Sam ran, grabbed him, and dragged him away.

It wasn't much of a burn, but Sam smeared it with cylinder oil, then with the help of an oiler carried the big fellow to his bunk. The first assistant engineer followed them up the stairs and to the black gang's bunk room, and, when Sam came out on deck, was waiting there with a wry grin, his little black shoe-button eyes gleaming with excitement or curiosity.

"What the hell's going on?" Singapore Sam's erstwhile companion wanted to know. "Who is this stiff?"

"Ask him when he comes to. Where's the money I left on that poker table?"

The black-eyed man answered uneasily, "Well, I wouldn't know the answer to that one, Red. But something I would like to get settled is, what's the old man got it in for you for?"

"I guess," Sam replied, "I would not know the answer to that one either, you double crossing punk."

The engineer grinned. "Maybe you will learn some manners by the time the old man gets finished with you. You're to do twelve hours a day down there—and like it."

SAM RETURNED to the hell hole without further comment.

He was going to play Duke Wrangle's game all the way—and find out in Soerabaya what it was all about.

The first assistant came in a little later, watched him shovel coal for a while, and presently said:

"The skipper's taken your boyfriend off the black gang. I guess he must be somebody of importance. He's up there now with the skipper, and they're drinkin' champagne. Who is that guy?"

"Ask him," Sam grunted, and returned to his work.

He took a half hour out for supper, then returned to the boiler room. At midnight he threw down his shovel and went on deck. He had done twelve hours' work and had lost approximately eight pounds in that withering heat.

He walked forward, sucking in deep lungfuls of the delicious cool night air. At the forward turn of the deck, above the forward well deck and below the starboard wing of the bridge, he stopped and dropped his elbows to the teak rail and looked from the sailing stars to the phosphorescent churn of the bow waves.

He heard a man tap the dottle from a pipe on the bridge wing rail, then a voice spoke that he recognized as Duke Wrangle's.

"I don't know what to make of it," Wrangle said.

There was a long silence, then another voice said:

"What will you do about following them now?"

"I'll pick 'em up."

"You trust that mugg?"

"I think he was telling the truth—yes. He doesn't know much."

There was a low chuckle, "He'll never know much. But how about this redhead?"

Captain Wrangle answered quietly—so quietly that Sam only caught it: "He will sweat and like it. He will sweat until he cracks; then maybe we'll know things we don't know now."

"That schooner—" the other began.

"Oh, the hell with that schooner. It was merely to confuse the issue."

The discussion stopped. Sam waited another half hour, and when it was not resumed, went to his bunk, puzzled and wondering.

The next day Sam was awakened at dawn by a rough hand at his shoulder. It was the assistant engineer, grinning.

"Turn to, tough guy. You got six minutes to grab breakfast."

Sam turned out, drugged with sleep, and had breakfast. The food was quite as bad as it had been last night. As he left the mess room he encountered face to face his faithful and hateful shadow—the man with sandy hair. He was standing with his back to the rail facing the doorway, his mouth open in a grimace, his little piglike eyes bloodshot with hate and squinting with determination. He was panting.

Neither he nor Sam saw Captain Wrangle round the after turn of the deck and walk catlike toward them.

"Listen, you poor sap," the redheaded man said wearily, "are you nuts? Will you tell me what this is all about?"

"You don't know, do you?" the big fellow snarled. The sun bursting over the horizon splashed bloody light on his cheek. "I'm gonna kill you for stealin' it!" His eyes looked it.

Duke Wrangle slipped the iron handle off a patent lifeboat lowering gear as he came striding along the deck.

"Wait a minute," Sam cautioned the big fellow.

But the big fellow was rushing at him. Midway, his hand encountered the iron handle in Captain Wrangle's hand, swinging in a brief arc. The man with sandy hair went down like a pole-axed steer, and Duke Wrangle said quietly, "A smart man like you should not have his trail cluttered so. You'd better start shoveling coal, Red."

Singapore Sam went to the fire room and started shoveling. He was still shoveling at a little after three, when the Moanga dropped anchor in the Straits of Madoera, off the mouth of the Kali Mas, and the greedy little engine was stopped.

From a greasy porthole, kept closed because of its nearness to the waterline, he saw Soerabaya glittering weirdly against the slant of the afternoon sun, and wondered if Captain Wrangle intended going into the Kali Mas and tying up at the Royal Packet dock, or entering the main harbor; but it was evident that the Moanga's master had neither intention, for Sammy now heard the after anchor going down.

The ship had swung a little, giving him a better view of the waterfront; and he suddenly saw, tied up to a dock in the Kali Mas, the familiar blue hull and white spars of his schooner! For a moment he was too excited to do anything. Then he ran to the engine room door, opened it—and came face to face with Duke Wrangle.

CHAPTER V

MURDER!

THE FAMILIAR IRONICAL look was in the captain's steel-blue eyes. He said, "What's the rush, Red? Not thinking of leaving us, are you? I wish you wouldn't. I'm getting to like you. Do you know what I've done for you? I've taken that dunderhead off the black gang and put him to work in the deck crew so he'd stop bothering you. What did you do to that poor half-wit, Sam?"

"You tell me, Duke."

Captain Wrangle stared at him steadily. "Just one big mystery, aren't you, Red? But I'm getting to like you more and more. I like the way you shovel coal. Don't skip ship, will you? I might miss you too much. Understand?"

"Yeah, I understand," the redhead growled.

"What's that?" the other asked in a tone of mild reproach. "You really need some discipline, Red. You really ought to learn respect for your superiors."

Sam's eyes were sultry. "O.K., big shot. So what?"

"Some Dutch officers will be aboard any minute, Red," Wrangle answered laconically. "I understand the authorities in Buru-Waru are interested in knowing how you broke jail twice. You know, Red, these Dutchmen are mighty curious about people who break out of their jails. So I'll pass it back to you—so what?"

Singapore Sam shrugged, walked on to the ladder, climbed to deck, and went to the black gang's bunk room. There he stayed until sunset. He did not know how he would escape from the Moanga. Certainly, Duke Wrangle would not let him at one

250

of the boats. Swimming was too dangerous. He had seen, from the bunk room porthole, too many black fins slicing in and out of the Kali Mas.

But with darkness he grew desperate. He wanted to find out what had happened aboard the Blue Goose, and he must somehow contact Mr. Z at the Oranje Hotel before midnight. That was an ironclad appointment.

He waited for the ship's lights to go on, and when they were on and had steadied he slipped down to the engine room, reasoning that the engineer on watch would have started the dynamos and then returned to deck.

But he was five minutes too early. The black-eyed first assistant was still in the engine room. He was at the switchboard, adjusting a rheostat handle and watching a voltmeter. He looked around at Sam, grinned in that unpleasant way of his, and said, "What's on your mind, sucker?"

"Only this," Sam mildly answered, and sent his right fist slashing up to the other's jaw.

The first assistant engineer rebounded from the switchboard and sprawled face down on the hot steel deck. He should, Sam reasoned, not be out of the anesthetic for ten minutes anyway.

Sam swiftly stripped to the skin, smeared himself from head to foot with black oil and then coal dust, and went to a porthole on the starboard side from which he could see the light in Wilhelmina Tower, and the twinkling lights of the Javanese city beyond. The engineer uttered a soft groan.

Sam crawled out of the oversize porthole, trusting to the film of oily black on his body to deceive any hungry shark he might encounter, for he was a firm believer in the superstition that a shark will never attack a native.

SAM DROPPED into the water and started to swim as quietly as possible. He was perhaps forty feet away from the ship's side when he distinctly heard in the immediate vicinity of the bows the faint splash of oars and the soft grunting of muffled oarlocks. These sounds were followed by a yell from the deck, then a shot.

The swimmer saw the red-blue flash of the firearm, and promptly dived. He swam a hundred feet or more under water; then, with a strong trudgeon, made for the mouth of the Kali Mas. There were no more shots. A long black shape passed close by, swimming through the water with a sibilant hissing sound, so close to him that he felt the disturbed water along his ankles. But the shark evidently had no interest in this oiled black morsel, and sped on.

A few minutes later, between him and the mouth of the wide ship's canal, Singapore Sam saw for several minutes a dinghy containing a lone man, both silhouetted against the bright gleam of the light in the Wilhelmina Tower.

The swimmer was tempted to call out, but thought better of it. He swam on. The dinghy vanished. The tide was running out of the Kali Mas. It was hard, slow swimming. But Sam at length entered the canal and, eventually, reached his schooner, which lay against the dock in the darkness.

He called softly, "Koja! Win Lok!" And when neither the *serang* nor the cook answered, pulled himself aboard. As far as he could judge, from the pale light flooding the deck from the dock lights, everything was in shipshape order. But where were Koja and Win Lok?

He went into the main cabin and lighted lamps. Here, as on deck, everything was shipshape. He looked in the sleeping rooms. All the bunks were made, the floors clean.

Before continuing his investigation he decided to scrub off the black oily film and get into fresh clothing. And when he found there was no hot water in the shower, he became even more puzzled. The lack of hot water meant that the galley stove had not been used since last night at the latest. That certainly meant that Koja and Win Lok had not been aboard since last night.

He soaped and rinsed himself a half dozen times before the oily black film was thoroughly removed, then he shaved, and dressed in fresh white ducks. A bottle of good whisky in the drawer under his bunk had not been disturbed. Nor had a black tin money box containing assorted currency of Malaya and Java to the total of about twenty-five dollars, gold.

He poured himself a stiff drink, then picked up a lantern and went about the schooner on a careful tour of investigation.

Koja's and Win Lok's clothes and sea bags were gone from the foc's'le. Sam went to the galley. It was beginning to appear that the Blue Goose was going to furnish one of those baffling and forever unsolved mysteries of the sea. Why had Koja and Win Lok taken the Blue Goose from Buru-Waru to Soerabaya? If they had gone out of the Buru-Waru harbor, wanting sea room because of the coming hurricane, why hadn't they returned to Buru-Waru? It was all utterly senseless.

But in the galley Singapore made a discovery that did make sense, and that provided him with an alarming theory to illuminate these few known, puzzling facts. Just above the sink, in the scrubbed hardwood wall, he found a bullet hole. He could see the bullet end glimmering in the hole. He dug the bullet out with an icepick. It was of thirty-eight caliber. That bullet had not been there when Sam had last been aboard.

NEAR THE stove, on the floor, he found what might have been other evidence—a faint red stain that had been zealously scrubbed. The shape of the stain indicated that a pool of blood had formed, on the floor, in front of the stove. Sam went to the doorway. Standing there, he was in line with the scrubbed bloodstain in front of the stove and the bullet hole above the sink.

Presumably—or at least theoretically—a man had stood in this doorway, had shot and killed Win Lok as he stood at his stove. The scrubbed blood trail to the door could only mean that the dead cook had been dragged out and put overboard.

Sam pigeonholed the idea of summoning help from the Dutch police, although he needed expert help. He was not a detective. If this matter reached the police, he would spend the next six months in admiralty courts.

He continued his exploration of the ship. And amidships on the port side, on the inner edge of the deck rail, so far down he had to bend low to see it, he found another clue—a patch of kinky black hair, stuck to the wood with dried and hardened blood. That would have been the hair from the Malay *serang's* fuzzy black head. Thus, if Sam were to rely on this slight testimony, was the fate of Koja and Win Lok to be accounted for. Both had—or might have been—murdered and thrown into the sea. By whom?

The mystery of it, the cold-bloodedness of the killer—if this theory was to be accepted—suddenly made Sam murderously mad. He wanted to slug and maul somebody. These two victims of an unknown killer—or killers—had stood by him through thick and thin. They were his closest friends. They had given him the utmost loyalty. Their mysterious murder made him tremble with fury. His wrath was followed by feelings of hopelessness and chill. Ever since he had been in the Far East, he had been dealing with the type of enemy who strikes in the back and in the dark, but he had never been outwitted so completely.

But there was a mystery behind a mystery. Why had any one deliberately murdered Koja and Win Lok, brought the Blue Goose to Soerabaya, and left it tied up here? It should not be hard to find out who had brought the schooner in.

Looking back over the past few days, his mind attached itself to a new suspicion. Who was the big, sandy-haired man who persisted in attacking him, whose belligerence had twice gotten the two of them into jail? On the first occasion, the Blue Goose had been mysteriously sailed out of the Buru-Waru harbor while Sam was a prisoner. If it had all been deliberate, then why had the big dumb-bell followed him aboard the Moanga—and who was the master mind?

He wished he could present the police with his problems, but he dared not. He went ashore. From a native night watchman on the dock he learned that the Blue Goose had reached port shortly before dawn this very morning. She had come in under power, with sails down, furled, and covered. There had appeared to be only one man aboard.

THE WATCHMAN had helped tie up the schooner to the dock, but he had not once seen the face of the man who had brought her in.

"But you saw him when he came ashore," Sam said impatiently.

"No, *tuan*. It was the great darkness before the dawn. He was aboard for perhaps half an hour before coming ashore. When he came ashore, he wore something long and white, like a cape. He wore a dark cap pulled down over his eyes. And I was not curious. Why should I be curious about a lone man coming ashore from a respectable schooner? How many ships do you suppose come and go here?"

"Was he tall or short?"

"I believe he was tall, *tuan*. Yes, he was a tall man."

And that was that. The murderer had been a white man, and a tall man—but that was all. Baffled, Sam walked along the steam tram tracks to Hendrik Street, and took a ricksha from there to the Oranje Hotel. He inquired at the desk for Mr. Z, wondering if that over-cautious old gentleman could shed any light on his mysteries, and wondering if Mr. Z was an honest man or a rascal. Sam was even prepared to be told that there was no Mr. Z, but there apparently was, and Sam was apparently expected, for the desk clerk instructed a bellboy to take him at once to Room 313. The door of Room 313 was opened to Sam's knock by the mysterious old man with whom Sam had talked at the Buru-Waru pottery. And Sam saw that his first impression of the man had been correct. The eyes in the heavy red face were just as cold, the mouth was just as cruel.

There were two other occupants of the room. One was a dark-haired girl of twenty-one or two in a white georgette dinner gown, who sat near doors opened upon a balcony, with a notebook on her knee, a pencil in her hand. She was beautifully tanned. In her large dark eyes meeting his across the room, Sam suspected he saw mischief. She was smiling at him somewhat mysteriously. She was, in all respects, pleasing to any masculine eye.

The old man did not introduce her. He did, however, introduce the other occupant of the room—a dog. It was one of the most remarkable dogs Singapore Sam had ever seen. He suspected that it had started off in life as a wire-hair fox terrier, but had grown into something else entirely. With its fatness and its tight white curly hair, it resembled a sheep. Its eyes were in the center of round black markings, and these eyes were small, suspicious, and mean.

"This," the old man said, with the closest approach to amiability Sam had so far seen in him, "is Angel Face, Captain Shay."

"Angel Face?" Sam said dubiously.

"My dog," the old man explained, in his harsh, unpleasant voice. He bent down and patted the dog. Angel Face made a low whimpering sound and wagged his portly rear quarters, then padded over to Sam and sniffed at his ankles and growled.

"Don't mind him, captain," the girl said. "Angel Face doesn't mean anything personal. He merely thinks your ankles are hamburger."

The old man sent her a glance, and there was such deliberate hatred in it that Sam looked sharply at the girl and was surprised to see in her own large and lovely eyes a reflection of this same emotion. For a moment, the ugly old man and the beautiful young woman locked glances, and it was so startling that Sam held his breath until his face grew red.

Then the old man said, "Captain Shay, my name is Avery Gallatin. Perhaps you've heard of me." And when Sam said nothing, he added, "I am an archeologist. I have letters to you from Dr. Hannibal and Mr. Frothingham, of Singapore. Perhaps you'd better read them, then we can get down to business."

Sam accepted the letters, then looked at the girl. She said quickly, in a gay voice, "I'm Joyce Gallatin, Mr. Shay."

"Are you on this expedition?" Sam asked.

She nodded. "Yes, captain. I act as his secretary." Sam noted then that she did not use the word "father." In the course of that evening he never heard her use the word.

SAM OPENED the letters and glanced at their contents. Both were practically the same. Both were letters of introduction, urging Sam to do his utmost for Dr. Avery Gallatin, the "famous American archeologist, who is in the East Indies on a very dangerous mission."

When he had read the letters, Dr. Gallatin said, "I understand you specialize, more or less, in chartering to scientific expeditions."

"I've chartered to several scientific expeditions," Sam admitted. "After the last one, I swore I'd never charter to another. They always run to dangerous ideas. My partner was killed on the last one."

Dr. Gallatin was looking at him with coldness. Evidently Sam's past adventures did not interest him.

"You have a reputation for liking danger," Miss Gallatin said. "That's why he wants you."

"I want you," the old man amended, "because you have a reputation for being resourceful, ingenious, and fearless. These men told me you were the best man I could find in the East Indies for the purpose."

Sam had the feeling that the cold eyes were weighing him as they might weigh a saddle horse. He felt uncomfortable. Why was he being offered ten thousand dollars, gold, to undertake a job worth about one thousand dollars?

The old man said, "You told me in Buru-Waru your schooner had been stolen,"

"It was," Sam acknowledged, "but I've got it back. It's here."

Dr. Gallatin looked a little suspicious, but he said nothing further just then about that mysterious theft and reappearance.

"Have you ever heard of the Kusa Archipelago?"

Sam's eyes narrowed. "Yes. It's a group of small deserted

islands fifty or sixty miles off the coast of Celebes. They're surrounded by a reef in the shape of a *kusa,* which is Malayan for elephant driving hook. Actually, the shape is horseshoe, and the only entrance is less than a quarter mile wide. There is no place where a ship can cross that horseshoe reef, even at spring tide. It's one of the toughest stretches of water to be found in the Banda Sea."

THE ARCHEOLOGIST took a folded, hand-worn chart out of his pocket and unfolded it. The Kusa group was sketched in it—about one hundred islands of varying size—all within the reef that was shaped like an elephant driving hook. It was an accurate chart.

With a shaking forefinger, Dr. Gallatin indicated an island that was marked on the chart with a small, red-inked cross.

"This," he said, "is the island. Yin. Do you know it?"

"I'm not sure, doctor. I've been in there for water a couple of times. They're all deserted islands."

"The situation, Captain Shay, is this. I have been sent here by the International Archeological Museum of Washington, to secure an archeological collection or store that is hidden on this island. The collection consists of artifacts—pottery, implements, weapons, utensils, and so on, made by a race of cultured people who flourished in these islands during the latter part of the neolithic period—some time between four and five thousand years ago. They were probably one of the most highly civilized races that ever inhabited the earth—greater artisans, we suspect, than the Mayas at the height of their glory.

"In the year 1856, an expedition was sent out to track down rumors. They found the ruins of ancient architecture on Yin. And they found this great archeological store. Before they could get it aboard their ship they were attacked by cannibals, yet they very bravely and cleverly hid the entire collection—tons of artifacts, I believe—and, in doing so, sacrificed their lives. Rather than attempt to escape, they stayed to hide the artifacts for a future expedition—and all were killed by the savages but one man, a young scientist named Thorley.

"Thorley managed to escape in a small boat. Every other member of the party was killed, and the ship was burned. Because of the horrors of that experience, Thorley went out of his mind. On his return to America, he was committed to an institution for the insane on Long Island. He died about a year ago, at the age of ninety-eight, and before he died, somewhat magically regained his reason—or as death approached vividly relived that portion of his youth so that we came into possession of the information.

"Dr. Paterson, the head of our museum, sent me to question the old fellow. He seemed to be rational enough. He told me everything. Next day he died."

"What makes you think," Sam asked, "that it wasn't just a crazy man's imagination?"

"I've checked up on too many details."

Sam was puzzled. If Dr. Gallatin was telling the truth—and Sam presumed that he was—then the price he was offering for Sam's services was exorbitant.

No collection of pottery, statues, and mummies, however old, could be very dangerous.

"What," Sam asked, "makes you think it will be a dangerous expedition?"

"Because, Captain Shay," the old man answered quietly, "many of the artifacts are of gold—approximately a million dollars' worth of them!"

CHAPTER VI

A DANGEROUS GAME

SAM TOOK IT standing up. He looked dazed. His brain was, for the moment, stunned. He had taken part in many treasure hunts, but never one in which such a tremendous sum was at stake.

He gasped, "Are you sure there's that much?"

"Quite sure," the old man said coldly.

"And you're sure it's there?" Sam asked with amazement.

"My museum," Dr. Gallatin answered, "is not in the habit of spending money chasing will-o'-the-wisps."

Singapore Sam was trying to think clearly, but the value of the treasure which the archeologist discussed so calmly was too staggering. A million dollars' worth of gold five thousand years old! It might account for anything. It was the largest chunk of shark bait he'd ever heard about.

The red-headed man's face no longer looked dazed. It became almost bored. As far as Sam was concerned, it was still a poker game with every hand unknown. In no sense was it a show-down. And it wouldn't be a showdown until he learned why Koja and Win Lok had been killed, and the Blue Goose brought to Soerabaya.

"How many people know about it?" he asked.

"Three," was the answer. "Myself, Miss Gallatin, and Anthony Wingate, our excavator."

"Don't forget Rufe," the girl said.

"Who?" Sam asked.

"Rufe. Rufus Pound. He was present at the conference in Washington."

Answering the inquiry in Sam's eyes, the old man said, "Rufus Pound is Wingate's shovelman, or handy man. We have not met Wingate, but we know Rufus Pound well. He carried sealed orders to Wingate in the southwest, where he was working, from the directors of the museum. We have taken every precaution to prevent a leak. That was why I went to such elaborate pains to meet you secretly in Buru-Waru. The four of us have come here by four different routes, timing it to arrive practically simultaneously."

"Where is Wingate?" Sam asked.

And the old man's expression told Sam that the question was, for some reason, annoying. He was striding up and down the room. With his big head set low on his bent shoulders, he looked like an evil gnome. He rasped, "Wingate has been here a week. He went on a snake-hunting trip into the jungle and has not yet returned. As a hobby, he collects snakes. We've been calling his room all afternoon and evening. Try him again, Joyce."

The girl picked up the telephone on the table beside her and called Room 204. There was no answer.

Sam said dubiously, "Doctor, I'm afraid there's been a leak."

Dr. Gallatin barked, "There cannot possibly have been a leak!"

Sam told him of the conversation on the bridge of the Moanga which he had overheard. The archeologist listened coldly, almost with contempt, and said with finality, "It had nothing to do with this expedition. Now, I think we had better have a discussion of practical details. How long will it take you to outfit your ship and get under way?"

"I'm not so sure I'm going," Sam answered laconically. "If there has been a leak, in spite of all your precautions, we would certainly all be killed if we went. It's shark bait. Even if there hasn't been a leak, things are still too hazy. For instance, do you know just where all this gold is—I mean, exactly where it's hidden on the island?"

"I do not," the other answered coldly.

"Didn't Thorley tell you where the treasure was buried?"

"He did not. He would not. Either he knew and would not tell, or he could not remember. But that doesn't worry me. Anthony Wingate is one of the most expert excavators in the world. We will find the treasure."

SAM REMAINED dubious. "How do you know this old lunatic didn't tell somebody else, and let the secret out that way?"

"I checked up on that very carefully, Mr. Shay. Thorley babbled all his life about buried archeological treasure—a maniac's fixation. Every one in the asylum where he lived and died was familiar with it. No one but me ever took him seriously—and no one but me was with him in those last rational hours of his."

"It doesn't sound so hot to me," Sam said.

"Whether the treasure is there or not," Dr. Gallatin answered with impatience, "you will be paid ten thousand dollars, Captain Shay—five thousand tonight, in the form of a draft, if you will consent to take charge of this expedition—and five thousand on the delivery of the gold to any civilized port. Is that satisfactory? I am really most anxious to get this settled and to make plans for our departure."

Sam shook his head. "It still doesn't sound so hot."

The archeologist made a noise in his throat of extreme annoyance. Suspicion visited his cold blue eyes again.

"Captain Shay, we cannot afford to pay you more than ten thousand, regardless of the value of those artifacts. Perhaps the figure I mentioned—a million dollars—has dazzled you. To us—to any true archeologist—these golden objects have no more actual value than objects carved from stone. We are not doing it for ourselves, but for the museum."

Sam drawled, "Don't get me wrong, doc. Ten thousand is plenty for what you want me to do. It isn't the money. I want to look at this from all angles. You represent a respectable and legitimate outfit—a museum. Why can't you simply ask for a Dutch gunboat and go there under Dutch protection? The Kusas belong to Holland."

"Impossible. We are going after this treasure under the direct authority and with the direct permission of the Queen of Holland. It was secretly arranged. The arrangement specifically excluded the local island governments from participation. We have made an arrangement with the Amsterdam Museum to share in this treasure. The colonial Dutch government here or elsewhere must not have an inkling of our plans, because of the jealousy and confusion that would result, or Queen Wilhelmina will withdraw her consent."

The archeologist's voice had grown angry and contemptuous. He said:

"Captain Shay, you can readily see the trouble we have gone to in undertaking this expedition. Everything is keyed to this night—this very hour. You are, I don't hesitate to say, our key man. If you will not undertake to help us, our whole plan will fail."

Sam liked neither the tone in which this was delivered, nor the facts at hand. He was sure that, despite the archeologist's emphatic denials, there had been a leak. A million dollars in gold was too much money. If the truth about the expedition were general knowledge, every cutthroat in the East Indies would be sharpening his knife for their throats. And Sam knew, also, that Dr. Gallatin was an impractical man; in that respect, typically a scientist. The responsibility would be wholly up to Sam.

On the other hand, if he did not somehow secure approximately ten thousand—actually eight thousand dollars would do—his old friend, Jake Fordyce, languishing in the Saigon prison, would be surely guillotined.

"O.K., doc," Sam said with sudden decision. "You can count me in."

For just a moment the scientist's cruel mouth and cold eyes became genial and friendly. It was a quick response no doubt to tremendous mental relief.

He said crisply, in his harsh, unpleasant voice, "That's fine, captain. Joyce, try Wingate's room again. Captain, how soon can we get under way?"

"How long," Sam countered, "will you want to stay on Yin?"

"From a week to a month."

"Give me four days."

THERE WAS a faint shriek from Joyce Gallatin at the telephone. "A python?" she said excitedly into the mouthpiece. "Listen," she said to Sam and her father. "He has a python in his room! He caught it in the jungles and just brought it in. It broke out of its box, and it's simply destroying his room!"

Sam grinned with appreciation, but Dr. Gallatin looked annoyed. The girl was giving them a sort of round-by-round description of the misunderstanding between Mr. Anthony Wingate, famed archeological excavator, and a python.

"He says it's swinging from the chandelier now!" the girl squealed. "Now it's coming down, and he's going after it! But he won't kill it. He wants to send it to a friend of his in New York."

There was a long, tense pause. Then, "He's got it! He put it into its box! What, Mr. Wingate? Just a moment."

Flushed and breathless, she turned from the instrument again. She said to her father, "He says he'll be up as soon as he cleans up. He says Rufus Pound has just come in."

"Tell him," Dr. Gallatin said angrily, "to come here at once. Tell him there is no time to lose."

The girl transmitted this message to the man in Room 204, then hung up the receiver and said, "So that's Tony Wingate!"

With curiosity, Sam asked, "Who is this Tony Wingate?"

"I never met him," the girl answered. "He's supposed to be the greatest archeological excavator in the world. He's done excavating in the southwest, in Carthage, in the Valley of the Kings, in Egypt, at Chichen Itza, in Yucatan, and in the Mongolian desert—the Gobi."

She suddenly stopped babbling.

Sam became aware that the light was gone from her eyes, the lovely flush from her cheeks. She was quite pale, and in her eyes, meeting her father's, was that look of cold hatred Sam had seen earlier. It was mystifying, and it was intriguing. But it made Sam uneasy. He guessed that these two hated each other enough to commit murder. And he wondered why.

His reflections were interrupted by a sudden knock at the door. The father and daughter wrenched their hating eyes from each other. Sam opened the door, and a tall, thin man of about twenty-six walked in, grinning. He was a striking figure, partly because of his exceptional leanness, partly because of his color, and partly because of his garb.

"I'm Anthony Wingate," he announced in a crisp and amiable voice. And he looked very much like the person Sam had imagined him to be. His lean, hard face was as brown as old saddle leather, and overlaid just now with a red flush from recent exposure to tropical sunrays. A week's beard bristled on his lean jaws. His eyes were keen and brilliantly blue. And he wore a stained and tattered khaki field costume—a buttoned jacket, breeches and eighteen-inch lace boots.

Shutting the door, he grinned at Sam, then at the girl, and finally at Dr. Gallatin.

The girl said, "This is Dr. Gallatin, Mr. Wingate. I'm Joyce Gallatin. And this gentleman is Captain Shay, of the schooner Blue Goose. He has just agreed to take charge of the expedition."

ANTHONY WINGATE shook hands with the three of them. He shook hands longest, Sam observed, with Miss Gallatin. And he was interested in noting that the girl's face had more animation, was of a brighter color than it had been before, and he guessed that she had been looking forward with considerable excitement to this meeting. In her business Anthony Wingate was probably a big shot—"the greatest archeological excavator in the world," she had said.

Shaking hands with Dr. Gallatin, the tall, thin man said, "I've just been reading your latest book on the origin of the Aztecs, doctor."

Dr. Gallatin looked pleased. "That so? How did you like it?"

"I didn't like it at all," the famous excavator answered heartily. "I don't agree with a word you said. I think you're off on the wrong track."

Before Dr. Gallatin could reply, Joyce said, "Then you've got two quarrels on your hands, Mr. Wingate. I helped write that book, and I firmly agree with everything in it."

"I love a quarrel," Mr. Wingate laughed.

He said nothing to Sam beyond a murmured, "Glad to know you, cap'n." But there was a complete exchange of views between them, in the unspoken language of the eyes. There was nothing challenging about this. It was merely a brief, hard look of mutual approval.

The fat dog was sniffing at Mr. Wingate's boots and growling. Dr. Gallatin had flushed angrily at the tall, thin man's scornful dismissal of his book, but he beamed now.

"This is Angel Face, Mr. Wingate," he said. "He won't bite you." And he bent down and bestowed an affectionate pat on the dog. It was quite obvious that he had far more affection for the fat little beast than he had for his own daughter.

Straightening up, he said, "Where is Rufe, Mr. Wingate?"

"In my room, taking a bath and getting into clean clothes, doctor. He'll be along directly. Captain, how long will it take to outfit and get under way?"

"Three or four days."

"I'll help all I can."

There was a knock at the door. Joyce Gallatin opened it. A tall, powerfully built man in fresh and badly fitting ducks stood in the doorway.

For a moment, Sammy stared at the big, sandy-haired man with paralyzed astonishment, and the big fellow stared at him.

"Captain Shay," Mr. Wingate was saying, "this is my shovelman, Rufus Pound. Rufe, this gentleman is taking complete charge of our expedition."

The big, sandy-haired man seemed not to hear. His mouth was working, and his blue eyes seemed to be turning pink. He suddenly shouted, "There's the low-down sneak-thief! There's the guy who stole my locket!"

"Rufus!" Joyce shrieked.

"Let me at him!" the shovelman roared.

CHAPTER VII

THE STOLEN LOCKET

SAMMY PICKED UP a chair and said, "Listen, you ape, I'm going to bash your silly brains out if you make a move. Now, calm down."

"Yes," Dr. Gallatin said angrily, "for Heaven's sake, calm down and get that look off your face, Rufus."

"You look exactly like a baboon," Joyce added merrily. "What's it all about?"

"This," Sammy explained, "is the big dumb-bell who's been following me around taking a sock at me every time we meet."

"He stole my locket!" Rufe panted. "He stole my locket with a lock of my girl's hair in it!"

"Where?" Joyce gurgled.

"In Buru-Waru!"

Looking no less menacing, with his great fists at his sides, the shovel man took a step toward Sammy, and Sammy picked up the chair and held it ready to swing.

"Rufe," Mr. Wingate said, "get hold of yourself and try to tell us what's bothering that poor, undernourished brain of yours."

"A fellow told me he stole my locket," Rufe growled.

"What fellow?" Sammy snapped.

He suddenly believed he was on the verge of clearing up a most important mystery—the mystery of the runaway Blue Goose and the murders aboard.

"A blond fellow in Hat Gow's ginmill, in Buru-Waru."

"Who is he?"

"I don't know."

Rufus Pound wasn't relenting. He was still glaring at Sam from the depths of his suspicious nature.

"You were drunk," Anthony Wingate guessed. "And that explains some other things. Captain Shay says there's been a leak in our plans. How many times have you been drunk since you left me in Calcutta?"

The big handy man looked uneasy. "I wasn't very drunk, Tony. I was just a little bit drunk."

"Drunk enough," Dr. Gallatin said angrily, "to go blabbing about our plans. Where? Buru-Waru?"

"I got a little bit drunk in Rangoon, too," Rufe admitted.

He looked ashamed. Sam thought he looked pretty ridiculous, this big, dumb bull of a man.

"And you talked," Joyce persisted.

"And you got a little bit pie-eyed on the Moanga," Sam added, "and you spilled the works to Duke Wrangle."

"Did you," Dr. Gallatin put in angrily, "tell any one the name of that island?"

"No!" Rufe said.

"Are you sure?"

"I'm positive, doctor!"

"Of course he's positive," Anthony Wingate said. "He didn't know. I didn't tell him. All he knows is what he overheard you saying in Washington. Rufe, just what did you spill?"

"I don't remember." Still glaring at Sam, Rufe said, "If you didn't steal my locket, why didn't you say so?"

"You didn't give me a chance."

"Huh! Just the same, you're a pretty suspicious character. If you're not, how did you escape so easy?"

"Right back at you, Rufus. How did you get out?"

"By doing what you did! I cut a hole in the roof and climbed out twice."

"The last time, you smashed that lamp in the corridor. How did you get off the Moanga?"

"Stole a boat and rowed ashore."

But Rufe was not interested in a friendly conversation with the redheaded man.

"Look at Angel Face!" he cried. "Even the dog is suspicious of you!"

AND AT that moment the overgrown fox terrier deserted Sam's ankle, waddled over to the handy man, and, with an irritable snarl, bit him in the ankle.

In the uproar promptly following, Sam said:

"I've got to get back to my ship. I've got to get things started early in the morning."

And Anthony Wingate remarked, as Joyce dragged the dog from the room and closed the door against his yelps, "I'm sorry you two men don't hit it off better. I was thinking Rufe had better go aboard your ship with you tonight."

"Have you," Singapore Sam asked the shovel man, "had any sailing experience?"

"Certainly. I was second mate on a lumber schooner once."

"We'll need a Malay *serang,* a cook, and another deck hand," Sam said.

"Yeah?" Rufe sneered. "I should think a guy as big and smart as you wouldn't need any crew at all."

"Don't let it slip your mind, Rufe," Anthony Wingate said sharply, "that Captain Shay is boss. You are to place yourself under his orders and obey him implicitly."

Rufe growled some insult under his breath, and Sam said, "You better get aboard now, Rufe. I don't think we should be seen together—any of us. The quieter we get away, the better." He told Rufe how to reach the schooner and where to sleep, and when the shovel man was gone the four of them had a discussion of plans. All were agreed that their greatest source of worry was

Platform, man, and box started downward

Duke Wrangle. There was no question in Sam's mind that Duke Wrangle planned to follow the schooner to the Kusas.

Dr. Gallatin asked him irritably how he would cope with a shipload of "virtual pirates."

"I'm thinking it over," Sam said.

"You were advertised," the archeologist remarked, "as a man of infinite resource and daring. You must prevent his following us."

"I'll think of something," Sam answered.

At the end of their discussion Dr. Gallatin gave Sam a draft for five thousand dollars. Sam left and returned to the schooner. He heard Rufe's snores issuing from the transom over the first mate's stateroom. Undressing, he felt more than a little uneasy. He didn't, with the unseen danger in the air, like the thought of taking full responsibility of this crowd of greenhorns. Doubtless, Rufe had let the secret out, either in Buru-Waru or in Rangoon. Certainly, it was in the possession of Duke Wrangle, perhaps others. A million in prehistoric gold gadgets! Too much! Enough, in fact, to start a war. Why, he wondered, had they taken that big dumb-bell into their confidence?

Sam fell asleep worrying, and he woke up worrying. He heard sounds in the galley as he was dressing. And as he passed the room in which Rufe had slept he looked in and saw an array of small and large boxes with coarsely screened holes.

RUFE WAS preparing breakfast for two in the galley, and the soft morning air was fragrant with frying bacon and boiling coffee. Rufe dropped the last of a half dozen eggs into a pan as Sam came to the doorway. On the galley table two places were set.

The big, sandy-haired fellow glared at him resentfully. "Don't think I'm doin' this because I like you," he growled. "And I still think you took that locket."

Sam grinned.

"Aren't those snake boxes," he asked, "in your room?"

"They are—and what of it?"

"So you're a snake collector?"

"Tony Wingate is a poisonous snake collector, and so am I, and who the hell has anything to say about it?"

Sam wagged his head. "I might have known that a great big bully like you would go around picking on little-bitty snakes!"

"Nuts!"

Rufe set out their breakfast. He was a good cook, but Sam goaded him by complaining that the bacon was scorched and that the coffee tasted like boiled lye. But it wasn't fair. Rufe was a simple-natured fellow. He became wrathful and profane.

"I take it back," Sam said. "Getting your goat, Rufe, is so easy that you ought to kick to the S.P.C.A. whenever anybody does it. Now try to tell me something about this blond guy who told you I stole your locket. Wait a minute! It's important. It was a gag. The same guy who told you that stole this schooner and killed my two hands. I know it's part of a plot, but I can't make out the rest of it. Try to tell me what he looked like."

Rufe stared at him dully a while, then slowly shook his head. His ugly big face grew red, and he lowered his eyes.

"I was tighter'n a tick," he confessed. "All I know is, I was in this ginmill, and the joint was crowded, and all of a sudden I miss this locket. I started yellin' about it, and then this blond-looking guy told me you had it, and where to find you. Said he saw you swipe it and duck out. That's all I can tell you."

"Was he tall or short?"

"Damned if I remember."

"Color of eyes?"

"I can't tell you."

"Accent?"

Rufe wrinkled his low brow until it resembled a puzzled ape's. "You've got me there."

The big fellow looked so miserable that Sam stopped questioning him.

Obviously, Rufe wasn't lying. He was too dumb to lie.

"Of course you don't remember what you told Wrangle?" Sam could not resist asking.

"No."

"Do you know what he plans to do, Rufe? He's going to follow us down and kill us off and grab that treasure."

Rufe looked unhappy. "My gosh, I'm sorry I talked, but what can I do about it?"

"We have to head him off somehow."

"How can you head him off? He's layin' outside there, right across the entrance to this canal! You can't slip out day or night but what he'll see you!"

"I'll stew about it," Sam said. He had a plan—a dangerous plan—for putting an end to the chase Duke Wrangle planned. But it could not be executed until night.

"I'm going ashore and order provisions and equipment," Sam said. "When they come, have 'em stowed. There'll be some heavy tackle to stow in the forward hold. All food supplies will go into the lazarette. Don't go ashore. Lie low."

SAM WENT ashore, to find that, some time during the night, a large white world-cruise ship, the Queen of Asia, had come into the big canal and was now tied up astern of the Blue Goose.

He went uptown and spent the day purchasing. But first he stopped at the bank, and, with the five-thousand-dollar draft Dr. Gallatin had given him last night, bought three drafts, one for two hundred dollars payable to Ah Fong, one for twenty-five dollars payable to the Buru-Waru pottery, and a draft for the balance made payable to Jake Fordyce. The first two he mailed to the American consul at Buru-Waru, and the third to the American consul at Saigon, French Indo-China.

He believed that the first two drafts would cause the Buru-Waru police to lose interest in him. Half that bill Rufe must pay, but he would settle with the shovel man later. He returned from his day of purchasing to find Rufe in his cabin.

The latter had kept out of sight all day, he said, except when the supplies came aboard. "And I've got your crew for you," he said with pride, "A Malay *serang*, a Chinese cook, and an island boy for deck hand."

"I thought you hadn't let the ship."

"I didn't. They came aboard. They looked O.K., so I took 'em on. They're all in the fo'c's'le gettin' settled. I just got through hiring them."

Sam went to the fo'c's'le, and found the three men, as stated, getting settled. He questioned them one by one. He examined their credentials. He was suspicious of them, but their credentials were satisfactory. Wong, the Chinese cook, had spent eighteen years in Royal Dutch Steam packets steamers; Simbi, the Malay *serang*, had a good record both in sail and steam; and Lakka, the deck hand, a Fiji boy, seemed honest and looked husky. He had nothing but a Chinese document, having worked for a Chinese on a pearling lugger, out of Macassar.

It was dark when Singapore Sam finished questioning them, and decided, in spite of mild suspicions, to let the three of them stay. He had supper and sat in the cockpit smoking his pipe until a few minutes before the moon went down. Then he went into the small bulkheaded compartment which housed the schooner's Diesel engine, hunted about until he found a small bag of fine, dark gray powder, which he dropped into a coat pocket with his pocket electric torch.

He went out on deck, pulled the dinghy alongside, and took out the oars. He wrapped each one for about a foot with canvas, which he tied in place with marlin. Then he oiled the oarlocks, got into the dinghy, and started rowing.

He rowed to the far side of the Kali Mas, so that the bright lights of the big white world-cruise ship would not reveal him, as he must be seen by no one.

Most of the way to the Moanga he rowed swiftly and without particular care for noiselessness, but when he neared the converted yacht he rowed with great care, taking pains to drop the oar blades into the water and to take them out without causing a splash.

His errand was a very dangerous one. If he were caught, Duke Wrangle would probably kill him, or, at the very least, make him a prisoner. Sam's heart, as he neared the silent black hulk lying in the roadstead, with its few dim lights, began to race; and, in spite of the cool off-sea breeze, he was sweating.

WITH UTMOST care he pulled up alongside the small steamer. He listened alertly, but heard no sounds aboard save those of a man loudly snoring. Aside from this, there was no sound to cover whatever noises he might make going aboard.

The only factor in his favor was the darkness of the night.

He could not rid himself of a feeling of strain. His hands were stiff and his fingers were clumsy. They shook when he made the end of the painter fast to the brass bolt of the engine-room porthole clamp alongside which he had maneuvered the dinghy.

Standing up in the dinghy, he looked into the engine room. It was dark except for a dim bulb that burned over the switchboard. He looked in and listened for some time before he made another move. Assured that he was not observed from above, and that the engine room was empty, he pulled himself carefully up and through the oversize porthole. His shoe scuffed noisily against a stanchion as he eased himself down. He waited in a panic of shaking muscles. When he heard no sounds he crept across the steel floor toward the sturdy little steeple-compound engine.

Near the crank-pit he stopped in sudden terror. A man was sitting in a chair just under the steam gauges! It was the first assistant engineer, no doubt delegated by Duke Wrangle to spend the night on guard here.

The first assistant engineer was asleep and faintly snoring, but his sleep was troubled. As Sammy stared at him, the first assistant stirred and groaned, and Sammy wondered why the war-drum booming of his frantic heart did not wake the man up.

It would have been a simple matter to knock the man directly from sleep into complete unconsciousness with a well-aimed sock in the jaw. But that would not do. It had sufficed for Sam's escape from the Moanga, but his plans tonight were of a much more delicate nature. His presence aboard must not be suspected.

The first assistant groaned again and made muttering sounds. He seemed to be on the verge of waking up. Sammy waited in an agony of suspense; but the man, with further groanings and mutterings, subsided and apparently slept soundly.

With utmost caution Sammy tiptoed to the crank-pit. He flashed his pocket light on the massive cranks and bearings, then glanced quickly at the sleeping man.

The first assistant was groaning and mumbling again.

Shaking in all his muscles, Sammy lowered himself into the pit. The bottom was covered with a sludge of grease and that with a layer of water. The footing was precarious. When he had braced himself as best he could, Sam removed the paper bag of gray powder from his pocket, and with great care dusted the powder down into the slot in the crank through which the bearing surface was exposed.

He emptied part of the bag into the slot, then went to the next bearing and dusted it. His footing was so insecure that he could stand erect only by hanging to such objects as presented themselves.

He was sifting dust into the last bearing when, with no warning, his feet shot out from under him and he skidded with a great splash under the big crank. There was only enough clearance for his body. He lay there, soaked with water and grease, with his heart triphammering, his body tense with terror, breathing the sickening smells of old oil and bilge-water.

A mumbling voice blurted, "What the hell was that?"

LYING IN the grease, Sammy waited. He had only one thing to be thankful for—that his pocket light was switched off when it happened.

He heard the first assistant get out of the chair, softly cursing. Sammy said to himself, "If I don't get out of this pretty quick, I'll drown in my own sweat."

A bright light flashed on, and he heard sounds of the first assistant stirring about, grumbling and cursing. He prowled about the engine room. If he found Sam Shay in that strange position, he would probably kill him with the first spanner he could lay hand to. And if he didn't kill him, Duke Wrangle would—when the emery dust was discovered.

In suspense more agonizing than he had ever known, Sammy lay in the grease and water and waited. The first assistant went to the far side of the engine room. If he found the dinghy's painter, it would be simply too bad.

Sammy, in his strange position, could not see him. He could see nothing but the gleam of the bright light on steel yellowed with old grease. The slow footfalls of the first assistant were now coming toward the crank-pit. Sam held his breath. But the engineer's course was evidently diverted by the bilge pump, for he went on around this and stepped over the thrust bearings. From that point, if he had looked down, he could have seen Sammy. Evidently he did not look down.

Grumbling, he returned to his chair, switched off the light, and sat down. Sammy heard the old armchair creak and give. There was an interval of silence, broken only by the intermittent dripping of water in a bilge, and the ticking of the engine-room clock; then came the sharp sound of a match being struck. A moment later Sam smelled strong pipe tobacco.

He waited, it seemed to him, for hours, for ages, for whole lifetimes. And suddenly he heard a faint snore, then another. When the snoring became measured, Sammy moved. He found it almost impossible to move. Everything he touched was so greasy. From head to foot he was smeared with grease. He wriggled half out, only to slide back.

On his fourth try he made it. He reached up, grasped one of the big nuts on the crank, and pulled himself out from under. At each move he made, accompanied by some sound, he waited. But the first assistant kept on snoring.

ONCE OUT of the crank-pit, Sam was faced by another problem. He must not leave a trail. Footsteps of thick grease left behind on the steel floor, unclean as it was, would arouse suspicion. He made his way to the waste box, took out great handfuls, and back-tracked to the pit. He wiped off his shoes. He wiped the spot clean where he had crawled out, then he backed around the engine, taking short steps, pausing at every step to eliminate his tracks and the grease that dripped from his clothing.

It seemed to him that dawn must certainly be at hand, yet the engine-room clock said three twenty. Reaching the porthole, he pulled himself up and cautiously lowered himself into the dinghy. But before he cast off the painter he carefully removed the gobbets and smears of grease adhering to the porthole rim.

He threw the waste into the sea, cast off the painter, and began to row. When he neared the Blue Goose, he again kept to the far side of the Kali Mas so that the lights of the Queen of Asia would not reveal him.

Reaching the schooner, he told Rufe to go at once to the Oranje Hotel and notify the Gallatins and Mr. Wingate that they were sailing immediately.

"Tell them to pack as fast as they can. We must be out of here long before daylight."

"But we ain't got everything we need," the shovel man protested.

"We're sailing as is," Sam said firmly. "And if you get a chance to drown that dog, I'll never tell a soul."

"How did you get all that grease on you?"

"It's too long a story. Beat it."

When Rufe had gone, Sam went below, stripped off his soiled clothing, showered, and dressed again, this time in sailing gear—dungarees and denim shirt.

He went on deck. He felt much better. Duke Wrangle was now eliminated from the picture. The expedition to Yin for a million dollars worth of gold artifacts could now be made in comparative safety. Quite pleased with his cleverness in having ridded the expedition of the menace of Duke Wrangle and his cutthroats, Sam walked forward to tell his crew the schooner was getting under way very soon.

A whispery voice hailed him from the dock.

"Hey! Singapore, that you?"

He stopped and stared, but saw nothing but a vague shape in the purple black shadow of the godown. A cigarette spark glowed in an unseen face.

"Who is it?"

"Brain Fever Addison. Come ashore."

CHAPTER VIII

DANGEROUS LATITUDES

SAMMY WALKED ASHORE, wondering. Brain Fever Addison was a mysterious figure, a young man Sam had known for years but had never understood. He thought he was a British spy, but he could never be sure, and Brain Fever Addison was the most evasive, most elusive, most mysterious figure he knew in all the Far East.

With no visible means of support, Brain Fever, so called because his initials were B.F., and he had once been confined to a hospital in Kuala Lumpor for eight months with brain fever, had a trick of appearing unexpectedly in the most unexpected places, and vanishing like a puff of smoke.

Sam had once fought off a gang of waterfront thugs in Singapore, standing back to back with Brain Fever, and the adventure had evidently left Brain Fever with a sentimental attachment for him. He was usually a purveyor of amazing secret information.

Brain Fever flipped the cigarette into the Kali Mas as Sam approached, shook his hand, and murmured, "One hears you are browsing around in a mess of trouble."

Sam felt the skin at the back of his neck creep.

"Where the hell did you hear that?"

"Softer, softer! The soul of discretion must maintain the usual Delphic attitude. A fat murderer named Papeete Pollario is combing Soerabaya for you with, I think, a proposition. I believe gold is concerned. Oh, gold, what crimes are committed in your pretty name! Of what possible good is gold to humanity, now that it is no longer a medium of exchange, or used for jewelry, but only as a filling for teeth? It keeps me awake—often."

"What about Papeete Pollario?"

"Ah, I think he owns a ship called the Lotus Lady, which is in Batavia at present."

"Stop being so damned mysterious. What do you know about my schooner being stolen in Buru-Waru, and my two hands being murdered?"

"It is dismaying and new. But don't you spend your life proving my point?"

"What point?" Sammy grunted.

"That these are dangerous latitudes. Why am I so much busier, why is life so much cheaper, why are crime and violence so much commoner, just a little down under than just a little up over?"

"You're nuts," Sam growled.

"Certainly I'm nuts," Brain Fever Addison agreed cheerfully. "I merely maintain that these latitudes just a few degrees south of the Equator breed more danger than any other latitudes on earth. Perhaps it's the awful heat, or the violence of the winds. Whatever it is puts savagery into a man's blood, be he white or yellow or brown. Now—you're in hot water. Why? Dangerous latitudes, my lad—dangerous latitudes! Good-by! I have work to do tonight."

Sam did not try to detain him. He never tried to detain him. He often thought that Brain Fever Addison fancied himself as a will-o'-the-wisp, appearing as magically as a slave of Aladdin's, vanishing as abruptly as a star behind a skating cloud.

Sam remained beside the godown for some time after Brain Fever Addison had vanished. He stared at the whitely glittering lights of the cruise ship, and he experienced successive waves of disgust, despair, and doubt. Dangerous latitudes!

How many East Indian tramp skippers knew about this expedition to Yin? Should he seek out Papeete Pollario, or avoid him? If Pollario's ship was now in Batavia, and if the Blue Goose got under way in an hour or two, Pollario could not possibly follow.

But how much did Pollario know?

He decided to let Papeete Pollario find him. The more he knew, the better could he cope with any situation that might arise.

A million dollars was bait for such hungry sharks!

SAM MADE his way uptown, where he permitted Papeete Pollario to find him with no difficulty. The overtaking took place in a Javanese grogshop, noted for its purple arrack, one whisky-glass of which, it has been said, will rob an ordinary man of his powers of locomotion within ten minutes.

A hearty voice proclaimed, "Singapore Sam! I'm lookin' fer yuh!"

The speaker was a short, thick-set, heavy-faced man with loose jowls and a somewhat flabby, or rubbery, mouth. A long large nose made his eyes look porcine. He reminded Sam at first glance of a jocular villain of the screen he had seen in a motion picture in Sarawak; an actor named Beery. There was the same oiliness to Papeete Pollario's face, the same droll look in his eyes, the same stubble on his chin.

"You don't know me, I guess," the thick-set stranger said. "I'm Papeete Pollario. Let's set down somewheres and drink some beer and git acquainted."

Over two mugs of beer, Papeete Pollario mentioned that he owned a small steamship named the Lotus Lady, now anchored in Batavia, and that he had come hurrying to Soerabaya by train for the express purpose of making Sam Shay's acquaintance.

In a soft, purring voice, Captain Pollario now said, "I know about this junket you're charterin' for, Red. I just thought we might have a friendly little talk about my cut."

Certainly Papeete was frank enough to suit anybody.

"Your cut?" Sam stalled.

"Your and my cut. Suppose we say fifty-fifty. I might as well tell you I know what it's all about. I'm a business man, Red. I always put my cards face up on the table."

"If you've got a ship and you know all about it," Sam said, "why bother with me?" Sam waited tensely for the answer to that one. Did Papeete Pollario know where the Blue Goose was going, or didn't he?

Papeete smiled amiably. A wolf about to gobble a rabbit might smile in much the same way.

"Listen, Redhead, I'm no hawg. My motto is, you help me and I help you. So just supposin', to save our wind, we agree on a flat fifty-fifty split."

Sam looked at him steadily a moment, met the flickering threat in the porcine eyes, and said decisively, "O.K., Papeete. We'll deal. You know how much there is?"

"I heard a million."

"You heard right. A million—gold. Worth going to some trouble for."

"You said it. When do you pull out?"

"Day after tomorrow. I've got to load supplies and equipment."

Papeete Pollario frowned. "I heard you had 'em loaded."

"Only part. Now, here is what I suggest, Papeete. Give us a week to get there, and two weeks to find the treasure. In other words"—Sam paused to calculate—"be there May sixteenth."

PAPEETE POLLARIO grinned. The corners of his mouth seemed almost to touch his earlobes. "Red," he said, chuckling, "don't try to fast-talk me. How do I know the perfessor don't know exactly where it is? How do I know it'll take two weeks to find? You're too smart for me, Red. You're plannin' to go there, load the gold—and blow. No, siree. That ain't fair to Papeete Pollario. I'm gonna foller you. I'm gonna stay just over the horizon behind you."

Sammy shook his head. Did or did not this fat greasy scoundrel know the Blue Goose's destination?

"It won't work, Papeete. You know how large that island is."

"Sure, sure."

"It's a pretty big island."

"I don't care."

"But nobody in the world can find that gold but the professor. The minute you drop anchor, the professor quits. That's human nature."

"I know somethin' else about human nature," Papeete said amiably. "Just take a pair of pincers and begin pullin' out a man's toenails and fingernails, and he does just about whatever you want. I guess we can make the perfessor find that treasure all right."

"And when you found it, you'd figure on killing everybody, including me," Sam said gloomily.

"Everybody but you, Sam."

Sam still looked gloomy and doubtful.

"I don't know, Papeete. I'm not so sure. How do I know I can trust you?"

Papeete Pollario chuckled.

"The way I look at it, Red, you've just got to trust me. But I'm a man o' my word. Ask anybody!"

"I like the idea of splitting it with you fifty-fifty," Sam said. "I'd rather have you for me than against me. The only thing I don't like is the chance of getting my throat cut, along with the others."

Papeete laughed uproariously. "Aw, don't let that bother you, Red. You can trust me like a father."

Sam stared at him with an air of hope.

"I guess I can," he said.

"I guess you'll have to," Papeete laughed.

"All right," Sam said. "It's a deal. Now, look here." Without seeming to, he watched the oily face shrewdly as he said, "I figure on anchoring on the north side of Jalwan. You'd better come in at night on the south side for a surprise attack."

There was no suspicion in Pollario's expression as Sammy said "Jalwan"; only an involuntary gleam of interest in the little eyes. Sammy experienced a sudden let-down from relief. He felt limp, and triumphant. If Papeete Pollario did not know where Jalwan was, he would speedily locate it on charts as being in the little cluster of islands just off the southwest end of Timor. He would hurry back to his ship in Batavia and set out for Timor as swiftly as possible. Which would suit Sam to perfection.

Papeete said, with a judicial air, "That sounds like a good bet, Red. I'll sneak up on the south side. If you ain't there when I get there, I'll just hang around."

Sam finished his beer and got up.

"O.K., Papeete, but God help you if you try to double cross me."

"And if you try to pull any fast ones on Papeete Pollario," the jolly villain laughed, "mebby you'll be kinda sorry, Red. So long and good luck!"

"So long, Papeete."

SAM RETURNED to the waterfront in a pleasant state of mind. Not only had he crippled the Moanga's engine this night, but he had given Papeete sailing directions which would take him approximately one thousand miles to the south and west of the Kusa Archipelago! He had outwitted two of the smartest and most dangerous scoundrels in the East Indies!

Sam felt pretty good when he went aboard. He felt even better when he found that the Gallatins and the tall, thin, sun-browned Anthony Wingate were aboard with their duffel, and were ready to sail.

Sam told them with considerable merriment of his busy evening.

"We've proved one important point," he said. "The news of the expedition may have leaked, but no one knows where the gold is. It looks to me like fair weather ahead."

Sam might not have been so optimistic if he could have glimpsed a little way into the tragic future.

Simbi, the new *serang*, and Lakka, the new deck hand, cast off the lines. Rufe started the Diesel engine. And with Sam at the wheel, the Blue Goose purred out into the Kali Mas and into the Straits of Madoera.

He steered for the Moanga.

When within hailing distance he shouted, "Moanga ahoy!"

There was an interval, then a voice answered, "Ahoy schooner! Who is it?"

"The Blue Goose—Sam Shay in command. Tell your skipper Papeete Pollario has been seen in Soerabaya, and that there's a rumor that he made a secret visit to your ship during the night. I thought Captain Wrangle might want to know. That's all."

Joyce Gallatin, who was standing near the wheel, asked Sammy what it was all about.

He grinned. "When in doubt, muddy the water."

"Isn't he the one who got Rufe tight?"

"Yes, Miss Gallatin."

"Let's be Sam and Joyce—Sam."

"O.K., Joyce. I'm kind of curious about you."

"I know," she said quickly. "Most people are. They wonder why I go along with him on these expeditions. One reason is, I'm really mad about archeology. I'd rather poke around in some ancient ruins than go to all the tea parties and dances in the world. The other reason is—he makes me."

"I didn't mean to pry into that," Sam murmured.

"You aren't prying. It's no secret. We hate each other. I hate him because he practically murdered my mother. It happened in Guatemala, when I was ten. We were both there with him. It was just before the rainy season. My mother was very ill. She seriously needed an operation. There was just time to go into the interior to see an ancient Mayan city, just discovered in the jungle, before the rains started. The choice was up to him—get mother out, back to civilization to a good hospital for her operation—or go into the jungle. He chose the jungle. She died in there."

Her father's voice behind them said harshly:

"I told you never to mention that subject to any one!"

THE GIRL whirled about. "You have absolutely nothing to say about it!" she said hotly. "What we think of each other is not a secret from any one. Certainly, you've never made a secret of how you hated mother and me!"

"Your mother was disloyal to me!"

"That's a lie!"

The old man was glaring at her with hot, malignant eyes. "You are being disloyal to me at this moment!"

"I am not! I hate you! I am being perfectly honest about it!"

"Go to your stateroom!"

"I refuse."

By this time Sammy felt decidedly uncomfortable. It was not so much what they said, but the tones in which they said it. Never, in human voices, had he heard such hatred.

The archeologist relieved the situation a little by retiring from the scene himself. He went below. The girl said nothing for a time. She was crying. Wiping her eyes with a handkerchief, she said:

"I'm sorry I brought it up, Sam. But you can't realize how it eats my very soul. He hated my mother because she was gay. She loved parties and people and fun. That's what he means by 'disloyalty.' He hated her because she wouldn't take archeology seriously enough."

Sam said nothing. He felt even more uncomfortable than before.

"I've never seen him show the slightest affection for any living creature," Joyce went on, "but that horrible little dog. How he adores that dog!"

After a moment of silence she said, "His attitude toward women has spoiled me for men. I'm a sincere man-hater. You have no idea how I looked forward to meeting Tony Wingate. For years, I've thought he was the most romantic figure in the world. When I finally met him, night before last, I wanted to cry—I hated him so."

"Right off the bat?"

"Right off the bat! I don't know why. He's all that I expected. I spent most of today with him. We went to the Botanical Gardens and had a terrific row. I was as polite as could be. And so was he. But first thing you know, we were like a strange cat and a dog. It was awful. We simply can't agree about anything. Do you think I'm crazy, Sam?"

"No."

"Sam, are you in love?"

The red-headed man grinned. "Yes. But it isn't doing me any good. She can look me in the eye and tell me how much she loves me while she's signalling to a thug behind me to wallop me with a club."

"Has she done that?" Joyce gurgled.

"You bet she has!"

"What are you going to do about it?"

"Nothing."

Joyce was standing so close beside him that he could smell the fragrance of the perfume she used. He suspected she was in love with Tony Wingate, and was fighting against it.

She was watching the spreading soft glow of yellow along the eastern horizon. It brightened to silver, then to shell pink, and the blackness of the Java Sea was suddenly alight. Light flowed into the sky, washing out the stars, turning the air overhead a soft and brilliant blue.

The girl sighed, stretched her arms, and said, "Ah, this is living!" Then she looked aft and cried, "Sam! That ship is after us!"

"Yeah," he said laconically. "She weighed anchor right after we passed. She won't be with us long."

His prediction was soon fulfilled. The steamer in their wake stopped, wallowing in the purple waves of sunrise. It was presently beam on. The Moanga remained in that position while the Blue Goose fleetly drew away.

Joyce turned and looked at Sam.

"I'm just a little bit scared of you, Sam. You're utterly unscrupulous. But I'm awfully glad you have charge of our expedition. I can sleep with a clear mind. And I'm going to do it now."

Sam turned in shortly afterward himself. He gave the wheel to Simbi, his new *serang,* and went below for some much needed sleep.

CHAPTER IX

THE STRANGER

HE WAS AWAKENED almost at once, it seemed, by a strange voice. He saw by the little brass ship's clock on the cabin wall that it was ten o'clock. He had slept less than four hours.

The strange voice shouted clearly, "Steward! Steward! Where the devil are you, steward?"

For a moment, lazily enjoying the gentle motion of the ship and the hissing of water along her stout skin, he wondered to which of his passengers the voice belonged. And when he realized that it had sounded like neither the voice of Dr. Gallatin nor Tony Wingate, nor yet Rufe, Sammy sat up in his bunk and reached for his pants.

Lakka, the island boy, was at the wheel, his long black hair blowing wildly in the strong beam wind. And Simbi was forward on the port side, wildly gesticulating to an apparition in the longboat.

Muddled eyes in a pale white face were staring at the *serang*, and Simbi was waving his brown arms and executing an angry little dance with his feet.

The apparition arose and stepped down on deck as Sammy walked forward. He was a slender man of about Sam's age, hatless, but otherwise attired as if for a dinner party. He wore a white, beautifully cut mess jacket, and white beautifully tailored trousers, both badly rumpled and wrinkled. A white carnation had withered and turned yellow in his buttonhole.

He blinked in the glare of midmorning sunlight and staggered a little. Sam had seen such an expression in men's eyes and faces plenty of times. He had seen it often enough in his own face. He did not have to be told that this fashionable young man was the private owner of a history-making hangover. He had that dazed, glassy look in his eyes, and there was that greenish tint around the dry and cracked mouth. The young man seemed to be having a hard time adjusting himself to his surroundings.

He grasped the rail of the longboat to steady himself against the gentle pitching and the slope of the deck. He looked with dismay at the bellying white sails.

"For the love of St. Swithin," he inquired in a strangling voice, "where am I? Give me a drink, somebody. Give me a drink before I die!"

Rufe Pound had come sauntering toward the little group.

"Who is this guy?" he growled.

"A stowaway," Sam answered. "Get him a drink."

"A long cold one," the stowaway croaked. And addressed himself to Sam:

"Are you the captain of this vessel?"

"Yep."

"What am I doing here?"

"Search me, mister."

"What day is this?"

"Thursday."

"Oh, my God! What time is it?"

"Ten."

"Oh, my God! The Queen of Asia pulled out for India an hour ago! Are you going to India?"

"Nope. The opposite direction."

THE YOUNG man with the hangover sat down heavily on the deck and clasped with both hands a forehead that must have been brutally throbbing.

"Can you possibly overtake her, captain?" he said.

Sam said gravely, "She makes twenty-five knots against our eight. Figure it out for yourself."

The fashionably dressed stowaway groaned again. "Oh, my God!" he groaned. "My aunt will be wild!"

"Is she on the Queen?"

"Certainly she is! I was chaperoning her on this cruise. She'll be positively insane with terror. Have you a radio aboard?"

"Nope."

Sammy heard a giggle behind him, and glanced over his shoulder. Joyce Gallatin, looking very fresh and clean in a white linen skirt and a canary-colored sweater, was standing with feet apart, her long, slim legs braced against the pitching of the schooner.

"Is it lost?" she laughed.

Sammy grinned and turned back to the stowaway. "How did you get aboard this ship?"

"Oh, come now," the stylish stowaway pleaded. "Ask me an easy one."

"You must," Joyce said sweetly, "have had a humdinger."

The blurred and bloodshot amber eyes tried to focus on her. The young man shook his head, but it apparently did him little good, for he continued to stare as if he still saw several of her.

He wrinkled his forehead. A dark groove appeared between his eyes. "The last thing I remember was dancing with a Javanese princess in the moonlight."

"Where was this?" Sam grunted.

The black-haired young man said, "In Government House. The governor's ball, you know. He gave it in honor of Admiral Jepson, who is a passenger on our ship—didn't he? Wait a minute! I remember taking a ricksha. Hold everything!"

He began a search of his pockets. He brought out a roll of Javanese florins.

"I wasn't robbed!" he cried.

Rufe appeared at that moment walking along the deck with a tall drink of water.

The young man saw it. "Water!" he screamed. "Did I ask for water? Don't tell me I'm among prohibitionists!"

Joyce was clinging to the longboat, weak with laughter.

"Rufe," Sam said, "go down into my cabin and bring the bottle of redeye you will find in the bottom drawer under my bunk. What the gentleman meant was a hair of the dog."

Angel Face came waddling up and began sniffing and growling at the stowaway's ankles. Dr. Gallatin and Tony Wingate also joined the little group.

The dark young man in smart Far Eastern evening dress stared from one face to the other. He looked uneasy. His eyes returned to Sam's.

"Look here, captain, where is this ship going?"

"To the Kusa Archipelago."

"I never heard of it. You've got to put back to Soerabaya and put me ashore! I haven't the slightest desire to go to the Kusa Archipelago!"

Dr. Gallatin was staring at the stowaway with amusement.

"Captain Shay, who is this?"

"A stowaway. He mistook the Blue Goose for the Queen of Asia."

"What are you going to do with him?"

"Look here," the stowaway said. "I'll give you five hundred dollars to take me back to Soerabaya."

"We can't put back to Soerabaya," Sam answered. "That's flat."

"Put him to work," Joyce suggested.

"Put him aboard some passing ship," Dr. Gallatin said.

Sam shook his head. "There won't be any passing ships. Since six o'clock we've been out of the steamer lane on this course."

"Go back to the steamer lane," Dr. Gallatin persisted.

Again Sam shook his head, with firmness. "We'd wait, maybe, a day or two for a ship to come along. We can't afford it."

RUFE RETURNED with a bottle of Bourbon and a small glass. The stowaway shakily poured himself a drink and drank it. He poured himself another.

Sam, Dr. Gallatin, and Tony Wingate discussed the problem in Sam's cabin. Much as they all objected to having the stowaway, there seemed to be no humane way of disposing of him.

"There'll be plenty of hard work to do on this ship," Sam said finally, "and plenty of hard work on the island. We can use an extra hand."

"He must, of course," Dr. Gallatin interjected, "be told nothing of the gold at Yin. And are you quite sure, captain, that the crew has no inkling of it?"

"Dead sure," Sam answered. "They understand that we're going there for pottery and old statues."

Dr. Gallatin was worried on this point. He mentioned that too many crews of treasure-hunting ships had mutinied and murdered their officers when the gold was found.

"There's no reason," Sam said, "why we can't keep it secret from them all, including this stowaway, even when we've got it aboard. It's simply up to us to keep our mouths shut."

"I'll speak to Rufe," Tony Wingate said grimly.

So the stowaway was added to that small, strange company.

His name proved to be Dudley Mallory. He was a New Yorker, and evidently used to wealth and all that went with it. He confessed that he had been a playboy since he was old enough to know the difference between play and work. As long as he did not have to work, he preferred to play, and he had apparently done a very thorough job of it. Most of his days, he admitted, had been spent sleeping off the effects of misspent nights.

"My only claim to distinction," he confessed, "is that I know the head waiter in every New York night club by his first name. I also know how to make eighty-seven different cocktails."

When he had sobered up and had learned the purpose of the expedition, he was delighted, he said, that he had missed the Queen of Asia.

"My aunt will worry," he said. "All my life I've been a thorn in her side, but maybe this will make a man of me. Put me to work, Sam. Don't stowaways have to chip the rust from the anchor chains? It has a familiar ring. The ne'er-do-well ships before the mast, and the blood mate—is Rufe a blood mate, Sam?—kicks the stuffing out of him, and at the end of the voyage the ne'er-do-well is hard and tough and clean of heart and never goes back to his old dissolute habits. So make me scrub a deck!"

Sam didn't make him scrub the deck, but he let him do odd jobs. And he kept the ship's liquor supply locked.

The evening of the stowaway's discovery aboard Rufe said to Sam, "I don't like that guy. He's too fresh. I think I met him in New York once. Or mebby it was in Hollywood. Anyway, we were out on a kind of a party. It seems to me he stole the girl I had."

"You weren't plastered, were you, by any chance?" Joyce asked.

"Mebby," Rufe said thoughtfully, "it was Detroit, Michigan. I'll have to ask him."

JOYCE AND Tony Wingate had another quarrel that evening. They were, it seemed to Sam, always disagreeing about something. It was hard for one or the other to make a statement without the other promptly dissenting.

Sam was puzzled. He liked them both. Joyce was a happy, fun-loving girl who laughed and joked most of the time. Tony proved, on closer acquaintance, to be all that Sam had expected of him. His adventures had made Tony pretty hard, at least on the surface. But he was always cheerful. He never boasted or expressed violent opinions except when Joyce aroused him.

Their clashes were always about archeology. On this subject they disagreed constantly, and, strangely enough, their disagreements often placed Joyce and her father on the same side of the fence, opposing the arguments of the tall, thin, weather-browned young man.

When these heated debates started, no quarter was asked or given. Tony would pump arguments at father and daughter with the rapidity and violence of machine gun bullets. The battles raged far into the night.

It began to look as if Sam's first guess was wrong, as if it wasn't, after all, a case of love at first sight between the tall, dark young archeologist excavator and the slim and pretty archeologist's daughter.

Sam once said to Tony, dryly, "You seem to like that girl an awful lot, fellow."

"That stubborn little dumb-bell?" Tony cried indignantly.

"She's no dumb-bell, Tony."

"Well, she's stubborn."

Questioned on the subject, Joyce said:

"I don't have to be a man-hater to hate him, Sam. Why, I could cheerfully murder that hateful, conceited creature!"

"He isn't conceited, Joyce," Sam argued.

"Well, he's hateful," she growled.

That evening Sam learned that Joyce's man-hating instincts were capable of being lulled on occasion. After a spell at the wheel after supper, he walked forward to see that everything was shipshape. He heard the murmur of voices in the bow, and he could not help overhearing a snatch of conversation.

The stowaway and Joyce were standing close together at the rail, looking out over the boulevard of moonlight, and Dud was saying, "Of course I'm worthless. But I have lots of fun. Join up with me and see the world. Why marry some stuffy professor?"

"Well," Joyce answered merrily, "I do prefer archeology to your calling, and I'd honestly prefer to share archeology with some man than a lifetime of mixed drinks."

"There's nothing for me to do," Dud said in a tone of mock sadness, "but become an archeologist. Will you teach me how, Joyce?"

THEY BOTH began to laugh. Sam turned about and went aft. It was none of his business, but he felt a little uneasy. Joyce had told him a good deal about her life on this archeological expedition and that. She had spent most of her life away from cities, and most of it in the company of a pretty serious-minded lot of men. Archeologists were usually good fellows, but their minds were generally on musty old ruins.

He assumed that Dudley must be a brand new experience to Joyce, with his frivolous viewpoint, his lack of serious interest in any weighty subject. Sam also knew that a girl, unless she was pretty hard-shelled, might be hurt if she played along too far with a fellow of Dudley Mallory's type. She wasn't hardshelled. She was spunky, but under her spunk was the innocence of a child.

Her fiery quarrels with Tony became less and less frequent as the voyage went on, and she spent more and more time gayly enjoying herself with the frivolous young man who had missed his ship.

Dud's presence was, in a way, welcome enough. Sam didn't care much for the violent arguments Tony, Joyce, and Dr. Gallatin had. When Joyce paired off with Dudley, it left Dr. Gallatin and Tony oftener together. They argued, but not violently. Their arguments consisted largely of drawing diagrams and of quoting books.

All in all, it was a smooth voyage. Simbi, who was fat and cheerful and well experienced, was a capable *serang;* Lakka was an efficient and obedient hand; and Wong was an excellent cook—a jolly Chinese who was always inventing strange and tasty desserts.

Rufe could not overcome his original dislike of the stowaway, and Sam sometimes suspected the shovel man of being a little jealous. Rufe continued to insist that Dudley had stolen a girl of his at a party somewhere.

At intervals throughout the voyage, Rufe would approach Dudley with an anxious frown and speak somewhat in this fashion:

"Dud, I know dog-goned well I've met you at a party somewheres. Was it in Duluth, Minnesota?"

"No, Rufus!"

"New Orleans?"

"No, Rufus!"

"By gosh, I'll get it yet."

Sam once suggested, "Try him on Timbuctoo and Kalamazoo, Rufe; they are pretty far apart."

Rufe, like all men of his type, hated being kidded. He was still suspicious of Sam. Although he never again accused Sam of stealing his locket, with a lock of his girl's hair in it, it was evident that the thought sometimes entered his mind, and when Sam kidded him Rufe would remind every one within hearing that anybody who could break out of jails as easily as Sam Shay could not be a very honest man.

It was a swift and uneventful voyage, although Sam would look back on it with a certain amazement.

CHAPTER X

TREASURE HUNT

THE BLUE GOOSE passed through the narrow opening of the horseshoe-shaped reef surrounding the Kusa group one day shortly after noon. They passed many islands and at dusk entered the small cove on the eastern side of Yin, and dropped anchor.

From the deck they could easily see either end of the island. It was thickly covered with nipa palms and other tropical vegetation, but there was no indication of human inhabitation. The entire Kusa group, so far as Singapore Sammy knew, was uninhabited. The islands were too small, too mountainous for practical purposes, and they were in the direct path of the savage hurricanes which swept up through the Arafura Sea from the southwest.

Both Tony and Dr. Gallatin were agreed that Yin would show them—if they could just find that treasure trove—a civilization quite as ancient as the Mayan.

"We are apt to find what Cortez found when he conquered Mexico," Tony told Sam; "that this ancient race knew nothing of the value of gold. To the Mayans gold was nothing but a soft, easily worked metal. They even used it for garden tools."

In the fading light Dr. Gallatin excitedly studied the island through binoculars. Yin was lower than any of the near-by islands, but there was a long eminence in the middle, a long, natural plateau, and on this, Tony believed, they would find the ruins of that ancient, forgotten culture.

Immediately after breakfast next morning every one aboard

but Wong went ashore to begin the treasure hunt. And Rufe took with him two of the stout screened boxes he had brought along for collecting poisonous snakes. Tony had said that Yin was a likely looking place for coral snakes and larger members of the cobra family. He expected to find on Yin hamadryads—bull cobras—the most dangerous snake that squirms or wriggles.

Studying the surrounding islands as they went ashore in the big longboat, Sam felt very contented. He loved any deserted island, and he looked forward to the excitement this one promised. A million in gold artifacts!

The rest of them shared his excitement. Even Tony, who generally kept himself pretty well under control, had a gleam in his eyes and a darker flush in his lean, dark cheeks.

Of them all, Joyce was the most striking. Sam had never before seen Joyce in her field outfit. It consisted of a khaki blouse, khaki shorts, and low lace boots. He had never noticed before what pretty legs she had. It occurred to him that, much as he liked Tony, the tall thin man was a damned fool to have wasted so much time quarreling with this slimly delicious young woman.

Going ashore, she sat with Dudley, and when they fell to work hacking a path through the jungle toward the little plateau, she and Dudley worked together, and they lunched together. Tony and Dr. Gallatin spent the lunch hour quarreling over the influence of the Mayas on the civilization of the ancient Aztecs.

Once the path was finished, Tony automatically took charge of the expedition's efforts. And Tony went about his job of finding the ancient treasure with an engineer's thoroughness. It was, to Sam, fascinating business. Tony's guess that the old city had once occupied the plateau proved correct.

OVERGROWN BY the jungle, surrounding a plaza, or square, were the ruins of many buildings, some only scattered heaps of masonry. Here and there a stone column still stood. The winds had partly covered these fallen buildings with soil, and the jungle had crept in and grown over the wreckage of the ancient city.

All of Tony's guesses proved correct. But they were not guesses. He had tackled too many ancient ruins to be misled by hunches. His theories were all based on experience. When Tony said, "That old crater over there was once their community house, and it must have been all of sixty feet high," Tony was not guessing. Some of the buildings, he explained, had had great underground rooms, so that, in collapsing, they had left craters full of broken masonry.

There were also eleven wells, beautifully built, some with collapsed sides but a few in excellent condition. Inspecting these with great interest, Tony said it was evident that the prehistoric people had been wonderful masons.

Every depression, every ridge in the plateau where the little city had stood, told Tony its story in a way that made Sam marvel. Actually, Tony was a modern detective at work in the realm of antiquity.

He found the remains of three great buildings and a burial ground where the 1856 expedition had done extensive excavating. But where they had hidden the treasures they had found remained a mystery. Tony had Rufe dig here and there; but their efforts revealed nothing.

When Tony did not need him, Rufe was busy with affairs of his own. He spent his time in the jungle with a snake stick. He had wonderful luck. In one day he captured a dozen coral snakes and three full-grown bull cobras.

And on the day which marked the end of their second week on Yin, Tony suddenly announced, as they were filing up the path they had hewn through the jungle from the beach to the plateau, "We have overlooked something! The tunnel!" He was excited.

Sam drawled, "What tunnel?"

"There's bound to be a tunnel under one end of the city!"

"I'll be damned if I see why."

"I think," Tony said, "you'll find it in the well at the far end of the plaza."

He tried to explain it. He couldn't explain it in terms that Sam understood. At the far end of the old plaza was a well perhaps sixty feet deep, round in shape—a splendid example of prehistoric masonry. It was, of course, choked with weeds. In the very bottom of it a jackfruit tree now grew.

They had all looked down the well Rufe had, in fact, been lowered into it by Lakka, the deck hand, in his tireless search for poisonous snakes.

Tony said, "There are far too many paths leading to that well for ordinary purposes. There are too many other wells just as easy of access as that one. A tunnel would be the quickest way for the population to move from one side of the island to the other, in case of warfare. It's logical."

Sam was still unconvinced, but he gave the orders for Simbi and Lakka to return to the schooner for heavy tackle.

"Rig it to haul up heavy masonry," Tony requested; and Sam saw that this was done.

WHEN THE tackle was rigged, Tony, in a bosun's chair, swung out over the weed-grown well at the end of a short, stout boom, and was lowered on the end of a rope by a low-gear hand hoist.

He took a crowbar with him. After a half hour of picking here and there, he let out a yell and ordered himself hoisted. His lean, dark face was flushed with excitement.

"It's there!" he proclaimed.

"The treasure?" Joyce cried. "The gold?"

"Treasure?" Dudley Mallory echoed. "What gold?"

Joyce hesitated, and said, "You might as well know. Yes. A gold treasure. No one was supposed to tell you."

"Your secret is safe with me," Dudley laughed. "I'll promise not to breathe it to a soul. Gold! Hey-hey!"

Tony had found the tunnel. He reported:

"It's about twenty feet from the bottom of the well. I think we'll find the other end without trouble."

But Tony did not find the western end of the tunnel, the existence of which he had so amazingly guessed, until almost night-fall. The slope of the plateau on the western side was completely covered with bushes and trees.

It was necessary to send to the schooner for a surveyor's transit. Among Tony's accomplishments—necessary to an archeological excavator—was that of surveying.

He ran a line due east from the center of the well, and told Sam and Rufe where to dig, approximately five hundred feet from the well. And after about an hour of feverish digging they broke through the dirt and rubble into an opening that gave off a breath of foul, damp imprisoned air.

A catastrophe was narrowly missed. Sam's pick had gone clean through the sudden opening. Earth and loose masonry fell away from the steep slope. Muffled sounds of these objects falling a considerable depth were given back with the sour smell of mold and dead air. Sam almost fell through this opening.

He sprang back and yelled, "It's a deep hole!"

It was now almost too dark to see, and the moon was just rising. Tony secured a flashlight and investigated. He reported that a flight of steps had at one time run down to the level of the tunnel, but that the steps were gone, rotted away, and that the drop into the tunnel was now almost sheer to a depth of about thirty feet.

"We'll have to go in at the other end," he announced.

The next morning they began. The men took turns, seated in the bosun's chair, picking away at the false wall of the well which covered the tunnel opening. Masonry had been cunningly fitted into place by the members of the 1856 expedition, perfectly matching the wall of the well.

In an hour a hole large enough for a man to crawl through had been picked out. A strong wind blew through the tunnel, clearing it of the foul air imprisoned there—if Tony's theory was correct—since 1856, when that ill-fated expedition had employed it for hiding an amazing archeological treasure.

But Tony would let no one enter the tunnel until the bad air was all blown out by the stiff sea breeze. And he insisted that Dr. Gallatin have the honor of being the first man to enter the tunnel.

So excited that he almost fell out of the bosun's chair as he was swung out over the well, Dr. Gallatin was lowered. Tony went next, followed by Joyce, Sam, and Dudley.

DR. GALLATIN was shouting like a madman when Sam's turn came to be lowered. The eminent archeologist was, by far the most excited of the lot of them. He had come upon the treasure, under a few inches of debris, within thirty feet of the mouth of the tunnel. And in the course of his twenty-six years Sammy had never seen a man so hysterically excited.

And for the first time since that remarkable quest had been mentioned to him, Sam lost his skepticism. He had actually not taken much stock in that story. He had heard too many treasure stories, and had gone treasure-hunting himself too often with bitterly disappointing results. But there was no denying what his eyes saw in that gloomy tunnel with its fungus-whitened walls and mossy ceiling.

All of the gold the 1856 expedition had found lay in a mound. When Sam slipped out of the bosun's seat and entered the tunnel, Dr. Gallatin was on hands and knees, clawing into the mound with the wildness of a man who has gone completely mad.

The old man was making yelping and growling sounds. He did not bother to clear off the accumulated layer of dirt and broken stones, but was plunging his hands into the mound, dragging out objects of fine yellow gold, and making these hysterical, animal-like sounds.

Sammy watched him somewhat cynically. The old man had told him emphatically that, while the rest of the world might be greedy about the yellow metal, to him, an archeologist, it was of no more importance than a fine old piece of pottery, or a well-preserved mummy.

Just beyond the pile, Sammy could see a great array of pottery and other items, none of which was gold. And he observed that Dr. Gallatin paid utterly no attention to these. At the sight of all that gold, the archeologist had betrayed that he was, under the skin, as susceptible to the feverish influence of gold treasure as any ordinary man.

But Sammy did not blame him. The sight of all that soft yellow gold was affecting him violently. His heart was hammering.

He was feverishly flushed. Chills of excitement raced up and down his backbone. All he saw was a blur of beautiful, glowing yellow.

Every one was babbling, but no one looked at or heard any one else. No one looked at anything but the heavy golden objects Dr. Gallatin was clawing out of that pile. And the archeologist growled and cursed at any one who came near.

His touch of gold madness would pass, but while it lasted he was not a pleasant spectacle. He clawed out heavy bracelets, anklets, and breastplates of pure gold. Some were studded with precious and semi-precious gems, and some were not. He clawed out heavy golden chalices, plates, and bowls. There were chains of gold almost too heavy for a man to lift. There were lamps similar to those found in Egyptian tombs. There were strange implements and objects which had no name. In this pile, valued at a million dollars, there was, indeed, an object for every use to which a prehistoric people could have put that rare metal.

DR. GALLATIN'S passion presently spent itself, leaving him faint and shaky. As if ashamed of having displayed that vulgar interest in gold, he made a pretense of examining the pottery and stone carvings piled up beyond.

But his interest was not in pottery or carved stone. Again and again his eyes strayed back to the great mound of gold.

He said presently, "Captain, this must be boxed and loaded as quickly as possible. Now that it's found, we must waste no time."

Sam appreciated this. He had been on gold hunts before, one or two of them successful, but not on such a scale as this. He knew what effect the finding of gold had on those who found it. Irritations and suspicions developed. There was a feverish excitement in the air, and all these symptoms were trouble symptoms.

Now that the gold was found, he again became the boss of the expedition. He emphasized what they had collectively agreed upon before leaving Soerabaya: the crew must not learn of the gold. The crew must believe that the boxes, as they came aboard and were stowed, contained nothing but pottery.

Dudley Mallory, now that he had been admitted to the secret, took it calmly. And he was willing to do anything Sam wanted of him.

Sam wanted speed. He had secured, in Soerabaya a number of small strong wooden boxes for packing the gold if it should be found. Perhaps optimistically, these boxes had been brought ashore a few at a time by the landing parties, and stacked in the bushes near the beach.

He distributed the necessary work of carrying the boxes up from the beach, bringing heavy lumber and tools from the schooner. While Dr. Gallatin boxed the gold—and he would permit no one else to assist him—Sam and the others built a stout platform at the mouth of the tunnel, and a ladder in sections for climbing into and out of the well. The upper section was detachable, so that it could be removed when the hoist was in operation. All this went forward speedily. By the time Dr. Gallatin had the gold boxed, the platform and the ladder were finished, and the hoist was strengthened.

Sam attended to other details. He saw to it that loaded rifles were placed in the tunnel and near the hoist in case unexpected trouble should happen. He anticipated no trouble. He kept a wary eye on all horizons for steamer smoke, but the Kusa Archipelago was so far from steamer lanes that this precaution was hardly necessary.

He was sure he had put all trouble behind.

The work of hoisting the boxed gold artifacts to the top of the well and transporting the heavy boxes to the beach was begun late in the afternoon following the discovery of the treasure.

There were, in all, twenty-seven boxes of gold, each containing about thirty-seven thousand dollars worth of the metal—as much as a man could lift and carry.

Dr. Gallatin and Tony stationed themselves in the tunnel, to drag the boxes to the platform; Sam stayed on the platform to rope up each box; Joyce and Dudley were at the hoist; and Simbi, Lakka, and Rufe carried the boxes to the beach.

IT WAS a well organized little crew, and it worked like a machine. When darkness fell, more than half the gold had been transferred from tunnel to beach. By the time they had finished a hasty supper the moon was up. It would be up all night.

Twenty of the twenty-seven boxes had been hoisted when an incident occurred which gave to the entire situation a new complexion. It came near to being the final incident in Singapore Sammy's life of adventure.

He was on the loading platform at the mouth of the tunnel, fastening the end of the rope about each box as Tony dragged it out to be hoisted. When the box was halfway up the well, something happened to the hoist. There was no shout of warning from above. Sammy, in fact, had no warning but the faint whirring sound of a pulley as rope under strain ran out. He had time only to step quickly aside, not time enough to jump back into the tunnel, when the heavy box crashed on the platform where he had been standing.

Strong as the platform was, it was not strong enough for that impact. With a splintering crash the platform gave way, carrying Sam and the box of gold with it.

Platform, man, and box fell the twenty-odd feet to the bottom of the well, with the man, fortunately, on top. The wind was knocked out of him. He was badly bruised about his left hip, and one elbow was raked to the bone by the swift passage past the rough masonry. But he was not, miraculously, killed. And he miraculously broke no bones.

There were shouts of anxious inquiry.

Joyce's voice shrieked, "Sammy! Are you hurt?"

He could speak now. "I'm all right," he said. "Hoist out this box and then send me the rope." The box, he had ascertained, had not been broken.

When the box had been hauled out, the rope was sent down and Sammy made it fast about himself, under his arms.

He was hoisted to the top. Joyce and Dudley were there. Sam's elbow was bleeding rather badly. Joyce bound it up with a handkerchief.

He felt shaken, and he was angry. "Who was working the hoist?"

"I was," Dudley said. "Sam, I can't tell you how sorry—"

"Stow it," Sam said curtly. "Where is Rufe?"

"He and Lakka and Simbi haven't come back from the beach," Dudley answered. "Sam, I'm terribly sorry, but the damned thing just seemed to slip out of my hands."

"Forget it."

"How about the platform?"

"We'll have to get along without it. We're almost through."

He did not believe definitely that the fashionable stowaway had let that box drop on purpose, yet—

Dudley Mallory was an unknown quantity. He had always been unknown. Sam had taken his story with a grain of salt. He did not believe it, and he did not disbelieve it. He did not know what Dud's game could possibly be, if that handsome young man was not all that he claimed to be. He only knew that Dud had left himself open to suspicion.

Joyce had sensed his suspicions in the manner in which he had talked to Dudley. Her sympathy for Sam's accident entirely ceased when she saw what his attitude was.

She was white with anger. She said spiritedly:

"It isn't like you, Sam, to intimate such things."

"What things?"

"That Dudley might have done it purposely."

He looked into her indignantly glowing eyes for perhaps ten seconds. And he wondered if what he had been hoping would not happen had definitely happened. She was in love with the fashionable stowaway—or wasn't she?

DUDLEY WAS still standing at the hoist, somewhat pale himself, looking apologetic. At this moment Rufe came up the path from the beach. He took in the tableau with his small, piggy eyes. He said nothing for a while.

He looked down the well, then he looked at Sam, and said, "You didn't get hurt bad, did you?"

"No," Sam said.

"Dud was on the hoist, huh?"

Dud said quietly, "Yes, I was on the hoist."

Rufe looked at him. The shovel man's sandy eyebrows were puckered, and there was a deep groove between his small, piglike eyes.

"Say!" Rufe said. "Say! Something is all of a sudden coming over me."

Dudley chuckled. "Is it measles?"

Something in the shovel man's attitude caused Sam and Joyce to stare at the pale, grinning face of Dudley, quite well lighted by the tropical moon.

"It's where I met you," Rufe labored on. "I know I met you somewhere, and I almost know where it was."

Dudley laughed softly. "Rufe, we have got to get the gold out of this hole. Let's play this game later. If you strain your mind now, you're apt to break down when we need you most."

Rufe gave a grunt. He whipped a flashlight out of his pocket. With his free hand he reached up, deliberately grasped a small handful of Dudley's hair—and yanked it out.

The stowaway yelped with the unexpected pain, and Rufe held the handful of dark hair against the lens of his pocket light.

"Sam!" he shouted. "It's blond! He's dyed it! The roots are blond! This is the guy!"

"Are you crazy, Rufe?" Dudley said indignantly. "What are you yapping about?"

Still Rufe stared, with that stupid expression, at the stowaway's face. "Sam," he panted, "this is the guy who told me you stole my locket! In Hat Gow's ginmill! In Buru-Waru!"

"Dudley!" Joyce wailed.

But Dudley was not there. Possibly he did not even hear the girl's cry of pain and protest. He was running. He was running down the path toward the beach as if the devil were at his heels.

CHAPTER XI

TREACHERY

SAM STARTED AFTER the stowaway, but Rufe was well ahead of Sam, overtaking Mallory. He saw Rufe go through the air in a flying tackle. Rufe's great, boom-like arms wrapped themselves about the flying legs of the fugitive, and Dudley Mallory sprawled, crashing to the ground.

He started to scramble up as Sam limped to the scene and, in a murderous fury, Rufe struck the stowaway on the jaw, knocking him back to earth again half-conscious.

Rufe was seated on the stowaway's chest, puffing, when Sam reached them.

"This is the guy, Sam!" Rufe panted. "This certainly is the guy! If I hadn't been so plastered that morning in Buru-Waru, I'd have recognized him the minute he showed up on the schooner! Only he didn't look like this. He was tricked out like a beachcomber."

Staring down at the glazed eyes of the half-conscious man, Sam realized, to his amazement, just who this man who called himself Dudley Mallory was. He did not know his name, but he knew he was the man who had stolen his schooner and murdered his old *serang* and cook. His first wave of amazement and fury passed. His mind leaped to the terrifying possibilities that this revealment opened up.

"Let him up. Don't let go of him," Sam said. "And get to hell away from me!" This last was addressed to Angel Face. The dog had followed Sam down the path, snapping at his heels all the way.

Rufe unseated himself from the suspect's chest, but held him firmly by an arm as the man got slowly and painfully to his feet. He said, panting, "You fellows have made a great mistake. You're as wrong as usual, Rufe. I never saw you in Buru-Waru. Sam—"

"You're a liar," Rufe said.

"Hold him!" Sam shouted.

But it was too late. As quickly as a cornered snake moves, Angel Face had charged at Rufe's nearest ankle, sinking his teeth into it.

With a yelp of pain, Rufe relaxed his hold for a moment. The stowaway darted behind Rufe, gave him a push which threw him off balance—and dived into the thick undergrowth. He vanished as swiftly, as completely, in that split second as a drop of rain water vanishes into the ocean.

Sam shouted, "Sic 'm, Angel Face!" But the dog did not know that simple command. Instead of following the stowaway, he came at Sam with savage barks and growls. And Sam was busy for the next few seconds defending his ankles.

Rufe had plunged into the jungle, but he soon returned. Sam listened. There was no sound. And Sam knew, from this, that Dudley Mallory, whoever he was in actuality, knew his way about the jungle—was no doubt one of the most slippery and cleverest crooks in this part of the world.

The handy man was almost sobbing with disappointment. He had wanted to kill Dudley Mallory with his bare hands, at least to choke out of him the secret of the stolen locket.

AS THE two frustrated men stood in the path, discussing it, there was a sudden sound like savagely torn canvas, and a bullet went through Sam's red hair, passing so close to the scalp that he could feel the wind of it. He was not wearing a revolver, nor was Rufe.

The two men ran back to the hoist, where Joyce was huddled

The cobras had done a thorough job

down, sobbing hysterically. The two rifles that had been near the hoist had vanished.

Sam shouted down the well: "Tony! Doc! Come up quick and bring rifles! That stowaway has double crossed us!"

Rufe hooked the detachable upper section of the ladder into place, and Joyce came to her knees, panting, "Sam! What is it? What does it mean?"

Sam did not answer her. Even now, he hated to voice the full possibilities of what it might mean. It might mean that every one of them would be cold-bloodedly killed.

Dr. Gallatin and Tony came swarming up the ladder, each with a rifle.

With that sound like savagely torn canvas, two bullets ripped past, and Sam verified at least a part of his dismaying suspicion, for the bullets had come from different directions, which meant, of course, that the man who had called himself Dudley Mallory was not alone in this treachery. More than that, it meant to Sam that the man with the amber eyes had coolly planned all of this, and was prepared to execute it ruthlessly. As far back as that morning at Buru-Waru, he had been cleverly, slyly building his plans for this.

A third bullet struck the heavy iron handle of the hoist and, ricocheting, went screaming away.

Not more than a hundred feet away was a crater-like depression where one of the ancient Yin temples had stood. With little ceremony, Sam hustled the bewildered archeologist, the hysterical girl, the stupefied shovel man and Tony into it. He thanked God for Tony. Rufe was courageous but dumb. But Tony was a man on whom you could pin your hopes for intelligent and fearless aid in a crisis like this.

Sam told them to crouch down, to say nothing. He had executed the maneuver so swiftly that he was sure the stowaway and his aid or aids had not seen where they had gone. The hoist at the well, where they had been standing, was in an exposed clearing, but from there to the crater they had been concealed by the jungle.

Once Sam determined where the enemy was, his plan was to instruct the others to slip out over the back wall to the beach, encircle the island where the small boats were, and to escape to the schooner. He would stay behind. With one of the rifles, he could hold the enemy off until Tony and Rufe, armed with rifles from the arms locker, could come ashore and possibly rescue him.

To execute this plan, it was necessary, first of all, that their enemy have no definite idea of their whereabouts.

He whispered: "Be absolutely quiet. No arguing!" And he proposed his scheme.

At that moment, his scheme was, at least in part, ruined by the sudden appearance of Angel Face. The dog came waddling into their hiding place and at once began to bark furiously. Sam reached out with the intention of smothering the barks, but the dog was too quick for him. It leaped at his outstretched hand, savagely bit one of his fingers, backed off, and continued to bark.

IN THE midst of this sudden uproar, Sam, peeking through a chink in the eastern wall, saw four dark figures flittering toward him with rifles. The leader he recognized as their stowaway. Behind him in the moonlight ran Wong, and next came Simbi, and, lastly, Lakka, the deck boy. Thus were his suspicions clinched.

Sam snatched up one of the rifles. He aimed quickly at the foremost man and fired. Dudley Mallory did not fall, but the bullet must have passed close to him, for he suddenly veered and dropped down into a crater about two hundred feet away, similar to the one Sam and the others were in.

Sam aimed and fired again. This time, there was no roar, only a hard click. There were no shells in the magazine!

He snatched up the other rifle, aimed it at Lakka, just as the Fiji Island boy jumped into the crater with the others. There was another click. Sam swiftly worked the loading mechanism. There were no shells at all in that rifle! Somehow, their stowaway had found a chance to remove all the shells but that one!

In short, they were unarmed and cornered by four men who had no plan but to exterminate the five of them as speedily as possible!

But the four men in the crater apparently had not heard those futile clicks as the firing pins shot home into empty firing chambers, or they would certainly not have hesitated. And it was evident that Mallory, in spite of his careful job in removing the shells, was not certain that they were without weapons. He was simply taking no chances. Actually, it wasn't necessary. He had Sam and his small band just where he wanted them.

As Sam put down the second useless rifle, Joyce panted: "Sam! Sam! Stop Tony!"

Tony, on hands and knees, was crawling toward the back wall of the little crater. He turned and said, "Your scheme's all wet now, fellow. There won't be as much as a cap pistol in your arms locker. I've got an idea. Bluff him off—and fast-talk him!"

With which the tall thin young man slipped out over the back wall and vanished.

Joyce panted, "What does he mean?"

Sam was too busy thinking to answer. Tony was smart. Tony's idea must be a good one. But it evidently did not strike Dr. Gallatin in that light. He had overcome his first bewilderment and terror at this sudden treachery of the stowaway and the crew. He became, suddenly, a wrathful old man. He accused Sammy of negligence for not having anticipated this. Sammy said nothing. But when the snarling old fellow declared that Tony had shown the white feather, had slipped out to safety, leaving the rest of them to the mercy of those cutthroats, Sam lost his own temper.

"Pipe down," he said softly. "They can hear every word. Tony never showed a white feather in his life. He isn't that kind."

Rufe, too, was angry at Dr. Gallatin's accusations. Never had he addressed the archeologist in tones that were not respectful. Now he said, "Bottle it, you old fool! If that gang knows Tony's gone, we're nothin' but crab fodder!"

The old man subsided, and Sam heard the buzz of voices from the crater across the way. He heard, in the sharp voice of Simbi, in Malay, the phrase, "and the girl—" and knew what that meant. For Sam recalled the manner, several times during the voyage, in which not only Simbi and Lakka but even Wong had stared at Joyce. He was aware that white girls are curiosities to men of these races, but it occurred to him now how deliberate their stares had been. Even then, they had been doubtless discussing which of them should possess the white girl.

Certainly, their plan was to kill Sam, Rufe, Tony and Dr. Gallatin at once. They would not kill Joyce until such time as they must—presumably, just before they reached civilization.

The prospect of her falling into such hands was suddenly more horrifying to Sam than the prospect of losing his own life.

SOME MINUTES had passed since Tony had slipped away, unseen by the enemy. Whatever his plan was, it would take him some time to execute it, but Sam thought that enough time had passed.

He called, in a voice which he forced to be amiable: "Hey, Dudley! If you want to make a proposition, we may be interested."

There followed a long silence in the crater across the way.

Then their stowaway said mockingly, "Step right into my office, Mr. Shay!"

"I'll sit tight, thanks," Sam answered, "and I'll shoot the first white, yellow or brown man who makes a move I can see. The trouble is, Dud, you haven't got us on a spot."

"No?" was the jeering answer. "Well, let's pretend it's a spot, anyway."

"To get out of here clean," Sam said persuasively, "you're going to have a lot of explaining to do. That is, if you figure on killing all of us."

"Stop putting ideas into my head," the stowaway laughed.

"You're going to have a job explaining the Goose," Sam went on leisurely. "Don't forget, I've got a pack of friends in this part of the world. You might even have to explain where we all are."

There was a period of silence. "Pardon me," the stowaway said presently. "I was laughing."

"Don't you want to make a deal?" Sam asked in a patient voice.

"I don't have to make a deal," was the cheerful answer.

"Talk it over with your boy friends," Sam suggested. "Dr. Gallatin is willing to go fifty-fifty with that gold and keep his mouth shut."

The archeologist started to protest, but Rufe placed his hand roughly over the old roan's mouth.

"By this time tomorrow night, after a day without water," the man across the way answered, "you may be willing to make an even more generous proposition."

"Well," Sam said, "supposing you make one."

"All right! If the five of you will come out with your hands up, we'll have a nice, cozy little chat."

"Would you promise not to shoot?"

"Of course I'll promise!"

"We hesitate," Sam said, "only because a burned child dreads the flame. You double crossed us once, Dudley."

Their stowaway laughed. Joyce began softly to whimper. Sam did not blame her. It was a blood-chilling laugh. If it were possible for a man's laughter to contain the note of murder, then that was what Joyce heard in the stowaway's laughter. Just as coolly and deliberately as he had murdered Sam's old cook and *serang,* that man would kill Sam, Rufe, Tony and Dr. Gallatin. And, later, when it suited his convenience, he would as cold-blood-edly murder Joyce.

IT SEEMED to be in the very air of that warm, moonlit trop-ical evening. From somewhere, Joyce had secured a small knife. Sam saw it glitter in the moonlight. She held it firmly in her right hand, the blade pointing inward.

He whispered hastily, "Don't, Joyce! Give Tony a chance!"

She had stopped weeping. Her enormous eyes in her white face stared at him. She said, "You know I didn't love that man."

"I know, Joyce."

"It's Tony. It's always been Tony! Oh, Sam—" She stopped. Their stowaway had begun talking again.

"You might as well come out, all five of you," he said. "It's going to be pretty hot there tomorrow. You haven't any water. You're going to be pretty thirsty."

"You wouldn't let us die of thirst, would you?" Sam asked.

"Well, what do you think?"

"I'm afraid you would."

"I'm afraid you're right, Sam. There isn't any proposition to discuss. I am a merciful man, but my men haven't much of the milk of human kindness. They want to kill all five of you—*now.* Simbi is getting ready to run amuck. He has a bolero he wants to cut your head off with. And Lakka and Wong are thirsting for blood, too. Come out and take it like brave people! We've got you. We're going to kill you in the end! Why prolong the agony? That's the only proposition I can make to you, Sam."

"Hasn't it occurred to you," Sam said mildly, "that you may get just as thirsty tomorrow as we will? The first man who sticks his head up is going to get a rifle bullet through it. Had you overlooked that, Dudley?"

Dudley's voice said jeeringly, "I see I've got to enlighten you on a few minor points."

He doubtless intended to say more. But at that moment, he was interrupted. A scream suddenly ripped the stillness of the tropical night. It was the scream of a man in sudden terror.

At the suddenness and frightfulness of it, Joyce uttered a faint shriek. The scream was joined by others. Men were screaming. The men in the little crater two hundred feet away were screaming with utter terror. And their firearms were blazing.

But at what? The uproar was so sudden, so deafening, that momentarily bewildered Sam. He got to his knees and looked over the wall. He saw men's heads darting about. One at a time, he saw these heads vanish, as if the men were falling. Then one of the men leaped out of the enclosing walls of the ancient ruin and began to run. After him, a tall, thin, familiar figure ran.

Sam leaped out of the crater and ran to the other one. What he saw suddenly locked about his heart an ice-like clamp. Three men lay inert on the floor of the old ruins, and about them long, black, rope-like objects glistened.

Cobras! On the back wall was a snake box. Tony had secured that box from the beach, craftily approached from the rear and emptied the box into the crater!

Three men were lying in attitudes of death, two with their faces upturned to the cold white moonlight, with horrible frozen grimaces about their mouths. The opened and glassy eyes of Wong and Simbi stared at the moon. Lakka lay crumpled on his side.

To Sammy's relief was added incredulity. He had heard that men struck by cobras do not die instantly, unless it is shock that kills them—the shock of the striking fangs plus the certainty that they are doomed to death. These three were certainly dead.

THE MAN who had escaped this neat trap was the stowaway. Behind Sam and Rufe, Joyce said faintly, "What happened, Sam?" She looked into the crater and faintly screamed.

Then the doctor came up and Tony returned from the chase. He said, "He's down there in that bunch of rocks. I want a rifle."

Sam said, "That was clever work, guy."

Joyce cried, "Oh—oh, Tony!"—then restrained herself when Tony looked at her with a strange grin.

Dr. Gallatin failed to see anything remarkable, brave or clever in what Tony Wingate had done. He said, "There's no time to waste, hoisting the rest of that gold and clearing out of this place!"

"With him at large—armed?" Sam asked.

"Can't you get him now?"

"He's in those rocks. It may take time," Tony said.

And Sam added, "One thing at a time, doc. A minute ago, none of us had a chance of seeing the sun come up tomorrow."

Even with their stowaway still at large and a real menace to all their lives, Sam felt tremendously relieved. They would somehow capture or kill the stowaway, then all would be clear sailing. They'd load the gold and, once beyond the great Kusa reef, would shape a course for the nearest port—Macassar. Macassar was less than a day's sail from the reef, if the wind didn't fail them.

He looked toward the southwest, where the wind came from this time of year, and saw dark clouds piled up on that horizon. It might mean a squall.

Dr. Gallatin said impatiently, "Captain, you and Rufe can attend to that scoundrel while Tony and I hoist the remaining boxes of gold."

He had hardly finished when Rufe said, in a strangled voice, "Say! Am I dreamin'? Is that ship there or ain't it there?"

Everyone looked where Rufe was pointing, with a trembling arm, at the cove where the Blue Goose lay at anchor. A small steamer had come in; was slowly swinging about with black smoke greasily pouring from her skinny, raked stack.

In a shaken voice, Sam said, "The Lotus Lady! It's Papeete Pollario!"

"How," Dr. Gallatin said harshly, "did he find his way here? You said you'd sent him a thousand miles away."

"I did," Sam said wearily. He was trying to think. He couldn't think. His brain was a noisy confusion. Suddenly gone was the happy relief of a moment ago. They were trapped now. They were inescapably trapped!

CHAPTER XII

SAM'S INSPIRATION

THOUGHT BEGAN TO emerge from the confusion. Far away, he heard the faint rumble of the Lotus Lady's anchor chain as it was paid out. He glanced hastily at those clouds on the southeastern horizon. There was a hush in the air. It would be at least a squall, perhaps a full hurricane. You never could tell, this time of year.

Tony had hooked a rifle out of the crater with a long stick. He said, "Well, Sam, how are you fixed for inspirations?"

Suddenly Sammy clicked his teeth. He watched the small steamer. A boat was being lowered. It reached the water. Men swarmed down the falls. Even at that distance, Sam could see the glint of moonlight on rifle barrels. There must have been ten or a dozen men.

"Wait a minute, Tony," he said softly.

They watched the boat. Oars appeared. The boat pushed away from the shadow cast on the water by the steamer. Oarsmen began to row the boat briskly toward the schooner.

Sam said nothing until after they had reached the schooner. Men swarmed aboard it, apparently made a brief search, then returned to the rowboat. They now settled down to the long row to shore.

Sam said, "I think I've got an idea. You'll have to help, Tony. It may work. It may not. But it's our only chance. We can't fight off that gang."

He briefly outlined his idea, then said: "Doc, you and Rufe

get busy and hoist up the rest of the gold. Joyce, you can help with the hoist. Tony, in the few minutes you have, see if you can't blast that rat off the face of the earth. When he knows Pollario's here he'll try to contact him—if he does, we're sunk! Tony, you've got to get him!"

Tony said grimly, "I'll get him!" and started toward the rocks where their stowaway was, or had been, hiding, and Sammy started at a trot down the path toward the beach. He was filling in the details of his reckless plan as he went along. He was shooting at the moon now. And he had to hit the moon!

He had only gone a few hundred feet when Tony shouted, "I've got him!" His cry was followed by a shot.

Sam waited a moment, then trotted on. The rowboat full of men was halfway between the schooner and the beach when Sam reached the cove. He went boldly out onto the beach, knowing that Pollario might without hesitation order his men to shoot him down. Instead of a shot came a shout. And it was the hoarse, well-remembered voice of that jolly villain.

"Hi, there! That you, Red?"

"Hi, Papeete! You bet!"

"What luck, pardner?"

"Gold, Papeete! More gold than you ever saw in your life! A million dollars' worth of it, Papeete!"

There was a small roar from the boatload of men, then Papeete said: "Good boy! Don't spend a dime of it till I get there!"

Sammy heard behind him soft, swift footfalls. He turned to see Joyce running toward him. His heart went even colder than it was.

She ran across the beach to him, panting, "Sam! Sam!"

He said angrily, "Oh, Joyce, why did you do this?" He had told her, under no conditions, to let Pollario or any of his men see her.

She panted: "He sent me!"

"Good Lord, why?"

IT WAS a moment before she caught her breath. "Tony didn't catch Dudley! It was a false alarm! Dudley got away!"

"But why did your father send you?"

"He couldn't spare Rufe, he said. He needed Rufe to help hoist the gold."

Sam groaned. "The best thing he does to the women of his family," he said bitterly, "is to throw them to the lions."

Papeete Pollario shouted: "Ain't that a lady with you, Red?"

"Yes, Papeete."

"You ain't gonna try to double cross me this time, are you, Red?"

"No, Papeete."

"That's right, Red," Papeete laughed. "Never try to put over fast ones on Papeete Pollario." And he laughed in a way that made Sam feel cold all over.

Joyce whispered: "He said you had to be warned. If Dudley gets in touch with Pollario somehow—"

"Sh! Not so loud. I know."

He tried to be calm and gentle, but he was boiling with anger. Her father's greed for that gold had led him not only to subject Joyce to the risk she must run with this mob of cutthroats, but to threaten Sam's dangerous and delicate plan.

"He said we must delay Pollario as long as possible. He said I would help delay him."

Sam said nothing. He could not understand any man's willingness to sacrifice his own daughter so heartlessly. His mild dislike for Dr. Gallatin blazed into sudden hatred and contempt. Then the bows of the rowboat scraped on sand, and men were swarming out and dragging the boat up on the beach.

Sam whispered a few hasty instructions to Joyce in the brief seconds that remained. Papeete Pollario was the first to reach dry sand. He carried an automatic rifle in his hands. A holstered revolver suspended from a bullet belt slapped his fat thigh as he strode up the beach. His big red face was oilier than ever, and it was split by that wolfish grin.

He slapped Sam on the back with such heartiness that it drove the wind from the red-headed man's lungs in a gasp. He grinned wolfishly at Joyce, and said "M'am, I'm pleased to make your acquaintance. You must be the perfessor's daughter."

"Yes," Joyce said in a frightened voice.

"I," the square-built, jolly scoundrel roared, "am Papeete Pollario!"

"How do you do, Mr. Pollario?" Joyce said faintly.

"I guess I gotta apologize for bein' so late," Papeete said jovially. "I sorta got off my course, Red. But Papeete Pollario don't stay off'n his course for long. No, sir! Red, you know where I went lookin' for you? To Timor! Can you beat that?"

He laughed with uproarious heartiness. "To Timor!" he boomed. "And here you was all the time! So I back tracked, Red; I back-tracked all the way to Soerabaya, and I found a feller there, a feller name of Wrangle, with a crippled ship, who told me what course you took. So I just come a-snoopin' along the course—and it brought me down to Kusa. When you was talkin' about the island that night, Red, I guess your g'ography must have been a little bit off. Huh?"

"It must have been," Sam laughed. "And I'll tell you why, Papeete. The professor gave me a bum steer myself. He didn't tell me we were coming here until we got under way."

"That so?" Papeete said with interest. "Well, that sure was a piece of bum luck for you, Red!"

One of the men growled: "To hell with this chatter, Papeete. Where's that gold?"

A SUDDEN small roar of men's voices echoed him. Sam had been counting on this. He had been aboard ships when treasure was in the wind. The best-trained crews were demoralized by the very word. He looked at the circle of eyes about him, but he did not have to look at them to know what type they were. They were the scum of East Indian waterfronts.

"Just to look at it," Sam said with excitement, "is enough to drive you crazy. There's a big pile of gold down there—this high! I mean solid gold. There's chains of it and big heavy bracelets and anklets of it. There's more gold in that pile than you ever saw anywhere any time. It looks like the mint!"

"Wait a minute—" Papeete began.

"How can I stop myself?" Sam demanded. "You never saw gold like it—this big mound of soft, yellow gold. It's enough to blind you, all that soft, yellow gold!"

Three of the men shouted simultaneously, "Never mind tellin' us! Where is it?"

Others excitedly ordered him to lead them to it.

Papeete Pollario tried to inject a note of reason into his mounting hysterical excitement.

"Stow it!" he roared. "I don't trust this red-headed guy. He double crossed me once, and no man alive can double cross Papeete Pollario twice."

A short, one-eyed man snarled, "Leave the bleddy blighter till later. Wot we wants is the gold, skipper. I arsks you, where's the gold?"

"Wait a minute!" Papeete bellowed. "It sounds like mutiny to me. No one gives orders over Papeete Pollario's head. Take it easy. Pipe down, you slobs. Let me do the talkin'. Red, where's the rest o' them?"

"The rest of who?"

"The crew! The gang!"

"My crew is dead. There's no one else but Miss Gallatin's father. When he saw you coming, he ran and hid. I don't know where."

"Red, if this is another double cross—"

"Where's the dead crew?" another man asked. "Show him your dead crew, Red, and then show us that gold."

"Who's givin' orders here?" Papeete roared. "I've told you guys, and I tell you again. This red-headed guy is too smart. He fast-talked me into goin' to Timor. Give him a chance, and he'll fast-talk us into hell!"

An irritable and impatient babble answered him. The gist of it was: To hell with all this palavering. Where was that gold?

Papeete could not stem this mounting tide of enthusiasm. But he cannily compromised.

"Let's see that dead crew, Sam. Start walkin'. You and the young lady walk ahead. The first move you make, Red, I warn you, I'll blow you apart!"

The stout cockney cried: "Orl I wants is the bleddy gold. The good old bleddy gold. Where is it, Red?"

"In a tunnel at the bottom of a well—near where the dead men are."

"All right! Show us!"

BUT PAPEETE Pollario stopped and brandished his thick arms. "This red-head is just trickin' you saps. In a tunnel at the bottom of a well! Boloney!"

In a moment of silence, Joyce said swiftly: "Mr. Pollario, Sam is telling the truth. We found the gold in a big tunnel at the bottom of a sixty-foot well. It was hidden there years ago."

"How big is this tunnel?" Papeete asked.

"About eight feet in diameter and I think it's five hundred feet long."

"And where does it go?"

"It dead-ends. It was their secret hiding place."

"It sounds like a trap to me," Papeete said.

"To hell it does!" a man shouted. "Lead us to it!"

Papeete put his hand on the butt of his revolver. "All right. Step lively, Red. You and the lady first. How come your crew is dead?"

"Cobras. There was a mutiny. We slipped up on them and dumped a box of cobras amongst 'em."

"Oh, yeah?" Papeete drawled cynically. "Well, we'll see. How many are there of you left?"

"Just Miss Gallatin, her father and myself."

"And he's hidin' in the jungles, eh?"

"I don't know where he is."

Sam and Joyce crossed the beach to the path and started up it. On their left, as they started, they passed the clump of bushes behind which the bulk of the boxed gold had been cached, but the bushes screened the boxes.

Going up that path, with the girl clinging to his arm for support, Sam felt utterly without hope. His scheme, so ingenious when he had hatched it, now presented a dozen drawbacks. It was too simple to be effective. And he could not depend on Papeete Pollario's singular nature. Papeete was too clever at smelling rats.

Yet he and his men seemed to be tremendously impressed when, reaching the small plateau, Sam led them to the crater in which the three dead men lay. One cobra remained in the crater. It moved sluggishly about, as if it were injured. It inflated its hood and hissed at the newcomers.

Sam wondered, and perspired freely as he did so, where the stowaway was. This was the stowaway's chance to align himself with the new enemy. Had Tony captured or killed him?

Sam wished he knew what had happened. He only hoped that all of the gold was out of that tunnel.

Papeete Pollario stared at the dead men and the snake and suddenly chuckled. "Red," he said, "I thought you was lyin'. All right. Now, where's the perfessor?"

"I told you I don't know."

There was a sudden volley of mutinous comments from the men. The cockney said, "Oh, to 'ell with the perfessor, mates. 'Oo wants to see the gold?"

At the ensuing uproar, Papeete bellowed, "Pipe down!" But they were pretty well out of control. Two men had hold of Sam, each taking an arm; Joyce stayed as close to him as she could.

"Where is it, Red? Show us where it is!"

Papeete's roars went unheeded.

Sam showed them the well and the ladder.

A man started down it. Papeete yanked him back.

"Back up, by God!" he roared angrily. "You're a pack o' saps! This feller is too smart for you! Red! Young lady! You two go down that ladder first!"

Sam, who had been coldly sweating, for fear that Pollario would not give this order, said, "All right, Joyce. I guess you've got to go first."

PAPEETE WAS looking doubtfully down into the blackness of the well. He turned on a pocket electric torch, and sent the beam skipping about. As the rays found the tunnel's mouth, the men shouted.

But Papeete was not to be hurried. "I want six men to stay on top. You, Stubbins; you, Marteen, you, di Paolo, Lin Fang, Arundel, Chin Foo."

The six designated profanely protested. And Sammy was reasonably certain they would desert that post.

Joyce was halfway down the ladder. Sain had not yet started. The men were yelling at him, but he was in no hurry. This was in accordance with his instruction to Joyce. She must descend as quickly as possible, and he must take it slowly.

Someone shouted: "Go on, Red! Snap into it!"

He grinned. "All right, boys, all right. I don't blame you. A million dollars' worth of gold is enough to make any man impatient."

He swung his leg over the ladder and started down. He went down as slowly as he dared. Joyce had disappeared into the tunnel.

Papeete followed Sam down, holding to the ladder with one hand, holding a ready revolver with the other. If there was an ambush down here, he announced, Sam was going to pay for it with the top of his head. And if it was any kind of deception, any kind of a trap, or if Sam was just stringing him along—if the gold wasn't is this tunnel—"You know what'll happen to you, Red? You'll get your fingernails pulled out with pincers. I mean that!"

Sam knew he meant it. Sam knew the chances of his getting out of this corner alive were no better than one in one hundred. He knew that he was probably living the last of his adventures. Papeete Pollario, when he found he'd been tricked, would kill him without mercy.

Reaching the tunnel mouth, Sam hesitated before swinging off the ladder. His heart was racing so fast he could hardly breathe. He listened, but could hear nothing in the tunnel because of the soft roar of excited men's voices above him. Papeete had kept his crew fairly well under control until now, but no crew can be kept under control when treasure is almost within grasping distance. And Sammy was counting on that.

Knowing that the next few seconds would spell life or death for him, Sam swung off the ladder into the dark tunnel. At the far end, moonlight sifting down through the opening they had made glimmered for a moment on an object that seemed to spring straight into the air and disappear. Sammy sucked in a breath of relief. That meant that Joyce, at any rate, was safe.

HE STARTED along the tunnel with Papeete Pollario at his heels. A certain spot midway down Sam's backbone felt numb and raw. It was the spot at which he was sure a bullet from behind would enter him.

The misleadingly jovial voice of the pearl poacher behind him bellowed, "Where is it, Red?"

"Follow me," Sam said steadily, but his heart was thumping like runaway hoofs.

"Where's that girl?"

"She's there ahead."

Papeete flashed on a light. They had reached the great dirt-covered mound of pottery and statues.

"It's down near the end," Sam said. He looked back. At least a half dozen heads bobbed behind Papeete Pollario. And more men were dropping from the ladder and entering the tunnel!

The guards posted above the well were deserting, as Sam had hoped. All were coming down the ladder!

He could not see the men's faces because of the gleaming lenses of their flashlights, which danced about like giant fireflies He looked ahead at the sharp wall of rubble marking the end of the tunnel. The time to act was now, and he must act with unfaltering decision. He was twenty feet from the rope, but he could not see it. Tony had planned to rub it thoroughly with dirt so that it would blend with the same color of the damp rock where the old stairway had been.

Papeete said again, "Where's that girl?"

Sam ignored the question this time. He said sharply, in a voice loud enough to carry above the sounds of scuffling and inquiry: "Here we are, Papeete!"

Papeete sent the beam of his light to the ground, as Sam had counted on his doing. As he did so, Sam suddenly slashed up with his right fist to Papeete's stubbed jaw. He rushed in as the blow smacked home. He seized the suddenly limp man by his belt, hoisted him swiftly into the air—and hurled him at the pack of oncoming treasure-hunters!

In the ensuing seconds, Sam pivoted, ran to the end wall and groped for the rope. He could not find it. Panting, almost sobbing with panic, he fumbled for it again—and found it. He gave it a healthy yank. And he felt, more strongly than ever, that numb, creepy spot in the middle of his backbone.

He heard a strangled roar behind him, then Papeete's agonized voice: "Get him! Grab him! Shoot him!"

Sam held firmly to the rope. He seemed to soar into the air. Below him, as he shot toward the small aperature at the top of the tunnel, men were yelling and shooting. Bullets ricocheted, screaming, from the old masonry walls. Dust sifted into Sam's eyes, blinding him. A sharp burning impact in the muscles of his left arm told him he had been hit by a bullet, but he did not relax his hold on the rope. Next thing, he was through the aperature, and Joyce was seizing him by the shoulders, pulling him away from it.

Tony was fifty feet down the slope, where he had run with the upper end of the rope. Now he dropped the rope and ran toward the hoist at the well. It was deserted. Not one of the Lotus Lady's men had remained! All were in the tunnels—trapped!

Tony grabbed the upper section of the ladder by its top rung, and pulled it out of the well.

The uproar from the men trapped in the tunnel was almost deafening. It would, of course, attract those who remained on the Lotus Lady. Certainly there was no time for delay.

CHAPTER XIII

MADMAN'S END!

TONY HASTILY RECOUNTED what had happened, while Joyce bound up the wound in Sam's arm. Dr. Gallatin and Rufe had had time to hoist all but one box of gold. Reluctantly enough, Dr. Gallatin had abandoned it. But while he and Rufe were carrying the last of the boxes to the beach, Tony had gone down the rope into the tunnel from the other end, made the box fast to the lower end of the rope, then climbed the rope and hoisted the box up. So that not one ounce of gold had been sacrificed!

"Where's that stowaway?"

"He got away. But I think he's wounded!"

With the uproar of the trapped men behind him, the three ran to the beach, the two men carrying the box of gold that Tony had recovered.

They found Rufe on the beach alone. He bad loaded all the gold into the longboat, and would have taken it to the schooner, but he had not known just what to do.

"Where's Dr. Gallatin?" Sam snapped.

"That's what," Rufe panted. "That's why I waited. He went back there."

"Where?" Tony barked.

"To the tunnel—to try to get that last box of gold."

"But Tony got it!" Joyce wailed.

"Well, he didn't know that. Neither did I. I tried to tell him not to go. He wouldn't listen. I think he's nuts. He didn't take the path, either."

Sam said: "Rufe! Tony! We've got to get him! Spread out. Joyce, you stay here. If a boat leaves the Lotus Lady, fire a shot, and we'll come."

Sam was furious. They had been at the point of making good their much-delayed getaway. He was sure he could have bluffed his way past the Lotus Lady, and once again, his plans were ruined.

The three men started off. It was impossible to hear anything but the muffled, strange roaring sound that came from the men trapped in the tunnel.

Sam climbed through the thick undergrowth to an eminence from which he was level with the small plateau. From here he could see the hoist. Beyond the hoist, in the southwest, the clouds he had been watching were piling up. The wind was coming in puffs. If it increased, if that cloud bank covered the moon before he could get the Blue Goose under way, all of his efforts would, once again, have been wasted.

Suddenly he saw a strange figure capering about the hoist. It was the old archeologist. With his strange antics he looked, in the moonlight, like a ghost. He danced to the edge of the well. Sammy shouted a warning. He was certain the old man had finally cracked under all the strain, was out of his mind. Certainly, he knew those men were in the tunnel.

It was useless for Sammy to shout. Dr. Gallatin could not possibly have heard him above that uproar.

Sam saw him bend out over the well. What happened made Sam turn sick and faint. A dozen rifles and revolvers must have been fired simultaneously from the tunnel mouth at the insanely shouting and gesticulating old man.

Dr. Gallatin must have been dead even before he started to collapse. With a feeling of nausea, Sam watched him fall to the edge of the wall, then watched the limp body carom off and vanish.

There was no question that he was dead before he began that sixty-foot fall. There could not be. And as Sam turned about to return to the beach, he heard a shout from Rufe. He supposed that Rufe had seen the tragedy, but Rufe had not. He had, however, come upon Dudley Mallory. This announcement across the night was followed by a rifle shot.

WHEN SAM reached the little clearing where Rufe had surprised the stowaway in the act of aiming a rifle at Sam, Rufe was once again seated on the man's chest.

Sam gasped: "Is he dead?"

Rufe had a sheath knife clasped in one hand. "Not yet," he growled. "But he will be in a minute."

"Don't!" Sam yelled. "He's worth much more alive than dead. There's bound to be a reward on him. I'm taking him to Macassar."

"It's risky, Red," the shovel man pleaded. "As sure as hell, he'll start trouble if you get him aboard. He's too smart. Let me cut his lousy throat!"

"No."

Rufe reluctantly unseated himself from the unconscious man's chest. Sam and Rufe carried him to the beach, where Sam at once broke the news to Joyce about her father.

She took it calmly. She did not cry out. Her eyes became enormous. She said, "I wish I could say I'm sorry, but I'm not."

Sam said glumly, "Yeah, and I wish I could say I'm not, but I am. We've got a fighting chance to get out of here. I took the job of getting all of you here and back to civilization. I wanted to make good on it."

"It wasn't your fault. He was out of his mind, Sam."

"Yes, but I wanted to get all of you to Macassar, with your skins on. What's that gang out there been doing?"

Crisply, Joyce reported that there appeared to be activity aboard the steamer, but that no boat had left it.

With their stowaway and the last of the gold aboard, with

Joyce in the stern to give directions, and Sam, Rufe and Tony at the oars, they started, after so many delays, for the schooner. At Sam's suggestion they took a roundabout way. If they rowed along the shore, their movements would be hidden from the steamer to a certain extent by the mangroves which overhung the beach most of the way. Then, when the schooner lay between them and the steamer, they would row in a straight line, always keeping the schooner between them and the Lotus Lady.

This plan was followed. Because of the weight of their cargo, it was a long and arduous row, made additionally difficult by the freshening puffs of the coming blow.

Angel Face, who had come waddling along the beach as they were about to push off, had been taken aboard by Joyce. At Sam's suggestion she had bound a strip of canvas around the dog's jaws to prevent his barking and betraying them again.

By the time they had reached the schooner, the cloud bank had almost reached the moon.

SAM THREW a tarpaulin over the boxes in the longboat. Tony swiftly bound a gag of burlap in their half-conscious prisoner's mouth, carried him below to his cabin, saw that the lashings at wrists and ankles were secure, and hastily returned to deck.

A puff of wind struck Sam with such violence that he almost went overboard. The moonlight seemed less silvery, less brilliant. He glanced up. The clouds were almost touching the rim of the sailing moon, and they extended to the southwestern horizon in a threatening, purple-black mass.

Sam glanced again at the steamer. He saw a knot of men gathered on her bridge; knew that, if he attempted to escape, they would follow him out.

The squall would give him a reefing wind for an unknown length of time, but the speed this would lend the Blue Goose would be offset by the fact that the squall would be accompanied by torrential rains, and Sammy, if he tried to take the schooner out ahead of the squall, must sail blindly between a dozen islands and an opening in the great Kusa Reef no wider than a quarter of a mile! An impossible undertaking. While the squall might blind his escape to the pursuit, its very blindness would wreck his schooner. But there was no choice. He must try to take the Blue Goose out.

For perhaps the hundredth time on this expedition, he wished that his old partner Lucky Jones were alive and here. Lucky had known how to handle a ship in any weather. He could send a ship through reefs in total blackness with skill and sureness.

A rising, roaring sound added its uneasiness to Sam's uneasy state of mind. The outer reefs were talking now. And the first hard puff of the squall lashed the cove as he decided on this desperate chance.

He issued orders sharply. "Rufe—Tony! Get that anchor up! Joyce! Make the longboat painter fast to the cleat aft. We'll have to take a chance with the gold, and unload when we're under way! Everybody—step!"

Everybody stepped. While Rufe and Tony hoisted the anchor, Sammy and Joyce hoisted sails.

When the main sail was up, the schooner swung around and pointed at the inlet of the cove.

He needed only his main sail and one jib to get under way: Sammy raced aft and took the wheel. He sailed the hook out of the mud, as the saying is. The sails had filled with the sharp and sudden pressure of another puff. The Blue Goose lay well over, then righted and seemed to leap ahead.

As she passed the Lotus Lady, there was sudden activity. Two rifles on the bridge blazed away. Sam saw holes appear in the canvas near his head, saw splinters flying from the boom. Above these sounds he heard the whirring of the steamer's deck engines, the grinding sound of her anchor chain.

Rufe and Tony came running aft. He shouted at them to lie flat on deck, and he crouched as low as he dared.

The men aboard the steamer continued to fire at the schooner until she was beyond range, then, with anchor up, the Lotus Lady followed.

The Blue Goose sped through the inlet in a hissing smother, making an easy ten knots.

The cloud bank reached the moon. Sam yelled at Rufe and Tony to raise the foresail just as the light of the moon went out. He wondered what Lucky would have done. Lucky had been a reckless devil. Would Lucky have shortened sail, left the fore-sail furled?

Sammy, knowing that Lucky Jones had been a master at this kind of seafaring, tried to do what Lucky would have done. He crowded on all the sail the Blue Goose carried, except, of course, for spinnakers and topsails.

He knew his compass course, and he had an excellent memory.

THE SQUALL struck with all its shrieking force a moment after the clouds had rolled across the moon. The Blue Goose seemed to lift in the hissing black water and take wing. Sammy, with strong legs braced well apart against rolling and 'scending, felt the wind square on the back of his tough neck and handled the wheel as delicately as ever a violinist handled his fiddle, determined to prevent a jibe with its inevitable consequences. Jibing in a wind like this would snap the sticks out of her.

He could see nothing but the bright glimmer of the compass disc in the binnacle. Rain came in a driving, uproarious wet madness. And the Blue Goose, straining every fibre of wood, steel, hemp and canvas of which she was composed, drove ahead.

It was very much like a nightmare in which nothing happens but roaring blackness. Sammy felt as if he were riveted to the deck. Every muscle in his tough body was as tight as a piano wire. Rain lashed down on his bare head; hard-packed, demo-niac wind shrieked and screamed against the iron-hard canvas. It was terrible and it was nerve-destroying.

He stared at the compass disc, gripped the wheel and used his head. Fortunately, the course was a straight one. It lay from the mouth of the inlet straight through passages between islands, straight through the narrow jaws of the Kusa Reef. Yet he must take into consideration the side current that flowed out from the other islands and the drift of his ship under such a terrific stern wind.

He knew that Rufe, Tony and Joyce were doing their best at unloading the gold, yet he had a sense of utter and complete aloneness. It was as if he were sailing his schooner through the uncharted blackness of a half-world, the half-world one entered, perhaps, after death.

He was alone upon a black and raging sea. Once he glanced astern, saw nothing. Either the pursuer had given up or was blotted out by the rain. Running with no lights, Sammy believed it would be impossible for anyone to follow him.

Yet he had no sense of being pursued. Crowding in upon him more and more as the minutes passed was this chill, this almost supernatural sense of aloneness. But as time went on, he had a new feeling—that he was not alone at the wheel; that an unseen man stood with him, gripping the spokes, too, guiding the schooner with a cleverness and skill that would never be Sam Shay's—a tall, black-haired Viking with eagle's eyes and a profane and wonderful scorn for all the winds that blew, and all the seas that ran.

Sammy's brain was numb. His hands on the spokes were numb. It seemed to him that all the blood had run out of him, had been replaced by some black and icy fluid. Yet he no longer feared the Kusa Reef.

Hours had passed. Lifetimes had ebbed away since that first sharp puff had sent the Blue Goose scooting past the Lotus Lady and out of the little cove.

And suddenly, dead ahead, he heard a tremendous sustained thunder. That was the surf on the great horseshoe-shaped reef. He might have spun the wheel, sent the ship toward a point in the roaring blackness where the thunder seemed less loud. But he was not tricked into that error. He did not twist the wheel a spoke.

THE THUNDER of the surf came closer and closer. Dead ahead, through the driving rain, he could see the phosphorescent glow of it. It was all about him now. Off to starboard and to port was a thundering froth of pale-green. The schooner began to plunge and yaw, but he held her firmly on her course.

At any instant, she might have ended her flight in a smashing blow on the unseen fangs of rock, but she did not. She sailed on. And presently Sammy was aware that the thunder was receding. An explosion forward, a jerk at the wheel, told him a sail had burst. He didn't care—he was through the reef. Single-handed, blindly, he had done the impossible. He no longer had the feeling of another, unseen presence beside him at the wheel. It must have been purely imagination, but as long as he lived, Samuel Larkin Shay would believe that the ghost of his dead partner had guided the schooner on that black and dangerous course.

The rain stopped. The violence of the wind abated. Behind him, in the night, Sam saw nothing of the pursuing ship.

Rufe relieved him at the wheel. Both men were on the verge of exhaustion, but Sam would have collapsed in another few minutes.

"Where we headin'?" Rufe wanted to know.

"Macassar. It's the closest port." And Sam gave him his course.

Tony reported that the last of the gold was safely stowed. He would, he said, relieve Rufe at the wheel a little later.

Sam turned in with his clothes on. He was soaked to the skin, but he didn't care. The Blue Goose and those aboard were safely out of danger. Once through the reef, it was clear sailing. On the short run to Macassar, the Lotus Lady could not possibly overtake them.

Once, during the night, he awoke. He imagined that he had heard that most hideous of all earthly sounds—a man screaming in terror. But the sound was not repeated.

He awoke shortly after dawn to find Tony sitting beside him, grinning at him. Blinking sleep from his eyes, Sam sat up.

"There've been two casualties during the night," Tony said. "Angel Face was washed overboard—and our stowaway is dead."

The red-headed man grunted. "What happened?"

"Sometime during the night, a coral snake got into his clothing somehow, stung him—and he died."

"Rufe—" Sam began quietly.

"Yes, I've talked to Rufe. He disclaims any part in it. He says the box containing the snakes was badly battered when it came aboard, and that one of them must have got out and bitten the poor devil. He says he has counted the snakes, and that all but one are accounted for. He caught the one that bit Mallory and put it back with the others. Do you want to talk to him?"

"Sure."

RUFE CAME and stubbornly denied having freed a snake in their stowaway's bed.

"Not that he didn't have it coming," Rufe said placidly. "Only don't blame me for an act of God."

"Were you in his cabin any time during the night?"

"Oh, sure," the big, sandy-haired man said amiably. "I had quite a talk with him. I wanted to know where that locket was."

"Where is it?"

"Somewhere at the bottom of the ocean between Buru-Waru and Soerabaya. He threw it overboard—right off this ship. He admitted it."

"Who is he?" Sam interrupted.

"He wouldn't say. I asked him, but he wouldn't say. He offered me a fifty-fifty split on the gold to double cross you and the rest, to kill you all off and to take the gold ourselves. He was a pretty hard guy, all right. Said he stole my locket and steered me onto you so's he could swipe your schooner and get to Soerabaya. Then he said he killed the *serang* and the cook to protect himself and so's you'd have to hire a new crew. And he kind of laughed and said he'd like to see you or anybody else prove it on him. Do you blame God for turning a coral snake loose in that guy's bed?"

"No," Sam said. "But the next time you get drunk, you'll tell somebody all about it."

"Not me. I'm on the wagon. And who the hell are you to criticize me for gettin' drunk?"

"And of course," Sam said, "you didn't throw that poor helpless little dog overboard?"

"Me?" Rufe said. "Me kick a poor sweet helpless little dog overboard?"

"You mean," Sam said dryly, "it was another act of God?"

"That's how I figger it."

He stared broodingly at Sammy for some time with his piglike blue eyes.

"Red," he said, "there's been a lot of talkin' goin' on. Tony is gonna charter a steamboat to go back and get the rest of the stuff on the island—the pottery, and statues and all. And Joyce has kind of realized how dumb she acted with Tony. Unless I'm crazy, she's gonna marry him at the next port. Anyhow, she wants to. It kind of leaves me high and dry."

"So what?" Sam growled.

The big man fidgeted and turned red. "Well, it's like this. They ain't goin' eat on no field expeditions for anyway a year. They'll be in Washington, sortin' out all this stuff and writin' the books they always write after their expeditions. Me, I don't like Washington. I look at it this way. I know you're a lowdown skunk that would steal the pennies off your dead grammaw's eyelids, but I was sort of wonderin'—" Rufe stopped.

Never much of a conversationalist, the big man was floundering in water too deep for him.

But the red-headed man's cold stare gave him no encouragement.

"I know you're a lowdown louse and all that," Rufe went on, "but I was sort of wonderin' if I could team up with you. I kind of like the life you lead."

"Yeah?" Sammy drawled.

"Yeah! Sure!"

"Listen, you punk," Sammy said heavily. "You're so dumb you

don't know your ear from a hole in the ground. You're so clumsy you almost kick your brains out every time you take a step. And I know you're a cold-blooded murderer. I know you put the snake in that fellow's bed last night."

"So what?"

"So, if you want to team up with me, I guess it can be fixed."

ABOUT THE AUTHOR

THE DECISION TO become a writer of fiction was made for me by fate. In 1914, in Panama, where I spent a week when I was a wireless operator on a little steamer that creaked up and down the Central American coast, I met an author who painted the joys of free-lancing so vividly that I could not resist the call. We were drunk. I was twenty. Since then, I have been trying to catch up with all of those joys he mentioned.

Starting to write stories in 1914 and, four years later selling my first one, marks up, I suppose, a very poor batting average. But in those years I was getting experience, seeing the world, and acquiring knowledge. I "punched brass" as a wireless operator all over the Pacific. I entered Columbia University in 1915, and one year later left because I didn't believe in higher learning. I still don't believe in it. I became a newspaper reporter, later a magazine editor.

Then came the war, which I won practically single-handed by writing high-pressure publicity to induce patriotic Americans to send books to Washington for camp libraries for soldiers and gobs. Books came by the carload, by the ton: McGuffy's readers, old almanacs, spellers, arithmetics, out-dated novels and just trash. The soldiers and sailors who read those books soon hated the war so bitterly, that they promptly got busy and ended it. That's how I won the war.

After the war, I wanted another look at China, and was sent

to the Far East by *Collier's* to write articles on China, the Philippines, India
and Malaya.

The first story I sold was written
while I was editing a motion picture
trade paper. It was bought by the
Argosy, and it was about a wolf named
Murg. Don't ask me why. In the intervening years I have written millions of
words. Perhaps it is Murg who sits so
patiently at my door!

*George F.
Worts*

I started writing fiction under the
pen name of Loring Brent, because it would have annoyed the
owner of the motion picture magazine to learn that I was writing fiction out of hours. He thought I fell asleep at my desk
because I was working so hard for him! When my income from
fiction exceeded my salary, I quit the job. Since then I have been
free-lancing exclusively, except for a two-year period when I
lived in a Florida swamp town and added to my writing the
duties of postmaster, game warden and deputy sheriff. Out of
that experience came a long series of stories about a Florida
town I called Vingo.

I have enjoyed most writing stories about certain established
characters. Apparently the most popular of these have been the
Peter the Brazen, the Vingo and the Gillian Hazeltine stories. I
stopped writing about Peter the Brazen (a swashbuckling wireless operator on ships in the China run) about ten years ago.
He was, incidentally, the subject of the only novel I have had
published in America. I am now starting a new series about him.

When I am not traveling I live in Westport, Connecticut. My
interests are horses, sailing and flying. I took up flying about a
year ago to write some articles on how it feels to learn to fly, and
was badly bitten by the bug. I can make a three-point landing
about five times out of ten.

I like New York, but would prefer to live in Honolulu. I smoke sixty cigarettes a day. I like murder trials. I have never mastered the noble game of poker, although I once wrote a book about it. In my spare time I study law and medicine. I have two young sons and a still younger daughter; an able crew for my sailboat—except that there is usually mutiny aboard the lugger!

www.ingramcontent.com/pod-product-compliance
Lightning Source LLC
Chambersburg PA
CBHW020640030726
47498CB00002B/294